FRANK SPINELLI

PERFECT
FLAW

FRANK SPINELLI

PERFECT
FLAW

ONE BLOCK
EMPIRE

Perfect Flaw
by Frank Spinelli

Published by **ONE BLOCK EMPIRE**,
an imprint of Blind Eye Books
315 Prospect Street #5393
Bellingham WA 98225
blindeyebooks.com

Edited by Nicole Kimberling
Copyedit by Dianne Thies
Cover by L.C. Chase Designs
Ebook design by Michael DeLuca

First Edition February 2022 Copyright © 2022 Frank Spinelli
Print ISBN: 978-1-935560-83-8
ebook ISBN: 978-1-935560-84-5

Printed in the United States of America

Dedication
To C.S., who makes me dream of murder

CHAPTER ONE

The way Angelo saw it, everyone deserved a miracle. He wasn't likely to win the lottery or discover a cure for cancer or learn to fly. But by some divine intervention, he had been chosen to join the Manhattan practice of Dr. Anthony Stanzione—*New York* magazine's top rated HIV specialist.

Sweaty. Shaky. Thinking he was going to pass out, Angelo assured himself he was ready. And why not? He had graduated medical school and completed an internal medicine residency. He had missed out on parties, holidays, vacations, and fun while he studied in the library, reviewed slides in the lab, and treated patients for years. He had worked long hours on hardly any sleep and stood for stretches at a time—swaying in a trance of boredom—rounding with his attending physicians each day, knowing it would all be worth it once he got that dream job.

Standing in front of Dr. Stanzione's office that morning, staring at the black wrought iron gate and the white marble entrance, Angelo thought things couldn't possibly get better. That's when he saw it.

A bronze plaque on the exterior wall bearing his name: ANGELO PERROTTA, M.D.

Deep breath, he said to himself. This is the first day of the rest of your life.

Angelo opened the door, juggling a box under his arm. The waiting room was empty. Bleached wood chairs and a glass coffee table loaded with perfectly fanned out magazines. Two large pieces of artwork hung on the walls that reminded him of Miami with their profuse use of turquoise and pink. Behind the receptionist window sat Tiffany, a slender Trinidadian woman. Her dark complexion highlighted her aqua blue eyes. Her face framed by strands of golden-blond cornrows.

"Good morning," he said.

She offered him a wan smile then returned to watching the door that Angelo knew from doing a rotation in this office, led to the exam rooms. Since the doors held her attention so closely, he turned his attention to them too, just in time to see them burst open.

A short, harried-appearing woman stormed out. It was Jackie, the clinical trial coordinator. She was followed by a tall, boyishly handsome man named Steven, the practice manager who was also Stanzione's husband.

"Go to hell, Steven," Jackie shouted, carrying an open cardboard box. Angelo, a man of average height, saw that inside the box were medical textbooks, a stethoscope, and a framed photo of a man he thought had to be her husband.

Steven crossed his arms over his chest. "Well, don't expect Tony to give you a good reference."

"Tell Dr. Stanzione he can take that reference and shove it up his ass." Jackie swung around and nearly collided with Angelo. "Oh, well if it isn't you," she said, with a haughty laugh. "Hi and good-bye."

Once Jackie had exited, Steven and Tiffany seemed to exchange a collective sigh of relief.

"Well, I'm glad that's over with," Steven said.

Angelo was paralyzed, feeling like he had stumbled into a crime scene. "What just happened?"

"We let Jackie go," Steven replied.

"Why?"

"With you on board, Tony felt he no longer needed Jackie's services."

"Who's going to manage the clinical trials?" Angelo asked.

"You, of course."

"I'm taking over as the coordinator?" Angelo shook his head, as if to dislodge the confusion.

"Yes, unless you have some tiny assistant in that box of yours," Steven replied. "Welcome to the business world of medicine, Dr. Perrotta. Fortunately, your job is to take care of the patients. My job is to manage the office. Right, Tiff?"

"Right," she said, hastily distracting herself with work to withdraw herself from the conversation.

"Just don't let Jackie ruin your first day," Steven added.

"I won't," Angelo said. "Besides, it's not every day you get your own plaque. Thank you, Steven."

"Well, you're part of the family now. It reminds me of when I came to New York fifteen years ago. I got my first gig as a catalog model for *International Male*. I must have stared at myself in that first issue for days."

Steven's so-called modeling career was something he had mentioned often throughout that month-long rotation. Angelo thought whenever Steven brought it up, he detected the wistful longing of a famous child actor who grew out of his cuteness.

"Come on," Steven said. "Let's get you situated."

The office was a two-story condo with a street entrance. There were five exam rooms, two bathrooms and two private offices on the main floor. Downstairs was an empty suite with two exam rooms, a waiting area, and a private office. Beyond the generic furniture and artwork was the sparkling white marble tile that shone so brightly it appeared as if the entire office was built on a frozen lake.

"Jackie should have been more professional," Steven continued. "Tony and I were expecting a smooth transition of responsibilities. Now you'll have to review the clinical trial binders and make sense of them on your own. The pharmaceutical business is an entirely different world."

Angelo set his box on the desk and sighed. Stanzione had never mentioned he would be taking on Jackie's role in addition to seeing patients. "Don't worry," Angelo said with the strained cheeriness of a wife whose husband brought home unexpected dinner guests. "I'll manage."

"Office hours begin at one." Steven had already retreated into the hallway. "Tony is having a stress test as part of a life insurance exam, and there's a drug rep lunch today at noon. Tony asked if you could speak with the rep until he gets here."

Angelo listened while marveling at the skylight overhead, the plush navy carpet, and the bare walls waiting for him to hang his diplomas. "You know, this office is bigger than my apartment," Angelo joked, but Steven was already gone.

In that moment of quiet, Angelo's anxiety returned like some ferocious animal emerging suddenly from the darkness. He gripped the desk, shut his eyes, and tried to imagine something to calm him. He gazed up at the skylight, took a breath, and felt the sun on his face. A flash of memory startled him, almost as if a spotlight were being directed on him. He saw his dead mother. *It's okay. It's okay.*

Angelo unloaded his textbooks and set them on the shelf. He hung up his lab coat, which was now completely wrinkled. Though he hated the mawkish sentiment of family photos, he treasured the one of his deceased mother, his older sister, Camille, and himself taken at a carnival on his tenth birthday. As children, Angelo and Camille were often confused for identical twins except for the scar on Angelo's face; the result of a dog bite when he was two that left him with a two-inch pink slither that ran along his right cheek like a second smile.

After he set up his office, Angelo prepped the exam rooms: checking the blood pressure cuffs, ensuring the ophthalmoscopes and otoscopes functioned properly, and stocking the cabinets with needles, syringes, and vials to collect blood. The time flew, and soon he smelled the aroma of the catered lunch wafting under the exam room door.

Angelo was familiar with the routine of interacting with pharmaceutical representatives. Typically, it meant eating with someone who spoke nonstop about their products. Often, reps relentlessly baited doctors into writing prescriptions. *Will you prescribe product x for your next three patients, doctor? Can you do that for me?* Angelo found their used-car-salesman-pitches discomforting, but there was no arguing that Angelo enjoyed eating their lunches. Reps tended to order better food than he would have had under normal circumstances, but eventually the allure wore off. Having to make polite conversation with overly effusive drug reps became exhausting. Still, he had to do it, partially because it was expected of him but mainly out of guilt for eating their expensive food. Stanzione, on the other hand, felt neither obligated nor guilty. Often, he ignored reps while he ate.

Once an older female rep tried to explain why he should use her brand of cholesterol-lowering medication as he shoveled pasta with broccoli in his mouth. In between bites, as she pushed her brochure under his nose, Angelo observed a change in Stanzione's demeanor. Slowly, his head turned to look at her with an expression that would have made children run away in terror. Afterward, a dramatic slow swallow followed. Stanzione said, "Excuse me, but after practicing medicine for twenty years, I think I know a thing or two about treating cholesterol." Then he threw his plate of food in the garbage and stormed off. Steven entered the break room as if on cue and wrapped up the leftovers.

Lunch was over.

The rep and Angelo stood there aghast, plates trembling in their hands, wondering what had just happened. Of course, that rep was never allowed back, having been put on Stanzione's persona non grata list, a collection of names Steven committed to memory. It was also the first time Angelo had a caught a glimpse of the prima donna lurking inside the beast that was now his boss. But he wasn't like that with all the reps.

Stanzione had specific ones he liked very much. Angelo referred to them as Stanzione's five-star reps because they were usually the ones who offered him more than a silly pen, pad, or clock branded with the company's logo. Stanzione had no need for low-level reps and their worthless tchotchkes. He was keen to the savvier ones who booked him for speaking engagements and asked him to enroll patients in their company's latest clinical trials. Those were his favorite kind of reps, and he spent long lunches cavorting with them like war buddies, often taking them back to his office for private conversations, particularly if they were young, male, and handsome. Stanzione had a notorious reputation at St. Vincent's Hospital for enjoying the company of good-looking men, and Angelo always knew when Stanzione had a crush because you could hear his obsequious laugh, a staccato of heavy breaths, as it echoed down the hall.

As a resident, Angelo paid little attention to reps, thinking of them as beleaguered punching bags for the attending physicians to abuse. During that month-long rotation at Stanzione's office, Angelo began to keep a mental tab of the costs Stanzione had incurred as a result of his relationship with various pharmaceutical companies and all for doing very little in the process.

But it went well beyond that. Stanzione was also an HIV thought leader. He met certain criteria established by the pharmaceutical companies, which included: operating a thriving practice, writing hundreds of prescriptions for expensive antiretroviral medications, and participating in clinical trials which were sponsored by pharmaceutical companies. It was a brilliant concept sprinkled with ski vacations at Whistler Mountain and lobster bakes in Nantucket. Yet, for all the glamour, there was an undercurrent of impropriety that didn't sit well with Angelo.

But he supposed he was being naïve. Like Steven said, medicine was a business. Physicians like Stanzione worked the system to their advantage, earning an additional six figure salary on behalf of pharmaceutical companies. How else could Stanzione afford a two-story Park Avenue office?

The rep today was a gregarious blond named Jill Abrams, a legendary five-star rep. In all probability, a total sycophant and likely a former college cheerleader. Not only was Stanzione the lead investigator for her company's latest clinical trial, but he was also their national speaker, and according to Stanzione, Jill's "close friend". Though Angelo already knew from his rotation that Stanzione and Steven had no friends, only business associates.

"You must be Dr. Perrotta," Jill said, thrusting out her hand. For a second, Angelo thought he was supposed to kiss it. Then he realized she was showing off her huge diamond engagement ring. "We haven't met. I've been away on my honeymoon. I just got married!" And then she held her hand up next to her face.

"Congratulations!"

"We just got back from Maui," Jill continued. "I didn't want to come home." Then she smacked the side of her head and rolled her eyes. "Where are my manners? Please, have something to eat. Here I am going on about my honeymoon, and you're standing there starving."

Jill had splurged on lunch, ordering from an Italian restaurant in Gramercy Park. Not a typical drug rep lunch, Jill had ramped up the sophistication level down to the white linen tablecloth and bottles of sparkling water with lime wedges. There were three aluminum chafing trays containing chicken piccata, pasta with vodka sauce, and mixed vegetables. In addition, there were loaves of fresh bread with honey and an assortment of cookies. All this to feed four office staff.

"I'm hardly starving," Angelo said. "Just hungry."

Jill's face went sullen as though he'd said something profound. "You know, I bet obesity is a huge problem for doctors. You're all so incredibly busy. It must be hard to find time to work out?"

"Not Dr. Stanzione."

Jill covered her mouth. "Oh my God. No. Not him." Then she began giggling hysterically until it broke into a shrill high-pitched laugh. "He looks amazing for his age. Not that he's old. God no." Then she whispered. "He doesn't like when I order so much food, but I do it for the staff." Jill wrinkled her nose for emphasis. "They deserve a treat instead of the usual boring sandwiches the other reps buy."

Angelo helped himself to the chicken piccata and the mixed vegetables. He ate standing as Jill navigated the conversation back to her wedding day. He imagined what her husband must look like. A muscular ex-football star. Jill would have selected him purely for the genetic implications for their children.

Stanzione entered the break room entrance, huffing like he'd sprinted to the office. The day Angelo met Stanzione for the first time, he thought Stanzione appeared trapped in mid-metamorphosis from Dr. Bruce Banner into the Incredible Hulk. A mammoth caricature with a wide back, big arms stretching the seams of his lab coat, and a black toupee that looked like a ferret had curled itself on top of his head. "Where's my Jilly?"

"There he is?" she said, kissing him on both cheeks. "Hi handsome."

"Sorry I'm late."

"Late!" she said, giggling. "You can't be late. This is your office. I'm here for you. Plus, this adorable young doctor has been keeping me company."

Stanzione flashed a faint smile at Angelo, who detected a flicker of hurt in his eyes before he turned to scan the buffet. "Oh, Angelo. Yeah, he is handsome and young."

"You two could be brothers."

Angelo continued to eat, amused by the superficiality of their conversation. Stanzione fished for compliments, and Jill took the bait every time.

"Come in my office," Stanzione said to Jill.

"Aren't you hungry? I brought all this food."

By the time she finished her sentence, Stanzione was already gone.

"Well, it was a pleasure meeting you," Jill said, holding out her hand again. "I'm sure we'll be seeing plenty of each other. You're coming to dinner tomorrow night, right? I'm taking the boys to that new restaurant, Duran's, just off Park Avenue."

Steven appeared in the doorway. "Jill, Dr. Stanzione is waiting."

"Oh, of course," she said, squeezing past Angelo. "Can't keep the big guy waiting." Jill dropped a company pen in his breast pocket right before exiting the break room. Steven handed Angelo a note and escorted her away.

And that was that.

Why had it been so important that Angelo be there to entertain and charm Jill like a father making uncomfortable conversation with his tardy daughter's date? It was okay as a resident. It seemed peculiar now as a future partner. But this was Dr. Stanzione's kingdom after all. Although Angelo had been promoted from pawn to knight, Stanzione had made it clear; Angelo was not part of the king's court. At least not yet.

Once they were gone, Angelo opened the note. *Patients are waiting for you!!*

Angelo hustled to chew the remaining piccata on his plate, but in his haste, a piece of chicken fell out of his mouth, staining his lab coat. Ducking into the bathroom, he blotted the stain with a moist hand towel, but only made matters worse. Steven called out his name. Angelo abandoned any hope of making a good first impression and hurried to greet his first patient.

The system was simple: once Tiffany checked in a patient, she placed their chart in the acrylic rack in the hall so Angelo would know a patient was ready to be seen. He picked up the only chart and flipped it open. The name of the patient was Demetre Kostas. He was last seen by Stanzione over eight months prior.

Angelo opened the waiting-room door.

Slouched in a chair with his foot on Steven's spotless glass coffee table, speaking loudly on his cell phone, had to be Demetre. For a brief second Angelo stood there fixated by the tan, rippled muscles of his belly peeking out from under a snug T-shirt. Demetre glanced up with menacing eyes that shifted instantly into sudden recognition, as though Angelo had just stepped off a plane and Demetre was waiting to greet him at the gate.

"I have to go," Demetre said, clicking off his phone.

"Mr. Kostas?"

"Yes," he replied, smiling. Demetre walked over and stood very close. Angelo noticed he was slightly taller, about five foot ten. Angelo tried to maintain eye contact although he was fixated on Demetre's buttery forearms as he crossed them over his chest, the taper of his waist and the curve of his thighs against his jeans. His body was perfectly proportioned. "You must be new."

"Yes, yes," Angelo stuttered. "It's my first official day."

"Does that mean I'm your first official patient?" Demetre's fascinated eyes seemed to graze Angelo from head to toe like he was studying a piece of art he was thinking of acquiring.

Angelo grinned but felt a traitorous blush rising up his face. "Yes, you are," he replied awkwardly. Angelo glanced down at his crumpled lab coat, now bearing a chicken piccata stain like the scarlet letter of a slob.

Demetre leaned against the doorjamb. The intensity of his expression unnerved Angelo. "I'm your first," he repeated, slyly and under his breath added, "does this mean I get to pop your cherry?"

Angelo stood, staring at Demetre. How long? He didn't know, but one thing was fixed in his mind, a concrete moment sharply etched in his memory; Demetre had taken his breath away.

"Ciao, Demetre!" Stanzione shouted from down the hall. "When did you get back?"

"Yesterday, and I'm so jet-lagged."

"Come in. Come in." Stanzione threw his arms around Demetre's neck and hugged him for what seemed like an inappropriately long time. Then he tore the chart from Angelo's hand. "I'll see Demetre," he said through a rictus smile. "He's an old friend."

Together, they walked with arms slung over each other's shoulders, carrying on like school chums until they disappeared inside one of the exam rooms.

"Demetre, huh?" Jill muttered. "Hubba-hubba." Tiffany giggled. "Am I right Tiff? Talk about a Greek god. That is one handsome man."

◆◆◆

The art of fine dining was a concept lost on Angelo, having been brought up on hotdogs, macaroni and cheese, tuna-noodle casseroles, and meatloaf stuffed with so much bread it hardly tasted of beef and more like cardboard doused in ketchup. Walking into Duran's, Angelo knew that he was in for a treat. The two-story restaurant had a barrel-vaulted ceiling. A giant waterfall stood in the center of the main dining room. Every table draped in white tablecloths and accented with an arrangement of white peonies and roses.

The maître d' sidled up to Jill. "You have a reservation?"

"Abrams party."

The maître d' escorted them to a table on the second floor.

"Regulars get the prime real estate." Jill jutted her chin toward the raucous out-of-towners exiled to the far corners of the main dining room. Angelo wended his way past tables, observing the other guests as if they were museum artifacts. Deep-pocketed executives in designer suits, insouciant model-types texting, and elderly women with hair like butter frosting and lips plump as shiny as labias. Each one looked at him as he passed, giving him a brief, ravenous appraisal, and then they looked away.

Jill had brought her husband, Ted. A man with chiseled features and solid body but much shorter than Jill. Stanzione sandwiched himself in between them. Angelo sat across the table next to Steven.

At once, a serious looking server presented their menus. Angelo opened the wine list by accident, his face burning at the prices. The cheapest bottle started around fifty dollars and there was a dessert wine priced at five hundred dollars.

Jill took the lead, ordering appetizers for the table and the first round of cocktails, while Stanzione ogled her husband. Since Ted was a rep for a medical device company, he was proficient in the art of making conversation. Although Angelo suspected his line of work didn't lend itself to much gay interaction, he handled Stanzione's advances well.

Angelo cringed as Stanzione stared into Ted's eyes with the intent focus of an actor on stage, gently touching his wrist to emphasize a point or wrapping his arm around Ted's shoulders with varsity camaraderie at the slightest joke.

They carried on as though they were the only two people at the table, and Angelo felt obligated to keep Steven occupied by rating the comparative cuteness of the servers zipping around their table. But the more he tried to engage

Steven in conversation, the clearer it became that he hardly had any opinions about anything outside of the office.

They dined on fluke carpaccio with cashew puree, pickled egg yolk, charred cuttlefish, and sweet carrot soup. Stanzione took the reins from Jill, ordering a different wine pairing with each course, consulting with the sommelier. "We have lots to celebrate tonight," he said. Jill offered Angelo a weak smile, but her eyes shifted nervously at the wine list, which Stanzione had placed by his feet and out of her reach.

"Congratulations, Angelo," she said holding up her glass.

Stanzione looked momentarily befuddled. "Oh yeah," he said, clinking Angelo's glass, "but I'm saving the big surprise for later."

By the time their entrees arrived, Angelo had so many glasses in front of him he felt as if he was a glasspiel virtuoso about to perform on the vaudeville stage. Jill had ordered an appalling amount of food. Their table was a hub of activity with servers constantly clearing away plates or filling up wine glasses. After they finished their main course, Steven nudged Angelo under the table.

"I would have rather had a Big Mac than another piece of raw fish." Being a corn-fed boy from Nebraska, Angelo suspected Steven felt just as out of place as him, maybe worse since he was wearing a T-shirt and corduroy pants. Everyone else was in business attire. Still, Angelo felt a sense of impoverished solidarity with Steven, and the two managed to have fun, shifting uncomfortably on fuchsia velvet chairs like two mischievous boys seizing an opportunity to sit on a king's throne.

Stanzione monopolized most of the conversation. Jill and Ted were rapt, or at least convincingly feigned it. Holding court outside his castle, Stanzione seemed enlivened by the prospects of the additional attention. At one point he leaned across the table and slapped Angelo's hand. "Better pass your internal medicine boards, kid. Otherwise, our deal is off, and you don't want to give up this life now that you've had a taste." Turning to Jill, he added, "You get to work with beautiful, smart women and gorgeous men like Ted." Stanzione then cupped his hand right over Ted's left pec. It was an awkward moment covered up quickly by Ted's exuberant laughter.

"Now, now, that one's taken," Jill chided. "You have a handsome hubby."

Stanzione's face soured, but then he offered an appeasing smile. "Oh sure, sure. Steven is great." Then he turned to Ted and whispered, "Talk to me after you two have been together for fifteen years." This caught Ted in mid-swallow. He laughed so hard he almost choked.

"Come on," Jill said. "Steven is gorgeous."

Stanzione ignored her. He was on a roll, despite the strained expression on Steven's face.

"You know what's gorgeous. This dinner. I want to meet the man responsible." If Stanzione's red face hadn't revealed his total inebriation, the slight slur would have. He beckoned the server to him. "I want to speak to the chef."

Angelo watched a harried expression on Jill's face emerging from behind her mask of composure.

"I'm serious," Stanzione insisted. "Get him out here right now. Do you realize how much money we've spent tonight?"

The server shot Angelo a look of rebuke, a warning to keep his drunken father in check, but the evening had taken a detour, and Stanzione was turning purple. He moved to stand up but lost his balance and immediately sat back down.

"Did you hear me?" Stanzione pointed his finger at the server with one eye shut. "I want to meet the chef. Go and get him now!"

Suddenly, Angelo was aware of the maître d', lurking nearby, listening with interest. "May I be of some assistance?"

Jill attempted to diffuse the situation, but Stanzione pushed his chair away from the table, knocking it backward so that it crashed to the floor. He stood up, wavered slightly, but then steadied himself by gripping Ted's shoulders. "We've spent a great deal of money here tonight, and we would like to thank the chef personally."

"But if he's busy . . . ." Jill interjected.

Stanzione clapped his hand on Jill's shoulder, silencing her. "Tell the chef he's got some big fans waiting to meet him."

"Happy to oblige," the maître d' said.

A hush befell their section of the dining room.

"See that," Stanzione said as their server hastily righted his chair. "That man understands." Stanzione teetered for a moment or two, then sat back down. Angelo was spellbound watching this mammoth man trying to commandeer the room, imagining that from his perspective it was like reclaiming his youthful charisma. Steven remained impassive, as though his partner's behavior was something he had grown to accept and ignore.

After several awkward seconds, during which Angelo sipped the remaining drops of wine from the glasses propped in front of him, Jill stood up and excused herself. Stanzione glanced at his watch. After five minutes, he exhaled with exasperation.

"Where the hell did they go to get him?"

Then magically, the maître d' reappeared, escorting a handsome young man dressed in white. The man exhibited a hint of annoyance in his eyes, forehead coated in a thin layer of sweat. "May I introduce Chef Steven Duran?"

Stanzione shook his hand eagerly, and then went into a longwinded compliment, something about being something of a chef himself. Jill returned minutes later and reacted as if a celebrity had stumbled up to their table. The chef kissed her on the cheek, and then he handed out signed menus to each of them before he graciously disappeared back into the kitchen.

The maître d' remained at the table, hands clasped behind his back, smiling smugly. "Will there be anything else?"

Steven placed a hand over his mouth. A gesture that portended he knew what was about to happen.

"Yes, a bottle of your finest dessert wine." Stanzione looked around the room magnanimously. "Spare no expense."

"Of course," the maître d' said.

Jill strained to smile through her anxiety, knowing Stanzione had just ordered a five-hundred-dollar dessert wine on her tab.

"This has been an amazing night," declared Stanzione, wrapping his arms around Jill and Ted like a proud father. "We have a lot to celebrate. Not only do I want to welcome Angelo to our practice, but it looks like we may have found a solution to our problem downstairs."

Jill gasped. "You found someone to rent the space?"

Stanzione grinned, nodding his head in slow emphasis. "Fingers crossed, but I spoke to an old friend yesterday. He owns his own aesthetic practice. You know, laser hair and tattoo removal, and all sorts of facial rejuvenation procedures. He just got back from visiting his family in Greece and said he was thinking about moving his practice. I showed him the suite downstairs and he *loved* it."

"Greece?" Jill asked. "Not that Greek god who was in your office yesterday?"

Stanzione snickered lecherously. "Oh, you remember him?"

"How could I forget?"

"Sexy, right?" Stanzione said. "We used to spend summers with him on Fire Island. Remember Steven? Hot, hot, hot." Stanzione shook his fingers like they were on fire, and he was trying to put them out.

"You're unbelievable." Jill swatted him playfully.

"I'm serious. Everyone wanted to sleep with him. Demetre was a go-go dancer. That's how he put himself through school."

"More like a stripper if you ask me," Steven said.

"But with the goods to back it up," Stanzione added, elbowing Ted in the ribs. "Know what I mean?" Then he bit his knuckle.

"Okay, simmer down now, mister." Jill pointed a thumb at Steven. "You're making your hubby jealous."

Stanzione waved a dismissive hand. "I'm telling you this is kismet. Having Demetre in the office will change everything."

"How so?" Jill asked, curling her fingers under her chin.

"If Demetre comes on board, we will eventually combine practices and open a medical spa."

"Well," Steven said. "Nothing's definite yet."

"Oh, it's definite," Stanzione said. "I know it."

The server arrived with fresh glasses for everyone. The sommelier presented the bottle. "Who will do the tasting?"

"We'll have none of that," Stanzione said. "I'm sure it's great. Just pour. *Vino per tutti.*"

CHAPTER TWO

Two weeks after that disastrous dinner with Jill, the five-star drug rep, Steven appeared in Angelo's office doorway, fanning himself with a white envelope.

"Is that what I think it is?" Angelo asked.

"Don't spend it all on one place," Steven said.

After work, Angelo went shopping at the local specialty market and liquor store. He walked back to his alcove apartment on West Twenty-Third Street, grocery bags filled with assorted cheeses, meats, a baguette, and wine to make a charcuterie board like the one he had read about in the *New York Times*. He was hosting his colleague, Tammy. They were celebrating his first paycheck since joining Dr. Stanzione's practice. Although they had taken divergent paths when it came to the types of practices they favored, it hadn't driven a wedge in their friendship.

Tammy craved the jolt of the emergency room, the dazzle of flashing ambulance lights, the whirl of sirens and a tension so palpable it seemed to envelop you the moment you stepped inside its white-tiled corridors. For no good reason, Tammy just assumed her best friend would follow her down the path of caring for the impoverished. So, it was a complete surprise when right before graduation, Angelo informed her at brunch one day that he had accepted a position at Dr. Stanzione's practice.

Tammy had nearly spit up her Bloody Mary. "You can't do this to me," she had pleaded. "Learn about *real* people with *real*-people problems."

Of course, he knew, she would never understand. She'd grown up the daughter of a wealthy lawyer and a stay-at-home mother, living in a suburb of Illinois on Loon Lake and enjoying the riches of a well-padded lifestyle, one that ensured the children didn't have to work after school, spent summers Jet-Skiing on the lake and snowboarding in the mountains in winter.

Maybe if Angelo had Tammy's childhood, he would have felt the same privileged guilt and chosen to spend his career slaving in a poverty clinic. But Angelo had lived a childhood going to those clinics, waiting for hours with the other poor, unfortunate people like him, dreaming about a world outside of the one he had been assigned.

Angelo fished in his pants pocket for his key, dreading the suffocating August heat that would hit him like opening an oven. At the precise moment he heard the lock disengage, an ominous foreboding tightened around him like a sphincter. He stepped slowly inside. Though the room was dark, he sensed someone was there. Cigarette smoke lingered in the air. *Blondie—Greatest Hits* played softly from the alcove bedroom. "Who's there?"

That question went unanswered, but Angelo already knew.

He stepped closer, peeking his head around the corner. Lying in his bed was a man. Pin-striped suit. Tasseled loafers. Ray-Ban sunglasses. It was his ex-boyfriend, Miles Scribner. Angelo turned on the lights.

"Hey buddy." Miles held a cigarette in one hand and an empty bottle of tequila in the other.

Gloria Gaynor's song immediately came to Angelo's mind. *I should have changed that stupid lock.*

"What are you doing here?"

Miles pressed out his lower lip. "You're not happy to see me?"

Angelo returned to the kitchen and began unpacking the groceries. Miles came up behind him. Gripping Angelo's hips, Miles thrust his growing erection firmly against his buttocks. Angelo didn't resist at first. If he had learned anything that year they had dated, it was that an inebriated

Miles was as unwieldly as a stack of dishes. A brusque twist of the nipple caused Angelo to recoil. "That hurts," he said, pushing Miles away. "You stink of liquor, and you know you can't smoke here."

Miles heaved an exasperated sigh. "Okay." He walked to the window and opened it. After one last puff, he flicked the cigarette into the balmy night.

"Are you crazy?"

Miles shrugged, dumbly. "What?"

"Someone could get hurt." Fortunately, no one was walking by when the cigarette butt hit the ground, still glowing red. He glared at Miles. "Take off those stupid sunglasses. You look ridiculous."

"Name calling already?" Miles removed his sunglasses to reveal bloodshot eyes.

"You look like shit," Angelo said, assessing Miles's face for other signs of intoxication.

"Come on. Let's have a drink." Miles staggered to the counter and removed the wine bottle from the bag. "Red wine," he said, disappointedly. "My, how you cling so ferociously to your Italian heritage. Don't you have any real hooch?"

"No," Angelo replied, reclaiming the bottle. He glanced at his watch. "You have to leave. Tammy will be here any minute."

Miles rolled his eyes exaggeratedly. "I see you're still playing house with Peppermint Patty."

"I would advise you not to call her that." Angelo resumed unpacking the groceries. When he turned around, Miles was snorting cocaine from a small brown vial. "What the fuck do you think you're doing?"

Miles held a finger to his lips. "The neighbors."

"Exactly," he replied. "What if they call the police?"

"The police," Miles repeated. He snatched the wine bottle and lurched toward the couch. "Screw top!" When Miles glanced up, he burst out laughing, and Angelo knew he was laughing at him. At his lack of refinement. Suddenly, the coke kicked in. Miles raised a cocked arm and sang with a hillbilly accent. "Err, nothing wound be finer than to drink this old cheap winer in the mornin."

"Just go."

"Would you just relax." It was that condescending tone that raised Angelo's hackles. Miles sank back against the couch, spread open his legs and thrust the bottle in between them. "Why don't you come over here and uh a . . . ." Then stroking the bottle neck added, "Have a sip, if you know what I mean?"

Angelo winced with disgust. "Don't even think about it."

Miles sat up, slamming the bottle down on the coffee table. "You know what your problem is? You pretend you're this *Pollyanna*, but the truth . . . the truth is that you're nothing but a pussy boy bottom. You just don't want to admit it. That's because you're also a little baby." He began sucking his thumb. "A real mamma's boy."

"Shut up!" The mention of his mother made him shudder like cold fish were swimming around his organs, chilling them.

"My bad. I forgot. You no longer have a mother."

Although Angelo charged at Miles, ready to slap his face, he wouldn't really do it. At least not without making Miles angrier. Miles grabbed him by the wrist. "You don't want to do that, Polly," he said, gritting his teeth. His hand clenched so tightly, Angelo's fingers went numb.

Miles seized him, forcing him to the floor. Kissing Angelo's neck with such fervor, it felt like a branding iron. Angelo resisted then relented, knowing that he would submit. He had submitted in the past even after they had broken up. That's why Miles kept coming back. Angelo had grown to accept his addictions. His cruelty. His violence. There was a time when Angelo felt drawn to Miles's ferocious sexual intensity. Alcohol transformed Miles into something more carnal, more brutal, but in the end, he saw that Miles was nothing more than an abusive drunk in expensive clothes.

He found himself now grappling with a feverish desire to revisit those former days when Miles transformed into that ferocious sexual beast. Should he allow Miles to drive his cock in his mouth until he gagged? Angelo knew if he did, that would satisfy the beast. Miles would feel satiated, and then he would slink out the door victorious.

Quickly, Angelo dismissed this thought as a ridiculous regression from all the personal growth he had achieved after leaving Miles, but it was too late. As soon as that thought had crossed his mind, it seemed to transmit directly to Miles because his eyes alighted with savagery. Angelo wasn't just afraid, he was splintering. The sharpness of Miles's grip left him feeling chipped apart.

He was confounded. Straining to imagine a scenario whereby the connection between Miles and himself made sense: they had met by chance. He remembered distinctly that Miles was leaving a party just as Angelo had arrived. Locked in each other's gaze, ignoring the pull of their friends, Angelo recalled Miles's perfect smile, the dimpled chin, and the black hair so slick and straight it shone like asphalt. Miles had said good-bye to his friends and returned to the party with Angelo. His mind gyred eagerly, hoping to conjure other happy memories, but in the end, he found none.

Miles always knew who and what Angelo really was, which is why he revealed himself so completely. There was no pressure to hide behind some vapid, manufactured personality since Angelo had accepted him and all his vices; he knew Angelo believed that his own self-worth was measured only by his proximity to privilege.

Miles reared up, shifting his body so that he was straddling Angelo, pinning his arms down with his knees.

Angelo gaped in anticipation. Awaiting the moment when Miles would unzip his pants. *Here it comes,* he thought. *Just do it. Just get it over with.* Instead, Miles chuckled once and spat on his face. Angelo blinked repeatedly, shocked by the humiliation.

Miles was standing now. He turned the music up. "This is my favorite Blondie song." He began singing along, loudly, and off-key. "*Soon turned out, had a heart of glass.*" He stood over Angelo with an air of frenetic insistence, peering curiously down at him as though he was strapped to a gurney in four-point restraints. "I think of you whenever I hear this song."

Angelo fought back the tears, but they came, unbidden. It was then that Angelo felt the beginnings of nausea, of fear, although he was unable to comprehend something vital, the warm excitement of work just a few hours earlier had vanished, and the world had reverted to an all too familiar icy harshness.

A knock at the door, distracted them. "That must be Peppermint Patty."

Angelo wiped the spit from his face, staggering quickly to his feet just as Miles let Tammy in.

There stood Tammy. Round face. Round glasses. Mousy hair pulled behind her ears. Wearing an oversized UPenn sweatshirt over scrubs. "What the fuck are you doing here?" she asked.

"He's all yours." Miles looked at Angelo and chuckled. "Isn't that right, Polly?" Then turning back, he added, "He'll always be yours, Peppermint *Patty*"

"The name's *Tammy*, asshole." She reached back and slapped Miles so hard his jaw clicked. Miles stormed passed her, and she slammed the door behind him. "What the fuck was that all about?"

"He was here when I got home."

"He still has a key?"

Angelo nodded, walking over to the sink to splash water on his face, trying to reclaim his dignity in order to move past this crushing embarrassment.

"Are you crying?"

"Please," he said, grabbing the wine bottle. Angelo poured them both a drink, and they sat on the couch in silence. Angelo hung his head, wiping away the tears. "This wasn't exactly how I planned to celebrate my first paycheck working at my *posh* Park Avenue office. The irony is not lost on me that Miles chose this day . . . of all days to remind me how shamelessly aspirational I am? I'm so pathetic." Angelo took a gulp of wine. He closed his eyes and when he opened them, he seemed to have regained his footing. "No," he said emphatically. "I'm not letting that asshole ruin this milestone."

"Old friend," Tammy said delicately. "I'm happy to hear you're not going to let that asshole ruin your celebration. Shamelessly aspirational? Yes. Pathetic? Only if you don't change those locks tomorrow."

Angelo nodded. "Will you sleep over tonight?"

She got up and sat next to him. Arms wrapped around one another. There was no other sound in that quiet apartment other than Angelo's sobbing.

"All right," Tammy said, refilling their glasses. "Enough whining and more wine." Angelo grinned thankfully. Tammy was able to pivot them away from what could have been a tragic night. "Tell me how it's going? Is working for the great Stanzione everything you thought it would be?"

Angelo stood up to prepare the charcuterie board. "It's even better than I imagined."

Tammy fell back against the couch. "Still besotted with the missing link, ugh."

Angelo snickered. "Tony is one serious weightlifter. I'll give you that. I worked out with him last week. He nearly killed me."

"Tony?" Tammy repeated. "You're on a first-name basis with Stanzione?"

"Under that tough exterior lies a nice guy once you get to know him. Plus, he's considered a national HIV thought leader. You realize working in his practice isn't just a job? He made me his clinical trial coordinator. Sure, it's more work, but I'll get published sooner than if I had started out in a clinic."

"Watch it, bub," Tammy chided.

Angelo set the board on the coffee table and stared into Tammy's eyes. "You know what this means for someone like me. I don't have an Ivy League education like you."

"Is the notoriety that important?"

Angelo's eyes were searing under dark brows, intense and unwavering. "It's not about the notoriety. I've been given a chance to work alongside a genius. Someone who can teach me everything there is to know about HIV. I have an opportunity . . . no, the obligation to make a change in these men's lives. I refuse to be apologetic for wanting to be the best."

◆◆◆

First thing Monday morning, Dr. Stanzione called a staff meeting to announce that SkinDem—an aesthetic practice focused primarily on skin rejuvenation using laser therapy as well as hair and tattoo removal—was moving into the vacant office space downstairs. Stanzione explained how this opportunity would transform the practice.

"The possibilities are limitless," he said with the enthusiasm of a carnival barker. From Angelo's perspective, the idea of incorporating aesthetics into a thriving predominately gay male practice seemed like an exciting venture, but Steven's skepticism was evident. He stood stone-faced. Arms crossed over his chest as Stanzione delivered the news. What was it about Demetre that Steven didn't like? Stanzione went on to add that he and Steven would be taking an extended long weekend to vacation in Provincetown, Massachusetts over Labor Day weekend, leaving Tiffany and Angelo to man the office alone.

The Friday before Labor Day, Angelo spent most of his time answering a steady stream of calls from patients requesting their monthly controlled substances before heading out for the long weekend. He refilled sedatives, sleeping pills, steroids, and hormones, which were commonly prescribed by Stanzione for his clientele.

Angelo sat up front with Tiffany, chatting to pass the time, but also because he knew, Demetre was moving in today, and he was keen on seeing him again. Angelo recalled his one and only encounter with Demetre, who appeared to operate on a blazing hot oven setting while they had briefly chatted. When Demetre entered the office around noon, Angelo's heart released a pattering of erratic beats. After a cursory look around, Demetre walked up to the desk.

"It's like a funeral parlor in here." The sound of rigorous laughter punctured the quiet atmosphere of the waiting room, and all at once Angelo realized only he was laughing. Demetre, too, seemed startled. "Hello again."

Angelo straightened. "Yes, nice to see you too."

"So, today's the big day," Tiffany said.

"Yes, it is." Demetre leaned over the counter, his expression turning serious. "Has anyone called here looking for me?"

"No. Why?"

He cocked his head slowly to one side, teeth clenched. "Damn it."

"Is everything all right," she asked.

"Yeah, is everything all right?" Angelo parroted.

Demetre turned around and began to slowly pace, one hand rubbing his chin, the other cupping his elbow. Tiffany and Angelo watched him in that curious, expectant way you stare at an actor on stage, thinking they've forgotten their lines. Then Demetre spun around and clapped his hands together loudly as though he remembered exactly what he'd intended to say.

"Listen, can you both do me a favor?"

"Of course," they said.

"Excellent." Demetre's face brightened. "Tiffany, I need you to call my assistant, Laura."

"At your old office?" she asked, picking up the desk phone.

"No, call her cell. I'll give you the number." He grabbed a pen off the counter and wrote on pad. "I think this is it. Tell her I lost my wallet, again." While Tiffany dialed, Demetre turned to Angelo.

"You," he said, waving his finger. Then he paused and smiled with shining, helpless eyes. "I'm afraid I don't remember your name."

"Angelo."

"Angelo," he repeated slowly, as though he was deciding whether the name suited him or not. "You look like you work out, Angelo. Am I right?"

"Yes."

"Well let's put those muscles to good use."

"Doing what?"

"Come with me, and I'll show you."

A rental van was double parked outside. It seemed odd to Angelo that Demetre hadn't hired a moving company equipped with a pack of muscle men who resembled a line of go-go dancers. Instead, Angelo found that Demetre was an army of one. Once Demetre unlocked the van doors, Angelo saw inside was something akin to a copy machine with a mechanical arm.

"What's that?" Angelo asked.

Demetre clutched his left pec, mouth gaping. "*That* my friend is the Ferrari of lasers. It can make anyone's skin look like a newborn's bottom, remove a regretful tramp stamp and above all, it can permanently eliminate the growth of hair. If that's your thing?"

Angelo held his stare, dazzled by the mischievous glint in Demetre's eyes and the whorls of dark chest hair sprouting up from his scrub top.

"No, that's not my thing."

"Good," Demetre said, raising a single eyebrow. "So, will you help me?"

"You want me to help you move the Ferrari of lasers?"

Demetre stepped closer. "Do I have to beg?"

It was no small endeavor, transporting the laser from the moving van into the building. It literally weighed half a ton. Part of Angelo, the sane part, thought this was ridiculous, but Demetre was so encouraging, especially as they maneuvered the laser onto the dolly.

"There you go," he said. "You should see your biceps. Now that's hot."

Pushing the dolly together into the office, navigating the sharp turns of the foyer, they did their best to avoid knocking into walls, knowing Steven would notice every scuff, scratch, or ding.

"Careful," Demetre said. "I don't want to piss off Lady Steven." Angelo chortled. "Oh, was that bitchy? Don't listen to me. I'm a horrible person."

Once they moved the laser just outside the elevator door, Demetre came up behind Angelo and threw his arms over his shoulders, hanging on him, hot and panting, like a Labrador retriever.

Inside the elevator, breathless and completely drenched in the smell of salty sweat and musk all around them, Demetre pulled Angelo toward him by the waist. "I want to let you in on a secret," he whispered. "Watching you just now actually gave me a little chub."

Angelo felt a tingling in his groin and heat burning his ears. The shocking delight of this glorious sexual friction, Angelo imagined himself naked under a silken duvet with Demetre pressed against his body.

Once it was done, and the laser was positioned in the exam room right where Demetre wanted, they walked back upstairs. Tiffany had spoken to Laura by then. "You left your cell phone and wallet at the van rental place."

Demetre held his hands up to the ceiling. "Thank you, Jesus!" Then he darted out the door but stopped short once he reached the sidewalk. He paused for a second, spun around and charged back inside. His faced flushed with embarrassment. "Thank you both so much for all your help, especially you Angelo. We make a good team, just like Batman and Robin."

Demetre seemed on the verge of asking him a question, but then he ran his hand through his hair, smiled, and nodded before rushing back outside.

◆◆◆

Walking home that Friday afternoon, the sun had nearly set, casting a penumbral light the shade of a bruise. None of that mattered to Angelo after seeing Demetre again. The blazing touch of his hands around Angelo's waist, his broad shoulders, and the smell of sweat as it soaked through his T-shirt played over and over in his head on a loop. His mind wandered, imagining what it would be like to see Demetre every day, that a harmless flirtation might evolve, and that he could develop a massive crush on a co-worker.

A disaster waiting to happen.

By the time he reached the bar on the Lower West Side where he was meeting Tammy, Angelo had come to his senses. He had convinced himself that he had blown this entire encounter way out of proportion. Demetre was an unabashed flirt, and Angelo was nothing more than victim to his charms. A child beguiled by a stranger with candy to help him move his laser.

Nothing more.

Angelo entered the bar, standing on his toes, looking over the crowd for Tammy. Women in jeans, baseball caps, and sports T-shirts. Manufactured haze hovered near the ceiling as flashing lights cut sharp lines through the dense air. Glass shattered. Two women scuffled. The crowd lurched back, and Angelo shimmied his way over to the bar. Tammy was sitting next to a beautiful Black woman with cornrows and a small gold ring in her left nostril. Angelo tapped Tammy on the shoulder. Her face lit up.

"Hey, you made it." She turned to the woman and shouted in her ear. "This is my friend, Angelo. He's the guy I was telling you about."

The woman's name was Val. She looked at him critically.

"Oh, so you're the famous Angelo."

Tammy was the Hugh Hefner of lesbians, with a new woman on her arm every time Angelo saw her. She was a serial monogamist, but most of her relationships lasted only a few months. Prior to tonight, Angelo had never heard of Val, and so he was left to assume that she was the new bunny on the block.

"*Tamara* was just telling me about your new job."

"What did *Tamara* tell you?" he asked, glowering at Tammy. Angelo signaled the bartender and ordered a beer. "Would you ladies care for anything?"

"No, thank you," Val said.

"I'll have another," Tammy said.

"So, what's it like working in private practice?" Val asked. She had the look of a gambler in her eyes, weighing the currency of her question against the odds of his response. Angelo burst out laughing, a defense mechanism he learned when he wanted to change the subject. He looked away, pretending to be distracted. Val reached over and placed her smooth hand on his. "Tamara here thinks you sold your soul to the devil."

Beers arrived. Angelo attempted to steer away from the subject again by making a toast. "To new friends," he said, holding up his bottle.

"To new beginnings," Tammy added, kissing Val on the cheek.

Then they drank, but Angelo was deluding himself into thinking Val was done with her interrogation. No sooner did his bottle touch the bar, she launched right back in again. "I told Tamara it's the pharmaceutical companies that are the real enemies. I bet they come by all the time bringing great big lunches."

"I'm not that easily swayed," he said casually. "I won't write a prescription unless it's completely appropriate for my patients. I don't care if the rep brings in cheeseburgers or foie gras. Besides, those lunches are a great opportunity to learn about new medicines."

Val smirked unevenly. "You know there're several independent studies that show doctors will write a drug if they've been given a pen or a pad by a drug rep. You're only playing into their market research. Reps get in the door by schmoozing physicians with lunches and branded office supplies. If it hasn't happened yet, you can expect to be invited to expensive dinners, and once that starts, you'll get fast-tracked toward becoming a speaker. Then you'll really start reaping in the rewards: laptops, tickets to Broadway, vacations for you and a guest. Just you wait."

"Sounds exciting when you put it that way," Angelo chided. "Right Tam?"

Tammy took a sip to avoid answering. Clearly, she didn't want to take sides.

"Just remember, all the expenses you incur trickle down to their products and guess who pays for it in the end?" Val asked. "The poor unsuspecting patient. But don't worry. Pharmaceutical companies explain their high drug prices by blaming it on research costs, but we know that if doctors didn't accept their generosity, then maybe they wouldn't charge so much."

Angelo continued sipping his beer, unblinking. Val's rant wasn't anything he hadn't heard before, except she was overdramatizing the facts.

Angelo aimed his ear at her. "And what is it you do for a living?"

She offered an appeasing smile.

"I'm studying Public Health at Columbia," she replied, proudly. "I'm part of a mission-driven workforce to recruit physicians into taking jobs in underserved rural areas. That would be *not* on Park Avenue."

Angelo glanced at Tammy and winked. "Oh, I get it. You two do-gooders are ganging up on me."

Tammy threw her arm around across Angelo's shoulders. "We're not ganging up on you Ange." It was clear she already had too much to drink. "Why would you say that old friend? You should listen to what Val has to say. She's an amazing person. Big pharma is evil."

"He's just being defensive," Val said coldly. "Apparently, someone has already drank the Kool-Aid."

"Oh, is that so," Tammy said. Then she looked Angelo in the eye with a glint of antagonism. "Why are you being so defensive?"

"I think I'm going to head out." Angelo finished his beer and put a tip on the bar. "It's been a long week, and I have to get up early to study. *We* have to take the boards in two weeks."

Tammy burped and took a step back as though it threw her off balance.

"This conversation is going in circles. I need to use the restroom." Val turned and walked away.

"Nice girlfriend you have there, Tam."

"Oh, don't mind Val. She's just busting your chops. What's got you all uptight?"

"I wish you'd stop talking to everyone about my career as though I was a drug dealer. There are worse things in life than being in private practice."

Tammy burped again. "Who said you were a drug dealer?" She was drunker than he'd thought; otherwise, he would have continued to berate her.

"You know what? I think I should go before I say something I'm going to regret later." Angelo pushed his way through the crowd until he reached the door. Once he stepped outside it was like walking into a sauna.

It seemed to take forever to navigate the ten blocks back to his apartment on West Twenty-Third Street. He was too upset with Tammy to care that the streets were crowded with handsome men walking up and down Eighth Avenue. He concentrated instead on the task before him: passing the boards. That was the only thing that mattered now. Failure was not an option. Stanzione had made that clear.

Once Angelo arrived at his apartment, he threw off his clothes, turned on the air-conditioner and fell on the couch. Though he believed Tammy had instigated Val to antagonize him out of spite, he never doubted her loyalty. Still, that weekend he felt himself cleaving into two different modes: the person he was with Tammy and the person he'd started to become working in Stanzione's office.

Angelo had a glimmer that the life he had known previously was going to change.

He fell asleep almost immediately, dreaming about his future and the rewards he would reap from the long days of hard work ahead. The next morning, he got up and showered. As he dressed, his phone rang. It was his sister,

Camille. He decided not to answer it. For the time being, he thought it was best if he didn't speak to anyone. His plan was to walk over to the French bistro on Seventh Avenue, have breakfast, followed by an entire day of studying.

It was more important for Angelo to live as he saw fit and not worry about what anyone else thought, especially Tammy. And to hell with being part of the mission-driven workforce because he had been granted his wish, a golden opportunity, the dream job he had always wanted. His life had crossed over, and now there was no turning back.

That weekend passed, and for Angelo it went by with take-out Chinese food, studying, and falling asleep on the couch. Nothing was lonelier than being in the city during the summer, but he knew his confinement was temporary. Once he passed the boards and proved himself to Stanzione, it would only be a matter of time before he would be frolicking on the beach in P-town and sipping cocktails on Fire Island surrounded by beautiful men.

He had to be patient.

◆◆◆

Sunday night the phone rang, startling Angelo from a nap. Outside, the sun was low, casting sharp lines through the blinds. Angelo had no idea what time it was when he answered the phone.

"Hey," Tammy sang. "Whatcha doing?"

"Napping."

"Napping!" she repeated mockingly. "What are you, eighty? Come out and join me for a drink."

He heard the music blaring behind her. She was at Henrietta's, and by the way she sounded, Tammy was already quite intoxicated. "I'm on call."

"Okay, so don't drink. Just come out and hang with us."

"I don't know," Angelo said. "Is Val with you?"

"Geez, Ange. You're worse than a chick when it comes to holding a grudge. Go splash some water on your face and get your little gay ass down here right now."

Click.

Angelo forced himself to get up. While he showered, his phone dinged, alerting him he had a voice message. It was from Dr. Stanzione. Angelo called him back immediately.

"Thank God," answered an exasperated Stanzione. "You need to go to the office. The alarm company called. Apparently, Demetre spent the weekend moving in and forgot to set the alarm before he left."

"Can't it wait until morning?" Angelo asked as he toweled off.

"No, it can't wait."

"Of course. I'll head over right now."

CHAPTER THREE

When Angelo arrived at the office building it appeared
dark from the outside. He slid his key into the lock only to
find it already unlocked. He switched on the waiting room
lights. The fluorescent bulbs slowly brightened as he made
his way down the hall toward the alarm box. Before he set
the alarm, he peered down the stairs. "Hello, is anyone
there?"

The stairwell was dark and quiet. At first, he assumed
Stanzione was correct in thinking Demetre had forgotten
to set the alarm but leaving the door unlocked seemed
careless. He returned to the alarm box and punched in the
code. Outside, he put his key in the lock and secured the
door shut.

"Can I help you?"

A dark figure stood behind him. Startled in a paroxysm
of fear, Angelo stumbled back against the door.

"Angelo, it's me." The soft cadence of his voice, those
piercing brown eyes set under a canopy of thick black eyebrows belonged to Demetre. A wave of relief washed over
Angelo but still, the shock precipitated a sudden release
of sweat. "I'm sorry if I scared you. What are you doing
here?"

Angelo's heart pounded inside his chest. "What are *you*
doing here so late?"

"Moving in. It's taken me all weekend. I must have this
place up and running by Tuesday. It's not like I have my
very own Steven to do all the grunt work."

Angelo let loose a snort of amusement. It appeared everyone knew Steven was more than just the office manager.

Stanzione had taught him how to take vital signs: blood pressure, weight, and temperature. Steven recorded them in the chart along with their chief complaint. In addition, Steven was a certified biller, handyman, a one-man cleanup crew and the boss's wife. He ran the entire office, handling the stress with a conciliatory manner and a perpetual smile. Stanzione was lucky to have him.

"Next time let the alarm company know if you're staying late," Angelo said. "Otherwise, they'll notify Stanzione or worse, dispatch the police."

Demetre nodded as though he were listening, but Angelo could see his eyes graze over him. "Well, let me back in. I have to grab my stuff."

Angelo followed him downstairs where he disappeared into one of the rooms. It was impressive how Demetre had managed to transform the space in such a short amount of time. The small waiting area was decorated with silver metal chairs arranged along the far corner, black-and-white nude forms hung on the walls, and over the receptionist's desk, there was a sign that read: SKINDEM.

"How did you come up with the name?" Angelo asked.

Demetre poked his head out. "It's an interesting story. Do you have a minute?" He motioned for Angelo to have a seat. "Wait. I have a better idea. We should have a celebratory drink."

"Sorry, I'm on call."

Demetre shrugged. "I'm not going to tell anyone."

"I can't."

Demetre sauntered over to Angelo and stood close. "Listen, one sip is not going to hurt you. There's no medical board watching us on closed-circuit TV."

"Okay, but just one."

"I'll be right back." Once again, Demetre disappeared into one of the rooms. When he returned, he was holding a bottle of brown liquid. "Do you like bourbon?"

"I don't think I've ever had it."

"Seriously?" Demetre paused for a half a second with a look that made Angelo wonder if he thought he was kidding. "Well, this is Maker's Mark. It's from Kentucky, and it's the best bourbon on the planet." He set the bottle down on the receptionist's desk and sprinted up the stairs, taking them two at a time. He returned, holding two plastic cups. "Sorry but I don't have any snifters." He poured enough to fill a third of the cup and handed Angelo one. "Sniff it first."

The scent reminded Angelo of burnt caramel. "Smoky."

Demetre snapped his fingers and pointed at him. "It does have a smokiness about it. Sniff it again." This time they did so at the same time. "Do you smell the spicy chocolate? There's also a hint of tobacco."

Angelo couldn't smell anything beyond the burnt caramel, but he was too nervous. Demetre's eyes were searing in their focus. Angelo felt like Demetre was administering a sort of refinement test and Angelo was failing.

"Well," he said, lifting his cup. "Here's to new beginnings and new friendships."

Angelo took a sip. This time he tasted the chocolate, the hint of tobacco, and even something that reminded him of leather, or maybe it was all in his head. "Wait!" he blurted out. "I'm the one who should be toasting you."

"It's not too late," Demetre said, holding up his cup.

Angelo cleared his throat. "When climbing the hill of prosperity, may we never meet a friend coming down."

Demetre drew his head back, looking impressed. "I will drink to that." They shot back the rest of the bourbon. "Would you like another?"

"No, I shouldn't have even had that one." Just then Angelo's cell phone rang. Tammy again. Angelo silenced the ringer and slipped the phone back in his pocket.

"Go ahead. Answer it. Is it your boyfriend?"

"No, it's just a friend."

"Do you have a boyfriend?" Demetre asked.

The question lingered unanswered as Angelo involuntarily relived his latest encounter with Miles. Finally, he shook his head. "Not for a while."

"Sounds like there's a story there."

"More like ancient history."

Demetre held Angelo's stare. He didn't press him further. Instead, he poured another round of bourbon while Angelo shifted uneasily in his chair.

"Handsome, single doctor like yourself shouldn't be tied down anyway. There's plenty of time for relationships. Enjoy yourself now while you're young. In fact, you should be out collecting phone numbers instead of sitting here with some old man."

Angelo picked up the plastic cup and downed the bourbon in one gulp. "You're not old."

"Old enough to be your father."

"That's not possible."

"I'm at least fifteen years older than you."

"How many fifteen-year-old fathers do you know?" Angelo asked.

"Still." Demetre stared into his cup briefly and downed the bourbon in one shot like Angelo had. "Okay, why don't you run along? I have to finish up here, and I promise to set the alarm."

"Thanks for the drink."

Angelo moved to walk past him, and Demetre came in for a hug. It was an unexpected and awkward moment that was made even more uncomfortable when Demetre stepped back and said, "You smell nice. What kind of cologne is that?"

"It's called dollar store soap. I took a shower right before I came here."

Demetre stared at Angelo. "Wait a minute. Were you going out when Stanzione called? Did I ruin your plans?"

"It's okay."

Demetre wiped his hand down his face. For a moment, his eyes were fixed on an empty space. Suddenly he snapped his attention back on Angelo. "That call you just received . . . you were supposed to meet someone?"

"Honestly, it's no big deal."

Demetre shook his head. "No one smells that good for no big deal."

Angelo chuckled, thinking if only Demetre knew he was meeting his lesbian best friend and her girlfriend. "My friend will understand."

"Go and salvage your night."

"But you never told me how you came up with the name SkinDem."

"Oh, it's nothing really." He shook his head at first, shrugging it off, but then he peered up and saw Angelo staring back at him expectantly. "Once I decided to leave my former employer, a nasty cunt by the name of Dr. Kathleen Eichhorn, I took six close friends out to dinner. I asked them to write down what they thought I should call my new company. Everyone agreed it had to have the word skin in it. Tim came up with the idea to add 'Dem' for Demetre, and there you have it."

"SkinDem," Angelo repeated. "SkinDem like kingdom. Right?"

"Something like that."

"Who's Tim?" Angelo asked.

"Tim?" Demetre repeated, running his hands through his hair. "He was my lover of five years." Demetre turned away, moving toward the stairs. "Okay, so now you know the story. Please, go and meet your friends. I feel horrible as it is."

"Don't feel horrible," Angelo said, taking the stairs. "Thanks again for the bourbon."

"My pleasure," he said, bowing, "and once again, my apologies to your *friend*."

Angelo glanced back, then *looked* at him with his physician's eyes, and for a split second he detected regret in Demetre's face, a forlorn expression like some brooding character from a Jane Austen novel. Angelo felt a vibration. The kind you sense between yourself and another person, but it was much more than that. He wanted to stay with Demetre but knew he couldn't. The moment, both ambiguous and delicate, would be ruined by any attempt to prolong it.

While walking to Henrietta's to meet Tammy, it occurred to him that what he felt was a spark. Something he hadn't felt toward another man since Miles, and knowing how tragically that relationship ended, Angelo was cautious not to make more out of it. The next man would have to prove himself. The next man, Angelo swore, wouldn't hurt him.

CHAPTER FOUR

On Monday morning Stanzione called Angelo, again in a panic. For someone who presented himself as larger than life, Angelo noted that Stanzione's carefully crafted exterior easily cracked under pressure to reveal a man who masked his inferiority with muscle.

"You have to go and admit a patient for me," Stanzione said, shakily. "He's having a procedure on Tuesday."

A half hour later, Angelo was standing over an ICU bed containing a man named Cal Hudson.

Cal was thirty-five, a fashion designer, and had severe lung disease related to HIV. Stanzione had been treating him with an experimental course of prostacyclin, which required monthly infusions under close ICU observation to monitor for life-threatening arrythmias.

At first glance, Angelo thought that Cal didn't look as ill as his medical history implied. Squared jaw, hazel eyes, and thick auburn hair that looked perpetually windswept.

"Do you have a boyfriend?" Cal asked. Angelo could feel the blood rushing to his ears as he focused on writing admitting orders. "I'm guessing no." Cal spoke slowly accentuating his southern drawl. "Don't worry. Cute guy like you won't have trouble finding one."

Angelo remained silent, feeling badly flustered. "I need to examine you."

Cal threw back the sheets, exposing his sinewy body covered in a perfectly symmetrical distribution of hair the same color of a red fox's pelt. He was wearing red silk boxer briefs and nothing else.

"Ready when you are Dr. Dreamboat," Cal said, clasping his hands behind his neck. "I even wore clean underwear. Just like my mamma told me to."

After a brisk but thorough exam, Angelo hung his stethoscope around his neck. "That's all for now. Do you need anything?"

Cal aimed his head at the door where a muscular policeman was stationed outside the next room. "How about him?"

"I meant a pillow or extra blanket."

Cal pouted with disappointment. His eyes scanned the room briefly. There was an empty paper cup on his tray. Cal snatched it up and crumbled it into a ball. Just as Cal was about to hurl it at the policeman, Angelo intercepted it.

"What do you think you're doing?"

"I'm trying to get his attention," Cal said in frustration.

"You can't just throw objects at strangers, let alone a policeman," Angelo argued. He took the crumpled paper cup and threw it in the trash.

"You're nothing like Tony," Cal said petulantly. "He would have been circling around that number like a vulture."

"I doubt that. Dr. Stanzione is happily married."

"So am I, sugar."

"Why don't you rest," Angelo suggested.

"They'll be plenty of time to rest when I'm dead," Cal said flatly.

It was then Angelo caught a glimpse of fear in Cal's eyes. It got him wondering if Cal's playful attempt to engage the policeman was his way of distracting himself from his upcoming procedure.

"Listen, if you want to talk . . . ."

"Come by later and meet my better half," cut in Cal. "Carlo is going to love you. He has a thing for scars." Instinctively, Angelo reached up and touched his cheek. Cal read his reaction. "Damn me and my big mouth," he said, sitting upright. "I have no filter, and sometimes I say things without thinking first."

"It's okay."

"What a horse's ass I am," Cal cried, pounding his fist against the mattress. "Listen, if it's any consolation that scar is pretty darn hot."

"Well, I need to call Dr. Stanzione. If you or your partner need to speak with me later, just have the nurse call me."

Cal's eyes narrowed. "I'm gonna get that policeman's name. Just you wait. He hasn't taken his eyes off you since you arrived."

Glancing over his shoulder, Angelo took in the policeman's appearance: average height, muscular body, and a face as cheerful and rugged as a Norman Rockwell painting. Part of him was astonished he hadn't noticed how handsome he was before.

◆◆◆

Later that night, Angelo returned home and tried studying. His internal medicine boards were less than two weeks away, and the burdensome yolk he carried was wearing him down. There was so much riding on this one exam.

He tried to focus, but he couldn't.

For so long, he'd been manically dedicated to work and avoiding any social circumstance that would have allowed him to reclaim a life for himself. Cal's words, still fresh in his mind, razed through the truth he had always known. That after his relationship with Miles Scribner, Angelo had avoided any opportunity for intimacy. Speaking with Demetre and today with Cal, he was surprised how easily they saw through him—like he was made of glass even though he had worked so hard to shed his pathetic past. After he ended his relationship with Miles, Angelo had made a conscious choice to pursue the only thing that mattered—his career. And now that he had the job he always dreamed of, he refused to risk losing it over another failed relationship. Whatever Cal or Demetre thought, it didn't matter, because his priorities remained the same.

Dr. Stanzione had returned from vacation a day early. Angelo met him at the hospital the next day. By now, Cal's room was cluttered with get-well cards, flower arrangements, and a silver Mylar balloon bouncing gingerly against the ceiling. Cal's partner, Carlo, was sitting on the bed when they arrived. Carlo was a slender man with a dark complexion that matched his curly hair and downturned eyes. He held Cal's hand while Dr. Stanzione explained the high-risk procedure.

Once Cal signed the consent, Stanzione excused himself, but not before he leaned forward and muttered, "What does a guy have to do to get arrested around here?"

Stanzione's head comically twitched toward the door. Standing there was the same policeman guarding the room next door.

Cal dropped Angelo a wink. "Told you. Tony don't miss nothing."

Once Stanzione exited the room, Carlo draped himself across Cal's body and kissed him. They were quiet for a while. Angelo was about to excuse himself, but Carlo stopped him. "Cal tells me you don't have a boyfriend."

Angelo shook his head, exasperated. "It's completely by choice."

"Get over yourself, honey," Carlo said. "Once Cal is discharged, we'd like to invite you to our apartment. We know many eligible men, like yourself."

Once again, Angelo felt the heat rolling up his back. How could he have been dragged into a conversation about his private life when it should be the last thing on their minds?

"Or . . . I can ask that handsome policeman if he's single?" Carlo said.

"No," Angelo said emphatically. "Now, if you'll excuse me."

"Told you he was a toughie," Cal said to Carlo.

The realization Angelo had no social life outside of his friendship with Tammy was never more apparent. He subsisted in a funnel of focus with only one purpose: passing the internal boards. But deep down, he craved the embrace of a man's body against his.

He thought about it more later that night. Excitement crackled inside him like a campfire, thinking he might have met a pair of new gay friends in Cal and Carlo. For the past four years, Angelo's social life was limited to the small circle of medical residents that worked alongside him. Long hours with only one full weekend off a month hampered any chance of making friends outside the hospital. Miles had introduced him to his friends, but he lost contact with them after the breakup. Maybe Cal and Carlo heralded a change? At the very least they had been an influence for him to try.

Angelo arrived at the hospital bright and early the next morning only to find Carlo in the lobby arguing wildly with a security guard, hands flailing, shouting in a hybrid of English and Spanish. Once their eyes met, Carlo bounded toward him.

"Dr. Perrotta, they're not letting me up to see Cal because I'm not family."

Angelo pulled in an impatient breath, annoyance that Carlo had been denied access because he was the gay lover and not a "real" relative triggered a swell of anger that was atypical of his personality.

"Too many people in the ICU at the moment," explained the security guard. "There were several traumas brought in overnight."

"My name is Dr. Perrotta . . . ."

"*Doctor*," said the security guard in a tone that reeked of end-of-shift weariness, "I don't care who you are. I have my orders, and right now I'm not letting anyone up unless they're family."

"But he *is* family!" Angelo insisted.

"Not according to this hospital."

Then Carlo interrupted, shouting in Spanish. The security guard clenched his teeth. Sensing the tempest forming around him, Angelo grabbed ahold of Carlo's arm and pulled him away. "What time is Cal's procedure?"

"Now!" Tears streamed down Carlo's cheeks. "He's up there all alone. Why are they doing this?"

The tension in Angelo's gut stretched like saltwater taffy. He had to do something, but what? Then a solution occurred to him. "Wait here. I have an idea." Angelo rode the elevator up to the ICU.

Once the doors opened, he walked into the din of chaos: policemen congregating in the waiting area, doctors encircling two ICU beds, a swarm of nurses working in tandem to adjust intravenous lines and attach electrocardiogram leads. Only the handsome policeman seemed unfazed, standing in the same position where he had been all week.

"What's going on?" Angelo asked him.

The policeman looked over his shoulder to see if there was anyone standing next to him. "You talking to me?"

"Who else would I be talking to?"

The policeman laughed at Angelo's directness, but quickly sensed his urgency. "A couple of cops got shot last night."

"Are you busy?"

"Not right now," he replied. "The perp . . . I mean, the patient I'm guarding is in surgery."

"You're guarding a criminal?" Angelo asked.

"Drunk driver," the policeman whispered.

Angelo was keenly studying the policeman's blue eyes, when he spotted a transporter—a spry, serious-looking man with gray hair—helping Cal into a wheelchair. "I need you to do me a favor?"

"Favor?" The policeman laughed mockingly. "I don't even know you."

"Name's Angelo," he said holding out an unsteady hand.

The policeman looked at it, noted the tremulousness, and said, "I'm . . . ."

Cal cut in. "They won't let Carlo up to see me," he sobbed, grabbing ahold of Angelo's pant leg. "Why are they doing this?"

Angelo leaned forward. "I'm working on it."

The transporter went to push the wheelchair, but Cal locked the brakes. "Excuse me, but I'm talking to my doctor."

"Please, just give us a minute?" Angelo pleaded with the transporter.

"You got ten seconds," replied the transporter with his hands on his hips. "I'm due for a break."

Angelo stood up and looked squarely into the policeman's chiseled face. For a moment, he forgot what he was about to say. "You've been here all week," Angelo began. "Do you remember what this man's partner looks like?"

"Latino? Slim? Five foot nine or ten?"

"Good memory," Angelo said impressed. "I really need your help."

One side of the policeman's mouth slid into a grin. "Are you always this forward?"

"Why?" Angelo asked. "Do you like forward guys?'

"Excuse me," interjected the irate transporter, "but I got more important things to do then to watch you two speed date."

Angelo squeezed his eyes, embarrassed. "Sorry," and then with pleading eyes said to the policeman, "I can explain everything but not right now. Won't you please just do me one favor?"

"Only if you promise to buy me a cup of coffee."

"Jesus H. Christ," the transporter cried.

"Hush up," Cal hissed to the transporter. "Angelo, if you don't promise this officer a cup of coffee, I swear I'm going to explode."

Angelo smiled. Turning back, he held out his hand again. "You have my word."

The policeman shook Angelo's hand, holding it long enough so that Angelo felt a trill of excitement shoot up his arm. "What do you want me to do?"

"Find this gentleman's partner. His name is Carlo. They won't allow him up so you have to escort him to the service elevators. They're on the other side of the main elevators. We'll meet you there in two minutes."

The policeman looked over at Cal who bulged out his lower lip. "Okay," the policeman said. "See you in two minutes."

Angelo followed behind the transporter as he wheeled Cal into the service elevator. Just after the transporter entered his key, Angelo pressed the first-floor button. Then he leaned against the wall and offered Cal a reassuring wink.

"Wonderful," the transporter said, reeking with sarcasm. "If I get fired for this, I'll want more than a cup of coffee."

Before the elevator doors closed, the very security guard who wouldn't let Carlo up to see Cal, stuck his foot in between the doors. "Going down?" Angelo was stunned into silence as the security guard entered. Over the next several seconds, as the elevator motor hummed, Angelo closed his eyes and said a silent prayer. When the elevator doors opened on the first floor, Carlo was standing there, waiting. The policeman had escorted him around back to the service elevator without anyone questioning him.

Carlo and the security guard were now face to face. "Hey, weren't you the one . . . ." and then looking at Angelo added, "I thought I told you . . . ."

Sensing the conflict brewing, the policeman intervened. "Are you getting out?"

"What's going on?" he replied suspiciously.

The policeman held out his arm to prevent the doors from closing.

"Important police business," and then he gestured to the open doors like a *maître d'* at a fine restaurant. "After you."

The security guard harrumphed, staring Angelo down as he exited.

Once the doors closed, Angelo breathed a sigh of relief. "You two only have a few seconds."

Carlo squeezed in between the scuffed metal wall and Cal's wheelchair. In the time it took for the elevator to reach the fifth floor, he watched those two men share a proper good-bye. Carlo kissed Cal on the sides of his face, on his eyelids and on his mouth while Cal stroked Carlo's cheek with the back of his hand. The doors opened. Carlo and Cal shared one last kiss.

"Jeez Louise," the transporter said, wiping his eyes. "Leave it to gays to make a five second elevator trip into an abridged version of Romeo and Juliet."

Every teary eye in the elevator locked onto Cal's wheelchair as the transporter wheeled him away. "He's going to be all right," Angelo reassured Carlo.

Carlo hugged him. Angelo glanced over at the policeman. "Thank you," he mouthed. Just then, Angelo's cell phone rang. When the elevator doors opened again, he excused himself. "I have to answer this."

"I take my coffee with cream and no sugar," the policeman shouted as Angelo hurried off.

◆◆◆

Stanzione remained at the hospital for the rest of the day while Angelo saw patients at the office. Steven helped, but Angelo felt overwhelmed not only by the number of people in the waiting room, but by the way the events of the morning had played out. Not only had he successfully united Carlo and Cal before his procedure but he was also finally introduced to the policeman, though he didn't know the policeman's name or how to get in touch with him.

And his internal medicine boards were in less than two weeks. Stanzione had promised Angelo he could take this week off to prepare, but clearly he hadn't factored in the chance of an emergency that would pull him away from the practice.

He hoped this wasn't indicative of all Stanzione's planning skills.

Once the last patient was gone and Angelo had completed all his notes, he threw on his backpack and walked up front to say good night.

Steven still toiled away at the billing and limply waved without looking up. "See you tomorrow."

Angelo stepped out into the chilly night. A dark car was double-parked in front of the office. "Dr. Perrotta?"

Angelo squinted to see who was calling him. "Do I know you?"

The man seated behind the wheel smiled brilliantly. "You owe me a cup of coffee."

Angelo regarded him carefully. It was New York after all. A memory clicked. "I didn't recognize you without your uniform."

"I try not to wear it when I'm off duty." They stared at each other for another second. "Do you not recognize me now? I can show you my badge if you want."

"What's your name?" Angelo found himself fighting not to blush.

"Jason Murphy.

The policeman had thrown him, he could hardly deny. Even in the dim light of evening he was ridiculously handsome. "How did you find me?"

"Um, I am a policeman."

Angelo shook his head, embarrassed. "Of course."

"Listen, do you need a ride home? I'm more than happy to drive you."

Angelo stood under the streetlight contemplating the long walk ahead, but also considering this is how most victims get murdered. Despite the nag of suspicion, Angelo couldn't resist this genial, attractive, and interesting man. "If it's not too much trouble."

Jason smiled. "Get in."

Angelo stepped inside the black SUV and sank back against the leather interior. For a second, he closed his eyes as exhaustion washed over him. Jason pulled away. At the stoplight, Angelo glanced over and found Jason staring back at him. "Tired?"

"Beyond tired. Too tired to study, but I have to."

"Doctors take exams?"

"Not just any exam. The exam of all exams. My internal medicine boards," Angelo said, pulling down the visor to assess himself in the mirror. "Whoa, how did you recognize me when I look like this?"

"Why don't we grab a cup of coffee?" Jason asked. "It'll wake you up."

Though coffee was exactly what he needed, Angelo was too preoccupied with his upcoming exam. "I'd love to, but there's too much riding on this exam. I really need to study." Jason didn't push. He asked Angelo for the address. Minutes later, the SUV pulled up to Angelo's apartment building.

Jason grabbed ahold of Angelo's arm before he had a chance to open the door. "What you did today—for those two men—that made my heart explode inside."

Angelo grinned suddenly, wide, and gleeful. "I couldn't have pulled it off without your help."

"Is there any possibility you might be free . . . after your exam?"

Angelo opened his mouth to speak, but his cell phone rang, giving both of them a jolt. "I'm sorry. It's my boss."

"I understand."

"Yes, Dr. Stanzione. Is everything all right?" Without thinking, Angelo got out of the SUV still listening to his boss prattle on about Cal. Inserting the key into his building's front door lock, it occurred to Angelo he hadn't thanked Jason or acknowledged his invitation to go on a date. Angelo let go of the door and turned around to catch him, but he was already gone. Fate had stepped in and made the decision perfectly clear.

CHAPTER FIVE

The next morning, Angelo hopped out of the cab, all too aware of the grinding urgency churning in his stomach. After speaking with Stanzione the night before, it was clear Cal's health was not improving. The alarm he felt was only exacerbated by Stanzione's long-winded explanation about how this wasn't his fault. Never once did Stanzione mention if he had spoken to Carlo.

"Hey Tiffany," Angelo said. There were two patients waiting. "Just give me a second to settle in." Based on his conversation with Stanzione, Angelo assumed he'd be at the hospital most of the day. Throwing his backpack on top of his desk, a note caught Angelo's eye.

Meeting in Dr. Stanzione's office. Now!!

Angelo knocked on the door and ventured in.

"Come in. Come in," Stanzione said.

Stanzione's office was a mirror image of his next door, but larger. A massive L-shaped desk took up most of the space. There was a small sofa to the right and two consultation chairs positioned in front of the desk. Bookshelves overstuffed with medical textbooks. Diplomas, certificates, awards, and magazine articles touting Stanzione as Top Doctor hung on the wall behind Stanzione's chair.

Demetre and his assistant, Laura, a middle-aged woman with dark hair faintly streaked with gray, and enormous blue eyes that seemed perpetually concerned, were already seated. Laura had a yellow legal pad on her lap, taking notes. Demetre appeared exhausted. Dark lines etched under his eyes. He wore scrubs and looked like he had just rolled out of bed.

"We were just talking." Stanzione stood behind his chair as if it was a podium. Steven sat legs crossed on the sofa, appearing completely disinterested and thoroughly annoyed. All eyes were on Angelo as he entered the room and sat next to Steven. "Now that SkinDem has officially moved in," Stanzione began, "I wanted us to meet. Demetre and I had some preliminary discussions about my medical spa idea. Angelo, the reason I asked you to join us is because I want you to spend every free minute you have downstairs shadowing Demetre. You need to learn what he does. Also, I was thinking you should attend an aesthetic workshop. They have them all the time. Usually, they're at some Marriott over a weekend. Am I right, Demetre?"

"Um, yeah." Demetre was slouched in the chair, fiddling with the drawstrings of his scrub pants.

"I can reach out to Abby from Silverlight," Laura offered as she wrote, "or the rep from Illuminesance and see if they know of any upcoming courses."

"Good," Stanzione said, clapping his hands together. "I want Angelo to be familiar with the different types of lasers, and what they're used for. Plus, he should learn how to administer Botox and fillers. Am I right, Demetre?"

"Sure," he said, peering over at Angelo. "That is, if Angelo is interested in performing those types of procedures."

"Of course, he's interested," Stanzione insisted. "Right, Angelo?"

Before he even had a chance to open his mouth, Laura interrupted, "Who will be the medical director?"

Demetre reached over and placed his hand on Laura's knee. "There's no need to worry about that right now."

"But we need—" Laura started.

"Not now," Demetre said, firmly.

Angelo sensed a deeper concern in Laura's tone. Her cheek flickered as if zapped by an invisible current.

Stanzione seemed mildly confused and offered, "I would be the medical director, of course."

Laura's face relaxed. "Oh, that's wonderful news. That solves everything."

"I mean, really, who better than me?" Stanzione asked. "I own the office. I own the practice. Therefore, I should be the medical director. Demetre and Angelo will be associate directors. Then once we're up and running, we'll hire masseurs, facialists, and whatever else we need to have a fully functioning medical spa." Stanzione took a breath that seemed to portend there was still more to discuss, but his gaze was directed toward the door where Steven now stood, tapping his watch.

"Okay," Stanzione said. "That's all for today. This was a great meeting. Really great everyone."

When Angelo stood up, Demetre's eyes were fixed on the floor.

"Angelo," Stanzione said. "I need to speak with you."

Steven said, "There are patients waiting, Tony."

"We'll only be a moment."

Steven slammed the door on his way out.

"Sit down," said a subdued Stanzione. "Cal Hudson died."

"Oh my God," Angelo's voice went soft. "When?"

"Early this morning."

The news of Cal's death was a pain Angelo had not felt before, though he couldn't quite articulate the feeling. Instead, he experienced a series of memories: Carlo draped over Cal's bed as they questioned Angelo, Carlo crying because they wouldn't let him up to see Cal the day of the procedure, and Cal and Carlo kissing right before he was wheeled into the operating room. Scraps of earlier memories—the get-well cards, the red silk boxer shorts, a silver Mylar balloon—whirred through Angelo's mind until he heard the jarring voice of Stanzione calling out his name. "Angelo!"

"How is Carlo?"

Stanzione clenched his jaw. "Death is a delicate matter. My lawyer suggested I not engage with Carlo. I don't have to since they weren't legally married."

Stanzione's callousness stunned him. Minutes earlier, he was outlining a plan for a medical spa with the enthusiasm of someone planning a surprise birthday party. All the while, he knew Cal had died; to shift so seamlessly into the role of the doleful doctor who had lost a beloved patient was horribly incongruous.

"The use of prostacyclin is controversial," Stanzione continued. "I'm meeting with the chief of critical care to review the case with the hospital's legal team later today."

"Legal?" Angelo repeated. "Do you feel culpable?"

Stanzione bristled. "Of course not."

"I'm sorry . . . it's just when you mentioned legal, I thought . . . ."

"You thought what?" Beads of sweat appeared just under Stanzione's synthetic hairline.

"Nothing," Angelo backtracked. "I . . . I don't know what I meant."

"Let me tell you something," Stanzione said, and although he wasn't yelling, his voice was deep and intense. "You don't get to be where I am without making critical decisions. That's what being a doctor is all about."

Stanzione reached for the door, opened it, and dismissed Angelo with a sweeping wave of his royal arm. Angelo found himself being pulled out of the office like he had been jettisoned.

Angelo paused at the threshold. "I know this isn't a good time, but I had asked you if I could take off a few days to study before my boards . . . ."

"Under the circumstances that's no longer possible."

"But you agreed."

Stanzione's eyes fastened on Angelo's. "Do you know why I hired you?"

"Dr. Stanzione, I'm not complaining . . . ."

"It was because you said that you would do anything for this job, that I was the one who made you want to become an HIV specialist. I don't know if you realize this, but I feel a certain responsibility towards you."

Stanzione asserted his paternal authority, against which the fatherless Angelo had no defense.

"I'm forever in your debt for this opportunity," Angelo said, "but keeping this job is contingent on passing the boards."

"There were several board-certified candidates, but I chose you. Maybe it was your Italian background. Maybe I saw myself in you, and after your interview I thought, this kid is going to work his ass off. One day he could be big, like me." Angelo was embarrassed. By the crazed look in Stanzione's eyes he felt, often, as if their interactions together were being timed, and that his job was to perform as quickly and efficiently as he could and never question his boss.

"I won't let you down, Dr. Stanzione." Angelo saw no use in arguing. Stanzione had made up his mind.

"By the way," Stanzione added before closing the door. "If you're not ready by now, then a few extra days studying won't matter. Now get to work. There are patients waiting."

Angelo had nothing to say to that.

◆◆◆

Later that afternoon, Angelo sat alone in his office. Normally, Steven would have tidied up his desk, stacking his mail and messages neatly in a pile. Like a maid in a five-star hotel, Steven's turndown service occurred reliably at three every afternoon.

But not today.

Through the wall, Angelo heard Steven and Stanzione

arguing. If he remained perfectly still, he could make out bits of their conversation.

" . . . is a nasty bitch . . . don't like the way she talks to Tiffany . . . ."

" . . . give them a chance to settle in . . . ."

"And I don't like that he calls himself doctor . . . he's a tech. Laura calls him Dr. D."

"You're making much more out of this . . . a relief that we've rented . . . they're paying us forty grand a month."

"He still owes the first month's rent . . . haven't seen a penny yet."

And suddenly, he could hear them perfectly as the pitch of their voices grew louder.

"Why can't you just be optimistic for once?" Stanzione shouted. "This is what we wanted."

"No, this is what *you* wanted," Steven countered. "Don't make it sound like I had any choice in the matter."

"Goddamn it! What do you want from me? Everything is on my back: the mortgage for this office, our apartment, my mother's apartment. All the bills come in my name. This fucking job is killing me. What would happen if I had a heart attack? Who's going to pay the bills then?"

There was an extended silence. Angelo hadn't worked there long enough to experience firsthand the interior quarrels of these two men. Since July, he saw Steven as the central figure bridging the man Stanzione was at home to the doctor he portrayed at work. Now it seemed that Steven was a shaky bridge, rattled easily under pressure. Angelo stood up and quietly closed his office door. He attempted to busy himself by reviewing labs, but it was impossible.

"I'm sorry," he heard Steven say. His voice, shucked of its usual undercurrent of sarcasm, sounded like someone else's. A little boy? Perhaps that was what Steven really sounded like when they were alone.

"*Ste*-ven," Laura called. "*Ste*-ven, oh, *Ste*-ven."

"I'm in Dr. Stanzione's office, Laura."

Laura clattered down the hall. "There you are." She settled right outside Angelo's door, firing off questions. "Why is there no one at the front desk? Is Tiffany gone for the day? And if she is, who will be directing Dr. D's clients downstairs? I just can't keep leaving my desk in search of clients."

"I'm sorry Laura. I'll make sure Tiffany lets me know when she leaves for the day. Try to be patient. It's going to take time for everyone to get used to all the changes. I'll be up front in one second."

"Thank you, I'll tell Dr. D." As she retreated, her heels clicked on the marble floor echoing down the hall like popping fireworks.

Angelo was reminded again that Steven called Demetre a tech. What kind of technician was he after all? Angelo brought up the SkinDem website online:

> At SkinDem Skin Care and Laser Center we are dedicated to providing the highest quality of care to our patients. Our professional staff is specially trained to offer the latest medically based, scientific technologies that are customized to fit your individual needs. With a passion for beauty, we offer expert skincare and laser treatments for blood vessel removal, electrolysis, laser hair removal, laser skin treatments, tattoo removal, and facials.
>
> Owner and Chief Laserist, Demetre Kostas, CPE has a Master of Science in engineering from RPI.

Angelo reread Demetre's credentials. For whatever reason, he had assumed Demetre was a doctor. But why? Then he tried to recall if anyone had said he was, but the more he thought about it, the more he realized that he had made that assumption on his own. And, of course, Laura's persistent use of the title had not added to his clarity.

Online, Angelo discovered that Demetre's CPE degree stood for certified professional electrologist, which he had earned in 1993, but Angelo was unable to confirm whether Demetre had a master's degree from Rensselaer Polytechnic Institute or whether Demetre had graduated from college. What Angelo did find was that anyone could purchase a laser, but that a licensed physician had to oversee its proper use as the medical director. Now it all makes sense, thought Angelo. That's why Laura was so eager to have Stanzione designated as SkinDem's medical director. But who was the medical director now?

Steven knocked on Angelo's door as he entered.

"Why are you sitting here in the dark?"

"I hadn't noticed," Angelo replied.

Steven switched on the lights. "Tony just left, but he wanted me to remind you he won't be seeing patients tomorrow. He has a haircut appointment, and then he's coming to the office, but only to take meetings."

Angelo's eyes never veered away from his computer screen. Great, he thought to himself. Another day working alone in the coal mine.

Steven stood in the doorway. "I'm heading out soon. It's been one of those days."

As much as Angelo wanted to avoid getting caught up in the tangled relationship between these two men, he realized that was not possible. "Change is stressful."

"You probably heard us arguing," Steven said. "We don't usually argue like that . . . it's just, like you said, this has been very stressful for me . . . and Tony."

"It'll get better."

"I hope." Steven turned to walk away but stopped. "You know. Sometimes I paint to relax."

Angelo's internal scowl melted to pity once he saw Steven's hopeful expression. "I had no idea you were an artist."

Steven lit up like an old jukebox. "I collect things out of people's trash. You wouldn't believe what people throw away. I make things out of the stuff I find. That's all I did while we were in P-town. I'm hoping Tony buys a place there. I think it would be great for him. You know . . . to have a place where we could go with the dogs. He could have a garden, and I could do my art stuff."

"Have you been looking for a house?" Angelo asked.

"Kind of."

"What's holding Dr. Stanzione back?"

Steven glanced over his shoulder. "If I tell you, will you promise not to tell anyone?"

Angelo wasn't prepared to hear a secret disclosure, and yet, he was riveted. "Yes."

"Tony had a heart *issue* last year," Steven said cautiously.

"Heart issue," repeated Angelo. "You mean, a heart attack?"

Angelo saw Steven's expression change. His clarification seemed to dredge up memories Steven likely had suppressed. His eyes welled. His lower lip trembled. "Uh-huh," Steven confirmed in a timid voice. He gripped the edge of the desk, knuckles blanching. "Tony's doctors said he had to avoid stress."

Angelo stood up and closed the door. He pried Steven's fingers from the desk and gently sat him down.

"Listen to me," Angelo said reassuringly. He was holding Steven's hands in his. "You need to speak with Dr. Stanzione. Not here, but alone. It's okay for you to be concerned, especially if he had a heart *issue*. But arguing with him, here, about work is only going to make the situation more stressful."

"I guess you're right," Steven said

"I know I'm right," Angelo confirmed. "Continue to make your art. It's very therapeutic. In fact, why don't you make something for the waiting room and get rid of those tacky paintings?"

For just a moment, Steven seemed ready to disclose something else, but then he cast his eyes downward. "Yeah, I guess those paintings are kind of old anyway." Steven turned to leave. Looking over his shoulder he said, "I think it would be good for Tony to have a place away from the city, away from the stress. Don't you?"

"I do. I really do."

Angelo sat in his office long after everyone else had gone home. The news of Stanzione's heart attack was stunning. Angelo could only imagine the impact it had on a man like Stanzione. A man who portrayed himself as strong and virile but was actually frail and sickly. It occurred to him that Stanzione's medical spa might be a great idea after all. What if Stanzione planned to finance the spa and retain ownership as the medical director, leaving the co-directors to run the day-to-day operations? When Angelo considered that possibility, and the very real possibility that he and Demetre would work closely together, he found himself smiling. With Stanzione and Steven living part-time in P-town it would give him and Demetre the ability to run the spa as they saw fit.

When it came to Demetre and SkinDem, there were still many unanswered questions, but that didn't stop Angelo from imagining what a budding relationship might look like between them. Again, he thought of himself lying naked with Demetre pressed against his body. He had convinced himself once that an office romance would only end in tragedy, but why couldn't this one be different?

And then Angelo was reminded of Jason, the police officer who had aided him in uniting Cal and Carlo. Had he dismissed Jason's advances in order to make room for Demetre? It seemed to Angelo that was exactly how the events played out.

◆◆◆

The next morning an unexpected thunderstorm wreaked havoc on Manhattan. September was notorious for hurricanes that swept up from the southeast. Most times, the storms subsided by the time they reached New York landfall, but that didn't stop the rain. Crowds rushed for busses that splashed them with water. Unwieldy umbrellas collapsed against the gusty winds.

By the time Angelo arrived at the office, he was drenched. It was no surprise when Tiffany informed him that several patients had canceled their appointments. Angelo sat alone in his office, studying. A knock at the door startled him back to the present. "Hiya handsome," Jill whispered, the five-star drug rep. "Is this a good time?"

"Come in."

Jill wandered in with her hands behind her back as though she was browsing for antiques. She was wearing a well-tailored emerald-green pantsuit. "This is a beautiful office." Then she pointed to the skylight. "Uh, well, that just changes everything. How fabulous is that!"

"It's more than I could have ever dreamed of."

She sat across from Angelo. Legs crossed. "So, a little birdie told me that Mount Olympus has granted you guys a gift from the gods."

"You mean Demetre?" he said, leaning back in his chair. "Yes, SkinDem has officially moved in."

"Good for you," she said, scrunching her nose. "Good for all of you."

"If Dr. Stanzione's happy, then I'm happy."

Then Jill turned serious. "You don't think Tony's idea of a medical spa is a good one?"

Angelo marveled at the remarkable way she was able to shift her demeanor so quickly. She was either slightly crazy or utterly brilliant, he thought.

"I have no idea, Jill. I just started working here. I'm still trying to get the whole private practice thing down."

She stared at him keenly then, tapped her finger to her temple, and pointed at him.

"Gotcha. I heard about Jackie the other night at dinner." Jill pressed out her lower lip. "I liked her."

"It was a surprise to me too."

"But what a coup for you." Jill slid forward so that she was sitting on the edge of her seat.

"If by coup you mean more work then, yes, it was quite a coup."

Jill rested her elbows on the desk, staring directly into his eyes. "You know when life hands you lemons, you make lemonade."

"I'm not following you."

Jill tossed her head back, shook out her hair. "How can I explain this without sounding . . . okay, forget that. Let me just state the facts. Now that Jackie is no longer the one enrolling patients into the clinical trial, that makes you the research coordinator. As the RC, you are obligated to attend the annual meetings. By the way, the last one was at the Four Seasons in San Diego." Then she winked. "Not bad, huh? Heard it was a blast. In addition to that, you automatically get assigned to our speaker's bureau so that you can deliver talks to other providers, nurses, and physician's assistants, regarding the outcomes of the clinical trial. Get where I'm going with this?"

Her forwardness was jarring. Angelo found this entire conversation somewhat inappropriate. "Why wouldn't you just have Dr. Stanzione speak? He is the lead investigator."

She laughed at the troubled expression on his face. "It's not a matter of choosing, sweetheart. We can use you both. There's plenty to go around." Then she made a twirling motion with her finger. "I'm talking twenty-five hundred for a one-hour dinner lecture, and if we fly you out of town that number doubles, plus airfare and hotel accommodations."

"I'd have to discuss this with Dr. Stanzione."

"What's there to discuss?" Jill smiled wryly. "All I need is your social security number. Lectures are always after work. Checks will be sent directly to your home. No one has to know." She raised an eyebrow and sat back. Dark clouds had converged overhead. The room was dim except for a stream of gray light filtering from above. Half of Jill's face was obscured in darkness, glowing through it, her blue eyes shone. "You're an up-and-comer. After a year or two you'll be a thought leader, just like Tony."

"I see." But what kind of thought, he wondered.

When she snapped her fingers, Angelo felt it like a thunderclap. "I knew you would."

"You're being very optimistic," Angelo said, smiling. "Remember, I haven't even passed my boards yet."

"Minor details," Jill replied.

In the hall, Angelo heard Stanzione cursing. Seconds later, he appeared in the doorway, drenched. "Can you believe this goddamn weather?"

"Time to build that ark," Jill said.

Immediately, Angelo noticed Stanzione's hair looked different. It was unnaturally black, like a Vampire wig, but much shorter with a crop of spikes on top.

"Did you get a haircut?" Jill asked.

Stanzione reached to touch his hair but caught himself. "Oh yeah, I did. It's a mess now because of the rain."

"No, I like it," she said, standing up to scrutinize it closer. "It makes you look . . . younger." Stanzione reacted with a visceral throb of excitement as if that was his intention all along.

"I don't know about that," he replied sheepishly.

"Do you need a moment to collect yourself or should I follow you into your office?"

"No, come in."

"We'll chat again," Jill said to Angelo before exiting, but not before she turned an imaginary lock to her lips and threw away the key.

CHAPTER SIX

By early October, Angelo was consumed with only one thing: the results of his internal medicine board exam. He returned home every night with a mounting trepidation. Each time he unlocked his mailbox, the warning voice of Stanzione echoed resoundingly about their agreement. The wait was driving him mad.

One afternoon, he slipped out to eat lunch by himself. Steven reminded him there was a pharmaceutical rep waiting, but he made an excuse about a dentist appointment. He strode through Union Square, the crisp fall breeze scouring his ears. He entered McDonald's and ordered two cheeseburgers, small fries, and a Diet Coke. Strolling through the square, amidst skateboarders abrading the concrete while attempting kick flips down steps, he ate lunch. The thought of eating fast food was brewing all morning, having dreamed of his mother with heartbreaking clarity and those afternoons she took him and his older sister, Camille, to McDonalds on special occasions.

His mother paid with crumpled dollar bills she pulled from her jeans, and the loose change they had recovered under the sofa cushions. She'd sipped coffee as young Camille and Angelo swiveled back and forth on school-bus-yellow fiberglass seats, holding a French fry in one hand and a cheeseburger in the other.

Now on the south corner of Union Square, Angelo sat on a bench overlooking the mega music store, chewing his straw when he saw the date flash overhead in the giant digital clock. October sixth. It was his mother's birthday. She would have been sixty-two.

Despite his disdain for reminiscence, his subconscious seemed tethered by it. It had been fourteen years since her death, and he still dissected the choices she had made in the months before she died, refusing chemotherapy, and telling him that she didn't want to die in a hospital. It was bewildering to think that the woman who encouraged him to become a doctor was the same person who refused to take their medical advice.

That year, he hated her for being a coward. In hindsight, he knew she had made the right decision. Still, that didn't quell the slap of disappointment he experienced when she told her children how long she had left to live. If only he could have compartmentalized his feelings then, the way he did now.

Then suddenly, cutting through his apparition of nostalgia, was Jason Murphy. The policeman from the hospital was heading toward him, smiling brightly, which rendered him even more attractive to Angelo. Though he had a narrow waist, his muscular arms and broad chest gave him a solid looking build, which was only accentuated by his fitted uniform. "Well, if it isn't Dr. Perrotta."

"Fancy meeting you here."

"My partner and I were driving around, looking for a place to eat lunch."

"Your partner?"

"Yeah." He pointed to the patrol car where a Black woman sat in the driver's seat."

"Oh, your work partner."

"You thought I meant partner, as in boyfriend?" Jason asked.

"Yes, I did," Angelo said. "Except I never got used to the idea of gay men referring to their partners as 'boyfriend.'"

"Too sissy for you?"

"No," Angelo said, realizing he had insulted Jason. "It's just . . . if you decide to be in a relationship with a man, aren't they your partner?"

"I like the sound of boyfriend," he said, sitting down. "How have you been? I haven't seen you since you roped me into that . . . I don't know what you call it but . . . ." Jason wagged his finger at him. "You're a sneaky guy."

"Desperate times call for desperate measures."

"Whatever happened to your patient?" Jason asked.

Angelo raised a fist to his mouth to choke back the unexpected emotional swell.

"Are you okay?"

Angelo remained quiet, fearing he might begin weeping if he uttered a word.

"I didn't mean to bother you on your lunch hour," Jason said. "I just wanted to say hi." He got up to leave.

"Don't go," Angelo said. "Would you like a fry?"

"I'd rather take you out to dinner."

"Can I ask you a question?" Angelo asked.

Jason smiled unevenly. His blue eyes seemed to reflect the sun and sparkled. "Can you answer mine first?"

Angelo inhaled sharply. "Cal . . . my patient, died."

Jason sat back down. They remained quiet in the charged silence that followed. "That's awful news," Jason said finally. "I'm so sorry."

"I still haven't recovered completely."

"I don't know how doctors do it," Jason said. "You must get so close to your patients, and for one of them to die . . . that must be like losing a family member."

"It is," Angelo confirmed. "Likewise, I can't imagine how scary it must be for you to go to work every day. It's not likely one of my patients is going to kill me. Isn't it exhausting, living in fear?"

"I don't see it that way," Jason explained. "The thing is, I see my job like yours . . . I'm helping people. It's not all cowboys and Indians. Remember, I was stationed outside a criminal's ICU room for a week."

"Is that part of the job?"

Jason's partner slapped her hand against the car door. "I'm starving here!"

"One minute," he replied. "To be honest, I had . . . a situation last year where I discharged my weapon. I had what they call a problematic recovery, so I see a mental health care practitioner. After an internal affairs investigation, it was determined that I had acted impulsively. So, I'm on a one-year probation, which includes seeing a therapist once a month. Good news is that I feel great, and my final evaluation is in six months."

Jason's partner honked the horn, startling them. "Doctor, please say you'll go on a date with him so I can eat."

"My partner's *hangry*," Jason said. "I should go."

Angelo fixed his eyes on Jason's, and for that one moment, everything seemed both possible and indescribably confusing. Why hadn't he accepted Jason's invitations? Was it to make room for Demetre? "Jason, wait."

And as if the cosmos were colliding at that very moment, Angelo saw something completely unexpected. Ambling across the square was Demetre, escorted by a short, stocky woman. Angelo felt buoyed by anxiety, a jittery sense that events were unfolding inexorably, and there was nothing he could do.

Demetre's eyes skittered from one person to the next, smiling, until his gaze fell upon Angelo, and then he wasn't smiling anymore. He turned away, and Angelo knew Demetre had seen the real Angelo Perrotta: poor white trash from Staten Island. He cast a rueful glance at his unfinished fries, the crumpled bag soused with grease, and the oversized soft drink in his hand. The clues were all there in the blinding nimbus of McDonald's golden arches.

Just as they passed, Demetre took one final glimpse and Angelo waved, buckling under the weight of his humiliation but determined to sustain an air of breezy indifference. And then they were gone.

"Hey, is everything okay?" Jason asked.

Then something else happened. Angelo received a call from Tammy. "Did you pass?"

"You got your exam results?"

"Yes, just now. I passed!"

"Congratulations!" Angelo yelled.

"Get your ass home and check the mail."

Click.

"I'm so sorry, Jason, but I have to run back to my apartment. That was my friend, Tammy. She got her exam results."

"Well, what could be faster than a police escort?"

"Police escort," Angelo repeated disbelievingly. "You're not serious?"

"Only if you'll let me take you out to dinner tonight to celebrate."

"Deal."

They hurried toward the police car. "Mary, this is Dr. Perrotta," Jason said to his partner as he opened the rear door.

"When I said 'Say yes' to going on a date," Mary kidded, "I didn't mean this very minute!"

As they drove away, Angelo glanced up again at the digital clock. He heard his mother's voice. *It's okay. It's okay.*

◆◆◆

"You're late," Steven said as Angelo walked into the office. "There are patients waiting."

"Tell them it was worth the wait." He slapped his exam results on the front desk and winked at Tiffany. He could hardly contain his exuberance, but in the short time he had been a doctor, he learned there was little time to wallow in self-pity or celebrate major victories when patients were waiting.

Two hours later Angelo listened to a patient explain why he was abandoning his HIV treatment in exchange for ozone therapy baths, when he heard a knock at the door.

"Sorry to bother you," Demetre said, "but when you're done can you find me?"

"Sure."

Fifteen minutes later, Angelo ventured downstairs. Laura sat behind her glass desk looking more annoyed than usual. Without a single utterance, she pointed a pen at the first exam room.

"Come in," Demetre said after Angelo knocked. On the exam table was an older woman, positioned on her right side. The slit in the blue paper gown revealed her leopard print bra and panties. "Violet, this is Dr. Perrotta. Doctor, meet Violet."

Violet was a reedy woman in her late seventies with a weathered face, red lipstick bleeding into the creases around her mouth, and varnished orange skin that was as thin as parchment. She wore magenta nail polish and strands of gold necklaces.

"So, you're the famous doctor I've been hearing about," she said in the husky voice of someone who'd smoked for decades. "You're a cutie." Then Violet did a double take, squinting up at him. "Where'd you get that scar, kid?"

"Violet," Demetre warned. "We're here to discuss you, not Dr. Perrotta."

"It's okay," he replied to ease the tension. "I got bit by a dog when I was two."

She stared at his face with cold appraisal. "Why don't you let Dr. D take care of it with his laser?"

Demetre glanced at Angelo, assuming the posture of a weary son embarrassed by his irrepressible mother.

"Moving on," he said. "I'm in the process of removing this hideous tattoo from Violet's hip." He gestured to a faded heart with the name, 'Sam', written in the center.

"It's a stupid tattoo for a stupid ass," Violet groused as she wrestled with the gown. "Not mine. The one I married."

"Well, you'll be rid of both soon," Demetre said.

"I've already gotten rid of one Sam," she said, followed by a long rickety breath. "Now, I just need you to get rid of the other pain in my ass." Then she launched into a coughing fit. "Well, get on with it," she said in between jagged breaths. "I ain't got all day."

"Okay, Violet," Demetre said. "Let's take it down a notch."

She jerked her head at him, insulted. "Watch your mouth or I throw you over my knee and show you who's boss." This was followed by wheezy laughter, another coughing fit and then, the expulsion of fresh mucous into a tissue she had tucked in her bra.

"There, there," Demetre said. "See what happens when you get yourself all worked up. Come on now. Let's show Dr. Perrotta." With surprising agility, Violet sat up without assistance. It was then Angelo realized just how small she was, probably no taller than four foot eleven and weighed at best ninety pounds. Demetre pulled the gown off her shoulder, exposing a constellation of various sized freckles, and in the center of this Milky Way of moles was a dark incongruous sun over her left scapula. "She noticed this a month ago but says it hasn't gotten any bigger," Demetre stated. "What do you think?"

Angelo leaned forward, pinching his chin as he examined the irregular borders and darkly pigmented center. "You obviously enjoy sunbathing."

"I told Dr. D to hit it with the laser," she croaked. "Can't stand the sight of it."

"It's nothing, right?" Demetre whispered.

"It looks fairly benign," Angelo said to Demetre. "Can you remove it using a laser?"

"What do you mean, can you remove it using the laser?" Then Violet yanked up her gown and turned her head to Demetre. "Is this guy a real doctor? I didn't come all the way downtown to be a guinea pig for some medical student."

"Settle down, Violet. Remember your pressure." Demetre gripped Angelo's arm, ushering him out of the exam room. "Let me talk to Dr. Perrotta privately."

Just outside the exam room, Demetre muttered, "Oy vey. I'm so sorry I dragged you into this."

"She's quite a character."

"She's what my mother would have referred to as a prickly pear." They laughed but were quickly hushed by Laura. "Listen," Demetre said. "What are you doing after work?"

"Dr. D," Laura said, tapping her wrist. "Clients are waiting."

Demetre tilted his head back—"Thank you, Laura"—then he goggled his eyes at Angelo.

"I'll let you get back to Violet." Then Angelo had a thought. "Come to think of it, you really should send her to a dermatologist. It's always best to err on the side of caution."

"I'll handle Violet Trautman," he said. "Come by later, after you're done for the day. I'll show you how to use the blue light laser."

Angelo stood there, feeling a thrum of excitement, but only in the way a harmless office flirtation causes a frisson of pleasure. "Is that the one you use to treat scars?"

Demetre reached up and ran his finger along Angelo's cheek. "I wouldn't change a thing on that face. Don't let anyone try to change you."

◆◆◆

Angelo crept down the stairs after his last patient. The office was dark and shadowy. "Hello?"

Demetre called out. "I'm in here."

Angelo headed down the dimly lit corridor and pushed open the door. Demetre was reclined in his chair, bare feet up on his desk with two cucumber slices over his eyes. Angelo laughed. "I hope I'm not disturbing you."

"No, come in."

"I wish I had brought my camera," he said, easing into a chair. "This would make a great advertisement for SkinDem."

Demetre sat up, popped off the cucumber slices and blinked repeatedly as though he'd just walked out of a dark movie theater. "Ah, that feels so much better. Even with the eye shields, I know the laser light is wreaking havoc on my eyes."

"Is that the blue light laser . . . the one you're going to show me how to use?"

Demetre waved away his words and opened the bottom drawer of his desk. He poured two glasses of bourbon and slid one over to Angelo. "Congratulations, I heard you passed your boards."

"Thank you." Angelo tipped his cup and drank.

"Besides, you're a fucking doctor," Demetre added. "I'm not going to teach you how to operate a laser like some trained monkey. Stanzione should be ashamed he even suggested such a thing."

Angelo stared confusedly. "I thought you'd agreed."

"I know he's your boss and all, but he doesn't know what he's talking about."

"So, you're not going to train me to use the blue light laser?"

"Angelo, if you want to learn how to remove hair then I'll be happy to show you, but I'm not going to force you to do something because of some bullshit scheme Stanzione cooked up."

"What about the medical spa?" Angelo asked. "I thought you were all in."

Demetre rubbed his chin. Angelo detected mischief in his eyes, and for a moment he wondered if Demetre was pulling his leg.

"So, what did you think of Violet?" Demetre asked, navigating away from the topic of the medical spa. "Some piece of work, right?"

"She's a colorful woman."

"That she is," he said, holding the cup to his lips before taking another swallow. "Her ex-husband, not Sam, the one before, owned a chain of stereo stores in Phoenix. After he died, she inherited everything and sold them off to PC Richards. You know how much that old bitch is worth?"

"I can't imagine."

Demetre snapped his fingers. "Hey, are you accepting new patients?"

"You're not thinking of pawning Violet Trautman off on me?"

"No, she has an arsenal of doctors already," Demetre said, laughing. "I do have lots of attractive male clients I can refer to you."

Angelo took another sip instead of responding. The warm syrupy taste coursed through his body so that he felt flushed. *Starting with you, I hope,* Angelo wanted to ask.

"Oh, that's right," Demetre said. "You're not looking for love."

"I never said that." Angelo cocked his head from side to side, cracking his neck. "I said, I'm currently not dating anyone. Besides, it's unethical to date patients."

Demetre walked behind Angelo and began massaging his shoulders. "Why so tense? Now that you've passed the boards you should feel relieved."

Angelo sat up. It was disconcerting to feel Demetre's strong hands kneading his muscles like they were clay.

"I am relieved," he said right before he moaned with pleasure. "It's these damn shoes . . . I have a blister."

"Come with me." Demetre grabbed the bottle and walked into an exam room. "Take off those shoes and lie down."

The cushiony, leather-upholstered exam table was nothing like the outdated ones in the exam rooms upstairs. Angelo kicked off his shoes and removed his socks, dusting the black lint off his feet. Demetre poured them another round.

"Here," Demetre said. They drank shots in unison. Demetre took the cups and set them aside. Pulling up a stool, Demetre ordered Angelo to lie back. "Let me see your foot."

"Seriously?" Maybe it was the bourbon or the utter relief he felt now that he had the boards behind him. Angelo let out a long exhalation of air and propped up his feet.

"Well, you have a blister on your heel," Demetre said, opening a drawer. He removed a packet, tore it open, and squeezed the ointment on his finger. Angelo sank into the cushion as if he were set in gelatin. All at once, he felt like he was floating.

"How does that feel?" Demetre asked as he applied the ointment to Angelo's blistered heel.

"Like heaven."

With Demetre kneading his thumbs into the sole of Angelo's foot, the tension faded.

"It's those cheap shoes," Demetre said. "You should spend a little of that hard-earned money and buy better shoes. Your feet will thank you in the end."

Angelo didn't respond. He was lost in the swell of the bourbon and the tingling running up his leg. He was neither insulted by Demetre's comment nor did he believe he was referencing his impoverished upbringing. At that moment, he didn't care about anything other than being touched.

"You have to take better care of yourself, Doctor." Demetre moved on to Angelo's other foot. "You want to end up a nervous wreck like Steven?"

"Steven is stressed out by all the changes," Angelo said. "Plus, Laura gets under his skin."

"Steven is a shelter dog. Cute. Sad. Eager to please. Except he has no identity. It's like Stanzione rescued him from certain death, and from that moment on, Steven ceased being an individual. Tell me, what do you know about him other than being a control freak?"

"I know he likes to paint," Angelo declared proudly.

Demetre chuckled. "You mean the trash art?"

"See, you do know something about Steven."

He leaned in, leering down at Angelo. "I wouldn't hang that shit in my waiting room."

"Those pieces upstairs are Steven's?"

Demetre cocked an eyebrow. "Original trash art by Steven."

Angelo sat up, his head spinning. "I told Steven to get rid of them. Fuck. I called them tacky. Why did I say that?" Angelo cringed as his spirits sank further, recalling Steven's wounded expression when he told him the paintings were tacky.

Demetre's eyes were bright with relish. "Don't ever stop being honest. The truth is brutal but necessary." He poured them another round. "Come on. Drink up. Let's toast to Steven, the shelter dog and his trash art."

"Now, you're being cruel," Angelo said. "Stanzione doesn't treat Steven like a dog. They've been together fifteen years. Okay, so maybe there's a power imbalance in Stanzione's favor, but that doesn't mean they don't love each other."

Demetre jerked up. Feet planted firmly on the floor. "You think Steven and Tony are really in love?"

"Yes, well . . . ."

"They sleep in separate beds."

"Well, how would I know that?" Angelo asked.

Demetre sat back down, grinning like he'd just beat Angelo in cards. "You know, for a doctor you're not very observant."

Angelo stood up quickly. For a moment, he felt wobbly. "I am very observant. I observe people all the time." Without realizing, he had doused his shirt in bourbon.

"Okay," Demetre said, reaching up to grab several paper towels and handing them to Angelo. "So, Dr. Observant, you think Steven and Tony are *really* in love?"

"Yes, I do," he said petulantly as he blotted his shirt.

When Angelo looked up, he was met by Demetre's eyes, studying him narrowly. "Tony is so miserable he looks perpetually constipated, and disguised under that strip of AstroTurf he calls hair and buried under that armor of artificial muscles is a sad little fairy his macho Italian father rejected years ago. But instead of realizing how lucky he is, how fucking amazing his life could be, what does the great Stanzione do? He bitches and moans and whines. And at the end of the day, he drags that poor little shelter dog home with him and projects all that anger and frustration upon him, throwing scraps of food on the floor when he's done eating so that Steven can chew them. Does that sound like love to you?"

Angelo clenched his cup with his teeth and began a slow clap. "That was poetic and harsh."

"I only speak the truth." Demetre stood up and took a bow. "Kid, if you learn anything in life it's that in order to survive you have to be indefatigable if not indestructible. When that bitch, Kathleen Eichhorn, refused to make me partner, even though I was doing most of the work, I saved my money and bought a laser. Now I own my own company, and every single one of my clients followed me. Having a Park Avenue address was the next step. I wasn't born with a silver spoon in my mouth. I had to fight for everything I have, and I would do anything to keep it."

"So, where does the medical spa fit in?" Angelo asked.

"Forget the spa," he said quickly. "What do you want? What are your dreams?"

Angelo cleared his throat. The conversation had veered from casual and celebratory to serious and interrogatory. "I don't know."

"Bullshit. Everyone has dreams."

So, drunk, he said the first thing that came to mind. "I hope to become partner one day."

"Good." Demetre drew a deep breath. "So, you have a goal in mind." Angelo hoped that Demetre would leave it at that, but then he said, quite softly and without inflection, "And you think Stanzione is going to let you become his partner one day?"

"Yes," he said timidly. "Why not?"

"Face it, kid," Demetre said, chuckling, snidely. "He's never going to give you that."

Angelo shook his head, fiercely. "We have a deal."

"Oh, so you signed a contract?"

"No, it was a verbal agreement," Angelo said. "I had to pass the boards first."

"And Stanzione said he would make you partner?"

"It was implied."

Angelo suddenly felt like Demetre knew more than he was letting on. Assessing his responses as though he was taking mental notes.

"Why do think Stanzione hired you?" Demetre asked.

"What kind of question is that?"

Demetre sat there grinning, a look of amused pity on his face. "I'm not here to burst any bubbles, but the truth is that Stanzione doesn't do anything unless there's something in it for him. Why didn't he hire someone already board certified? Did you ever think about that?"

"Yes, Stanzione said he hired me because he knew I'd work harder than any of those board-certified candidates."

"Or perhaps it's because they asked for too much money, or maybe he picked you because you're young, cute and eager to please."

Angelo gaped at him for a wounded second. "Are you implying that I'm a shelter dog like Steven?"

"Are you?" Demetre asked. "I don't know you well enough yet."

"I refuse to eat anyone's scraps." Angelo sat up, insulted. He picked up his socks and proceeded to put them back on.

"Guess I hit a nerve," Demetre mocked. "I'm sure you're making more money now than you ever made in your life, but eventually, as the years pass, you'll realize just how much Stanzione has been screwing you, and bitterness will fester inside you until you grow as old and miserable as him." There was a long pause. Angelo fought to hide the hurt and confusion he was experiencing. "That's enough shop talk for one night," he said turning amiable and charming again. "We have bigger fish to fry."

"What?"

Demetre leaned forward. The V of his scrub top buckled to reveal the deep cleft of his chest swathed in tufts of dark hair. "Listen to me," he said, clutching Angelo's knees. "Appearance is everything, and while you are an attractive man, you dress like a high school teenager attending the freshman formal."

"You're being cruel again."

"Don't act wounded. I'm just being honest. I believe you have dreams. You set your sights high and landed in a very good place, but what happens next depends completely on you. Being better than who you are sometimes means pretending to be someone you're not. You're a Park Avenue doctor. You should be eating caviar, not burgers from a bag, and dating princes not policemen."

"Fuck," Angelo said. He'd forgotten about his date with Jason. Angelo froze like a cornered mouse.

"Yeah, fuck him. Just don't date him."

"Fuck, fuck, fuck!" Angelo shouted, standing up. How could he have forgotten? It didn't seem possible that a dinner date with Jason had slipped his mind like forgetting to call someone back. Was Demetre right? Was Angelo not as observant as he thought he was?

"What is it?" Demetre asked.

"I have a date with that cop tonight."

"Cancel it."

"Wait. What?" He couldn't deny that was exactly what he wanted to hear from Demetre, that somehow it made his actions excusable. "I can't do that."

"Why not?" Demetre asked. "Text him right now."

"I've blown him off once already." The hope he felt about this burgeoning relationship with Demetre felt worth it—like a microscope gone into focus—new and refreshing and with endless possibilities.

"You're a doctor," Demetre said, grabbing Angelo's hips. He pulled him until their faces were so close Angelo could smell the bourbon on Demetre's breath. "Tell him something came up at the hospital. Tonight, we celebrate like kings. The day after tomorrow, you and I have unfinished business."

◆◆◆

The next morning, Angelo woke up sticky and peevish, replaying events of the night before, as much of them as he could remember. He cringed at the thought of himself lying on Demetre's exam table, slobbering like some moony-eyed drunk girl, his voice cloying and breathy. Angelo was disgusted and panicked. He jumped out of bed, ran into the bathroom, and threw up. Afterward, he stripped off his underwear and took a shower. He let the water envelope himself, but his body refused to relax under its calming stream. His stomach clenched, he vomited again. Brown saliva clung to his lips.

By the time he arrived at the office, Steven and Laura were conversing in the stairwell. It looked as if Laura was complaining. Her shoulders were practically touching her ears. As soon as they saw Angelo, she stopped talking and darted down the stairs like she'd forgotten to turn off the oven. "Morning," Angelo said, walking to his office.

Steven followed and closed the door behind him. "Apparently there was a little party here last night."

Angelo's stomach convulsed. "What do you mean?"

Steven slid into the chair and leaned forward like a neighbor bursting with gossip. "When I got here this morning, I noticed the lights were still on downstairs. So, I went to turn them off, and that's when I smelled the smoke."

"Smoke?"

"Yeah, so I checked all the rooms, and wouldn't you know, one of the exam rooms looked like there was a frat party: empty bottles of booze, cigarette butts and the worst smell of cigarette smoke." Steven's voice trailed off long enough for him to shiver with disgust. "I swear it's like a saloon down there. So then, I came up here and guess who I find sleeping on Tony's sofa?"

"Who?"

Steven glowered dramatically. "Demetre."

"What!"

Steven put his finger to his lips and jerked his head toward Stanzione's office. "Tony's meeting with him right now. When I woke Demetre, he said that he had worked late and didn't want to drive back home to New Jersey. Said he was worried about falling asleep at the wheel. I was like, *oh yeah, working late, huh.* Then I called Tony and told him he'd better get over here right away."

From down the hall, Laura called. "*Ste*-ven? *Ste*-ven?"

He rolled his eyes ferociously. "Back here, Laura."

She opened the door a crack and wedged her face in. "I'm sorry to bother you, but do you have any more Lysol?"

"I'll be right downstairs to help. Don't worry, we'll get rid of the smell."

Laura pouted with exasperation. "This is why I hate basement offices. No windows. Now it truly feels and smells like a dungeon." Then she disappeared, but Angelo could still hear her whining from down the hall.

"I'd better go help her," Steven said, getting up.

"Wait," Angelo whispered. "What do you think Dr. Stanzione is going to do?"

Steven shrugged. "He's not happy, but it's not like Demetre broke the law."

It was then the door to Stanzione's office opened. Demetre came out, hands in his pockets, bobbing along with a springy walk. Stanzione followed behind him. When he saw them staring anxiously, he stepped inside Angelo's office and closed the door. "We had a long talk," he said, gripping Steven's arms. "Demetre apologized, and he understands that if it ever happens again, he'll be asked to leave."

Steven looked skeptical. "And what about the smoking?"

"I told him we don't tolerate smoking, partying, or sleepovers." Stanzione's tone was imbued with a certain, fatherly tone as if Demetre was their reckless teenage son. But despite his assurance, Angelo could see by the look on Steven's face that he didn't believe any of it.

"Well, I guess that's that," Steven said facetiously. "Now if you'll excuse me, I have to go disinfect *the dungeon.*"

Once Steven was out of earshot, Stanzione looked at Angelo intently for a moment or two. "You have no idea how lucky you are."

"What do you mean?" Angelo asked with hesitation.

"What I wouldn't do to be your age again."

Then he walked back into his office and closed the door. He hardly came out again for the rest of the day.

CHAPTER SEVEN

Angelo woke up Saturday morning with a visceral pleasure, anticipating the day ahead. "Finally," he said, "I have a
thrilling reason to get out of bed."

Sweeping aside the events that unfolded the day before,
he saw no need to pick and pry them apart. He'd leave that
for Steven and Laura to hash out. All he remembered was
that Demetre and he had drunk bourbon and talked for
hours. They certainly hadn't smoked, and if anything,
Angelo remembered being in bed by midnight. What occurred after Angelo had left was unimportant to him even
though Steven was buzzing over the scandal for the entire
day. Angelo was less concerned with why Demetre slept
on Stanzione's sofa and more bothered that he hadn't confirmed their plans to go shopping. He assumed Demetre
would be there. He believed it wholeheartedly, but even
as he showered, the doubt seeped in like the soapy water
running in between his fingers.

He was still feeling good when he arrived at Barneys
at noon. Making his way to the men's section, he walked
through the department store as though it was an airport,
and he was leaving for vacation. As he stepped off the esca-
lator onto the fourth floor, he told himself for the umpteenth
time to relax, that there was nothing to worry about; he'll be
there. But once Angelo turned the corner and saw the crowd
milling through racks of shoes, Angelo felt an unshakeable
fear that Demetre had forgotten all about their date, and
he was home sprawled out on the sofa reading a magazine.
Though the bustling shoppers made Angelo smile, his eyes
leaped from one to the next searching for Demetre.

"May I help you?" A clerk appeared, looking delighted to see him.

"Actually, I'm meeting a . . . ." in midsentence he saw the back of Demetre's head. "Would you excuse me?" Of course he was excited and relieved, but as Angelo strode across the floor, he stopped to catch his breath. Angelo spoke casually, trying to contain his enthusiasm. "I bet you're one of those people who can't help but buy something for themselves even when they're supposed to be helping someone else."

Demetre turned around and smiled. He was wearing a black T-shirt with an obscenely deep V-neck and a pair of dark jeans. Immediately, he covered Angelo's eyes with his hand. "What size shoe do I wear?"

Angelo wrung his hands, trying to imagine Demetre's feet. "Ten?"

"Sorry Dr. Observant." When Demetre withdrew his hand, Angelo saw he was shaking his head. "Good guess, but I'm an eleven and a half."

"What's your point?"

He shrugged, picking up a black loafer. "I wanted to see if you paid attention to detail." Then he set the loafer back on the stand. "Okay," he said, clasping his hands together. "Where shall we begin?"

Angelo felt a flicker of tension run across his neck. "This store is so intimidating."

Demetre put his hand on Angelo's shoulder, massaging it a little.

"What are you intimidated by? Shoes? Shirts? Suits? Don't let anything intimidate you. You must learn to resist that. Don't look at yourself through anyone else's eyes except your own." Angelo was staring in Demetre's eyes when he felt that first scent of euphoria, an odd sensation intended for someone else, not him. "I know how you see yourself. Let me help you see who you really are."

Demetre guided Angelo back to the clerk.

"Do you trust me?" Demetre asked.

Angelo trusted Demetre completely.

◆◆◆

"Another bottle of Veuve, please," Demetre said in a raised voice.

"I don't think he's our server," Angelo said.

They were having an early dinner at Mr Chow in Tribeca. After several hours of shopping and several thousands of dollars later, Demetre decided they should reward themselves with carbs and champagne. Angelo had never spent more than a hundred dollars for any single purchase in his life and yet, today, he had been persuaded into overcoming any fear, albeit with Demetre's encouragement, and bought an entire new wardrobe. It felt all at once liberating and intoxicating charging twenty-eight hundred dollars to his credit card. Afterward, Angelo wandered around in a blissful daze like after a night of heavy drinking. He refused to allow himself to dwell on the financial aspect. Instead, he wanted to savor the thrill of being able to afford it all.

Carrying shopping bags rife with Burberry shirts, Theory pants, Ferragamo shoes and Ralph Lauren polo shirts, he felt like an heiress on a shopping spree with her stylist.

Even in the cab ride downtown, Angelo thought this day had felt so delicious—so glamorous—that he didn't feel like himself. As the world slurred by in a haze of color past the cab window, he caught a glimpse of his reflection in the glass and envied the person he saw. This day marked a change; Demetre had shown him a world Angelo hadn't known, and there was no turning back.

"I wanted to be a doctor when I was young, but my father had a landscaping business." Hunched over the table with his hand supporting his face, Demetre spoke without punctuation. Angelo listened eagerly but watched his fingers as they brushed through his hair and scored figure eights on his water glass. After a bottle of champagne, he seemed to relax, speaking as candidly as ever, tossing out personal truths without a second thought. "Papa said, 'you work with me. Do man's work.'"

"Somehow I don't see you tilling soil."

Demetre took a sip of champagne, dipped his finger in the glass and flicked it at Angelo. "Yeah, well, there was no saying 'no' to Papa. A summer job turned into a career. After he died, I inherited the business. I don't know if you know anything about landscape design, but I did very well for myself."

"What happened?"

"I got sick of dirt," he said irritably. "Some people don't mind getting their hands filthy. Tim loved it." Then he stared off into the distance, shaking his head. "I only kept it going for so long because of him."

"Why did you break up?"

Demetre turned his head to the side and exhaled slowly. "He got hooked on crystal meth."

"Oh, I'm sorry I brought it up."

"It's okay. I don't mind talking about it. I gave Tim an ultimatum: he had to get help or get out. Thank God he decided on rehab." Then Demetre laced his fingers together and set his hands on the table in front of him. "While he was away, I had time to think about what I wanted. By then I was too old to go to medical school. One day I was reading *New York* magazine. There was an article about lasers, and I decided that was for me. So, I sold off the business and went back to school. Everything I have is tied up in SkinDem. Now you understand why I won't give up my autonomy to Stanzione and his pipe dream? What idiot would do that?"

"Maybe you don't have to. Maybe Stanzione will make you an equal partner. He knows nothing about lasers."

Demetre shook his head, "You're so young and naive."

Angelo decided to drop the subject, but his natural curiosity only latched onto another line of questioning. "So, what happened after Tim got out of rehab?"

Demetre offered a hollow laugh. "Funny thing about rehab—once you get clean, you're not the same person anymore. I guess sobriety made us realize that we were better suited as friends." Demetre took a big gulp of champagne. Setting down the flute, he excused himself.

The server came just then and asked Angelo if he cared for another bottle of champagne. He shook his head, even though he really wanted to continue drinking. He wanted to drink buckets of champagne. That's because he was feeling amazingly good, better than he had in years, and it had everything to do with Demetre. It was like Demetre had burned off whatever shameful residue had tarnished Angelo's life, burdening him with guilt for wanting a better future. It was no longer enough that he had become a Park Avenue doctor. Now he was starving for experience and whatever else Demetre had in store.

Angelo sipped champagne contemplatively, a dumb smile growing on his face. Then, he had this sudden, unbidden image of Demetre and him as a couple like Stanzione and Steven but as equals, and from that one image came another until it spun into an idea where he saw them owning their own business together—a medical spa—just like the one Stanzione had talked about except that theirs wouldn't be some ridiculous plan orchestrated by a greedy doctor. No, Demetre and he would open a high-end spa for men with HIV where Angelo would take care of their health, and Demetre would make them look beautiful. They didn't need Stanzione. They had each other.

When Demetre returned, Angelo was excited to tell him all about his idea. Demetre plopped down in his chair and began snapping his fingers. "*Garçon, une autre bouteille de champagne. Tout suite. And the check, s'il vou plait.*"

Demetre seemed changed somehow to Angelo.

All day Angelo felt cushioned by the layers of conviviality between them, and over the course of those hours they had dissolved, one by one, drawing them closer as they'd gotten to know each other better. But this new familiarity made itself known by the reappearance of regret in Demetre's eyes, and Angelo wondered if all this talk about missed opportunities and lost love had made him sad.

The server brought over another bottle of champagne and placed the check on the table in between them. Demetre and Angelo reached for it at the same time. Just as their hands touched, Angelo felt a pulse of electricity shoot up his arm. "I got this," Demetre said.

"Are you sure?" Angelo could hardly contain his excitement, smiling crazily as his hand lingered.

Demetre snatched the check. "You know what I'd like to do tonight more than anything else in the world?"

Angelo caught his breath, anticipating that if Demetre suggested going back his apartment to have sex, he would faint. "What?"

"I want to go dancing."

They took a cab to Angelo's apartment so he could drop off his bags and change his shirt. Afterward, Demetre and Angelo walked to a club called The Roxy on West Eighteenth Street. A clot of cabs had formed at the club's entrance, releasing men into the street. They joined the crowd outside the warehouse doors where a skinny, pale doorman with yellow hair and piercing eyes was holding a clipboard. Demetre tried to enter the mob, pushing forward, only to be extruded back out like a belch. He cupped his hands around his mouth like a megaphone and shouted, "Blaine! Blaine!"

The doorman's head twitched anxiously like a bloodhound picking up a scent, and all at once he locked eyes with Demetre. His vacant expression turned familiar, almost fawning. "D!" Then he unhooked the velvet rope, and suddenly the crowd magically parted as if they were pulled in by Blaine's invisible tractor beam. Once they were on the other side, Angelo watched as Demetre exchanged hyperbolic compliments for free passes and drink tickets. Angelo and Demetre entered the club and ascended the stairs through the thumping darkness.

The dance floor was one enormous amebic mass of flesh under the glittering lights. Angelo followed Demetre to another velvet rope where a very large Black man stood with absolutely no expression. Demetre handed him two comp tickets, and they were allowed up a flight of stairs to a glass enclosed room with its own DJ.

At the bar, Demetre ordered tequila shots and water. "Drink tickets don't cover shots," a frustrated bartender said. Demetre threw down his platinum American Express. They drank back the shots with salt and lime. Afterward, they sat on carpeted blocks overlooking the dance floor, watching the crowd below as though they were gods. Angelo felt the thumping shock of the music in his chest like electricity. It was something he had never felt before, and he realized that it was excitement. Here he was for the first time, sitting in a VIP lounge among throngs of shirtless, dewy men, their muscular bodies rippling like piano keys under the flashing lights. Everyone was moving. Bodies in motion. Angelo could feel himself moving, although awkwardly.

"I guess you used to come here all the time," Angelo shouted.

Demetre leaned in, pressing his lips close to Angelo's ear. "What?" Angelo could smell his cologne even through the fog of artificial smoke. "I said, 'I bet you used to come here all the time!'"

Demetre nodded. Then put his arm around Angelo's neck and spoke directly into his ear, the moisture of his breath sent a ripple of pleasure down Angelo's back.

"Yeah, but that was a long time ago. Blaine is an old friend and a client."

"Speak of the devil," Angelo said, for there was Blaine hovering over Demetre. They spoke without shouting, a trick Angelo supposed they'd learned through years of clubbing. Blaine looked over at Angelo, his eyes lingering for an extra second before pulling away. He reached into his pocket and slipped something into Demetre's hand. Then Blaine kissed the air on both sides of Demetre's face before disappearing down the stairs.

"What did he give you?" Angelo asked.

Demetre put his hand on Angelo's knee and squeezed it. For a while, he just stared out at the crowd. Angelo wondered what he was thinking. Where earlier he saw regret in his eyes, now he saw bliss, but then Angelo wondered if those blissful eyes were mirrors reflecting the dazzling scene below them, and Demetre was taking it all in like a little boy at the circus.

"Do you trust me?" Demetre asked.

"What kind of question is that?"

He put his hand in his pocket and pulled out two thick white pills. "Blaine gave me some ecstasy. Care for one?"

Angelo shook his head. He had never taken ecstasy before, and up until that night, drugs had never been a part of his world. Since Angelo was still drunk from all the champagne and the tequila shot, he was afraid adding drugs to the mix would literally have a deadly consequence.

"Come on," Demetre urged. "It's like floating."

"How long will it last? What if I get sick? Who will take care of me?"

"You seriously need to relax. I'll be with you the whole time. Nothing is going to happen."

The idea of floating over the dance floor with Demetre was intriguing because he suspected that if he took that pill, they'd wind up naked back at his apartment, their bodies intertwined like snakes, and that thought had him so aroused that he found himself nodding.

"Okay," Angelo said, reaching to take one.

"No," he said. "Like this." Demetre placed the pill on his tongue. Without warning, Angelo felt the warmth of Demetre lips, his tongue pressing the ecstasy against the roof of Angelo's mouth so that it dissolved immediately, like a communion wafer. He washed the metallic taste with water. Then Demetre grabbed Angelo's hand and led him downstairs.

They joined the mob, drifting among the men until they were in the center of the dance floor, directly below the giant mirror ball. It was then Demetre stripped off his shirt and secured it to one of his belt loops. He ran his hands through his hair, threw back his head, and closed his eyes. Angelo watched his face undergo a succession of metamorphoses as he succumbed to the music, the crowd, the blinking lights until he appeared utterly insouciant. Angelo was fascinated staring at him. Others noticed him too. They swam around them, waiting for the opportunity to breach their inner circle, as Demetre danced.

Only when a tall muscleman with a shaved head and an elaborate tribal tattoo scrolling up his left arm and across his chest shimmied up to them, did Angelo start to feel the first wave of euphoria bubbling up like a carbonated beverage. Angelo closed his eyes, swaying to the cacophony roaring around him. In that moment, Angelo submitted to this feeling, allowing himself to skim along the dance floor. He didn't care that he was a doctor or that someone might recognize him. He was lost in the sensations, feeling everything all at once and then, the pressure of Demetre's chest pressing against his, rising and falling with each breath. Angelo lifted his face to Demetre's lips and kissed him, first lightly, and then, as if that one single kiss had dislodged a critical rock, Angelo fell in an avalanche of kisses, pushing his tongue deep inside Demetre's mouth, pressing his hands up and down his back while Demetre squeezed Angelo's buttocks.

When Angelo drew back to catch his breath, he opened his eyes. To his complete shock, Angelo discovered that it wasn't Demetre he had been kissing. It was the tall, muscleman with the tribal tattoo, his eyes reflecting the dazzling lights so that they appeared blazingly red. Angelo staggered back as the young man moved to kiss him again. In the glittering light, Angelo noted the deep pockmarked skin. He backed into someone else who wrapped their arms across Angelo's chest, enfolding him like a blanket. Glancing over his shoulder, he saw it was Demetre.

For a moment, they stopped dancing. Demetre spun Angelo around. They stood very close, so close Angelo could feel Demetre's breath against his neck.

"You have no idea how beautiful you are," Demetre whispered.

Their bodies were pressed tightly against each other's, moving to the music as a cloud of smoke enveloped them. It was so thick Angelo could hardly see Demetre's face. He closed his eyes and allowed the music to judder through him, feeling Demetre's body grinding up against his. Their arms wrapped tightly around each other. Angelo found it almost so unbearably sensual that he could hardly breathe. When Demetre grabbed ahold of Angelo's hand and pressed it against his groin, he was nearly on the brink of collapse. He flushed, feeling Demetre's erection pulsing beneath his jeans. For the first time in a long time, Angelo felt the shocking delight of a cock rubbing against him.

"Let's get out of here," Demetre said.

But the delicious thrill of giving himself to Demetre rapidly began to dissolve once Angelo stepped out into the scouring wind. He felt exactly two different ways: seized by the feverish eroticism to lie naked with Demetre, and dogged by his unflappable conscious, cautioning him not to succumb to this whim.

What are you doing? Who are you? You can't go home with him.

Demetre's arm slung over Angelo's shoulder like he belonged to him.

You're high and drunk. This is a recipe for disaster.

Angelo walked shakily through the chilly night, feeling the grip of Demetre's hand, its strength, its possessiveness, and underneath it all, quivering with anxiety, was Angelo.

"Ange?"

In the blurry haze of his serotonin overload, Angelo saw two figures standing at the corner.

"Tammy?" he shouted, breaking free from Demetre's grip. "Oh my God, I'm so happy to see you." Angelo hugged her tightly, feeling the warmth of her body against his, penetrating his soul so that he felt breathless and energized. "What are you guys doing here?" He slid over to Val and assaulted her with newfound love. "Oh, my God. I'm so happy to see you too. Val. Oh my God. You're so pretty."

"Okay," Tammy said. "Someone's feeling no pain." Then, looking at Demetre she asked, "Are you responsible for this?"

Demetre was standing there, eyes half closed, a dumb expression on his face. "Evening ladies. How are you both doing?"

They found themselves perfectly silent. Next came the terror, or so Angelo thought at first, an overwhelming, guttural churning that made him double over. "Are you okay?" Angelo wasn't sure who had asked. He was gulping up air, inhaling it while his knees wobbled.

"He looks like he's going to be sick." A wave of nausea rolled over him. Angelo's vision pinholed as he swayed, awaiting the crack of asphalt against his face, but by some miracle, as his world tilted to one side, he felt hoisted by a pair of shoulders, buoying him in place. "Taxi! Taxi!" was the last thing he heard before passing out.

◆◆◆

Angelo woke up still dressed and clammy. Tammy sat on the sofa drinking tea, watching cartoons with the volume turned down. "Oh hey! Look who's up? Sleeping Beauty."

Angelo opened his mouth to speak but felt a twinge of pain. "My jaw is killing me."

"Oh, that's the ecstasy," she said. "You were grinding your teeth pretty badly last night. I almost had you bite down on a leather strap."

Angelo stumbled to the refrigerator for water. "My mouth feels like someone stuffed it with fiberglass insulation."

"Also due to the X." Then she started naming symptoms, tapping them out on her fingers one by one. "Expect to feel tired, depressed and very dehydrated. Good news is that it'll all wear off. Bad news is that you'll want to kill yourself tomorrow. Black Monday."

"When did you become a party drug aficionado?"

"There is no limit to my knowledge," she bellowed, resting her head backward against the sofa to stare at him. "Did you forget I moonlight in the ER? Oh, and avoid mirrors at all costs. You look like shit."

Angelo curled up on the couch next to her. "I can't believe you slept over. We haven't had a sleep over in a dog's age."

"We've had a few wild nights in our time. I felt I had my fair share of waking up and not remembering how I got there. I figured I owed you one, and last night you looked like you needed my help."

"What do you mean?"

Tammy wriggled her head. "Girl, please. Your eyes

were off in two different directions, you could hardly walk, and you were dragging some old man like you were taking grandpa out for his nightly constitutional."

"What old man?"

Tammy took a sip of tea, set the mug on the table. "I don't know. Demetrius or Deter? Something like that."

"Demetre is not an old man," argued Angelo. "I happen to think he's very sexy."

"Sexy for an old man. Now, if you want to go out and troll for daddies, I'm not going to stop you. Just don't try to pass off grandpa like he's anywhere near your age."

Putting it into words didn't make Angelo feel any better. "You're so judgmental."

"What happened to hot cop?"

Absolute silence fell. "What do you mean?" Angelo asked.

"I don't know. One minute you're getting a police escort home, and the next minute he's out of the picture."

Angelo pulled up his knee and wrapped his arms around it. "We text. It's just . . . it's just, we have conflicting schedules."

"Who'd a thought you'd be that guy," she said pointedly.

"What guy is that?"

"The kind of guy that goes out clubbing. The kind of stupid idiot that gets so high he stumbles down the street in his own neighborhood where people can recognize him as their doctor. Weren't you worried one of your patients might see you?"

"You really know how to kick a guy when his serotonin levels are down." Angelo caught his breath and waited for the shock to subside, but he had known all along that Tammy spoke only the truth. In fact, he had been bracing himself for it.

"Did grandpa slip you a roofie?" Tammy asked. She stood up and searched his cabinets for liquor.

"Stop calling him grandpa, and for your information, I accepted the ecstasy willingly."

Tammy shuddered in disbelief. "Who is this old man you gave up hot cop for?"

"I told you. His name is Demetre."

"Is he a doctor?" Tammy found a bottle of wine and searched the drawer for a corkscrew.

"He owns the aesthetic practice downstairs."

Tammy picked up the remote and turned off the television.

"Are you out of your fucking mind? Angelo, you don't go out with a coworker and get high. Those are things you do with your friends. What if your boss got wind of this?"

Angelo was jarred by her clarity. "Demetre won't say anything."

"Are you sure? How much do you know about this guy?"

Being the focus of Tammy's laser-sharp scrutiny caused Angelo to panic. He sat very still, trying not to think, but flashes of memory came then unbidden, each one more strikingly embarrassing than the other. Angelo felt Tammy's eyes on him, staring for several penetrating moments; he had to concentrate to keep from turning away because if he had, she would have realized he knew very little about Demetre other than what he had been told.

They spent the rest of that Sunday in Angelo's apartment watching TV, ordering take-out food, and drinking wine. Tammy took care of everything, nursing him through his post-ecstasy hangover. He thought she did it partly out of guilt for having been so hard on him when he was at his most fragile. After that, neither said another word about ecstasy or Demetre.

That afternoon, they hardly moved from the couch except to answer the door or use the bathroom. Angelo had taken the comforter and two pillows off the bed, and they nestled on either end of Angelo's sofa bed, snuggling as they watched a *Real World* marathon on MTV. Angelo took several naps throughout the day. Each time he woke up, Tammy was either on the phone with Val or sipping wine, or both. At one point, his gaze drifted over to the kitchen. By sundown, there were six empty bottles of Cabernet lined up by the garbage can like bowling pins.

It was many hours later before Angelo began to completely comprehend what he had done. "Tam?"

"Yeah."

"What do you think I should do tomorrow?"

Tammy turned to face Angelo, balancing a wine glass on her belly.

"Let him know that you don't blame him," she said tenderly, "and that you take full responsibility for your actions but that moving forward, your relationship must remain professional."

They had been friends for so long that Angelo often took Tammy's intelligence for granted. Despite her excessive drinking, she was a very astute person, which is why she was an exceptional physician. Her uncanny ability to solve problems was a corollary of her logical thinking, and he marveled at how well she was able to analyze the situation and present it calmly so that her impressions were without pity, without fear, without anything but a mature exegesis.

Just after ten o'clock, they said goodnight. It was then Angelo noticed he had received several text messages from Demetre. Nothing urgent. Simple words of concern.

Just checking in. Hope ur okay.

Angelo didn't text him back. They'd talk tomorrow like Tammy had suggested. Once he had made that decision, he felt fatigue overwhelm him, felt it ease the tension and the frustration that had been building up. Then, Angelo fell asleep and slept soundly until he was awakened by the alarm.

CHAPTER EIGHT

Monday morning, after a fitful night's sleep, Angelo woke up deliberately early and dressed in his new pants, shirt, and shoes for work. Outside it was chilly and overcast. He was not in terrific shape. His eyes burned, his body ached, and an awful trembling was passing through his nervous system like a runaway train. But on the outside, he looked good.

As per Tammy's instructions, he started off the day by having a large breakfast—bacon and eggs on a bagel—and drinking plenty of water. When he finally reached the office, Steven was standing at the front desk bursting with excitement. Angelo was happy to see him looking so chipper. It calmed his nerves. "I think Tony's going to buy that house in P-town," he blurted out before Angelo had a chance to say good morning. "We spoke to the realtor last night. The owner accepted our offer."

"That's great news," Angelo said. Steven followed closely behind, describing the house in more detail than Angelo cared to hear at that exact moment. A copy of *New York* magazine was opened on Angelo's desk, displaying an advertisement for SkinDem.

"Oh, that reminds me," Steven said. "There's going to be a meeting at noon."

"More medical spa stuff?"

"Uh-huh." In his current state, Angelo was not looking forward to a meeting, but he had no choice.

"Must have cost a fortune," Steven said.

"Excuse me."

"The ad in *New York*. It must have cost Demetre a fortune."

Angelo contemplated the ad. It took up half the page. Most of it consisted of a black-and-white photo of Demetre, which had to be old or airbrushed to death. Though it captured that look: those pleading eyes, the thick brows, and that glistening head of hair. It reminded him of one of those celebrity headshots from the fifties—dark and shadowy—all that was missing was a smoldering cigarette.

"To tell you the truth," Angelo said, "I would have expected something more professional."

Steven chuckled in appreciation and walked out.

Angelo entered the exam room of his first patient shortly thereafter. Mia Garcia sat on the exam table, texting. She looked up and smiled. Once he introduced himself, she slipped her phone inside her purse and dropped her head so that her long, mocha hair cascaded, partially obscuring the right side of her face.

At first glance, Angelo thought she looked much younger than her age, which was listed on the intake sheet as twenty-eight. Dressed in a suit, she appeared like a little girl in her mother's clothes—legs so short her feet dangled—but on closer inspection, Angelo realized this was a very well-groomed, well-dressed woman: nails beautifully manicured, teeth perfectly straight, and skin so golden brown, it appeared as though she'd just gotten back from vacation.

"So, you were referred by Demetre Kostas?" he asked.

She nodded enthusiastically. "You come highly recommended."

"That's nice to hear." One of Angelo's new roles as part of Stanzione's medical spa plan—in addition to shadowing Demetre and learning all about lasers—was to provide SkinDem clients medical clearance for Demetre to perform procedures on them. A standard practice that Angelo considered routine. "I see you're having a procedure. Is this your first?"

"Oh, Dr. D and I go way back," she said, holding a loose fist to her lips. "Initially, I saw him a year ago to have a tattoo removed. You know. One of those hideous tramp stamps I got after a night of tequila shots in college. That took seven sessions. Then he did a laser facial on me after the holidays to even out my skin tone. Recently, he bought a new blue light laser that treats scars." Then Mia lowered her hand, and Angelo saw that she was hiding a cleft lip scar that threw off the symmetry of her lips so that her tooth was exposed, giving her the subtle appearance of a sneer. "I'm so excited. You have no idea."

She stared at him in that anxious, hopeful way you listen to a fortune-teller. Angelo suspected she wanted to hear his opinion. He didn't have the heart to inform her that even if Demetre could magically erase her scar it still wouldn't correct the defect.

"Does it really bother you?"

She put her hand back up to her mouth.

"Of course it does. I work on Wall Street. Every time I shake a client's hand, I feel their eyes on my face. Whenever I give a presentation, if I hear someone giggle, I think they're laughing at me."

"I understand," Angelo said. "As you can see, I too, have a facial scar."

She inhaled sharply. "It's not the same. Scars are more acceptable on men. Besides, you can always grow a beard."

"You're right. I can't argue with that, but from where I'm sitting, I can hardly see the scar. Do you wear makeup to cover it?"

"I wear tons of concealer, but halfway through the day it wears off. Sometimes I forget. Then I catch a glimpse of myself in the computer screen and there she is. *La coneja.* That's what they used to call me when I was a little girl living in Mexico. By high school everyone knew me as *rabbit* girl." Mia turned away. Angelo thought she might be on the verge of tears.

"Children can be so cruel," he said.

Mia took a deep breath. When she turned around, she smiled directly at Angelo. "Listen, I'm not looking for sympathy. I have it pretty good compared to most people. My job pays me very well, which is crucial since New York is a very expensive place to live. You wouldn't believe how much I spend on clothes, shoes, makeup . . . and cosmetic procedures." "Mia's smile widened. It was obvious to Angelo that she had crafted this narrative as a form of armor to protect the little rabbit girl who still lived inside her. "Hey, there's no shame in my game," she added. "I make no apologies for wanting to look good. Why shouldn't I have it all?"

Angelo sat down, planting his feet on the floor so that he could stare directly at her.

"There's nothing wrong with treating yourself as a reward for all your hard work as long as you understand that there is no cosmetic procedure in the world that is going to be a substitute for peace of mind. At the sake of sounding trite, beauty does come from within. As for this blue light laser, make sure you do your due diligence. Manage your expectations. Otherwise, you may come away feeling disappointed."

Mia gave him a sly look. "Demetre was right about you. You're very sweet. Too bad you're gay."

Mia's candor was endearing, and it made Angelo smile because behind those warm, dark eyes, he saw a little of his own ambitious self. That made him want to protect her, to explain that this procedure was going to be a waste of her hard-earned money, and that in the end she would be disappointed. But it was apparent to him that nothing he said was going to change her mind.

"Well, now that we're BFFs," he began, "why don't you tell me how many cosmetic procedures you've had?"

Mia took a deep breath, eyes cast upward as she counted. "Well, I had a scar revision on my lip, a nose job, breast implants, and liposuction. Plus, I get Botox twice a year."

"Your plastic surgeon must love you."

She tossed her head back, laughing. "I don't pay New York prices. I have all my procedures in Mexico. Demetre is the only one I see in New York. Plus, he gives me a friends and family discount."

After Mia's consultation, Angelo walked back to his desk to complete his notes. Tucked in Mia's chart was a SkinDem medical clearance form. Angelo filled it out, wondering how many more of Demetre's clients he would have to provide medical clearance and whether this new role was taking his career in the wrong direction.

◆◆◆

At ten after twelve, Angelo knocked on Stanzione's door. The usual assemblage was waiting. Demetre dropped Angelo a slow wink, and he smiled back. "I was just telling everyone that I got some amazing news," Stanzione said. "Steven and I put a bid on a house in P-town, and it was accepted."

"The Cape," Laura said. "That's where I grew up. My parents owned an inn. You're gonna love it."

"And . . ." Stanzione's voice wavered as if he were about to announce the winner of a contest. "Steven and I have just been invited to Turks and Caicos with my friend Jill as her guests!"

"Turks and Caicos," Demetre repeated. "When do you leave?"

"Tomorrow night," Stanzione said.

Angelo watched as Stanzione glanced at him, waiting to see if he was going to object. "That sounds cool," he muttered, careful not to react enviously. But Angelo was envious. More than envious, he was annoyed. Another trip. Another in a series of days off. How could Stanzione justify taking so much time away from the practice?

When Angelo accepted this job, he wasn't under any illusions that it would be nothing less than long days of hard work, but seeing patients without Stanzione was difficult enough, not having Steven for support made it unbearable.

"Where are we as far as training Angelo with the lasers?" Stanzione asked.

Demetre took a breath. "I've been showing him how to use the blue light laser. He's gotten quite good, actually."

"Excellent," Stanzione said. "By the way Laura, the ad in *New York* magazine is terrific."

"Thank you." She flushed with pride. "I'm glad you like it."

"Seriously," Stanzione said, pausing for emphasis. "No kidding. Great job."

"How far along are you in creating a partnership agreement with your lawyer?" she asked.

Stanzione's jaw clenched as if her question caught him off guard. "Uh, well, my lawyers are putting together some ideas. Sort of like a Chinese menu. You know, create your own dinner, picking one from column A and then another from column B. I want what's fair for everyone involved. Doing it this way, we can tailor it to our needs."

Laura nodded eagerly. "And you'll still be the medical director?"

Demetre put his hand on her knee. "Laura."

"That's all right Demetre," Stanzione said, with edgy indifference. "She's only protecting you. I admire that. And to answer your question, all the details will be ironed out in the contract. You have my word."

◆◆◆

Later that evening, after everyone had gone home, Demetre knocked on Angelo's office door. "Why are you still here? I can hardly stand up I'm so tired. Did you sleep in yesterday?"

"My friend Tammy and I watched TV and ordered takeout."

"Tammy," he repeated, frowning. "The dirty blond who looks like Peppermint Patty?"

Angelo chuckled with condescension. "The last time someone called her that, she knocked them in the jaw."

Demetre collapsed in the chair, rubbing his back. "I spent the whole day lying in bed with a heating pad, popping anti-inflammatories every six hours. It's official: I've hung up my dancing shoes for good. Damn sciatica kept me up all night. Do you know if Tony is still here?"

"No, they left early to have dinner with his mother."

"Mama Stanzione. Have you met her yet?"

"No."

"Consider yourself lucky," he said, attempting to swivel from side to side but with apparent distress.

Angelo felt the desperate pull of Tammy's advice to speak directly with Demetre about the other night. "Listen," he said with reluctance. "About Saturday. I'm afraid I embarrassed myself."

Demetre regarded him carefully. "Not at all."

Angelo laughed with discomfort. "That's kind of you to say, but I was a mess."

Demetre narrowed his eyes. "Is that how you feel or is that how Peppermint Patty made you feel?"

Angelo looked down at his trembling hands. "The truth is that I take responsibility for my actions. It was careless of me to lose control like that in public. Thankfully, you were there to help, but we work together. From here on out we must maintain a professional relationship. Don't you agree?"

"Absolutely." Demetre smiled. "Just don't beat yourself up over this. Give it a few days. You'll see that it really wasn't as big a deal as it seems to you right now. It's common knowledge that most people experience a bout of depression the Monday after taking ecstasy on Saturday night."

"Black Monday," Angelo said. "Heard all about it. This isn't about any ecstasy-induced depression. I'm more concerned about moving forward professionally. I'd rather this not get back to Dr. Stanzione."

Demetre inhaled slowly. "Angelo, you have nothing to worry about. As far as I'm concerned, we're buddies. We had a crazy night out, and what goes on between you and I after hours is no one's business but our own. You have my word."

Relieved, Angelo was eager to change the subject. "Mia Garcia came in to see me today. Thank you for the referral."

"Such a sweet girl. Talk about the American dream. You know she came from nothing. Now she's a successful stock analyst on Wall Street who supports her mother and is putting her brother through school."

"I like her a lot."

"Listen," he said, massaging his back. "Could you do me a favor?"

"Sure," Angelo said.

"Would you mind writing me a prescription for pain killers? Just a few so that I can get some sleep tonight. Tony's given them to me in the past. You can check my chart if you like." Angelo sensed Demetre read the hesitation on his face because he quickly added, "I understand if you don't feel comfortable. It's just that I haven't been able to sleep. I meant to ask Tony all day, but I was so busy."

"It's just that Dr. Stanzione is pretty possessive when it comes to certain patients."

"I see." Demetre struggled to stand up, wincing with pain. "Don't worry about it." He hobbled to the door. Just as he reached the threshold he turned back. "I just figured, you know, one hand washes the other."

At first, Angelo wasn't quite sure what he meant, but then it occurred to him. Demetre suggested a quid pro quo: his discretion about their night out in exchange for narcotics. Of course, that's not the way he presented it, all hunched over and wounded, but Angelo knew that's exactly what he was implying. Despite everything, Angelo felt a reflexive sense of resentment. Within seconds he wrested it under control. How could he resent Demetre after he had only shown him kindness? Honesty? Just because Angelo had developed a crush why should he leap to the wrong conclusion now?

Black Monday, he thought to himself. Don't let a post-ecstasy funk fuck up the first real friendship you've made with another gay man.

Without uttering a word, Angelo opened the file cabinet against the far wall where he kept his controlled substance prescription pads issued by the State of New York, which were encoded with a serial number. After he wrote the prescription, Angelo tore it from the pad and handed it to Demetre.

"You're the best," he said, making no attempt to conceal the satisfaction in his tone. "What are you doing tomorrow for lunch?"

"Lunch?" Angelo laughed. "I've been so busy these past few weeks I haven't had time to take lunch. Normally I eat in between patients, and what with Stanzione going away again I'm sure tomorrow will be insane."

"All the more reason you should come with me tomorrow. I'm having lunch at that new sushi place on Park."

"What will I tell Steven?"

He looked at Angelo, dumbfounded. "Jesus Christ Angelo, tell him you're going out to lunch. What's he going to say? Besides, he'll be too preoccupied thinking about which swim trunks to pack."

"Let me look at the schedule and get back to you."

Demetre's gaze was firm and impassive. "You're having lunch with me tomorrow at noon and that's that."

Why not, thought Angelo. It's Demetre's way of returning the favor.

◆◆◆

At a quarter past twelve, Demetre entered Angelo's office wearing a snug, black, V-neck sweater and jeans.

"You're late," Angelo said. "Maybe we should do this another time."

"Don't be silly," Demetre insisted.

"Okay, but I have to be back by one otherwise Steven will release the hounds."

They started toward Park Avenue near Union Square when Demetre said, "Did I mention we're having lunch with my friend Rachel? She's a rep for a high-end skin care company called Jeune Toi."

Angelo stopped dead in his tracks. "You invited me to a drug rep lunch?"

"It's skin care," he said, pulling on Angelo's arm. "Tons of celebrities use it. Besides, this sushi place is next to impossible to get a reservation."

Rachel Sims was at the table when they arrived. Angelo recognized her as the woman he saw walking with Demetre through Union Square that day he gorged on McDonald's. She was a diminutive, wearing a short skirt and flats that accentuated her markedly fat legs. Demetre introduced Angelo, and she thrust her arm straight up so that it looked like it was protruding out of her ear. The poor girl had no neck whatsoever.

"So nice to meet you, Dr. Perrotta. Dr. D has told me so much about you. Please sit down. Lucky me. I get to have lunch with two handsome men. God, I love my job!"

The server came by, eager to take their orders since the restaurant was in the midst of a lunchtime frenzy.

"I'm just going to have a California roll," Rachel said, sipping her Diet Coke with lemon. "But go ahead and have whatever you like."

"Do you know what you want Angelo?" Demetre asked. "The *Times* raved about the ikura and maguro."

"Whatever you say."

As Demetre whispered to the server, Angelo glanced over at Rachel who was wriggling with excitement.

"I'm so glad you both made time to see me today," she said. "This place was almost impossible to get a reservation, but I managed. I didn't want to let down Dr. D."

"You could never disappoint me," Demetre said once he dismissed the server.

Rachel shifted gears and launched right into her pitch. "Jeune Toi is trying to position itself exclusively in upscale markets. We're not available in stores. You have to order directly through me. Right now, as far as the world is concerned, we are a first-generation alginate that comes directly from only one source in the South Pacific."

Almost immediately, the server brought over a bowl filled with salted edamame and two sakes, which he placed in front of Demetre and Angelo.

"Oh, I'm sorry," Angelo said, "but I'm not drinking."

"Seriously?" Demetre's jaw went crooked. "Guess that leaves more for me."

By now, Rachel had laid a brochure on the table listing the various products. Angelo watched as Demetre ran his finger down the page studiously. Among the lifting masks, firming creams and lightweight serums that came in both satiny and velvety finishes, were the corresponding prices that ranged from a hundred and sixty-five dollars up to two thousand, depending on the number of ounces. Angelo willed himself still to hide his shock at the exorbitant prices.

Demetre jumped in with, "We're looking to make Jeune Toi the exclusive skin care line of SkinDem."

This prompted Rachel to clap profusely. "That's music to my ears."

Their lunch arrived. Angelo took a moment to gander at the beautiful presentation. His plate appeared as a giant flower with petals made of translucent slices of pink salmon and ruby red tuna. In the center was a dollop of caviar surrounded by bright green shreds of pickled seaweed. Glancing at his watch, he had only minutes to devour his lunch, but at the same time he wanted only to stay. Each exquisite bite, a combination of briny fish mixed with sriracha, was committed to his taste memory. Added to a catalogue of decadence where he stored the experiences too expensive for him to revisit on his own.

Demetre held his chopsticks, ready to eat, but then leaned forward until he had Rachel's attention.

"We are on the verge of launching an entire media campaign: magazine ads, radio commercials, and television spots."

"How exciting," she said, slowly chewing her roll. "Which PR agency are you using?"

"Have you heard of Ellis PR?"

Ellis . . . thought Angelo. Wasn't that Laura's last name?

"No," Rachel said, sipping her Diet Coke. "I have a friend who works for a big PR firm. She knows how to get this sort of thing out there: talk shows, high-end glamour magazines, and celebrity endorsements. How do you think we got a certain Oscar-winning actress?"

Demetre picked up a piece of tuna and devoured it. "Get me your friend's contact info, and I'll give her a call. But only if she's serious." He took a dramatic pause. "I don't want to be competing with ten other aesthetic clients."

Rachel swallowed down hard, her eyes wide. "Oh, no! She's not like that at all." Then Rachel lowered her voice. "And just between you and me, once you officially make Jeune Toi the exclusive skincare line of SkinDem, I think I could help you financially with your advertisement budget." Then she gave a curt, self-satisfied shrug as if that were her final ace in the hole to seal this deal. "Just tell her Rache from Jeune Toi sent you—she will really help." Rachel's eyes glittered with the kind of madness one would expect to see in a cartoon after a pirate uncovered buried treasure.

Angelo glanced at his watch. It was just after one. "I'm sorry, but I have to get going. I have patients waiting." He stood up to leave.

Rachel wiped her mouth. "Oh of course. I understand. Just one thing." She pulled out a pen. "I need you to sign here." Rachel slid a sheet of ivory colored stationery across the table toward him.

"What's this?" he asked.

She cast a concerned look at Demetre.

"Oh, it's nothing," he said in a reassuring whisper. "Rachel needs our signatures for compliance reasons."

"Yes," she said. "We don't just take anyone to the trendiest Japanese restaurants in New York." From the moment they sat down, Angelo had listened to their discussion in silence like a dutiful wife accompanying her husband to a work function, but now it was obvious why Demetre had asked him to attend. Pricey lunches were usually reserved only for physicians. "And how much will you be ordering today?"

"Excuse me?" Angelo asked.

Rachel forced a smile, but the corners of her mouth tugged down with evident unease. "Dr. D help me out here. Didn't I just hear you say that you intend to make Jeune Toi your exclusive skin care line?"

Angelo stood there in stupefied silence, waiting to hear how this had anything to do with him.

"Rachel, I'm placing the order," Demetre said. "Angelo doesn't have a clue what to buy. He's a doctor." Then he laughed.

Rachel's mouth curled upward into a genuine smile. "Oh, I understand. You two make quite a team: cute and cuter. Just sign here Dr. Perrotta, and Dr. D and I will finalize the details." Then she held out her pen again.

Angelo nodded, wanting to walk away, but he couldn't seem to do it. Scanning the sheet of paper, it was addressed to him in response to an apparent query he had sent to learn more about Jeune Toi's products. There was no mention that he was required to buy anything as a result of being taken out to lunch, and so Angelo took Rachel's pen. Just then, as he signed, full comprehension seemed to overwhelm his vision. He squeezed his eyes shut and then opened them again, and all at once he saw it there in black and white: Angelo Perrotta MD, Medical Director, SkinDem, Inc.

Angelo teetered for a second, feeling as if he might fall. Demetre grabbed his arm and Angelo gazed at him, unable to comprehend why Demetre had used him.

"Go on," Demetre urged. "I'll stay here with Rachel."

Back on Park Avenue, Angelo let the cool breeze clear his head.

"Medical director?" he asked out loud. "Why would he tell her that?" But then he thought, *perhaps he didn't.* Maybe Rachel had just assumed he was the medical director in order to justify splurging on an expensive lunch. And even if it was all just a big misunderstanding, it didn't mean anything really. But the more Angelo thought about it the more he realized how wrong it all was—there's no such thing as a free lunch, only the power to buy people with it. It was just as Val had predicted: the tchotchkes, the fine dining, the vacations, a steady stream of expenses designed to ensnare physicians into their web of pharmaceutical influence.

"Excuse me, sir," someone called out. "I'm going to have to issue you a ticket for jaywalking."

Angelo turned in the direction where a police car was following him. Jason Murphy drove alongside him. His muscular left arm hung across the police car door. Angelo saw Mary, his partner, wink from the passenger seat. Angelo and Jason stared at each other for a long moment, then Jason flashed his badge.

"You remember me, don't you?"

Angelo took another second to pull himself together.

What an afternoon this was shaping up to be.

Jason's mysterious appearance had thrown Angelo, he couldn't deny it, and he felt flush with embarrassment aware of the reason why. He had treated this person with such disregard, yet he found himself happy to see Jason again. He looked incredible, light-blue eyes glittering in the sunlight, face chiseled in perfect symmetry.

"So, am I getting a ticket, Officer?" Angelo clarified now that he was in on the joke.

"I think we're well past that," Jason said, smirking. "I believe it's my duty to arrest you."

Angelo stopped and glanced over at Mary. She wriggled her head excitedly to indicate that she was simultaneously mortified and thrilled to be witnessing this scene.

"Your duty?" Angelo repeated with incredulity. "Am I a threat to the community?"

"Not so much a threat to the community but to my heart," Jason said, bulging out his lower lip. He held out a card. Angelo knew that this was Jason's final gesture. He reached to take the card. Jason brushed his index finger against his, and in that moment, Angelo wanted only to feel Jason's strong arms around his body, to feel the warmth of his embrace, and to know that all was forgiven.

On the back of Jason's business card was his cell phone number and a message reading: Call me. I'm a nice guy.

At that moment, Angelo glanced at his watch. "Shit!" he shouted. "I'm late. I'm really late." But as honest as that declaration was, Angelo saw the look of disappointment in Jason's eyes, and the comforting grip Mary provided to Jason's shoulder just before they drove away.

By the time Angelo arrived at the office, Laura was standing in the waiting room. Once Angelo entered, she pounced. "There you are. Is Dr. D with you?"

Steven was behind the front desk. Angelo ignored Laura and walked over to him. "Do I have anyone waiting?"

"Tony took the first patient."

Angelo leaned against the counter. "Can I talk to you privately?"

Steven's mouth hung open. "Sure."

"Where is Dr. D?" Laura insisted. "I have clients waiting downstairs."

"He's having lunch at that new Japanese place on Park Avenue. Would you like me to go fetch him?"

She looked at Angelo oddly, and then pulled out her cell phone. Steven and Angelo marched back to his office. Angelo shut the door behind him. They stood there in that quiet room, light streaking through the skylight. Angelo had dragged Steven back there to ask his advice, to get some reassurance, and to ease his conscience about unintentionally misrepresenting himself as a medical director in exchange for a plate of raw fish. But for some reason, Steven's presence made him acutely aware of how stupidly he was behaving. Angelo had already signed the letter. It was over. There was nothing anyone could do about it, especially Steven.

"Is everything all right?" Steven asked. "You look pale."

Angelo fumbled for an answer. "Laura is getting on my last nerve. I can't work like this. You and Dr. Stanzione are leaving tomorrow. Tiffany and I can't work with Laura hovering over us all day."

Steven smirked. Angelo sensed his vindication; he saw it on his face. "I told you she's a problem."

Angelo narrowed his eyes, pretending to think. "She's always asking me where Demetre is like I'm his manager. Why doesn't she know where he is? Isn't that her job?"

"Don't worry. I'll take care of Laura Ellis."

CHAPTER NINE

"We have a problem," Stanzione said. The sound of calypso music played in the background. It had to be a huge problem, thought Angelo, for Stanzione to call all the way from Turks and Caicos. "Guess who forgot to set the office alarm?"

Angelo glanced at the clock. It read twelve fifteen. "I'm on my way."

Walking back to work through the dark, deserted New York streets, Angelo felt a shiver of discomfort, some gnawing in his stomach. He knew exactly why. It was the fear that he was going to find Demetre passed out on Stanzione's sofa.

They hadn't spoken since their lunch with Rachel Sims. If Angelo had his way, he would have kept his distance since he hadn't quite reconciled what it was he wanted from Demetre, if anything. From the beginning, Demetre brought the promise of extravagant escape, harmless mischief, but lately Angelo saw the crackle of delinquency in Demetre's eyes as something more calculated, less breezy. Finding him in the office tonight meant having to confront him, and Angelo was simply ill-prepared.

At that late hour, Angelo walked down Twenty-Third Street, which was a broad thoroughfare unlike Eighteenth Street where Stanzione's office was located. Other than the occasional taxi, there were hardly any cars on the streets. Stores were all closed. Buildings alive with the bustle of lights, sounds and people during the day were now dark and empty like mausoleums. New York at night was like a cemetery to Angelo who had grown up on an island where nothing was within walking distance.

Angelo knew that braving the streets alone at night required a constant, cautious consciousness to avoid the menacing threats lurking in the dark: the reaching hand of the homeless begging for money, the hushed offerings for illegal drugs and of course, the pervasive threat of robbery or injury. Angelo walked quickly and turned down Park Avenue where there were more cars. He sighed with relief as he approached Eighteenth Street.

The front door opened easily. It had not been locked. Inside, it was dark except for the light in the stairwell. It had been left on. Angelo crept down the stairs, listening to the dulcet sounds of trance music. Peering over the handrail, he was shocked to find a tall, muscular man wearing only a black jockstrap. He had a shaved head and an elaborate tribal tattoo. Angelo remembered dancing with this man that night at the Roxy. He watched as the young man cut lines of white powder on Laura's glass desk using Demetre's platinum American Express card.

"Yossi, do you want more bourbon?" Demetre entered, shirtless, his erection tenting his scrub pants. Angelo squeezed his eyes shut, feeling the guilt of a voyeuristic intruder, at the same time enthralled by Demetre's audacity. They snorted two lines. Yossi squatted, his buttocks ballooning through his jockstrap like melons. He freed Demetre's cock from his scrub pants and gripped it in his palm. Yossi peered up at Demetre, grinning, and took his cock in his mouth. Demetre held Yossi's head, guiding it slowly, up and down. Demetre threw his head back, eyes closed. Angelo was paralyzed with shock on the stairs, listening to Yossi's moans, the wet suckling sounds of his mouth and hand on Demetre's cock. Angelo started to back away when suddenly Demetre looked up and locked eyes with him.

"Shit!" Angelo said, bounding up the stairs.

Demetre hurried after him. "Angelo, wait!"

Angelo had his hand on the handle, but Demetre pressed his body against the door. "Where are you going?"

Angelo looked at Demetre's anxious, jittery face. "Answer me."

How was it, Angelo wondered, that this man was able to adjust to this shock and look him in the eye as though he was the one in the wrong? Like Angelo was the nerdy boy in school who found the cool boys smoking and was going to ruin the party for everyone.

"You forgot to set the alarm, again," Angelo said.

Demetre shouted downstairs. "Yossi, did you turn off the alarm?"

"Yes." Yossi climbed the stairs and stood in the stairwell threshold. Angelo could make out his muscular silhouette. "Don't you remember? We had to let my friend in."

Demetre looked back at Angelo and offered a befuddled shrug. "That explains it."

"What's wrong with you?" Angelo could no longer hold his anger back.

"Relax," he said. "Yossi's an old friend. We were just hanging out. Come down and join us."

Angelo glanced over at Yossi as he massaged the bulge inside his jockstrap—a hint to take Demetre up on his invitation.

"Are you insane?" Angelo asked Demetre. "Seriously, are you literally, certifiably insane?"

"You're hysterical." Demetre was standing so close Angelo could feel his cock against his leg. He wondered if Demetre was so high he didn't realize or whether this was his way of winning him over. Angelo reminded himself over and over that this was wrong, but he could not unsee that scene: Yossi's head bobbing expertly over Demetre's throbbing cock. The lines of cocaine cut on Laura Ellis's desk. Angelo squeezed his eyes to force the images out of his mind, but he was blinded by them.

If he wanted to join them—be one of the cools boys— no one would know. It wasn't like Angelo hadn't fantasized about having a three way. He had sworn to himself that once he left Staten Island, he would stop dreaming of the experiences he wanted to have and actually have them. Angelo slid his hand down the front of his leg and felt Demetre's erection. He managed a weak moan, fighting to go with the moment and embrace the situation even as the voice inside his head begged him not to. And then, it happened. Angelo's cell phone rang. It was Stanzione. "Did you set the alarm?"

"I'm here now, Dr. Stanzione," Angelo said.

"They're going to dispatch the police," Stanzione warned. "Set the alarm and go home."

"Don't worry," Angelo said. "I'll handle it."

After Angelo hung up, he backed away from Demetre and stared him squarely in the eyes. "You need to leave now," he said. "They already warned you once. You know they don't like when you stay after hours. What if it was Steven or worse, the police, who caught you instead of me? You think the undynamic duo wouldn't think twice about kicking you out on the street."

"Undynamic duo," Demetre repeated, grabbing Angelo's shoulders and grinning. "Listen, I'm sorry Stanzione made you come back, but I pay forty grand a month for this office. I should be able to come and go as I please. Now let's go downstairs. Have a drink with us. Yossi's cool. He was in the army. Boy knows a trick or two. You'll like him. Trust me. I know he likes you."

Angelo stepped back, brushing Demetre's hands away. "The alarm company was about to dispatch the police. What's going on downstairs is illegal. What part of this don't you get?"

"Okay, okay," Demetre soothed. "Don't get upset. I knew the undynamic duo were away. If it'll make you happy, we'll clear out and lock up." Then he hugged Angelo, pressing his mouth against his ear. "Just don't be upset. I hate seeing you upset. We're a team. Remember? Batman and Robin."

"Batman and Robin?" Angelo snapped. "You . . . you really don't see the problem here?"

"I only see you making it into one." His icy tone was chilling.

"I want you and your friend to clear out of here. I'll wait until you're gone. Then I'll set the alarm and lock up myself."

Demetre took a step back. "Okay," he said, turning away but then looked back. "You won't mention this to Stanzione, will you?"

Angelo drew in a deep breath and exhaled. "No, I won't tell Stanzione."

"Cool." Then he slipped into the shadows and back down the stairs.

◆◆◆

Back in his bedroom, angry and exhausted, Angelo wanted more than anything to pull down the shades and lie in bed for the next twenty-four hours. But that was impossible since he had a day's worth of patients waiting for him the next morning. He closed his eyes and again saw Yossi in his jockstrap, performing fellatio on Demetre, the white lines of cocaine on Laura Ellis's desk.

As a teenager, he never imagined his career as a physician would include locking up the office for his boss and breaking up an after-work sex party.

Angelo's mother had raised her two children alone for most of their childhood. The year Angelo started middle school she married Don, a tall, skinny, soft-spoken Texan who referred to himself—a cross-country sugar salesman—as the confectionary sandman. For luck, Don sprinkled sugar on the sidewalk before every meeting. He was a calm person with a quiet candor. Since Angelo grew up without a father, he collected father figures. Don was the first, and he was a solid one—patient and supportive—the kind of man who knew exactly when Angelo needed a hand on his shoulder for encouragement or an open ear for Don to listen.

Soon after they were married, Don made his mother quit her job because he didn't think a respectable woman should work. Having a firm idea of how men and women should behave was very important to Don. After dinner each night they left the women to clean up and walked to the beach and back.

"Angelo," Don used to say, "men work to support the family, and the women take care of the house and children. Since your father ran out on you, I don't want you to think all men are like that. Real men take responsibility for their families."

Angelo never verbally disagreed with Don even though his mother had raised two children on her own for years. It seemed too trivial, and in all honesty, Don was a welcomed member of the family, a lifeboat collecting the remaining three survivors from the Perrotta family wreckage.

Then two years later, just as Angelo was about to start high school, just as Camille was entering college and they were finally a normal family, Angelo's mother developed back pain. She died ten months later from metastatic lymphoma. After that, Angelo didn't recall much about his childhood other than a sad collection of events: Don moving to Japan for work, Camille dropping out of college to get a job, and as for Angelo, all he recalled was wearing the same pair of red Converse high-tops every day for the next year.

Angelo opened his eyes. He woke up in his apartment with the sun shining through the blinds. Walking to work that morning after discovering Demetre and Yossi, Angelo was still angry. Once again, Demetre had put him in an awkward position and he had agreed to lie. Angelo decided then that he had to speak with Demetre, one-on-one. He was going to tell Demetre that Stanzione had placed a great deal of trust in his hands, and for Demetre to ask him to lie meant Angelo was betraying his employer. The reality was that Angelo hated confrontation, but Demetre left him no choice.

Just as he entered the office, he heard someone call his name. "Dr. Angelo Perrotta?" A young man stood there smiling uneasily.

"Yes."

He handed over a white envelope and then, the young man was gone. Angelo fumbled to see what was inside. His eyes landed on just a few sentences.

Notice of Medical Malpractice Action

Violet Trautman

vs

Angelo Perrotta, M.D.

Angelo caught a glimpse of himself in the glass door. That image of him—gripping legal papers in his fist—flattened Angelo with blunt disappointment, a sense that he was falling down a chasm. What little hope he had for salvaging his self-respect by speaking to Demetre was annihilated now that he was being sued by one of his clients.

Laura was staring at her watch when Angelo entered. "Thank God you're here. Where is Dr. D?"

"How the hell should I know?"

"He's not responding to my calls," she said. "We have clients waiting downstairs and that smell is back."

"Hey Laura, newsflash: I don't work for you, and I'm not Demetre's assistant. You are. If you can't manage him then maybe you should find another job."

Sitting at his desk, he decided that he needed to operate in a funnel of focus, concentrating only on his patients' needs. At noon, he walked up to sit next to Tiffany. "Did Demetre ever show?"

She shook her head in silence.

In the hall, Angelo heard the shrill tone of Laura's voice.

"Dr. D is unavailable today." She was speaking with Rachel, the Jeune Toi representative.

"But he promised he was going to place a large order," Rachel insisted. "He said that Jeune Toi was going to be SkinDem's exclusive product line."

"That is a conversation you'll need to have with Dr. D."

"What about Dr. Perrotta?" Rachel asked. "He is the medical director."

Angelo crouched down behind Tiffany's chair so that Rachel wouldn't see him as Laura escorted her out the door.

"I'll be sure to tell Dr. D you stopped by," Laura said. "Good day."

◆◆◆

That Monday, just four days after the incident with Demetre and Yossi, Angelo found himself in the office of his malpractice lawyer, Lawrence Meers. A man with a white mane of hair, a nob of nose and heavy eyelids like a bloodhound. The room was quiet. Amid the tense silence, Angelo's stomach growled. He coughed, hoping Mr. Meers hadn't heard. Angelo had been too nervous to eat that morning. He glanced over at the coffeemaker, the open box of doughnuts. Meeting with his malpractice attorney, he didn't think it was a good idea to grab a snack in the middle of their first session.

"Mrs. Trautman's lawyer contends that there was a delay in diagnosing her melanoma," Meers said finally.

Angelo held his stare until it morphed into something like a glare. "Why am I being named in this suit?" he asked. "Mrs. Trautman isn't my patient."

"Mrs. Trautman states that Mr. Demetre Kostas brought you into the exam room to assess a mole, which you said, appeared benign. She was made to believe you were a dermatologist."

Angelo sighed. "I never said I was."

Meers closed his eyes in frustration. "Dr. Perrotta, I'm simply explaining the details of the suit. Mrs. Trautman went to see Mr. Kostas to have a mole removed. He recommended a second opinion. You were asked to consult. According to Mrs. Trautman, you said the mole looked benign. Did you say that?"

Angelo felt his face burning. "Yes, but—"

"In the notes we obtained from Mr. Kostas's office, it states that's exactly what Mr. Kostas heard as well."

"Demetre wrote that?"

Meers displayed a photocopy of the notes. Angelo sat there staring at the documents in utter disbelief.

"I admit I said that initially, but I changed my mind while Demetre and I spoke in the hall. My exact words to him were: you really should send her to a dermatologist. It's always best to err on the side of caution."

"Unfortunately, you did not document that in your consultation," Meers pointed out. "In fact, you neglected to write a consultation note at all."

"That's because it wasn't an official consult. Demetre knocked on my door. The next thing I know he's asking my opinion about this woman's mole."

"By entering that room, you entered into a doctor patient-relationship with Mrs. Trautman." There was a hint of annoyance in his voice.

Angelo collapsed against the chair, heaving. "So, what happens now?"

Meers sat back with his hands intertwined behind his head. "We wait for them to disclose the damages, but in all likelihood, I'll recommend we settle."

"Settle?"

Over the years, Angelo had navigated through his fair share of awkward questions, judgmental looks, and uncomfortable silences, but none compared to the situation he found himself in now.

"Dr. Perrotta, no one wants to go to trial. In fact, she's

only seeking damages because there was a delay in diagnosis. Chances are some hotshot dermatologist planted this seed of litigation in her head. Anything to make a quick buck."

"But she's already rich."

"Ever heard the expression, *the rich get richer*? Now you know how they do it."

"I guess," Angelo said, only half listening. All he could think about was that he hadn't even been in practice a year, and he was already being sued. "Will my malpractice carrier inform my boss about this lawsuit?"

Meers took a sip from his coffee cup. "Let me ask you a question. Who pays for your malpractice?"

"My boss."

Meers swallowed down hard. "Well, he's going to know something happened when your rates go up."

Angelo had a flash of memory, Stanzione gripping the back of his neck and saying, *"Hiring you was one of the best decisions I ever made. Don't prove me wrong."*

"Mr. Meers, my boss can't find out that I'm being sued. He'll fire me. I have student loan payments. I'll lose my apartment."

Meers stood up and poured a glass of water for Angelo. "We have to allow this to play out, but if I were you, I'd tell your boss the truth."

"Couldn't you speak with the malpractice carrier? Ask them to hold off on increasing my rates until I can figure out a way to explain this to my boss?"

"Don't get me wrong. I don't like exposing people to painful realities, but losing your job is the least of your problems. Just pray this woman's dermatologist caught her melanoma in time."

Panic slashed through Angelo. "What's the worst-case scenario?"

"You really want to know?" Meers raised an eyebrow. "If her melanoma has metastasized or she needs chemo or radiation, then we'll be forced to pay a much larger settlement.

Millions. Should that happen, your malpractice carrier will likely drop you. On a positive note, Mrs. Trautman hasn't reported you to the Office of Professional Medical Conduct."

"Medical conduct?"

Meers's voice was cold, even accusatory. "Documenting a patient's visit is medical residency 101."

The cold slap of truth shocked him into a deliberately frozen stare.

"In the future, kindly refuse to offer curbside consults and have the patient make an appointment. Above all, document their visits. Any self-respecting doctor would have done exactly that."

◆◆◆

By the time Angelo returned to the office, he had made up his mind to inform Dr. Stanzione he was being sued. Having just returned from Turks and Caicos, he hoped Stanzione would be in a good mood. Once Angelo arrived at the office, he found Steven behind the front desk. Instead of looking tan and relaxed, Steven appeared pale and startled. His eyes darted around the room like an anxious cat. There was a tall, blond man standing just off to the side. Steven was speaking on the phone but covering the receiver so that no one could hear him.

The airy, casual way Steven usually carried himself had been replaced by an unmistakable panic as though this blond stranger had Steven in his thrall. Angelo took the opportunity to get a better look at him. He was over six foot with a fair complexion and blond hair flopping forward. He stood with his hands folded behind his back, wearing pleated khakis, a navy polo shirt, and a blue blazer. He looked at Angelo expectantly and smiled. Just then, Steven put the phone down and said, "Tim, Dr. Stanzione will see you now."

Angelo bristled with anxiety. *Could this be Demetre's ex?*

Walking back to his desk, keeping a respectful distance from Tim, Angelo's curiosity morphed into an obsessive fixation. Angelo hoped to learn more eavesdropping. No sooner had he set down his backpack, the phone rang. It was Steven informing him that a patient was waiting.

Fifteen minutes later, Angelo escorted his patient to the front desk to schedule a follow-up appointment. Tim was in the hall talking with Laura in hushed whispers. As Angelo passed them, he glanced in their direction. Rather indiscreetly they looked at Angelo in unison, as though he had been the topic of their conversation. Tim's expression was both wary and taut. Tim then kissed Laura on both cheeks and exited.

Stanzione's office door was open when Angelo headed back to his desk. He poked his head in. Stanzione sat, scratching his head vigorously; something Angelo had never seen him do. Steven was at Stanzione's side, pulling his hand to make him stop scratching. "Is everything okay?" Angelo asked with caution.

Stanzione glanced up at Steven and then looked at Angelo. "Come in and sit down."

Angelo sat on the sofa. "What's wrong?"

Stanzione took a deep breath. "Demetre's partner, Tim, was just here. He said that Demetre had been working long hours and sleeping late most days since he moved his practice. More recently, he's been staying in the city with a friend, concerned that he was too tired to drive. Thursday night Demetre never came home, and Tim has not spoken to him since."

"Has Tim contacted the police?" Angelo asked.

Stanzione looked pensive, rubbing the back of his neck. Even Steven had begun to mechanically arrange the magazines on Stanzione's desk.

"Is there more to this story?" Angelo pressed.

Stanzione gave Angelo a hard look. "It's really inappropriate for Tim to have come here. Demetre and I have a professional relationship. Plus, he's my patient. I couldn't say anything to Tim even if I knew something."

"What more do you know?" Angelo asked with a straightforwardness that must have seemed out of character, but under the circumstances felt completely warranted.

Stanzione cleared his throat and started up again. "Three years ago, Demetre entered drug rehabilitation. He spent six weeks in a clinic upstate. During that time, Tim paid the bills to support Demetre's business while he was away. Once Demetre was discharged, he went right back to work. After a successful year, they bought the house in Hoboken and moved in together. For years Demetre has been sober, but recently . . . Tim noticed that Demetre had been withdrawing large sums of money from their account. Demetre explained that it was to cover expenses incurred from moving to the new office space, but once he started staying out all night, Tim suspected he was using drugs again."

Angelo stared at Stanzione in disbelief. "You knew Demetre had a drug problem?"

Stanzione shot Angelo a quick flash of anger that took him aback. "Of course, I knew. I'm his doctor, but this most recent behavior is news to me."

There was a long silence. The only thing Angelo could hear was Steven's hands tightening a magazine into a taut cylinder. "Angelo, you've been hanging out with Demetre," he said. "Did you notice anything strange?"

"No," Angelo said. Steven stared at Angelo in a peculiar way. It came to Angelo that he might have answered too quickly because Steven had a suspicious look in his eyes. "How did you leave it with Tim?"

Stanzione rubbed his eyes with his thumb and forefinger. "I explained that as Demetre's doctor I was bound by confidentiality, and that he should follow up with the police. Of course, I said that if we heard from Demetre we would tell him to call home."

Stanzione's intercom buzzed. Steven answered. "Yes, Tiffany."

"If it's Tim again," Stanzione said, "tell him I'm with a patient."

Steven hung up; face etched with stunned alarm. "Demetre's here. He's on his way back now."

"Jesus Christ," Stanzione muttered. "What else could go wrong today?"

The door opened suddenly. Demetre stood there, breathless.

"Tony, can we talk?" He looked like he hadn't slept in days.

Stanzione nodded, and Steven and Angelo filed out of the room in silence.

"Wouldn't you like to be a fly on that wall?" Angelo said, but Steven had already started down the hall and didn't hear him. At any rate, he didn't respond.

Angelo sat at his desk, thinking about what Stanzione had said, and how his story conflicted with the one Demetre had told him. According to Demetre, Tim was the one who had gone to rehab, not him, but Stanzione was Demetre's doctor. Certainly, he knew the truth. *Maybe they had both gone to rehab*, thought Angelo. *What if Demetre had omitted that detail because he didn't want Angelo to know he had fallen off the wagon? And if that was true then hadn't Angelo been an enabler all this time?*

The phone buzzed. Angelo had a patient waiting. Pulling his stethoscope from his lab coat pocket, Jason's card fell to the ground. Angelo picked it up, staring at the cell phone number on the back. "Call me," he read out loud. "I'm a nice guy."

◆◆◆

That night, Angelo stepped into Bo's Noodle Shop on Sixth Avenue. He was seated at the table when Jason stepped through the doors. He walked to the host, who pointed in Angelo's direction. When their eyes met, Jason's face lit up.

Jason wore a navy button-down shirt, dark jeans, and Converse sneakers.

Converse sneakers!

His shirt had crease marks, and Angelo wondered if Jason had bought that shirt earlier just for tonight.

Right away, the server brought over the pork buns and steamed chicken dumplings Angelo had taken the liberty of ordering. They sipped tea from small white porcelain cups. The red glow from the neon sign reflected in the glass tabletop. "Have you been here before?" Angelo asked.

"My partner, Mary, has taken me to every restaurant within a two-mile radius of the police station."

Angelo removed the paper wrapping from his chopsticks and rubbed them together. "How is Mary?" he asked.

Jason took a pork bun on his plate and cut it in half using his fork. "She's good."

"Did you tell her we were having dinner?"

"Yeah, I did," Jason said. "She was excited to hear you called and asked me out on a date." Jason stopped abruptly, eyes bulging out of his head. "That is what this is, right?"

Angelo hadn't considered this a dinner date; he wasn't sure Jason was even interested in him like that because of the way he had treated him. If anything, he wanted to take Jason out to apologize. "Of course, it's a date," Angelo said going along with it to avoid an uncomfortable situation. "That is, if you still want to date me?"

Jason's shock gave way to relief. "I think you know how I feel about you, Angelo. Why don't we see how this night turns out?"

Angelo took a bite of a dumpling. After a long swallow he said, "Jason, more than anything I want to apologize. I'm not the kind of guy that leads guys on. There's so much going on at work. It had nothing to do with you."

Jason pushed the remains of his pork bun around the plate with the tines of his fork, staring at the treacly brown sauce. "I appreciate you saying that. It was confusing. At the hospital, you seemed interested, and then you weren't. I just assumed there was someone else."

"That's just it," Angelo explained. "There is no one else. It's just that work is so confusing. My boss hired this man, Demetre, who runs an aesthetic practice."

"A what?"

"It's laser facials and hair removal stuff."

"Demetre," he repeated. "Was that the guy you were staring at the day I ran into you in the park?"

"Yes," Angelo said. "That was Demetre. Why do you remember him?"

"You seemed pretty distracted." Jason's lips tightened. "Not bad looking for an older guy."

Angelo sipped water. "To be clear, I did not blow you off because of Demetre. In fact, the reason why I've been so preoccupied is that in addition to seeing patients, my boss wants me to learn about lasers. His plan is to merge businesses, but Demetre doesn't feel the same way. I'm hearing conflicting stories from each of them, and I don't know who to believe anymore."

Jason sat back, nodding. Angelo wondered if this was how Jason imagined their first date. "How long have you known this guy, Demetre?"

"I just met him a couple of months ago."

"And how long have you known your boss?" Jason inquired further.

"I've known Dr. Stanzione for three years. He was my medical mentor."

Jason shrugged. "My advice would be to trust the man you've known the longest. Stanzione hired you. Doesn't he deserve your loyalty?"

Angelo looked down at his hands for several long, charged seconds; he wondered how a complete stranger had assessed his situation better than he had himself.

"You know my mother always says," Jason began, "when someone shows you who they are, believe them the first time."

"Your mother sounds like a smart lady," Angelo said.

"She is." Jason flashed his charming smile. "My mother thinks she's a doctor, a lawyer, and the CEO of Murphy, Inc." Angelo felt a pang of envy that Jason had a mother he loved so clearly. "All the Murphy women are know-it-alls."

"How many Murphy women are there?" Angelo asked.

Jason held up four fingers. "Besides my mother, Eileen, I have three older sisters."

"You're the baby and the only boy?" Angelo clarified.

Jason was grinning so that his cheeks were ripe, like plums. "I'm the prince."

"You are a prince," Angelo said. "Thanks for giving me a chance."

Jason reached over and held Angelo's hand. He looked down at the comely hand, smiling. It felt warm and leathery, like a catcher's mitt. Immediately, Angelo imagined what those hands would feel like on his naked body.

"This was fun, right?" Jason asked.

"It was." They sat quietly for a few seconds longer, holding hands in the middle of the restaurant, feeling like they had moved past whatever obstacle had blocked their paths to unite them. Still, in the back of Angelo's mind, the malpractice case and Demetre's reckless behavior gnawed at him, but for now, he wanted only to enjoy Jason's company.

CHAPTER TEN

That next morning it was chilly and rainy. Angelo walked to the corner bagel shop to buy a cup of coffee. Sipping while he waited for the bus, his mind rustled, considering all the events that had transpired.

The reckless progression of Demetre's behavior was evident to him now. Back then, he didn't notice or perhaps he didn't want to see the truth because he was so infatuated. After learning Demetre had pointed the blame of Mrs. Trautman's melanoma diagnosis toward him, that he had lied about breaking up with Tim and cleverly gained Angelo's sympathy, had posed as a supportive partner when all along it was Demetre who was the addict; Angelo was overwhelmed with a familiar sense of shame.

He could feel it descend upon him last night after having dinner with Jason, could feel it inside him, and with it a special shame for allowing himself to believe that Demetre saw him as someone better than the person he was. Staring out the bagel shop window, veins of water swirling down the glass, Angelo began to seethe with anger.

His biological father's abandonment left a black speck of longing that grew from his rage over the years, hardening into an indestructible piece of glass. He imagined it as a glistening, black piece of obsidian wedged underneath his sternum. Last night, as he tried to sleep, he felt a deep ache in his chest. As he tossed and turned, it occurred to him that he was very familiar with this pain.

When other children boasted about their rich and successful fathers, Angelo had lied and said that his traveled to every country in the world writing. But the truth was that he never knew his father, had not even seen a photograph, and Angelo's mind had filled in an imaginary outline he had drawn throughout the years. Gradually, he forced himself to think about his father less and less until eventually, Angelo stopped imagining him at all. But the link between the father he had created in his mind and the men he clung to in real life was obvious to him now.

Despite Angelo's best efforts to be strong, he believed the men in his life conspired against him. Although he knew that succumbing to this conspiracy theory prevented him from being the man he fought so hard to become, it felt like he had squandered years of education for another man's approval, and protecting Demetre, even when he knew better, was proof of that.

By the time the bus pulled up to the stop, the crowd sloshing through puddles to gain access, Angelo stood caught in the folds of his shame. He stared out the shop window, the rage churning inside him like a motor until he was roused back to the present by the sound of his cell phone. "Angelo?"

"Jason," Angelo said. "I'm rushing to catch the bus. Can I call you later?"

"Are you all right?" he asked. Angelo sensed the urgency in his voice. "I was going to call you last night, but it was late."

Angelo said, "What are you talking about?"

"You don't know?"

Angelo caught a glimpse of a headline on a stack of newspapers at the bagel shop entrance.

"Phony Physician at Posh Park Avenue Practice Performs Laser Surgery"

"Your office!" Jason said. "It was on the news last night. That guy, Demetre, was caught on hidden camera. He lied about being a doctor, and they caught it all on video. They showed your office, Angelo. I saw your name on the plaque outside."

Angelo picked up the newspaper and read the first paragraph.

Demetre Kostas, CEO of SkinDem on Park Avenue, never went to medical school and doesn't have a medical license but refers to himself as a doctor and operates a high-tech laser to remove hair, scars, wrinkles, birthmarks, tattoos, and moles. Our investigation of the phony physician found that Kostas dropped out of college, has no professional license, and has overstated his qualifications.

"Are you there?" Jason shouted.

Angelo was startled back to the present. "I can't believe this is happening. What am I going to do?"

"Tell me where you are. Don't go anywhere. I'll pick you up."

"My life is ruined."

"Tell me where you are?" Jason pleaded. "We'll go to your office together."

A collection of dark umbrellas had assembled outside the office entrance. Jason and Angelo marched straight to the front door, avoiding the reporters' questions. Once Angelo grabbed the door handle, he felt an exquisite tension gathering around him. Blinding lights clicked on, bleaching everything white. The sound of camera shutters ticked off in rapid fire like someone squeezing bubble wrap. Reporters hurled questions at them.

"Did you know he was a fake?"

"Are you a patient of Demetre Kostas?"

Inside, the waiting room felt eerie. There were several patients seated. They looked like startled deer. Angelo forced a smile.

"Morning," he said to Tiffany. "Is Dr. Stanzione here?"

"Yes," she replied, staring plaintively back at him like a hostage too frightened to speak. Angelo and Jason walked through the door and down the hall, propelled by the pull of dread.

Stanzione was on the phone, scratching his head. Steven stood beside him, rubbing his shoulders.

"No, we haven't heard from him . . . what about the reporters? Of course, we won't let them in." Overhead the rain was beating on the skylight, sounding like a marching army. "I don't know where he is. How should I know if he's under arrest? They just aired the fucking story last night! I didn't see it!"

Angelo pulled Jason into his office. He had heard enough. Jason closed the door behind them and threw his arms around Angelo. He held him for several long minutes until Steven knocked on the door and invited them back in.

Jason explained that three separate undercover investigations of Demetre Kostas had taken place: one by a reporter from the *Daily News*, another by a local television news station, and a third by the New York state attorney general's office. All three had been tipped off by Demetre's former employer, Dr. Kathleen Eichhorn, after she saw Demetre's ad in *New York* magazine.

Angelo saw patients that day even though the office felt like a tomb. Once he closed the exam room door, eyes would flash open, postures sprang up straight, waiting for him to spill the gory details. Of course, he knew only what he had read in the newspaper that morning not having seen the news the night before. Jason had said that there was footage taken from inside the exam room using a hidden camera, and that Demetre admitted he was a doctor, having graduated from New York Medical College. "He appeared drowsy," Jason had said, "slurring his words like he was on something".

Angelo thought back to last Thursday night when he found Demetre downstairs with Yossi. The undercover reporters had already been there earlier that week. Demetre looked tired that night too, with dark circles under his eyes. Angelo wondered what those undercover reporters thought when they saw him looking like that.

By the end of the day, Angelo sat at his desk rubbing his temples. There were several messages taped to his computer screen: one from Tammy, another from his sister, Camille, and the last one from Steven. *Meeting tomorrow morning at 8 a.m.!!*

That night Angelo went home and lay face down on his bed, consumed with guilt-ridden exhaustion. His cell phone never stopped ringing, and he was too tired to return anyone's calls except Jason's. "How are you?"

"I don't know how to answer that," Angelo replied. "It still hasn't hit me."

"Well, remember, what happened isn't your fault."

"You're so nice. Why are you being nice to me? I've only been a dick to you."

Jason chuckled. "I don't know about that. I'd say that on the dick scale, you've been a micropenis."

Angelo burst out laughing. "I don't know if that's good or bad?"

"You were a little dicky. It's not like you were a monster dick. Just a mini one."

"This is why you'll get into heaven," Angelo said. "You can make someone laugh even when they don't deserve your kindness."

"All right," he said, turning serious. "Enough with the pity party.

"You're right. Time to shut down this pity party and go to sleep."

Seconds after hanging up, Angelo received a text from Demetre.

Can you talk?

Angelo took an instant to gather himself, then he threw his cell phone on the bed. Angelo sat frozen, toying with the idea of texting him back but convinced himself no good would come of it. The pull of curiosity was so intense. What could Demetre possibly say? The ding of a second text rattled Angelo.

Call me. I miss you.

Angelo powered down his cell phone and walked into the bathroom shaking his head.

Throughout the night, Angelo drifted fitfully on waves of unsettling dreams until he woke up in a panic that he had missed the meeting, but it was still dark outside. The glowing numerals on the digital clock read 4:13 AM. Minutes ticked by, and whatever had lulled him to sleep had now worn off because he was wide awake. In a trance, he walked to the bathroom, urinated, and fell back in bed. He looked at the clock. Only minutes had gone by. Angelo got up and rifled through the kitchen cabinets until he found an old bottle of whiskey. He poured a shot and drank it. Then he drank straight from the bottle for several long seconds, hoping inebriation would help ease his mind.

He had a thought: What was Demetre doing right now? He imagined him sitting at the kitchen table with Tim. Hours of talk had passed with Tim wending his way through Demetre's lies until they came to some mutual conclusion about what to do next. Angelo felt some consolation in knowing that Demetre wasn't alone, and yet, he hated himself for that.

Angelo flinched awake, eyes searching for the clock. 7:30 AM. He stumbled out of bed, racing drunkenly toward the bathroom. In the medicine cabinet mirror, he caught a glimpse of himself: hair tussled, eyes irritated and tired. By the time he showered and dressed, he peeked in the mirror again and thought he looked more or less like himself.

Walking to the office he was unsteady. His face felt flushed and raw. He could still smell the whiskey on his breath. Coffee, he thought, but the thought of stopping at the bagel shop sent a coil of revulsion through him. A cold wind blew against him. It felt oddly refreshing. He hurried the rest of the way. When he turned the corner of Park Avenue, the crowd of reporters waited. By the time he reached the door, he was assaulted by the din of shouting with a familiarity that caught him off guard: *Dr. Perrotta, how well did you know Demetre Kostas?; did you know he wasn't a doctor?; Dr. Perrotta! Dr. Perrotta! Dr. Perrotta!*

They were all there when Angelo entered Stanzione's office, including Laura Ellis, sitting around like survivors hoping to be rescued.

"I can't believe they're out there again today," Angelo said.

Stanzione squinted at him. Angelo could feel his eyes graze over his face. Angelo wondered if he appeared exhausted, hung over, or both. Under normal circumstances, Stanzione's stare would have seemed rude, but these were not normal circumstances.

"This is going to destroy us," Stanzione said, tugging at his lab coat. "I should sue Demetre." Steven massaged his shoulders, but Stanzione wriggled away. "Fucking bastard. I can't believe this. What a nightmare."

"Why don't you begin the meeting," Laura proposed.

Silence fell all around them as Stanzione collected his thoughts. Hands trembling, he intertwined his fingers and set his hands on the desk. "It has come to my attention that Demetre has turned himself over to the police."

Steven and Laura nodded as if a separate colloquy occurred prior to Angelo's arrival—one in which the details had already been explained.

Angelo leaned forward and dropped his voice. "When?"

"Tim called last night. They've retained a lawyer, and Demetre was advised to turn himself in. The charge is practicing medicine without a license." Stanzione looked to Laura who nodded slowly with encouragement. "This morning, I was informed that Demetre was released on a five-thousand-dollar bond."

"Oh, so he's not in jail," Angelo clarified.

"Yes. Yes. That's what I'm saying. My attorney insists that no one speak to the press. They are not allowed in the office, and they're certainly not allowed to film any of our patients. If they do that then it's a privacy violation, and we should notify the police immediately."

Stanzione spoke slowly, his every move calibrated. Except for these few simple facts he recited back to them like a hostage reading demands with a gun to his head, Angelo saw no resemblance to the intimidating man he'd met during his interview. The incorrigible king who drank expensive dessert wine and commanded the chef to genuflect. A different Stanzione might have thrived on the challenge of restoring order, walked around them reciting his speech as if he were a general and they were his troops preparing for war.

The intercom buzzed. Steven stood up to answer it. "Yes. Oh. We'll be right there," he said, hanging up. "The police are here with a search warrant."

Stanzione's face turned white as flour. "This will destroy us. How will we ever recover from this?"

At that moment, Angelo didn't know what was more surprising. That the police were waiting to search the premises or that this giant man he once admired had been reduced to a wavering, quivering minion, hiding behind his desk like a frightened elf in the forest.

At any rate, it didn't matter because Laura stood up and set down her yellow legal pad.

"It was nice knowing you," she said, "but I can't be a part of this anymore."

Sometime around three o'clock, Angelo was applying leads to a patient's chest to perform an EKG when he heard a loud hullabaloo outside the exam room door. "You can't be here. Do you understand? I want you to leave." Angelo opened the door a crack and saw Demetre and Stanzione by the stairwell. Steven loomed nearby.

"I spoke to Tiffany and told her I was coming," Demetre argued.

"We only assumed you were coming to pack up," Steven insisted. "The next thing I know clients started showing up for appointments."

"I need to work," Demetre said. "I'll go bankrupt."

"No, no, no!" Stanzione shouted, covering his ears. "You can't be here. You just can't."

Demetre held up a finger about to say something, but then stopped himself and walked downstairs.

"Call the police!" Stanzione said to Steven. "I want him out of here."

Angelo stepped into the hall. "What if you call Tim? Maybe he can get through to Demetre. You don't want to attract any more attention by having the police here again. It'll only scare the patients and give the reporters something to film."

Stanzione's head started shaking. "I don't care who you call. Just get him out of here." Then he lumbered back to his office, scratching fiercely at his head.

"Tony is being irrational," Demetre said to Steven. They whispered in the stairwell as Angelo listened.

"I don't think Tony's the irrational one in this scenario," Steven said. "Let me talk to him."

"Okay, I'll be downstairs packing up," Demetre said, inching closer to Steven. "You know you have incredible skin. Has anyone told you that?" Demetre held Steven's jaw, moving his head from side to side, inspecting his complexion.

"I moisturize." Steven grinned like a moony schoolgirl flirting with the varsity quarterback.

"You always look good," Demetre said. "It's not just your skin. I mean look at those biceps." Steven flexed spontaneously. "They're enormous."

"Let me speak with Tony," Steven said. "I'll be down in a bit."

Angelo ducked into an empty exam room before Steven noticed he had been eavesdropping. Why would Steven acquiesce to Demetre's compliments when he had proven he himself a liar? It didn't make sense to Angelo, but then he recalled his own struggle the night before, and how he was tempted to speak with Demetre even after all that had happened. Angelo had and still believed he was a victim to Demetre's charms. Unbidden, the memory of Demetre's sexually charged flirtations that day Angelo helped him move the laser into his office reconstituted itself before his eyes. Now, he understood that Demetre was motivated by pure ego and a total disregard for consequences.

In the end, Demetre agreed to evacuate the office in return for his security deposit along with the month's rent he'd already paid. Stanzione went home early complaining of chest pain. Steven urged him to call his cardiologist, but he simply left without saying good-bye.

Once the last patient was gone, Angelo sat at his desk sifting through messages. It was after seven in the evening. The sky overhead was dark. Leaves collected on the skylight leaving little room for the moonlight to streak through. When Angelo looked up, Steven was standing in the doorway.

"Why don't you ever turn on the light?" he asked, flipping the switch. Angelo squinted at him. For a moment, he remained in silhouette until his eyes adjusted. "It's over."

"What's over?" Angelo asked.

"Demetre's gone. His friend came by and helped him move. Some shaved-head muscle guy with tattoos."

Yossi.

Steven slithered into the chair, eager to talk.

"I told Tony not to trust him. I knew something was up from the beginning. I never liked the whole Dr. D thing." Then he leaned forward and added, "I think Laura was in on it. She had to know what was going on."

"Well, like you said, it's over now. He's gone. How is Dr. Stanzione feeling?"

"Tony is so upset," Steven said. "I'm trying to convince him to go up to the Cape this weekend."

"I think that's a good idea. It's all in the police's hands now. There's nothing more we can do."

"You should see it downstairs," Steven said. "What a mess. It's going to take me hours to clean up."

For one horrible second, Angelo had this vision of Steven rifling through Demetre's garbage, searching for art supplies. "Did you find anything interesting?"

Steven shifted uncomfortably. "Well, he took all the medical equipment but left his waiting room chairs and receptionist's desk. He even left the nude photos. Talk about tacky. I realize the art up here is outdated, but who hangs nude photos of themself?"

"I didn't know those pictures were of Demetre."

"Weird right, but not really when you think about it. Demetre is so full of himself. I don't know why Tim put up with him for so long. When we first met Demetre he was a real party boy who bounced from boyfriend to boyfriend. Then he started dating Mitch Lyon. He's the one that put an end to Demetre's crazy lifestyle."

Angelo stared at him, uncomprehending. "Who's Mitch Lyon?"

Steven had a devilish, secretive expression. "He owned a spa in SoHo. Mitch hired Demetre to do construction work, and they started dating."

"Construction? I thought Demetre was a landscape designer."

Steven laughed condescendingly. "Yeah, I heard that too. The truth is that Demetre was a construction worker by day and a go-go dancer by night at some bar in New Jersey called Feathers. He was living the real-life version of *Flashdance*."

"How do you know all this?"

Steven pursed his lips, savoring his words as though they were too delicious to speak. "We met them on Fire Island like ten years ago. Mitch was Tony's patient. One summer he brought Demetre out, prancing him around like some show pony. I'll admit that Demetre was a sexy guy, but it's not like Fire Island doesn't have its share of gorgeous men. Anyway, Mitch was the best thing that happened to Demetre. He trained him how to use lasers, paid for his education, and eventually Demetre became certified. But everything went downhill once Mitch died of AIDS."

There was something almost diabolical about Steven's revelations, and Angelo wondered why he kept all these secrets from him. When Angelo looked at him, he was grinning with a playful malevolence as if Demetre's downfall was his plan all along.

"Come with me," Steven said. "I want to show you something."

Downstairs, the office looked like it had been looted. Chairs were turned on their side, loose papers scattered on the floor.

"See here," Steven said, showing Angelo a tangle of wires by Laura's desk. "The police took the computers." Then he opened the file cabinet to show him that the client charts had also been confiscated. The exam rooms were all empty except for a stool in one and a silver tray still prepped with gauze and alcohol pads in the other.

Demetre's office appeared the most ravaged with papers everywhere. Desk pushed into the center of the room. A mesh of wires where the computer once stood. Angelo opened the file cabinet to see if it was empty too. Among the remaining folders, he found one labeled Jeune Toi. When Angelo opened it, he found the product brochure Rachel had presented to them at lunch along with the pricing table.

And there it was.

A copy of the letter he had signed, the one designating Angelo Perrotta as SkinDem's medical director. Of course, there was no reason the police would have thought to take it, but how fortunate this was for Angelo.

A quick glance over his shoulder showed Steven was collecting supplies from the cabinets—alcohol pads, gauze, tape—throwing them in a fresh garbage bag to take upstairs. Angelo took the letter from the file and slipped it in his pocket when Steven wasn't looking. "I think I'm going to head out," Angelo said. "Are you going to stay?"

"Yeah, you go on home. I'll be here just another hour."

Angelo walked back to his apartment, dreading the thought of being alone. Even with the blaring city sounds all around, nothing could distract him from the images of Demetre that paraded in his mind: drinking bourbon, shopping at Barneys, dancing at the Roxy, and catching him downstairs with Yossi. Angelo tried to jerk his head to shake them away but after a little while, they started up again like some relentless video, playing over and over on a loop.

He texted Jason, but there was no response.

Lying in bed, Angelo picked up the phone and called Tammy. She seemed sleepy and a little drunk. "Did I wake you?"

"Nah, how are you?"

"I guess you heard."

"Uh, yeah," she said. "It's been in the newspaper every day. Heard that jagoff is in jail."

"He's out on bond. You know he actually came in today to see clients."

"Are you fucking kidding me?"

"I'm completely serious," said Angelo.

"What a nut. You really dodged a bullet with that one. Thank God Val and I saved your ass that night."

Angelo absorbed that, knowing that this man they were talking about was not completely out of his life.

"Tammy," Angelo said, but his voice gave away.

"What's the matter?

Angelo couldn't breathe. His heart rate sped up. "I'm being sued by one of Demetre's clients."

"For what?" she shouted.

"This old lady . . . . She had a mole . . . . Now she's suing me for delay in diagnosis."

"Jeez Ange! Have you spoken to a lawyer?"

Angelo rubbed his fist against his sternum. "Yes, he's hoping she settles."

There was a long pause where neither one said anything. Angelo thought he would feel better after he told Tammy the truth, but he was foolish. His confession had only awakened the obsidian. Its sharp edges prickled his ribs like cactus needles. Angelo wondered what Tammy would have had said if he had told her about the night he caught Demetre and Yossi partying in the office after work? How she would have scolded him for not informing his boss immediately. And now that Demetre's lies had been exposed in the media, it only compounded what he already knew about himself; he was a needy child desperate for another father figure.

A pathetic, psychiatric cliche.

"Listen, Ange, it's late," Tammy said flatly. "We'll talk more in the morning. You've had a long day, old friend."

"Thanks for listening," he said. "Goodnight."

CHAPTER ELEVEN

Over the next several weeks, the practice slowly came back to life, stretching and yawning as if they had been hibernating. In the wake of the scandal, Stanzione had Steven cancel all scheduled lunches and dinners. Drug reps were not permitted to enter the office, not even the five-star ones like Jill. Eventually, the reporters disappeared, moving on to some other, more current stories. Stanzione and Angelo focused on the patients. Saving the practice became their mantra.

For all the time and effort it took to incorporate Demetre into the office, it was amazing how quickly all evidence of him was removed. In the days after his departure, Steven had the remaining furniture hauled away. He even repainted the former SkinDem suite himself. Once he was done, he invited Angelo downstairs to have a look. The walls, so sparkling white, were hauntingly sterile. The only smell was the pungent scent of fresh paint, like glue. As Angelo wandered around, it felt as if SkinDem had never existed there at all, that it was nothing more than a nightmare he'd dreamed, and he felt swaddled in the safety of his denial. For a moment, he closed his eyes and struggled to organize his impressions, but his memories of Demetre were fading even then, leaving behind but a vague residue he hoped would fade completely under that fresh coat of paint.

With the holidays approaching, Angelo welcomed the distraction. His relationship with Jason had shifted into a comfortable stride. No worries about whether he should text or call, but just doing it without feeling needy. Jason reciprocated with the same measure of spontaneity, surprising Angelo at his office so they could grab dinner together.

There was even a discussion about spending the holidays with his sister Camille and her husband Trace, but Angelo wasn't ready to submit Jason to the man he considered was the biggest loser he had ever met. Instead, they celebrated Thanksgiving with Tammy and Val.

And yet, for all the positive changes, Angelo's mind wrestled with doubt that his relationship had become too easy too fast, particularly on those nights he slept alone. But then, the next day, he'd wake up to a text from Jason, *Morning Sunshine*, and that gnawing beast of doubt was silenced.

Angelo thought Steven decorated the office to an excessive degree, perhaps hoping to camouflage some of the lingering embarrassment with a holly branch or a poinsettia set in a vase covered in reflective red paper.

Taking a seat at his desk one afternoon in early December, Angelo saw a message taped to his computer screen with Steven's trademark double exclamation points.

"Thank you for returning my call," Detective Farrell said to Angelo. "I need to discuss a matter regarding Demetre Kostas." A spider of panic crawled up Angelo's back. "Can I come by your office around noon?"

"Today?"

"Is today not good for you."

"No, please," Angelo said regaining his composure. "Come by."

◆◆◆

Angelo imagined what it would be like if he were a Kafkaesque insect on the ceiling looking down at him. Detective Farrell was just as he had imagined: a short, barrel-chested man with a meaty face, shaved head, and an unwavering stare. "Thank you for seeing me," he said. "I'm sure you're busy so I'll get right to it." Angelo noticed Farrell had liver spots on his nose and cheeks. They were quite large, and he wondered if he was an alcoholic. "Last night, Demetre Kostas was pulled over in Madison, New Jersey. He was unable to produce a driver's license, registration, or proof of insurance. When the officer inspected the car, he found cocaine."

Angelo gaped at him. "I'm not surprised."

"You probably don't know, but after his arrest in November, his lawyer arranged for a plea bargain with state prosecutors. His prison sentence was cut to six months. In return, Kostas agreed to help the attorney general's office investigate two doctors suspected of insurance fraud. He even agreed to contact these doctors, nosing around for more information. Essentially, he was providing evidence for the same doctors who were writing prescriptions for him while he pretended to be a doctor."

"Unbelievable," was all Angelo could muster.

"His arrest last night may have cost him his plea bargain agreement."

"Serves him right."

"His friend bailed him out this morning." Farrell cleared his throat. "The reason I'm here is because the arresting officer also found several controlled substance prescription pads in the backseat of Mr. Kostas's car. All with your name on them."

A brutal stab of betrayal and absolute panic followed. "My name!"

"Does that mean you didn't give Mr. Kostas your prescriptions pads?"

"What! No. Of course not."

"Do you know how he could have gotten his hands on these prescription pads?" Farrell asked.

Angelo stood up and opened the file cabinet where he stored them. "I keep them right here." There were stacks of them right where they had always been, but now, it was clear the stacks had mysteriously shrunk.

"Did Mr. Kostas have access to this room?"

"Demetre had access to the entire office. He was an old friend of Dr. Stanzione's, the physician who owns this practice. We never imagined Demetre was a thief let alone a person who would perpetrate himself as a doctor."

"You didn't notice any prescription pads were missing?"

"Not until just now."

"Do you keep a log of the controlled substance prescriptions you write?"

"Why would I do that?"

"So you can keep track of them," Farrell replied, deadpan.

Angelo detected a hint of sarcasm. It seemed inevitable that this nightmare should continue. The endless shockwaves. The false sense of back-to-normal security.

Farrell continued, "At any rate, I hope you decide to lock them up from now on. I hear stories like this all the time, patients stealing prescription pads from their doctor's desk or cabinet when they're not looking. Kostas must have known where you kept them. He had five or six pads on him. They also found prescription bottles for Percocet and OxyContin. All prescribed by you."

"Me?" Angelo was in shock, staring at the remaining prescription pads, imagining Demetre wandering into his office once everyone had gone home. "I only wrote him one prescription. Is there any way we could check with the pharmacies to prove the signatures are forgeries?"

"Listen doc, considering Kostas's prior arrest, you have nothing to worry about. I just wanted you to know."

Angelo shuddered spontaneously as though Demetre's ghost had passed through him, reminding him that even though he was gone, his chilly spirit lingered.

"Creepy isn't it," Farrell said. "To think someone would have the balls to steal right out from under your nose. Can I ask why you still use paper prescriptions? Fancy place like this, you would imagine everything would be electronic."

This was a topic of contention for Angelo as well. In the end, it came down to money and Stanzione's unwillingness to part with it. "We're working on that. Until then, I assure you that I will keep my prescription pads locked up from now on. Is there anything else?"

"Actually, there is one more thing." Angelo saw Farrell's demeanor shift from confident to hesitant. "You didn't happen to grow up on Staten Island?"

"Yes, I did. Why?"

"I used to work on Staten Island years ago," Farrell informed him. "I knew a woman named Rose Perrotta."

"Rose Perrotta is my mother's name."

"No kidding." Farrell drew back, shocked. "I figured it was a long shot. How is your mom?"

Angelo felt it almost impossible to spit out what he wanted to say. "She passed away fourteen years ago."

"I'm so sorry for your loss." Farrell shook his head slowly. "I remember you had a sister."

"Camille," Angelo interjected. "She still lives on Staten Island."

"You were both so young back then. Cute kids." Angelo watched Farrell scan his desk until his eyes latched on the photo of him with his sister and mother. He picked it up. "Do you have any children?"

"Medicine is a jealous mistress," Angelo joked. "May I ask how you knew my mother?"

"Let's just say your mother called the police regularly back then," he said in a tight voice. "I don't know how much you remember about your father."

"You knew my father?"

Farrell tilted his head from side to side as if he were weighing his response. "I knew he was a nasty drunk. Your mother called the police on him several times after he'd been out drinking."

"All I know is that he ran out on us when I was a baby."

"Well, he used to beat your mom up pretty bad," Farrell said. "We arrested him a few times, but she always took him back. Then there was that last time."

"What happened?"

Farrell bit his lip. Angelo could see him struggling to find the words. "You were just a baby. Maybe two or three years old. We got a call from one of the neighbors saying your father was on another bender, trying to get in the house, but your mom had locked him out. By the time we got there, she had already called the paramedics. They were trying to stop the bleeding."

"Bleeding?" Angelo caught his breath, anticipating the shock to come.

"You don't remember?" he asked. "I figured your mom would have told you once you got older."

"Told me what exactly?"

Farrell appeared uneasy. "Your mother said she was packing up to leave him. Your father came home so drunk he threatened to kill you all if she left. They got into a bad fight, and well, he picked you up out of the crib and . . . cut your face."

Angelo reached up and touched his cheek, hoping that it would spark a memory of that night, some horrific flashback of images, his mother and father scuffling, Camille cowering behind the couch and Angelo, standing in his crib, crying. Then the exquisite pain of cold steel on his skin, blood everywhere, followed by the flashing red lights and police sirens.

But Angelo recalled nothing.

"Listen, I didn't mean to open up any old family wounds," Farrell said. "It's just that some cases leave a lasting impression on a young cop. After we arrested your father, I got close to your mother. I guess you could say we kind of dated for a while, but that didn't last." Then he pressed his lips together. "I figured she would have told you the whole story once you got older. I guess she had her reasons not to. I'm very sorry if I upset you. It's just, when I saw your name on those prescription pads, I couldn't help but wonder if you were Rose's son. I had to come here and see you myself."

Angelo didn't say anything. For a long while, he was lost in his thoughts. "Thank you, Detective Farrell," he said finally, holding out his hand. Farrell stood up and shook it. "For years, I have had . . . so many questions about my father. Now you've answered many of them. I never wanted to believe my father was a bad person, but we don't get to choose our parents. As disgusted as I feel right now, I'm glad to know the truth."

Farrell looked at Angelo with concern. "Again, I'm sorry for all the trouble, but it's nice to see you made something of yourself. This is some office," he said, glancing up at the skylight. "I'm sure your mother is looking down at you, thinking how proud she is."

"Thank you for saying that."

Farrell quietly took a card out of his wallet and set it down on Angelo's desk. "Call me if you have any other questions. Use my cell phone. I'm always here for you."

Once Farrell was gone, Angelo picked up the phone and called Camille at the law firm where she worked as executive assistant. "Did you know I wasn't bitten by a dog when I was two?" Angelo asked without identifying himself.

There was a long pause. Angelo heard Camille breathing over the chatter of the busy firm. "Who told you?"

"The detective who arrested our father the day he cut my face." Angelo regarded her with such loathing his tone surprised even him. "That's who."

"Are you kidding me?" she whispered. "I really can't talk about this now."

"All these years I've been wondering why he left us, and all along, you knew the truth. How could you keep this from me, Camille?"

"I don't remember what happened that day," she snapped. "I only remember the fighting. The police. That crazy drunk man who terrorized us."

Then she hung up, leaving Angelo to stare at the dead phone receiver in shock.

◆◆◆

After work, Camille called Angelo and explained why she had kept their father a secret. He hung up, dissatisfied with her explanation, and texted Jason to meet him back at his apartment. Angelo sat at the kitchen table mulling over her excuse. "What kind of fucked-up sister keeps a secret like that from her only brother?" Angelo demanded.

Jason opened a bottle of wine. "Are you two close?"

"We used to be very close until she married that loser, Trace."

"Look at it her way," Jason said, pouring the wine. "She was only trying to protect you."

"That's exactly what Camille said, but don't you see? At least I would have known our father was an abusive drunk. Instead, I blamed myself for him leaving. When a child loses a parent, for whatever reason, they always experience some sense of guilt. She could have spared me all that pain." Angelo drank back the wine and poured another glass.

"That's true," Jason said, kneeling to hug Angelo. "Sometimes families keep secrets for the wrong reasons. Your sister only wanted you to believe your father was a good person."

"Good people don't walk out on their family. They don't leave their children to think they're unloved."

Angelo never imagined it could be possible to feel such outrage toward his only sibling, and keeping this secret wasn't simply a betrayal, he questioned how well he knew his sister at all.

"That's true," Jason said, nuzzling his face in the crook of Angelo's neck. "All the more reason you should accept the truth and move on."

"Move on," Angelo repeated with sarcasm.

"Camille is the only family you have. You can't shut her out for trying to protect you."

Angelo could not bring himself to reply. Here was the problem, here was the concern scurrying around in his head like roaches startled by the light. For the past several weeks, he had reassembled the broken pieces, the tiny bits of his ego that were shattered by Demetre, a man he had known for all of four months. Angelo's head was still churning with confusion, recounting the events that led him to latch on to this stranger, hoping to substitute that piece of obsidian for something less abrasive, more loving.

Jason stood up. "Come on. Let's eat."

Angelo sat with icy indifference, still stunned by his sister's deception. His father's identity was the final piece of the puzzle, the reason why he craved the attention of cruel men. Like his mother, it was a perfect flaw in their DNA. Even the self-described Prince Jason, who sat across from him, had been on remand for discharging his weapon when they'd met. Was this person who seemed so sweet just a front? If they got to know each other, would Angelo find himself on the receiving end of that weapon one day?

Jason served dinner and sat down at the table. He began eating, glancing up occasionally at Angelo, whose eyes were glazed over.

"Come on," Jason encouraged. "Food's getting cold."

Angelo blinked and looked directly in his eyes. He reached out to hold Jason's hand. "Hey, let's promise not to keep secrets."

Jason squeezed Angelo's hand. "Okay. You tell me a secret and I'll tell you one."

"Right now?"

"Right now."

"Okay," Angelo said, "but no judgment."

Jason raised the three middle fingers of his right hand. "Scout's honor."

Angelo began, "When my mother was diagnosed with cancer, she refused chemo and signed a do-not-resuscitate order. We knew she didn't want to suffer, but cancer can be a cruel sadist. Toward the end, she was in home hospice, lying in bed, writhing in agony. Even after they put her on a morphine drip, she was still in so much pain." He flushed guiltily, pausing only to swallow. "Finally, after months, Camille and I came up with a plan. We ground up Don's sleeping pills." Angelo began sobbing, rubbing his eyes. "We knew it was wrong, but she was no longer our mother. Just a skeleton shrieking in agony."

"Did you go through with it?"

Angelo nodded. "We dissolved the pills in water one night while Don was out walking. She was barely conscious, but when we put that cup to her lips, her eyes opened wide, and she drank. It was like she knew what we were doing." Angelo turned away, unable to look Jason in the eyes. "The next morning, she never woke up."

"Weren't you afraid Don would notice his pills were missing?"

"He did," Angelo said, staring down at his trembling hands, "but he never said a word about it."

"So, Don . . . ."

"He knew what we had done," Angelo sobbed with a kind of sheepish guilt. "The nurse said it was God's plan, and that was that. Don moved to Japan shortly after the funeral. I guess he couldn't bear to live with his dead wife's murdering kids."

Jason reached over and held Angelo's hands. "I'm sorry you had to go through that. It couldn't have been easy."

This reaction surprised Angelo, but he felt an astonished relief that Jason didn't bolt out the door.

"Watching someone die has a way of gutting you," Angelo said, wiping away his tears. "Do you think I'm a terrible person?"

"No," Jason whispered. "Just the opposite."

"Now it's your turn."

Jason puffed out his cheeks and exhaled slowly. "The reason I see a counselor is because I discharged my weapon," he said, coughing nervously into his fist. "What I never told you is that we were responding to a domestic violence call. When we arrived at the building, we heard screaming. Mary and I entered the apartment, and right away, we heard this couple arguing in the bedroom. It was pandemonium. Children crying. Broken glass. Furniture toppled over. Led Zeppelin music blared. We identified ourselves but weren't sure if they heard us. Mary darted toward the kids' room. I pounded on the bedroom door, announcing again it was the police. The woman cried, 'He's got a gun!' I took out mine." Jason reenacted, holding up his shaky hands. "My heart felt like it was punching through my chest. I kicked open the door and found this guy with his hands around the woman's throat, choking her." Jason dissolved into tears, covering his face with his hands. "And then the gun went off. I shot him. I shot him."

"But he was going to kill her," Angelo reasoned.

Jason shook his head like a bawling child. "I shouldn't have been so impulsive. Don't you understand? I didn't see a gun. I only saw her bloody face. Her bulging eyes. Something snapped inside me, and I shot him."

Angelo felt like an intruder listening to Jason recount these events like eavesdropping on a therapy session.

"Were you charged?" Angelo asked.

"No," Jason said, heaving. "His girlfriend had a restraining order against him. The investigation concluded that I used appropriate force based on the fact he was strangling her at the time. Lucky me, right? Still, I felt guilty. I couldn't go back to work. That's when they decided it was best if I saw a counselor for a year."

Angelo stood up and swept Jason in his arms. "What you did wasn't impulsive; it was instinctual. You didn't kill an unarmed man for jogging down the street wearing a hoodie. What you did, was save a woman's life."

Jason pulled back and cupped Angelo's face with his hands, as if it were something fragile. Angelo stood up. "Let's go to bed."

Jason rose to his feet and reached for Angelo's hand; he didn't hesitate for a second to take it. The light was low in the apartment. Angelo guided Jason to the bed. Until that moment, Angelo had only shared his bed with other men, but this time, it suddenly seemed very important. As if he had made a conscious choice that would change his life.

Jason stood at the bed and pulled off his T-shirt, exposing his beautiful hairless flesh contouring smoothly over his muscular body, like pastry dough. Angelo licked Jason's abdomen as he unbuttoned his jeans.

To Angelo, Jason appeared somber with the weight of his confession still lingering on his mind. He reached down and stroked Jason's cock through his boxer shorts. Angelo's gaze was desirous under his dark brows, intensely proprietary of Jason's firming erection in his hand. Jason squeezed his eyes shut as Angelo freed his cock and knelt down. Jason let out a heavy sigh. Shock. Relief. Expectation. Angelo wanted to please him, wanted to release any residual doubts, and now that they had shared their worst secrets, he was consumed with confidence that their relationship had crossed over into something more akin to love.

Up close, Jason's throbbing erection, red and swollen, left Angelo staring for several seconds. His hand fastened tightly around it. His mouth watered. And then, he took it in, gliding his lips down Jason's shaft until his nose pressed against Jason's pubic hair. The musky scent drifted into his nostrils, arousing Angelo with such ferocity. He stood up to pull down his own pants, stroking his cock.

Jason sat on the bed, gripping the dark curls of Angelo's head, guiding his mouth along the shaft of his cock. Angelo peered up, smiling confidently as Jason's cock swelled in his mouth, stroking it simultaneously with his hand, knowing instinctively that Jason was near climax.

Angelo knew exactly what to do. Not rushing into it with too much rapidity or suction, he slid his lips along Jason's tumescence, bobbing and sucking it gently. The sensation roused such a heightened reaction in his own cock that he was about to climax, but he stopped stroking himself.

Angelo wanted to strip off his clothes, fall back on the bed and spread his legs to allow Jason to enter him. But he couldn't free himself from stroking and sucking Jason's cock long enough to allow that to happen. He couldn't bear for it to end. Neither could Jason, apparently. He seized Angelo's head, gripping his hair, intertwining his fingers with Angelo's curls to navigate his mouth on his cock, maintaining a rhythm that quickened until Jason offered an aching pause. A confused moment of silence. And then Jason pulled out and came on Angelo's chest.

Jason moaned and collapsed on the bed, panting. Angelo wiped his lips, smiling. He leaped onto the bed beside Jason, kissing him deeply and passionately for several long seconds. "That was amazing," Jason said, panting.

Angelo struggled to respond, still dazed with a euphoric sense of vertigo. "I've been waiting to do that for such a long time," he replied. Jason wrapped his arms around him and squeezed him with such warmth and intensity Angelo felt frightened initially, but lying there together, Jason's strong arms encircling him, he realized it wasn't fear he felt. It was security.

Chapter Twelve

Two months had passed since the night Angelo and Jason shared their dark secrets. It was a Sunday morning in late February. The temperature had dipped below freezing. Scattered mounds of frozen snow, left over from the last storm, lay in the curb so soused with soot and mud they looked like heaps of coal. Angelo was heading to meet Tammy for brunch at the Empire Diner on Tenth Avenue. It was a converted subway car that served the best French fries in Manhattan.

Tammy sat in the back by a wall of pin-up girl photos, wedged between Betty Grable and Rita Hayworth. When Angelo stepped up to the table, Tammy was slumped down, chin resting against her chest. *She's lost weight*, he thought. Her features were sharper, edgier. Tammy's signature blond hair had grown back to its natural dark tone. "Dr. Hathaway!"

Tammy jolted upright, her eyes searching. "Holy crap, I fell asleep."

"Late night?" he asked, sliding into the booth.

Tammy was wearing a bulky gray sweater over her scrubs, hair in a ponytail, glasses covered in fingerprints. "We got slammed."

"You got so thin."

"You think?" she asked, glancing in the window at her reflection.

"I mean, in a good way."

"When is being called thin not good?" she asked, staring at him. "Your hair got long. Who knew it was so wavy?" Angelo combed his hand through his dark curls, smiling.

"Oh, and those dimples. Still a cutie. I guess Park Avenue is treating you well."

A stodgy-looking waitress came by to take their orders.

"Just coffee for now," Angelo said.

"Same for me."

Angelo raised an eyebrow. "No Bloody Mary? No mimosa?"

Tammy swept her hand officiously over the surface of the table, brushing off any remaining crumbs. "Nope. I've been alcohol-free since New Year's."

Angelo pressed out his lower lip, impressed. "Cheers to you, doctor."

"Val and I decided to take a little breaky break from the alcoholic bevies. You know, to prove that we can have fun without being intoxicated."

"Val really has her hooks in you?"

"To be honest, not drinking sucks," she said, turning serious, "but it's not like I'm never going to have another drink again. I'm just letting my body know who's boss." The waitress came by with their coffees. "Speaking of New Year's resolutions, Val and I were wondering if you might be interested in going on a double date?"

"A double date?" Angelo chuckled. "What's become of us?"

"We're growing up," she said, sliding out of the booth. "I have to use the bathroom."

Angelo contemplated the tangled interactions of his professional and private lives. A double date was the first optimistic sign one was moving in the right direction.

Angelo was sipping coffee when his cell phone rang.

"Hey, it's me," said a familiar voice.

Angelo didn't answer, silenced by the spasm of panic running through his body.

Again, Demetre, "Are you there?"

Angelo replied, "I'm here."

"You have to help. Something went wrong. She was fine. I don't know what happened, but she just started shaking."

Angelo stared fixedly at the photo of Rita Hayworth, taken aback by the intensity of Demetre's voice. "Who is shaking?" he asked. "Where are you?"

"Jesus Christ, I need you to come here. Please, help me."

"Calm down," Angelo said. "What did you give her?"

"Lidocaine! I only gave her a few ccs of lidocaine. Then she started shaking! Angelo, you have to help—"

"Listen to me very carefully," Angelo cut in. "You need to hang up and dial 911. Do you understand me?"

"Isn't there anything I can do to stop her from shaking?"

Angelo heard the fear in Demetre's voice, mixed with an irrational hope that this situation, however awful it was, could be contained somehow without notifying emergency services, and by extension, the police.

"Wake up!" Angelo heard him yell as an ambulance siren blared in on Demetre's end, drowning out his voice. Once it passed, Demetre was sobbing. "Jesus Christ, wake up!"

"Demetre listen to me," Angelo said in a monotone, hoping to instill calm. "You have to call an ambulance. They can resuscitate her. You need help."

There was a long pause. For a moment, Angelo thought they were disconnected or worse, he had hung up. "Wait," Demetre said. There were several precious seconds where Angelo couldn't hear what was going on. Muffled voices. Shuffling movement. "She's coming around."

"Call an ambulance anyway," Angelo said emphatically.

"Thank God," Demetre sighed. "She's okay."

Then he hung up.

Immediately, Angelo called him back, but it went directly to voicemail. "Hey, it's me," Angelo said in a cheery voice. "Text me the address. I'll come right away."

Tammy returned from the bathroom, having also been on the phone.

"I've got to go," she said, pulling on her coat. "They need me back at the ER ASAP. I forgot to fill out a death certificate. Sorry to leave you with the bill old friend. Call you later."

Angelo stared at his phone, hoping Demetre would text the address so he could call an ambulance. He waited several minutes before he threw some cash on the table and ran outside. Racing down Ninth Avenue, he was desperate to find Demetre and undo what damage he'd already done, but he had no idea where to go.

Angelo dialed Demetre's cell phone again.

"Angelo, I was just about to call. She had a reaction to the lidocaine. I panicked, but she's fine now." Demetre maintained that soft-spoken manner he was notoriously known for, but underneath Angelo detected the thrum of anxiety in his voice.

"Are you sure she's okay?" Angelo asked.

Demetre laughed nervously. "She's fine."

"Let me talk to her."

"That won't be necessary.

"Demetre . . ." Angelo began, but he had already hung up again.

◆◆◆

That night the rain fell, pattering against the windows while Angelo lay in bed with his eyes wide open. Immediately after Demetre's call, he subsisted in a state of near hysteria, biting off every fingernail, and then starting on his cuticles, tearing them with his teeth until the skin underneath flared and bled. Demetre's voice echoed in his head, wavering like a flag of panic. Only after they spoke the second time and Demetre assured him that everything was fine, that the woman had recovered, did Angelo begin the process of dispelling any lingering doubts. But even as he tried to extract himself from this situation—packaging it away by assuring himself the woman was safe and sound—he stumbled from moving forward because Angelo knew Demetre could not be trusted.

Angelo picked up his cell phone and called Demetre.

"What's the matter?" Demetre asked, sounding thoroughly annoyed. "It's after midnight."

"I was just checking to see how you were doing?"

"Thank you but that's unnecessary," he replied. "I spoke to her this evening. She's fine."

Fine.

There was that word again, he thought. Angelo imagined Demetre's face when he said it, a flicker of anger, or possibly fear.

"What have you done?" Angelo asked with the controlled mildness of a psychiatrist.

"Done?" Demetre repeated with irritation. "What are you talking about?"

Demetre was breathing heavily through his nostrils, and then it struck Angelo like running full speed into a plate-glass window. This woman, who Demetre refused to give a name, was not fine.

"If there's anything you need to tell me, now would be the time," Angelo whispered.

There was a pause, and then in a brisk tone, Demetre said, "It's late. Go to bed."

The click of the phone disconnecting caused Angelo to flinch. He held the phone up to his ear for several long seconds. The dread poured in all around him like rushing water, dread swirling with fear, and something stirred in him. It was as if this call had released a vertiginous sense of empowerment. Suddenly, he was galvanized with strength. His old self slipped away as the new one stepped up to take its place.

Angelo picked up his wallet and found Farrell's card. He dialed his cell phone. As the phone rang, he contemplated whether this was an awful idea. What if he had jumped to the wrong conclusion? But deep inside, Angelo knew his worst fears were likely true.

"That's some story," Farrell said.

Angelo heard Farrell struggling to get out of bed.

"I know it's late.

"Don't worry," Farrell assured him, "like I said, I'm always here for you." Farrell gave a mighty yawn. "Tell you what I'm gonna do. Let me see if I can get a patrol car to go by Kostas's house."

Angelo heaved with relief. "Seriously?"

"Yes," Farrell confirmed. "Now do me a favor and get some sleep. You got people to take care of in the morning."

◆◆◆

The next day, Angelo called Farrell once he got to work. "The local police spoke with Mr. Kostas last night after you called me," he told Angelo. "Kostas gave the same story you told me except he denied administering lidocaine."

"So now what?"

"Legally, Kostas can still perform laser hair removal."

"Do you know where he's working?" Angelo asked.

"No, but I'll do some digging."

Angelo heard a steady stream of phones ringing in the background. "What about the woman?"

"Kostas was unwilling to give her name without her consent." A man began speaking to Farrell. "Tell them I'll be right there."

"Can you get a search warrant?"

"On what grounds?" Farrell asked. "Listen, I'm busy right now, but I'll follow up with you later. Okay?"

Angelo fell silent, allowing the facts to sink in. He wondered where Demetre could possibly be seeing clients. It seemed unlikely anyone would hire him considering his arrest. He had been in all the newspapers and on television news. The laser itself was too big to carry to clients' residences. That left Demetre's house as the only option. But who would go to someone's house for laser treatment? No one in their right mind, surely, but what if he was wrong?

Demetre was great at talking, and especially existing clients might still believe whatever lies he'd told about being set up or cheated or misunderstood or whatever cover story he'd concocted for what happened at Stanzione's office.

Just before he left work that day, Angelo pulled Demetre's file and got his address. Then, he took the PATH train into New Jersey. Demetre's house was within walking distance from the station. As he made his way among the tall bare trees down Whitman Street, it was without any clear intention other than to see Demetre's house, he convinced himself.

The neighborhood was quiet, with rows of grand one-family homes. By now the sun was setting. There was still so much snow on the ground that it made the neighborhood appear bleak and dismally empty. A February stillness that was so unsettling. Demetre's house was at the end of the block. Standing out front, Angelo was impressed by the three-story Craftsman-style home that was set far back from the street and surrounded by a high wrought-iron fence.

Angelo stood, arms crossed over his torso, imagining Demetre and Tim living there, making plans for their future. How exciting it must have all seemed at first? Angelo wondered how long it took before Demetre started sliding back into old habits. Working for Dr. Eichhorn, Demetre said he felt cheated out of success, and even though he saved up to buy his own laser, he would never have what he really wanted: a medical degree. And to live with the dissolution of his dream, never to be a doctor or the kind of man his father would accept, he masked that pain with drugs.

It occurred to Angelo then that he wasn't standing in front of a technician's house. This was the home of a successful doctor. How sad it seemed that Demetre's sole ambition was to be a success even if it meant sacrificing his integrity and breaking the law to achieve it.

The house was dark. Angelo walked around to the side. At the end of the driveway was a two-car garage with a small apartment built on top. The light was on. Angelo pressed his head in between the bars of the wrought-iron gate, hoping he'd see something. He waited in the cold, shivering. After several long minutes, he decided to leave.

No sooner had he made that decision when a figure emerged, exiting the garage apartment, hurrying down the back stairs. Angelo ducked behind the brick pillar, panting in the darkness. When he peeked back, it appeared as though the person had entered the garage and turned on the light. Driven by some ineluctable force, Angelo started toward the garage, if only to see Demetre's face.

Slowly, and against his better judgment, Angelo pushed open the gate. Surprisingly, it was unlocked. A car was parked outside the garage. In a low crouch, Angelo padded up the driveway. A buttery circle of yellow light emanated from the garage windows.

He could barely make out the figure of a man. The garage window was caked with grime. Several bags of cement mix. A shovel. A suitcase. Waiting to see what would happen, Angelo had a harrowing suspicion someone was behind him. He spun around and saw another dark figure marching up the front walkway ten yards away. It was Tim Meadows, his coat flapping open. Tim stood at the front door, banging loudly.

"Demetre, let me in!" The light inside the garage went out.

Demetre had gone back into the house and opened the front door. "What are you doing here?" he asked. Angelo cowered behind the car, listening.

"I came to get the rest of my stuff this afternoon," Tim said, "but you changed the locks."

"You shouldn't be here."

"Don't worry," Tim said. "Just let me get my stuff, and then I'll be gone for good."

Angelo squatted as low as he could to stay out of sight, but he lost his balance and faltered, causing a minor stir in the gravel beneath his feet. Angelo froze, awaiting to be discovered.

"Come inside." Demetre gleamed with false kindness—even now, his eyes blinkering on and off, swaying with the drugs and liquor, he was too distracted to notice Angelo's presence. Once they entered the house, Angelo hurried back down the path and ran the entire way back to the train station.

◆◆◆

Back in his apartment, Angelo felt relief at first, but that changed once he began unpacking the facts. The walls of his studio felt like they were expanding and contracting like a giant, failing heart. Finally, he felt he knew the truth. That woman had not woken up as Demetre insisted. She wasn't *fine*. In fact, she was most likely dead. Angelo had seen the last vestiges of a desperate man: a shovel, bags of cement mix, and a suitcase likely containing her body folded up like a piece of origami.

Even though he picked and tore apart his theory like the leaves of an artichoke, hoping finally he'd see an alternative truth at the core, his clinician's mind knew the truth all along. He'd seen the clues.

Angelo called Jason. "He killed her."

"What are you talking about?"

And then Angelo explained what he saw in Demetre's garage. Jason could barely comprehend all that Angelo had just described. "Can I ask you a question?"

"Of course," Angelo said.

"Why didn't you call me immediately after you spoke with Demetre when you were at the diner?"

Angelo struggled to come up with a valid reason. It hadn't occurred to him at the time, but in hindsight, he saw how that should have been the obvious next thing to do.

"I'm mean . . . I'm proud you called the police," Jason said, "but going over to Demetre's house is weird."

"I was obsessed," Angelo offered, "but my decision had nothing to do with you."

"Didn't it?"

"What's that supposed to mean?" Angelo asked.

There was a long pause. "Maybe you chose not to tell me because you were afraid I'd tell you not to go."

"I didn't need your permission."

"True," Jason said. "So why not tell me?"

Angelo was thinking it over, nibbling what was left of his thumbnail. "Jason—"

"I thought we agreed we weren't going to keep secrets?"

Angelo's stomach seized, flooding his throat with acid.

"I think on some level you wanted to see Demetre again," Jason explained, "because you're not really over him."

The pained tone in Jason's voice made Angelo hunched forward. "That's not true."

"Angelo, you believe Demetre is a murderer, and you went all the way to his house in New Jersey, just to see him."

"I didn't go all the way to New Jersey to see Demetre," Angelo insisted.

"And yet, that's exactly what you did."

Jason's assessment rattled Angelo so viscerally his body shuddered. Like hearing the door to his prison cell slam shut, Angelo was stupefied by guilt. Had he really gone to New Jersey in the hopes of seeing Demetre? Of course, that wasn't his intention, but hearing Jason retell it back to him, there was a shred of truth embedded within his rationale. A tiny ring Angelo had ignored riding the PATH train into

New Jersey until Jason just brought it up. Angelo heard it now echo loudly in his head.

You wanted to see Demetre!

Jason heaved a long sigh. "I think we need to take a break."

"Why?" Tears streamed down Angelo's cheeks. It hadn't occurred to him until then that he should have considered Jason's feelings, that he had acted selfishly, and if he had called Jason before going to Demetre's house, he might not have gone at all. "I don't want to take a break."

Jason coughed. Angelo heard him choking back tears. "Maybe break is the wrong word. Maybe we should break-up."

"I think you're overreacting," Angelo said in a voice imbued with the detached objectivity of a physician, but inside, he was a dying man clinging desperately for his life. "Let's sleep on it?"

"Angelo," Jason said in a quiet voice. "I know you're a good person, but right now, I need to think about what's best for me. My therapist said to avoid drama at all costs. My final evaluation is in two months. My career is riding on it. I don't want you to feel like I'm leaving you high and dry. You've been through so much, and I've been support-ive, but this guy Demetre—he's got a hold on you that eats me up inside. It's fucking with my head, and I can't handle it right now. Understand?" Jason once again silenced Ange-lo as abruptly as a smack across the face.

"I understand," was all Angelo could muster before clicking off his cell phone. Alone in his apartment, Angelo experienced a lurch of abandonment so tsunamic, it felt like he was hemorrhaging.

CHAPTER THIRTEEN

When Angelo opened his eyes the next morning, for a moment he thought it had all been a nightmare—the suitcase, the bags of cement, the shovel—but that moment was fleeting. He knew Demetre had done something terrible. Still, he held hope it wasn't too late. And then he thought of Jason. For him not to be part of his life, it didn't seem possible. The sound of Jason's voice on the phone last night—the mixture of pain and confusion—gutted Angelo.

There were several times during his sleepless night where he thought about calling Jason. There was a short-lived plan to go over to his apartment to beg for forgiveness, but he quickly dismissed these ideas for Jason's sake. *Angelo wondered in how many therapy sessions Jason had brought up Angelo's relationship with Demetre?* The anger those conversations provoked, and all the while Jason kept his emotions bottled up, hoping Angelo's obsession with a con artist would end. Angelo's trip to Demetre's house had been the final straw. How could he have been so blind?

Rushing to dress, Angelo decided to call Farrell first instead of discussing his findings while at work. The mention of Demetre's name had become a dog whistle Stanzione's keen hears picked up. "Doctor, I understand how you might have come to that conclusion," Farrell reasoned, "but you realize that many people keep cement mix, shovels and even store their suitcases in the garage."

"Then go see for yourself."

Angelo heard Farrell sigh. He imagined the frustrated expression on his face. "The house has been sold. Mr. Kostas is required to perform several fix-up jobs on the property. He and Tim Meadows split up after his last arrest. I spoke to Meadows yesterday. He didn't have anything nice to say about Kostas. Apparently, he's still doing drugs and has accumulated over two hundred fifty thousand dollars in debt. Eighty thousand of which belonged to Meadows. He did, however, assure me that Kostas has not been treating clients at the house."

"He's lying!" Angelo shouted.

"I find it highly unlikely that Meadows would cover for Kostas," Farrell explained. "He's very angry. Meadows did say that for the past several weeks Kostas had been leaving the house daily and returning home late at night."

"Okay, so he found a place to work," Angelo conceded, "but there is a woman's body in his garage."

"If it were up to me, I'd search his house, but that's not how it works. You realize that without any evidence getting a search warrant is impossible."

"I didn't imagine that call, Detective," Angelo insisted. "You didn't hear Demetre's voice. Something happened to a woman."

"I understand, but it's very difficult to look for a victim when you don't know their identity."

With a sinking feeling in his chest, Angelo slumped in his chair, running over the details again and again in his mind.

"Doc, we're gonna catch him," Farrell assured him, "but it has to be legally. Now promise me you aren't going to do anything stupid. I don't want you going near his house again. Okay?"

◆◆◆

It was almost impossible for Angelo to focus on work. The time dragged by with an agonizing slowness. An air of unreality permeated his day so that he felt as if he was walking through a dream. The thought that Demetre was a murderer was absurd, terrifying; nonetheless, he obsessed over it, convinced there was no other explanation.

At lunch, he sat alone at his desk. He couldn't eat. He wasn't hungry. Minutes crept by. He texted Jason even though he swore he wouldn't, but his texts went unanswered. Angelo listened to one of Jason's older voice messages and wept, thinking he'd lost the first man he had ever loved.

Though all evidence of SkinDem had been removed from the practice, Demetre's presence was still palpable to Angelo—a ubiquitous phantom, consuming the oxygen in the room. There were times he smelled Demetre's cologne. For no possible reason, he felt Demetre's presence behind him, peering over his shoulder.

And it wasn't only him. After Demetre had been completely extricated from the practice, Stanzione checked in with his lawyers constantly. Angelo passed the time listening to Stanzione through the wall. His dependence on their advice bordered on obsessive, but it was more than that. Stanzione, like Angelo, had changed completely over the past several months. Though Stanzione's transformation was physical as well as psychological.

Most days they hardly saw each other. Then one day Angelo arrived at work and discovered a stranger sitting behind Stanzione's desk; he was that unrecognizable. The sunken cheeks, the ashen skin, and the ill-fitted toupee on top of his head. Angelo stood in the hall for a long while, stunned. Stanzione was staring fixedly at the wall. He didn't even notice him.

Later, Angelo saw Stanzione by Steven's desk, it was then he took a long hard look in the bright fluorescent light: the drooping shoulders, the deflated chest. His muscles appeared to have liquefied and settled in the center of his body, forming a flabby paunch. It was startling. Most astonishing of all was that it took Angelo by complete surprise, as if he had just watched it unfold like a film in fast forward. If Stanzione only knew Angelo suspected Demetre of murder, he thought, the old man might collapse and die.

So, Angelo told him nothing.

◆◆◆

Two days after Angelo reported his findings to Farrell, Tiffany had come back from lunch with a gash across her palm after falling in the street, shattering a glass bottle in her hand. Angelo was suturing the laceration when Steven interrupted. "The police are on the phone for you."

Angelo hovered the needle over Tiffany's wound, unable to continue. "Did they say what they want?"

Steven stared woefully back at him. "It's about your sister, Camille. She's in the emergency room."

It had been weeks since they last spoke, and even longer since they had seen each other. Camille's betrayal in withholding information about their father's drunken violence, although plausible only because of Jason's rationale, left him feeling chilly. He had decided to remedy the situation by icing her out of his life until he could reconcile what she had done to him.

"Let me finish up here," he said to Steven.

"Are you out of your mind?" Tiffany snapped. Her tone, imbued with such outrage, startled Angelo. Normally a mild-tempered person, Tiffany's reaction made Angelo wonder if she thought he was in shock or simply that dumb. "Go!"

◆◆◆

Hours later, Angelo brought Camille back to his apartment. He set her suitcase alongside the bed. "Would you like some tea?" he asked. She stared at him with no expression. The right side of her face was swollen and bruised. A rectangular strip of gauze covered the stitches on her cheek.

All he knew was what the police had told him, that Trace had assaulted Camille, and that he was in custody. At first Angelo was in shock, but at the same time thankful that Camille had called the police at all. On his way to the hospital, his only wish was that she wasn't badly injured. Once she was released from the emergency room, they went back to her house and packed her clothes. It felt like a heavy weight had been lifted when she agreed to return with him to the city. Angelo was afraid she'd decide instead to stay in Staten Island.

Trace's history of abuse should not have come as a surprise to Angelo. Camille and Angelo had never interfered in each other's private lives. It was an unspoken rule to avoid exploring the many cupboards in which they had secreted themselves. Now he saw the parallel that existed between his mother and him extending to include his sister as well.

She shook her head to his offer for tea.

"I'll make some anyway."

Camille walked to the window, distracted. Angelo put the kettle on the stove and checked the refrigerator. It was nearly empty except for some flat club soda and a stick of butter he had no idea how long had been in there. Thankfully, there was a box of tea bags and some sugar in the cupboard. When Angelo glanced over at Camille, she was staring out the window, shivering.

"It's so cold," she said tonelessly.

"I'll turn up the heat."

Angelo adjusted the thermostat, and the vent kicked on. He was aware that Camille's hands were clenched into fists. He reached over and interlaced his fingers with hers. She was so tense but then she relaxed. They stood without saying anything for a while. Angelo stared at their reflection in the window. Camille was short like their mother, but they both had dark, wavy hair, narrow faces, and wide eyes.

"You've had a busy day," he said. "Why don't you take a nap, and we'll have dinner when you wake up?"

Camille nodded and curled up on the bed like a little girl, facing the wall. Angelo removed her shoes and placed them on the floor. Then he fixed himself a cup of tea and sat on the couch staring out the window as snowflakes whirled against the glass. He meant to close his eyes for just a moment, but when he opened them again, it was morning. Angelo woke up drowsy. A blanket had been thrown over him.

He heard the shower running. Camille emerged minutes later wearing jeans and a baggy sweatshirt. She forced a smile as she moved toward the couch, toweling her hair dry. It was then he saw the wound for the first time. She had removed the bandage to wash. There was a comma-shaped incision with multiple tiny black sutures along her right cheek. It looked like a small caterpillar had curled up on Camille's cheek.

"How do you feel?" he asked.

She took a long breath. "I have no intention of dragging you into this. I can handle this on my own. I just need a day or two to get myself together."

"I want you to stay here for as long as you like."

She shook her head. "You say that now but . . . ."

"Camille," he cut in. "I'm sorry for not being there for you. I wish I could go back and do it over again, but I'm also very proud you found the courage to leave Trace. For now, I don't want you to think about where you're going to live; you're staying here with me. I'm certain there are a million things running through your mind. I can't imagine what you've been through or for how long, but you're safe now."

Camille turned her head away, wiping her eyes quickly. "I feel so stupid."

"You're not stupid."

Camille stopped suddenly in mid-sob and, sniffing noisily, ran back into the bathroom and closed the door. Angelo didn't chase after her. What good would that do?

Somewhere he heard the low buzz of his cell phone. It was still in his back pocket. He fumbled to answer it.

"Dr. Perrotta," Farrell asked. "Is this a good time?"

"Yes, of course."

"I wanted to follow up with you. Yesterday, I drove out to Mr. Kostas's home, but he wasn't in. I even called his lawyer, but she refused to let me question him."

"Did she tell you where he works?"

"No," he said.

Angelo experienced a pang of panic so startling, he couldn't catch his breath, realizing that with every passing hour the likelihood of finding that woman alive dwindled significantly. "So, what's next?"

"I don't have an answer for you," Farrell said. "At least not the answer you're looking for."

"Which is?" Angelo asked.

"Which is, I don't have enough evidence to compel a judge to issue a search warrant of Kostas's home."

"I understand," Angelo said, knowing no good would come from taking out his frustration on Farrell. "Thanks for the update, Detective."

"Anytime."

At that exact moment, Camille started wailing. Angelo dropped the phone as she ran screaming out of the bathroom as if she were being chased. "I'm bleeding! I'm bleeding!" She threw her arms around Angelo's neck.

"What's the matter?"

"I'm dying! Help me!"

He gripped her arms, trying to pry her off him, but she wouldn't budge. She clung to him, crying hysterically.

"I'm dying! I'm dying!"

"Camille, tell me what's wrong?" She cried hysterically, trembling in his arms. Angelo saw no blood on her face or torso, so he pulled her off him and ran into the bathroom. There in the toilet, blood swirled in the water like crimson smoke. He came out of the bathroom and asked, "Could you be having your period?"

"No," she cried. "It happened when I peed."

"Listen to me," he said calmly. "I'll call a colleague of mine. He's a kidney specialist. We'll see him this morning. Now, I understand how scary peeing blood is, but to be honest, there was not a lot of blood in the toilet. We'll go as a precaution. Okay?"

Camille nodded. Angelo saw in her eyes, calm had returned.

A short while later, Angelo sat in the waiting room of his nephrology colleague while Camille was being evaluated.

As children, Angelo always thought Camille was so durable, so strong. She was the self-assured one, displaying not an ounce of hesitation in every decision she made. Angelo lived in the shadow of his older sister who was very protective of him. Their father's desertion consumed Angelo. Camille was wounded by it too, but not to the same degree as Angelo, or so he thought.

It occurred to Angelo, sitting in the waiting room, how very wrong he was. Camille was deeply affected by their father's abandonment. She just hid it from him. Over the years, she led him to believe that as a daughter, she still had their mother. As a son, it was natural for him to feel deprived of the one thing he deserved—a father figure. Classic Camille, thought Angelo, deflecting her pain so that he was the focus of attention.

The truth, he knew now, was that Camille wasn't as strong as the image she projected, and fiercely guarding the chairs at McDonalds or dropping out of school to support Angelo were her noble attempts to hold their family together, to maintain order, not just for him but for herself. Their father's brutality left a scar on her memory that was as indelible as the one on her baby brother's face, and every time Camille looked at him, it sent a roil of panic through her. As an adult, she bottled up her emotions and exuded strength, but things suppressed had the potential to explode.

"Dr. Perrotta," the receptionist said. "Dr. Wang will see you now."

Wang sat behind a large oak desk. "I performed an ultrasound on your sister," he said. "She has a small hematoma on her right kidney. I was surprised how small it is, considering her other injuries."

"What other injuries?"

Wang gaped. "Angelo, I thought you knew."

"Knew what?"

Wang hesitated. "She was badly beaten. There are bruises of varying degrees all along her back. This abuse has been going on for a long time."

Angelo vigorously rubbed his forehead. "Why didn't the ER physician catch this?"

"She didn't tell them," he explained. "It's quite common for abuse victims to minimize their injuries. Camille couldn't hide the laceration on her face. Later, when she saw the blood in the toilet, she panicked. I assured her that the hematoma is small, and the bleeding will resolve on its own. She needs to drink plenty of water and avoid strenuous activity. Of course, I'll want to see her again on Friday to repeat the ultrasound."

Angelo breathed a deep sigh. "Can I see her?"

"Of course," he said, standing up. "She's still pretty shaken so be gentle. She thinks you're mad at her."

"What?"

"Don't take it personally," he said, putting his hand on Angelo's shoulder. "It's a common reaction. She's concerned you had to miss work on her account. I told her not to worry, but you know how family members can be."

"Thank you for squeezing her in today. I really appreciate it."

"My pleasure," he said, walking Angelo down the hall. "She's a tough woman. Feeling this vulnerable can't be easy for her."

Once they left Wang's office, they walked out to the street, and Angelo hailed a cab. There was traffic heading west on Twenty-Third Street. Neither had spoken a single word since they left Wang's office, when Camille glanced over and offered Angelo a twisty little smile. That one simple look warmed his heart because it said everything they couldn't say.

Right before they arrived back at the apartment, Angelo had the idea to order pizza and invite Tammy and Val over for dinner. If anyone could cheer up Camille, thought Angelo, it was Tammy. After letting Camille into the apartment, Angelo ran to the grocery store for snacks. He considered buying wine, but he knew Tammy and Val weren't drinking and, most likely, Camille wouldn't either. Although he could have used a stiff drink, Angelo decided against buying any alcohol.

Hours later, Tammy knocked on the door. "Hey, old friend, how the hell are you?" She entered, arms stretched out for a hug. "And look who it is," she said, moving toward Camille. "There's my girl." Tammy leaned in and kissed Camille—not on the cheek, but on the lips.

Camille took a step back, adjusting her hair. "Well, that was some welcome. How long has it been?"

"Too long." Tammy turned to the door and yelled, "Hey, come on in and meet Angelo's sister."

Val stood in the doorway. She had cut off most of her hair. The dramatic change was a surprising shock, and Angelo wondered if he would have recognized her on the street.

"May I come in?" she asked Angelo sheepishly.

"You look different," he said. "I like the change."

Val patted her hair. "Sometimes you have to change things up."

"Val, come in," Tammy said, her voice booming. Then she aimed her head at Camille and muttered, "This is my old lady. Tell her she's pretty." Then Tammy darted to the bathroom still wearing her coat.

Angelo clapped his hands together, wringing them nervously. "Val, can I get you something?"

"Some green tea would be nice," she said, removing her coat.

"I only have regular tea."

"That'll be fine." Val looked around. "Angelo, your apartment is cute. I love L-shaped studios."

"I know, right," Camille said, gesturing toward the couch. "That way your bed isn't in the middle of the room."

"My first apartment had a bathtub in the kitchen," Val said.

"Seriously?" Camille asked. "I don't know how people live in such tiny apartments. I'd go crazy."

As Angelo filled the kettle, Tammy came out of the bathroom.

"How's your sister doing?" she asked in a hushed tone.

"I think she's holding it together pretty well. All things considered. Care for some tea?"

Tammy rolled her eyes and stuck a wad of gum in her mouth. "I'll pass." Then she slapped him on the back and sat down with the girls. She appeared to have gained weight. Her complexion was ruddy, and her cheeks bloated.

Angelo had this ridiculous thought of flopping down in the center of the living room and telling them he suspected Demetre of murder because it was just then he felt the stirring in his chest. It was the obsidian, waking up. *No*, he said to himself. *Tonight, is all about Camille.*

He owed her that much.

Tammy monopolized the conversation, which kept Camille blissfully distracted. For the most part, they avoided all medical talk. Much of the chatter revolved around Tammy's obsession with the television program *Law & Order: Special Victims Unit.*

"That Mariska Hargitay," she said, pounding the table. "Damn is she hot."

"Excuse me, but do you always talk like that in front of your girlfriend?" Camille kidded.

"Oh," Tammy said, putting her arm around Val's shoulder. "She knows I don't mean anything by it. Right Val?" Then Tammy planted a loud smooch on Val's cheek.

"We don't keep secrets from each other," Val said. "But I will not be disrespected."

"But isn't that kind of talk a little disrespectful?" Camille said quietly.

"Actually, it's not," Val corrected, "but I can see why you think so. The truth is, I know where Tammy's coming from. She's not being malicious."

"I'm sorry," Camille said. "Who am I to judge? Everyone's relationship is different. It's just that when my husband said things like that, even when he was referring to someone on TV, I knew he was trying to get at me." Camille paused for a second, her eyes welling. "You know, if more couples were honest with one another then maybe . . . I don't know . . . they wouldn't fight so much."

Angelo rubbed Camille's back. "The problem with your marriage wasn't honesty. Your husband is a violent drunk."

"I agree," Val said. "Violence is never the solution. Even when communication breaks down completely there's always another option." Then she reached out and held Camille's hand. "What you did was courageous. Many women choose not to leave an abusive situation even though everyone thinks it's the obvious choice. Often making the right choice is the most difficult."

"Why is it difficult?" Tammy said with dramatic frustration. "I don't understand why the victims blame themselves. Trace hits his wife, and Camille's the one who feels bad.

Same thing for that jagoff Angelo worked with, Demetre. The guy practiced medicine without a license, and Angelo, for some reason, feels responsible. Why is that?"

Angelo bristled at the mention of Demetre's name. He'd hoped to steer clear from any discussion involving him.

"It's not that easy to explain," Val countered. "I worked at a women's detention center in Texas. There were hundreds of women and children running away from abusive relationships. All of them felt guilty for uprooting their families to leave these horrible men. We blame ourselves because we trust people. Then, when they betray our trust, we automatically think the character flaw lies within us."

Tammy shook her head, unconvinced. "That still doesn't answer my question. Logically, the brain interprets the truth. Why do our emotions override this process?"

"We're ruled by our emotions," Camille said. "At least, I know I am."

"I think that's a load of horseshit," Tammy said. "Not everyone is led by their emotions."

"You're right," Val said, crossing her arms. "They're called sociopaths."

"Ah-ha! Now that's a smart answer," Tammy said, grabbing Val's face and kissing her on the lips. "I love you honey bunny."

Camille looked directly at Angelo. "Do you really blame yourself for what Demetre did?"

Tammy leaned forward, grinning. It was then, Angelo caught a glimpse of that familiar glassy look in her eyes. It got him wondering if Tammy had been drinking tonight, sneaking to the bathroom for a quick nip. That would explain why she'd been chewing gum the entire evening, hoping to camouflage her liquor breath with peppermint.

"Right before it all went down," Tammy explained, "Angelo suspected the guy was shifty."

"Okay," Camille said, "but that doesn't make what he did Angelo's fault."

Angelo glared at Tammy for bringing up the subject. "I know it's not my fault."

"Come on, Camille," Tammy said, raising a brow. "You know your little brother. He's not very good when it comes to choosing men." Then she cocked her head to one side. "Remember that drunk, Miles?"

Camille darted her eyes from Tammy to Angelo. "Were you and Demetre dating?"

"No!" A churning began again in Angelo's chest. "There were certain things I witnessed, which I should have reported to Dr. Stanzione sooner, but I didn't because Demetre and I were friends."

"Oh, you two were more than just friends." Tammy raised her fist her mouth, pantomiming oral sex.

"See," Val said. "Angelo entrusted Demetre, and once that trust was broken, Angelo felt culpable."

"I don't blame myself," he insisted. "I just feel . . . ."

"I called that one," Tammy cut in, pointing her finger in Angelo's face. "I knew it the minute I laid eyes on him. Fucking bastard. How dare he impersonate a doctor! What if he hurt someone?"

Angelo shot up and ran into the bathroom. Staring at himself in the mirror, his skin wan, he washed his face. All he could think about was Demetre's voice on the phone, that suitcase in his garage, and the crippling fear that he had killed someone. Tears swirled with the water in the sink. At first, he was unaware that he was crying, but then he heard sobbing. He looked up at his reflection, staring with a curious detachment—like he was observing a patient, not himself.

When he returned to the table several minutes later, the women were laughing, which for some reason made him feel worse.

"There you are," Tammy said, reaching for his hand. "Thought you fell in, old friend. You're not sore that I brought up that jagoff, are you?"

"No." The truth, he knew, was that Tammy would never talk to him like that unless she was drunk, that her usual warm and friendly demeanor had vanished, and inebriation had unleashed Tammy's merciless candor.

"Besides," she continued. "You got hot cop now who is way hotter than that old jagoff."

"Who's hot cop?" Camille asked.

Tammy's mouth gaped open. "You haven't told your sister?"

Angelo squeezed his eyes shut. The conversation was a pinball, bumping from topic to topic Angelo desperately hoped to avoid. "There is no hot cop."

"No hot cop?!" Tammy slammed her palms down on the table. "Don't tell me you fucked up that one too."

"Tammy you're on a roll tonight," Angelo said with a humorless laugh. "It's good to know you're as much fun even when you're not drinking."

"I don't like your tone," Val said. "If you were a good friend, you would respect Tammy's sobriety instead of mocking it."

"That's why I stuck with you," Tammy said, kissing Val's cheek. "You always have my back." She glanced at Angelo, scratched the back of her neck, and then looked quickly away.

Angelo had no intention of confronting Tammy in front of his sister and Val, but for Val to turn a blind eye to Tammy's obvious intoxication made him believe she had become her enabler. Further proof of Val's theory that people in abusive relationships blame themselves and remain quiet instead of leaving.

Camille stood up and began clearing the table. "Would anyone care for more tea?" she asked, but no one responded. Val whispered in Tammy's ear before excusing herself to use the restroom. Camille washed the dishes as Angelo and

Tammy stared at each other in silence. He wanted to confront her. His mouth worked with hesitation, but he said nothing.

Tammy stretched out her arms, yawning. "I'm on call tomorrow," she reminded Val once she returned to the table. "We should get going."

Angelo stood up to stare out the window. His back to them, watching the scene in the glass as Val and Tammy kissed Camille good-bye.

"Thank you for having us," Val said out loud to Angelo.

Angelo did not respond. He had nothing left to say. How long he stood there, eyes fixed on his reflection, he didn't know. Shocked, silent, and disappointed—nearly catatonic—before he noticed Camille stood beside him and reached for his hand.

◆◆◆

That night, Angelo dreamed about her.

From the couch he looked over, expecting to see Camille sleeping, but instead, there was a suitcase, lying flat like some felled animal. He heard muffled cries coming from within it, along with the scratching of fingernails against the canvas lining. She begged him to let her out, but Angelo was frozen. A hand burst suddenly through, stiff fingers reaching out to escape.

When he woke up with a start, Angelo knew the police would find her body. It was inevitable. Still, he dreaded it.

Chapter Fourteen

Angelo spent the weekend with Camille. Being with her drew them closer and distracted him from thinking about Demetre and Jason. On Friday, Camille followed up with Wang. As predicted, Camille's kidney hematoma had nearly resolved.

Monday at work, tension lingered in the air like a mist. Stanzione and Angelo worked as if they were husband and wife during a divorce but still living in the same house. They exchanged terse greetings as they passed each other in the hall, but most of the time Stanzione stayed in his office with the door closed when he wasn't seeing patients. Even Steven seemed distant. They had ceased to operate like the well-oiled machine Angelo had joined in July, but more like a sputtering, stalling, steaming jalopy.

In between patients, Angelo busied himself reading journals, trying to convince himself that everyone was still recovering from Demetre's betrayal. Yet, Angelo couldn't shake an unfamiliar sensation that something ominous was stirring, skittering out of the corner of his eye like a dangling eyelash.

After his last patient, Angelo found a note on his desk. *Office meeting now!!* He entered Stanzione's office to find him seated behind his desk. Steven sat on the couch, legs crossed, arms folded. He appeared like his usual fit self, wearing a tight polo shirt and snug jeans. Unlike Angelo and Stanzione, the controversy swirling around the practice hadn't stopped Steven from working out.

"Angelo," Stanzione said. "Come in. Have a seat."

It was still a shock to see how much Stanzione had aged since Demetre's arrest, but it was more than that. Even the way he spoke, his gestures, they had aged too, taking on a halting quality that was so unlike the man that had hired him.

"How is your sister, Camille?"

"Good, thank you for asking," he said, sitting. "She's staying with me for the time being."

Stanzione glanced at Steven, smiling. "Family. That's what we do. We take care of each other."

Steven smirked. "That we do."

"Thank you for allowing me to take off the time."

"Please," Stanzione said, sitting back. "Family comes first. You know, being part of a practice is like joining a family. Don't you agree?"

Angelo cleared his throat, worried where Stanzione was going. "Yes."

"Particularly Italian families. What's the old saying? 'We're as thick as thieves.'"

"That's right," Angelo agreed though he hadn't been brought up in an Italian household. A fact, he knew, Stanzione was aware of.

"You were raised without a father, right?" Stanzione asked.

"Yes, but . . . Italian blood still runs in my veins."

Again, Stanzione smiled at Steven, but when he looked back at Angelo, he was no longer smiling. "I hoped you would have seen me as a father figure, having taken you under my wing, but . . . ." Stanzione paused, closed his eyes. "That wasn't meant to be."

"We know about the malpractice case," Steven cut in. "The insurance company sent a records request for Violet Trautman. When I informed them we had no record of this patient, they explained Demetre had asked you for a consultation."

"Dr. Stanzione—" began Angelo.

"Ah, ah, ah," Stanzione interrupted. "No reason to explain. I understand. Families keep secrets from one another all the time." He paused after each word, leaving the strand of the conversation dangling like the end of a stray party streamer. "On top of everything that has happened, I always knew I could trust you. That is, until now."

Simultaneously, Angelo experienced a churning in his chest and abdomen. A dueling set of obsidian, grinding so intensely he was unable to defend himself. "Let me explain?" he began.

"You're fired," Stanzione said. "Effective immediately. Now get out."

Steven handed Angelo an envelope. He opened it and read the enclosed letter.

Dear Dr. Perrotta,

This letter confirms that your employment with Park Avenue Medical is terminated effective immediately.

You will receive two weeks' severance pay. You will receive the severance payment once you have signed and returned the enclosed Release of Claims document and confidentiality agreement. You can expect a separate benefits status letter that will outline the status of your benefits upon termination. The letter will include information about your eligibility for Consolidated Omnibus Budget Reconciliation Act (COBRA) continuation of group health coverage.

Please let us know if we can assist you during your transition.

Regards,

Anthony Stanzione, MD, FACP

Angelo walked back into his office to pack up. "Don't take it personally," Steven said, standing in the doorway, holding a cardboard box. "This is business."

Don't take it personally, Angelo thought. *You just fired me.*

Angelo saw no point in arguing with Steven. They had all been entangled in Demetre's lies, but Stanzione was not the king he pretended to be. Angelo saw him now as someone akin to a targeted mafia boss. By withholding the lawsuit, Angelo had become the much-needed scapegoat—the rat who betrayed the Cosa Nostra—and like all rats, he had to be exterminated.

"Tony has his reputation to think of."

Angelo haphazardly threw items into the box. "I hope Tony is up to handling the patient load."

"We'll manage," Steven said, handing him another envelope.

It was a bill for Angelo's malpractice insurance.

For one horrible instant, Angelo wanted to tell Steven what he really thought; that Demetre was right about him all along. Steven was nothing but Stanzione's pathetic little lap dog, doing his dirty work because he was bound to him. They both were, but now, Angelo was free.

Angelo grabbed his coat. There was nothing more to say. He glanced in the box—textbooks, a picture frame, a mug Camille had bought him that read #1 Doctor—and realized there wasn't anything he wanted to take with him. Why not leave everything behind and start over fresh?

"You know what?" Angelo said. "I don't need any of this garbage. Why don't you keep it? Make some art."

Steven escorted Angelo to the door. As he walked down the hall, head held high, he noted the gleaming white marble floor. This is the last time I'll ever see the inside of this office again, he thought. The one he once thought looked like it was built on a frozen lake. The same one which felt like it was cracking beneath his feet.

He stood on the sidewalk, drawing in a breath, trying to maintain his self-control, but inside, he felt something collapsing. The icy water of despair threw his entire body into shock. He stared up at the sky, hoping to see beyond this crushing defeat. One last breath before drowning; it was too overwhelming. All he could think about was Camille. He had promised to take care of her, and the very next day he lost his job.

He turned to look back one last time, but he regretted it once he saw his once shiny bronze plaque had already been removed.

◆◆◆

Angelo walked aimlessly, thinking of his next move. His cell phone rang repeatedly, but he refused to speak with anyone, so he turned it off. Hours later, he returned home to face Camille. She was watching television when he entered.

"What are you doing home so early?" she asked, rising from the couch. "Is everything all right?"

Angelo shook his head. "They fired me."

"I'm so sorry," she said, walking over to hug him. "You'll get through this. We'll get through this together."

The television news blared in.

"Police are on the hunt for a Hoboken man after identifying the remains of a young woman found buried in his garage. Demetre Kostas is wanted for questioning in the death of Mia Garcia."

Mia Garcia!

Angelo lurched forward, turning up the volume.

A somber newscaster solemnly announced, "The young Wall Street analyst was reported missing on Tuesday after her mother informed police she hadn't returned home from work. A search of Miss Garcia's apartment revealed she had an appointment with Kostas the day she disappeared. Kostas had been charged for practicing medicine without a license. He had been awaiting sentencing when he set up shop again in his friend's West Twenty-Second-Street apartment in Manhattan. During a search of Kostas's Hoboken home, police noticed a fresh slab of concrete in the garage. Miss Garcia's remains were discovered buried inside a suitcase. Miss Garcia was only twenty-eight years old."

"Jesus Christ," Angelo said. Two thoughts, separate but equally shocking, came to mind. *Demetre is a murderer. My patient is dead.*

"What is it?" Camille asked. Angelo watched her reach for her cheek where Trace had clobbered her. A tell she had developed anytime she experienced panic. "What's wrong?"

"They're talking about Demetre," Angelo said, pointing at the television. "That's the guy I worked with."

The landline phone rang, startling them. Angelo answered it. "Did you hear the news?" Farrell asked.

"Just now on television. I'm still in shock."

"I called you on your cell phone, but it went right to voicemail," he explained. "Apparently, Kostas was seeing clients out of his friend's apartment. A Mr. Yossi Cohen."

Yossi!

"I'm thinking that while you were on the phone with Kostas on Sunday, Garcia stopped seizing. Kosta probably assumed she was dead and panicked. He must have thrown her body in a suitcase and carried her back to his house in New Jersey. He likely buried her the same night you went there."

A chill crawled down Angelo's back. The thought of that poor woman, unconscious in a suitcase, was terrifying. Had she woken up and realized she'd been buried alive? The horror of it all was too much. Angelo dropped the phone and clutched his spasming stomach.

"Angelo, what's wrong?" Camille asked. Angelo shook his head at the revolting thought that Mia Garcia, that ambitious young woman who had her whole life ahead of her, died of suffocation alone in the dark. Entombed in cement. Camille picked up the phone. "Hi," she said to Farrell. "I'm Camille, Angelo's sister. He's going to have to call you back."

"No," Angelo interrupted, taking the phone away from Camille. "Where is Demetre now?"

"That I don't know," Farrell replied. "I may come by your office tomorrow to review your statement."

Angelo let out an uncomfortable snort of sarcasm. "I no longer work there. Come by my apartment instead."

"Give me the address. I'll be by around ten a.m."

After Angelo hung up, he explained everything to Camille. Her eyes flickered and darkened like a pilot light had been blown out.

"Are you involved in this in any way?" She held his stare, unflinching and scrutinizing.

"No, I swear Camille. I only went to his house because I knew something bad had happened, and even after I told the police what I saw, I tried to convince myself that I was wrong. But I wasn't wrong Camille. Oh, God, I wish had been."

His body felt like it was collapsing upon itself—bones fracturing, blood pulsing, synapses misfiring. He fell to his knees, arms over his head, sobbing uncontrollably on the floor before his sister. How long he huddled on the area rug that smelled damp now soaked with his tears or stared at Camille's foot nervously scratching at her other one, he did not know, but it felt like hours.

The door buzzer rang. "Should I answer that?" she asked.

"No!" he shouted.

"Okay, I won't answer it."

The landline phone rang again.

"Jesus Christ!" He swung his arm, hurling the phone to the floor. Camille's entire body convulsed at his sudden violence. "Camille, I'm sorry I yelled."

She retreated to the table, rubbing her facial wound.

The buzzer rang again. This time, Angelo answered. "What do you want?"

"It's Jason. I came as soon as I heard."

Angelo buzzed him in and minutes later, Jason was at the front door.

"I've been calling you all day," he said.

Angelo flung his arms around him and sobbed.

Camille watched them in silence for several long moments. "Why don't I leave you two alone for a bit," she said, grabbing her coat and handbag.

Once they were alone, Jason and Angelo lay on the bed, holding each other.

"I'm sorry," Jason said. "Your instincts were right. I was just so goddamn jealous."

"I'm so happy to see you." His mouth was open and warm. Angelo felt the nudge of his tongue against his teeth, sliding past, entwining itself with his tongue. It was a hungry kiss of reconciliation. A kiss that announced a burning passion.

Stripping off their clothes until they were completely naked, their cocks gliding against each other, Angelo felt protected, shielded, with Jason's arms moving over his body. For a brief moment in time, Angelo allowed himself passport to compartmentalize Mia's death, and basked in the arousal that came from Jason's naked body against his. Somehow this felt like more than just sex. This felt like a confirmation of something new. Angelo knew it was ridiculous but at the same time, making love to Jason for the first time felt like a consummation.

Afterward, they collapsed on the bed. Angelo's body, still tangled with Jason's, panting and sweating, provided the welcomed reprieve Angelo needed.

"I missed you," Jason said.

"I missed you too."

They heard Camille struggle with the lock.

"I'm back," she said, balancing bags of groceries in her arms.

Jason was buttoning up his jeans when Camille marched directly toward him, her arm fully extended.

"I'm Camille," she said, shaking his hand. "You must be the hot cop."

Angelo winced when Jason glanced over at him.

"Nice to meet you, Camille. The name's Jason."

"Are you hungry, Jason?" She dropped Angelo a slow wink. Jostling off her coat, she began putting the groceries away. "I'm making fettuccini. There's wine. Angelo, why don't you pour us a drink. I think we all could use one."

On the table, Camille dropped a stack of newspapers: the *New York Times*, the *Daily News*, and the *New York Post*. All three reported Mia Garcia's death with photos of Mia and Demetre on the front page. "You should read while I make dinner," Camille said to Angelo.

CONCRETE COFFIN AT QUACK'S HOUSE

A "friend" of phony doc, Demetre Kostas, tipped off police with information that linked him to the disappearance of Mia Garcia. Her remains were discovered entombed in a concrete coffin in Kostas's garage. Now the quack, who was awaiting sentencing for his arrest for practicing without a license, is on the lam.

The medical examiner positively identified Garcia's body after matching the serial number on her breast implants. Detectives are investigating the possibility that Garcia died during a botched procedure Kostas was performing illegally on her out of his friend's West Twenty-Second-Street apartment, and that he buried her to hide the evidence. A police insider said real-life doctor, Angelo Perrotta, contacted detectives after Kostas called him last Sunday to ask his advice when an unnamed patient began seizing. Perrotta instructed Kostas to call emergency services right away. Had Kostas listened, said the insider, Garcia might still be alive.

Dr. Perrotta worked with Kostas at his Park Avenue office where he served as SkinDem's medical director. Police sources said they believe that Garcia most likely died when something went wrong with the use of anesthesia. The state prosecutor said that Mr. Kostas is not licensed in any medical profession. Kostas's lawyer said she had lost contact with her client several days before Garcia's body was found. At this time, Kostas's whereabouts are unknown.

Angelo didn't recall how delicious Camille's fettuccini tasted or whether she had served them dog food. The three spent the entire meal reading. Finally, when they were done, having read the same story told three different ways, they put down the newspapers and sat in silence. Camille poured another round of wine. "It's an unbelievably horrible story," she said finally, "Now the police have to find that murdering bastard."

"They will," Jason said.

Angelo gave a deprecatory laugh. "I hope so."

"I know this has been difficult for you, Angelo," Camille said, "but think of that poor girl's family. They're sitting around a table right now mourning the loss of their daughter and sister."

Angelo smiled appreciatively. Up until that moment, he felt like the victim of some complicated game, a systematic set of traps that he had suddenly stumbled into, but Camille, once again, offered the perspective he needed. Angelo knew he would run through the *what ifs* and *if onlys* that would play over and over in his head, but he had to acknowledge Camille was right. The one thing that would propel him through this miserable set of circumstances was the fact that everything he needed was sitting around his kitchen table.

◆◆◆

Jason and Angelo took a walk after dinner. Having read the reports of Mia's death in the newspapers and watching it on television, it felt like the buildings were collapsing all around him, forming cracks in the sidewalks and streets so that eventually they would expand into huge gullies, but that wasn't all—he knew the news of her death would send shockwaves throughout Manhattan in three-hundred and sixty degrees, across the surrounding waters, spreading indefinitely so that eventually everyone would know that Demetre Kostas was a killer on the loose, and Angelo was the doctor who had signed off on Mia's case. It didn't matter that Demetre had fooled him too. He would remember this case through a scrim of shame, embarrassment, and severe self-castigation that arose from being overly eager to please and overlooking every red flag.

Thinking that poor woman's final moments alive were spent buried underground, waking up not knowing what had happened, made Angelo shudder with revulsion. He decided then that he would attend her funeral mass.

"Do you want to stay at my place tonight?" Jason asked.

"I do," he replied, "but Camille . . . I don't feel comfortable leaving her alone yet." "I understand." Jason kissed him on the mouth in full view of everyone. It was the kiss of a lover, and it occurred to Angelo at that moment that he wanted nothing more than for that to be the kiss of his boyfriend.

Jason walked back to the apartment to thank Camille for dinner before heading home. Camille refused to let Angelo watch the news. He sat on the couch staring at the blank television screen. Still, he felt smothered by the horrifying final hours of Mia's life. The images and thoughts he contrived in his head played over again until he was exhausted and fell asleep.

The next morning, Angelo turned on the television. "Don't even think about it mister," Camille said, reaching for the remote. "Why don't we get out of here today. Let's wander around the city. It'll do us both good to enjoy the time off while we're still not working."

The thought hadn't occurred to Angelo, but it suddenly seemed like a perfect idea.

After they washed and got dressed, they rode the elevator down to the lobby. Once they stepped outside, a crowd rushed toward them. A single mass of flesh lurched with adrenaline, surrounding them like a rugby scrim. Video camera lights clicked on. Camille and Angelo froze in the dazzling glow of electric light. Men and women wearing suits pushed microphones in their faces. "Dr. Perrotta, what did Kostas say to you on the phone?"

"Was Miss Garcia your patient?"

"Where is Kostas now?"

"Has he called you again?"

Angelo held up his hand to shield his eyes from the explosive burst of light. He moved through the throng desperate for air.

"Leave us alone!" Camille curled her arm around his. "He's not the criminal."

Angelo pulled her along, marching steadily down the street, but the reporters had formed a circle around them so that he didn't know where they were headed. Worse, the wind was blowing against them. He had never encountered such insanity. "Are you Dr. Perrotta's wife?"

Camille turned to respond, but Angelo jerked the sleeve of her coat. "Just keep walking," he said brusquely.

A video camera grazed the side of Angelo's head. Instinctively, he knocked it away. The man stumbled and fell to the ground. Angelo crouched down, staring vacantly at the man, when Camille tugged at his sleeve. "What are you doing?"

Angelo had no idea.

◆◆◆

They had been holed up in the apartment for two days after being hounded by reporters waiting outside the building's entrance. Camille ventured out to fetch groceries while Angelo searched online for updates or watched the television news. Once he discovered the date of Mia's funeral mass, he informed Camille he planned to attend.

"Don't go," Camille pleaded. "You'll only draw unnecessary attention when this should be about that poor dead woman, not you."

"I've made up my mind, Camille."

"Then I want to come with you."

He never considered allowing Camille to accompany him for one second, knowing she was still dealing with the assault charge she had pressed against Trace in addition to filing for divorce. "I'm going alone and that's final," he said.

The morning of the funeral was a sunny day, but still very cold and windy. Angelo asked the superintendent to let him out the rear exit to avoid reporters. He tried to hail a cab when a voice called out, "Dr. Perrotta." A camera shutter caught his shocked expression. He'd been identified. Within seconds, a stampede followed. A cab pulled up, and Angelo threw himself into the back seat.

"Go," he shouted. He ducked until they were a safe distance away.

The church was located in Paterson, New Jersey. Thirty minutes later, he saw the giant spire several blocks away. The gothic stone building emerged once the cab turned the corner. Angelo stood on the corner and waited until ten minutes after the mass was scheduled to begin before he entered. He didn't want to cause a scene.

He took a seat in the last pew. The priest stood at the pulpit addressing the mourners. There were so many people dressed in black, rows of them like ravens on a line. Light shone through the stained glass windows, projecting a kaleidoscope of colors on Mia's coffin. Throughout the church, the hollow echoes of weeping and sniffling were deafening.

Angelo slid to the other end of the pew to see the front row. A small, elderly woman sat clutching a framed photo of Mia. A pair of black rosary beads dangled over the edge of the frame. A young man sat beside her, his arm slung around the old woman's shoulders, consoling her as she wept. Suddenly, Angelo felt embarrassed for being there. What right did he have to mourn Mia with her family?

Once the mass was over, the priest stepped down off the pulpit and gave Mia's mother a hug. The young man escorted the old woman down the aisle. Angelo watched as she reached out and ran her hand over the smooth surface of the coffin. The church was quiet for a few moments except for the creaking of the pews under the shifting weight of mourners and a few stifled coughs. Two men in black suits opened the church doors. A ray of sunlight sliced down the aisle. A procession began, starting with the priest, followed by the altar boys and then, the pallbearers carrying Mia's coffin on their shoulders. Mia's family walked in a state of stunned bewilderment.

Just as they passed Angelo, he wanted to say something, apologize, but when the old woman's eyes met his gaze, he couldn't bring himself to speak. Grief had etched her face so that it collapsed under the weight of her loss. He really shouldn't have been there at all, but then, she reached out and held his hand. "Thank you for coming."

Angelo remained still, lost in the sadness of her gaze until she released his hand and exited the church.

The organ music swelled suddenly. The entire congregation filed out of the church, absorbed by the blinding light of the sun. There was no wailing or crying. Just silent grieving. Death had laid its soothing hand upon them, and they were joined in their love for Mia.

Then the church doors closed, and Angelo was left sitting in the back, alone and shivering.

CHAPTER FIFTEEN

In the days after Mia's funeral, the newspapers found it impossible to avoid the story of Demetre's downward spiral. Every day a new development, another theory to explain how this seemingly normal man killed an innocent woman and buried her body in a suitcase. Eventually, the story of Mia's death gained national exposure. Across the United States people wanted to know how something like this could happen, and if it could happen to them. Their outrage and fear fed by ruthless reporters hoping to sell newspapers sensationalizing Mia's story. One even compared Demetre to a serial killer, tracking him down with bloodthirsty fervor. The hunt for an insane monster had begun. The only thing missing were the crowds bearing pitchforks and torches.

Most days, Angelo stared at the television even though it was off, choking back the anger and guilt, and ducking from reporters. Camille did her best to keep him occupied, maintaining a routine that included dinners together and no evening news. Angelo enjoyed her company. It was a welcoming distraction, but there was always an opportunity for him to wallow in despair.

It surprised Angelo that Stanzione and Steven never contacted him once the newspaper articles named him as the physician Demetre contacted as Mia seized. Angelo assumed Stanzione's lawyers had advised him against it.

Each night he dreaded the thought of sleep. In bed, the dreams were always like this: Mia's body convulsing, Demetre holding her down and Angelo, standing over them, watching it all happen quite calmly—without fear, without urgency, but with the curiosity of a stunned medical student observing a surgical procedure gone wrong.

Then he'd wake up.

The suffocating darkness surrounded him like gauze, and he trembled. *Oh, God, when will this end?*

Two weeks after Mia's funeral, Angelo received a call from his malpractice attorney. "Dr. Perrotta, I have some bad news and good news." He imagined Meers shaking his white mane of hair and reaching under his glasses to massage the fleshy pads under his eyes.

It had been weeks since Angelo had thought about Violet Trautman's lawsuit.

"At this point," Angelo said. "I don't think things could possibly get any worse."

"Don't ever tempt the gods of law," Meers said. "Trust me. Things can always get worse."

"Let me guess, Mrs. Trautman wants more money now that she knows Demetre is a murderous fraud?"

"Her attorney didn't phrase it that way but yes. What's frustrating is that we were close to a settlement agreement, and then, suddenly, the deal was off. I can't help but think that this latest development with Kostas is a motivating factor."

For weeks it felt like Angelo was forever falling apart, breaking down, disintegrating. "What happens next?" Angelo asked.

"We keep negotiating until we come to an agreement. The good thing is that you didn't bill her for the consultation. Had you done that without documenting your recommendation, you would have found yourself being investigated for medical misconduct. In addition, the court must weigh your testimony against Mr. Kostas's. It goes without saying that the balance is now in your favor."

"Thank God for small favors."

Meers's voice softened, taking on an uncharacteristic quality that Angelo could only perceive as encouraging. "We'll get through this. That's a promise."

The sensation of being comforted by Meers was so foreign and unfamiliar that it made him squirm. "Thank you," Angelo managed. And yet, Meers's tone strengthened his resolve to get through this lawsuit, although the outcome, he knew, was completely out of his control.

It was time to get back to work—if anyone would let him. He called the chief of medicine at the hospital where he completed his residency and begged for a job. A physician was going on maternity leave, and he needed someone to cover her clinic sessions. Angelo jumped at the opportunity, and the chief happily agreed. Never once did the chief ask about Mia Garcia or his involvement in her death. Angelo found a great deal of comfort thinking, maybe, the story was no longer front-page news.

The following Monday, Angelo started work. The clinic was a far cry from Stanzione's Park Avenue office with its white marble floors and affluent gay clientele, but Angelo experienced a sense of pleasure treating men and women who waited for hours to see a doctor. Many of them had no education beyond grammar school. Few had jobs. But they were all gracious and treated him with such respect. He finally understood what Tammy and Val had been telling him all along, and the stories they told about experiencing such pride. This indescribable feeling he experienced working long hours, was this pride? Whatever it was, he didn't care to analyze it. He only hoped that he would feel this way forever.

Just one month after Mia was finally laid to rest, Angelo was riding the bus heading to the clinic on the Lower East Side when he received a call from an unknown number.

"Morning," Angelo answered.

"Don't hang up. It's me."

Angelo's heart hammered in his chest. "Demetre?" Angelo stuttered. "What do you want?"

He whispered, "I had to speak with you."

"Where are you?" Angelo asked.

"That's unimportant," he replied. "I know there is nothing I can say to make you understand what happened, but I didn't mean to hurt her."

"You fucking killed her!" Angelo's voice pierced the otherwise quiet, crowded bus. Several older women scoffed their disapproval. Angelo hopped up and got off at the next stop even though it wasn't his. He headed down the avenue, hoping to convince Demetre to turn himself in. "This won't end well. You know that."

"It is what it is," Demetre said with a tinge of glibness that reignited a churning in Angelo's chest.

"Everyone is looking for you," Angelo insisted. "Don't you read the newspapers or watch television?"

"When I can find them in English."

"Well, if you're not going to turn yourself in," Angelo said beyond mortified, "I have nothing left to say to you."

"Wait," he snapped. Angelo experienced a plunge so chilling it felt like jumping into ice water. He stopped walking, frozen with panic. "I need you to do me a favor." Demetre's voice sounded strange. Desperate. Dangerous.

It took a couple of seconds for Angelo to respond. His mind raced. His eyes searched the streets, hoping an answer would magically present itself.

"You're a murderer," Angelo gritted. "Why would I do anything for you?"

"I can make your life miserable," Demetre said, his voice gaining control. "Maybe you won't go to jail, but I will destroy you."

Nothing else seemed important enough to give in to his emotions, but Angelo could not imagine a life beyond medicine. All around him the city came back to life. Traffic sped by, commuters hurriedly brushed passed him, but it was the wail of an ambulance that jolted him as if he'd been struck with an electric prod. "Don't ever call me again," Angelo warned. "Turn yourself in. You owe that much to Mia's family."

Angelo hung up and called Jason immediately. "He probably used a burner phone," Jason explained. "Did he say what kind of favor he wanted from you?"

"No," Angelo replied. "I wasn't on long enough to hear him out."

"Where are you?" Jason asked.

Even with rush-hour traffic, Angelo heard a call coming through. "It's the clinic," he said. "Shit, I'm late." Angelo, alerted by whatever psychic connection had interlocked his life with Demetre's, now veered perilously into threats of warning. He couldn't think straight. "Jason, what do I do?"

"Angelo," he said. "Go to work. I'll call Farrell. Text me the number Demetre called you from."

"Can you trace a burner phone?" Angelo's mind ran through a succession of horrifying possibilities, like experiencing the stages of grief at lightning speed. "He said he would destroy me!"

"It'll be all right," Jason assured him.

Angelo did not share his optimism.

Throughout the day, Angelo spoke to Jason and Camille several times. As Jason predicted, Farrell planned to contact the cellular service to trace Demetre's call. They hoped he had used it again or left it on, which would make it easier to trace. "It's a long shot," Farrell said, "but I'm optimistic."

Angelo thought Farrell said that only for his benefit. The truth, he knew, was that Demetre planned to destroy him, whatever that meant. At any rate, it was more important that he brace himself for whatever Demetre had planned than to hope he got caught first.

Before Angelo left for the day, Camille reminded him that Tammy and Val were coming over for dinner that night. At first, Angelo suggested they cancel, but Camille nudged him. "You'll only watch the news," she said, and so he agreed.

Later at dinner, Angelo seemed too distracted to notice Tammy and Val acted like mourners at a funeral. Angelo and Camille skirted around topics, avoiding any mention of Demetre's call, when Tammy finally announced, "I can't go on like this."

Val sat next to her, holding Tammy's hand in silence.

"I've come to a decision," Tammy continued, staring down at her untouched meal. "I'm entering rehab."

"Rehab," Angelo repeated. "Are you sure?"

"One hundred and ten percent," she assured him. "If I don't go now, I don't know what's going to happen to me." Tammy slowly lifted her head, reaching under her glasses to rub her eyes. "I can't live like this. I've been lying to you. I've been lying to myself." She glanced at each of them, her eyes round and glassy. "I feel like I've let you down. I'm sorry. Just please, don't be angry with me. I can fix this."

When Angelo glanced over at Val, she was sobbing. Angelo recalled the night they came for dinner after Camille moved in. That night, he had judged Val for being an enabler, but what part had he played in enabling Tammy? Not once had he reached out to her to offer his support. Instead, he cut her off, just has he had done with Camille when he discovered she had lied about knowing about their father. Only after Camille was badly injured did he realize how selfish he had been, icing her out, and instead of learning from that mistake, he made it again with his best friend.

Angelo stood up and knelt next to Tammy. "I'm sorry," he said, giving her hand a squeeze. "I'm sorry I wasn't a better friend. Can you forgive me?"

Tammy hugged him, and they sobbed into each other's shoulders. If Angelo had learned anything these past few weeks, it was that Camille, Jason, and Tammy were all that he had, and instead of leaning on everyone for support, he had to try to be a better man and support them.

CHAPTER SIXTEEN

The days that followed blurred into a welcomed, un-eventful series of weeks, which allowed Angelo to focus on work.

One Friday morning, he walked to the hospital to make rounds before heading to the clinic. He paid little attention to the budding flowers or the fresh spring breeze because he was too preoccupied revisiting his first year in practice as though playing over the events in his head might some-how alter their tragic outcome.

When the elevator doors opened on the fourth floor, Angelo spotted Steven outside the ICU. *What is Steven doing here*, he wondered. For a moment, he debated whether he should step out and speak with him, but the doors closed before he had a chance to hold them open. Once on the ward, Angelo sat at a computer and typed a search of ICU patients. Anthony Stanzione had been assigned to bed six. The realization startled Angelo. He became aware of his breathing.

"Dr. Perrotta," an intern said. "We're ready when you are."

After rounds, after he finished co-signing the notes and wrote medication orders, then took the elevator down to the fourth floor, Angelo pushed open the ICU doors and stepped inside. He felt a sharp twinge of panic, recalling those long nights he stayed up when he was an intern on call. Angelo smiled at the nurses as he made his way to bed six. Walking past patient after patient, he recalled the time he admitted Cal Hudson and how that encounter brought Jason into his life.

He passed the glass enclosure where the interns gathered to write notes, eat a quick meal, or take a nap. Angelo poked his head in. "Any of you assigned to bed six?"

"I am," a young woman with curly auburn hair and wire-rimmed glasses said, "but we've been given strict orders to not touch Dr. Stanzione."

Angelo smirked. "What's the diagnosis?"

"Massive myocardial infarction," she said, her voice hushed. "They're operating tomorrow."

"Thanks."

Angelo proceeded with trepidation toward bed six, which had been curtained off. Not sure what to say, he felt compelled to speak with Stanzione, to recall the reason why he wanted to work for him and resolve whatever ill feelings remained between them because in the end, Stanzione had given him an opportunity. Just as he was about to pull back the curtain, he froze. The heart monitor bleeped very slowly. The ventilator swooshed as it pumped air into his lungs. These sounds heralded an ominous sign that Stanzione was not in any shape for visitors.

Still, he had to see him.

Slowly pulling back the curtain, Angelo blinked in flustered amazement. Frail, pale, and bald, the mighty Stanzione had been replaced by a comatose corpse. The next few minutes transpired in a haze, and Angelo wondered if there was any hope for his recovery.

"They said he's lucky to be alive," the intern whispered as she sidled next to him.

"Unbelievable."

She turned to walk away, glancing over her shoulder as if she were inviting him to follow her. "He had nearly one hundred percent occlusion of the left anterior descending artery," she said. "That's the widow-maker."

Angelo offered a slightly condescending smile. "I know what the widow-maker is."

"Then you know he's lucky to be alive," she said, pausing near the main doors. "Apparently, he's being investigated for insurance fraud."

"Dr. Stanzione?"

The intern glanced over her shoulder. "It's worse than that. There's a rumor he was selling opioid prescriptions."

Angelo took a moment to answer, wondering if Demetre had a hand starting these rumors. *How could Demetre orchestrate such a plan without tipping off the police? Someone had to be helping him, but who would align themselves with a murderer on the run?*

"No wonder he had a massive heart attack," Angelo said, fishing inside his jacket pocket for a business card. "Can you text my cell if his condition changes?"

The intern studied his business card before inserting it in her breast pocket. "Dr. Perrotta," she said, drawing out his name. "I've heard of you." Angelo had to quell the riotous acid ascending his throat. It still surprised Angelo whenever someone recognized him.

As he walked to the clinic, he felt extremely sad, but sad seemed too miniscule a word to describe the epic nosedive Stanzione's entire life had taken. The part about insurance fraud didn't make sense to Angelo, knowing Stanzione was many things but not a crook. More and more Angelo thought all Demetre had to do was flick the domino of doubt, setting off a chain of events that would lead to months of chart and finance reviews by several insurance companies, which would throw the practice into a bureaucratic cesspool.

Angelo, for his part, was focused on work. He had to be but walking the crowded city streets, he no longer saw strangers projecting their medical clues. Now they wore Mia's mask, armies of them, marching on the sidewalk, reminding him that a woman had died at the hands of a greedy bastard. He could no longer hide from them. The intimidation of their physical presence inoculated him with a fear he had never known, and he accepted this punishment because he felt incredibly guilty. Angelo taunted himself with these thoughts; they galvanized inside his chest, switching on the obsidian like some combustive turbine, ripping and tearing its way out of his body.

Hours later, he waited for Camille to return home. She had been temping at a law firm, unable to find full-time work. As soon as she opened the door, he blurted, "Dr. Stanzione had a massive heart attack."

"Can this day get any worse?" she said, sitting at the kitchen table, slumping in the chair like a ragdoll.

"What is it?"

"After you got fired, I wished something bad would happen to him," Camille confessed. "I never imagined it would be this bad."

Angelo laughed. "Camille, this has nothing to do with you."

"No, I'm not kidding," she insisted. "I knew today bad things were going to happen."

Angelo was not surprised. Even as children, Camille had a superstitious streak. Bad things happened in threes. Angelo knew she was thinking: first, Demetre's threat, second, Stanzione's massive heart attack, but the third? He didn't know.

Camille held her forehead, squeezed her eyes shut. "I received a message at work today from someone named Yossi."

"Yossi?"

"He wants you to call him." She reached into her purse and pulled out a Post-it note. "Here," she said, handing it over. "That's his cell phone number. Do you know this person?"

Of course, he knew this person, but Angelo considered his sister's current emotional state. He didn't want to bring up Demetre's name. What good would it do? But he grappled, knowing the truth would surely come out in the end.

"Demetre used Yossi's apartment to see his clients after Stanzione kicked him out. That's where he killed Mia Garcia."

Camille burst into tears. "How does this Yossi person know my name or where I work?"

"I don't know." Angelo paced, scratching the back of his head. "Did you actually see him?"

"No, he came by while I was at lunch." Camille started hyperventilating. "Should I be worried? Is he some crazy stalker?"

"I'll call Jason," he offered. "He'll know what to do."

Camille wasn't satisfied, hearing his voice waver. Her face contorted with unease, knitted brows, downturned mouth. Angelo had seen that face hundreds of times, if not thousands.

"Listen," he said, sitting across from her. "Don't make yourself sick over this. I'll take care of Yossi."

Camille nodded her head. "Maybe this is what Demetre meant by destroy you. What if he wants to destroy me, too?"

"Camille," Angelo said in a stern voice. "I'm so sorry I got you involved in all of this. Let me call Jason before you melt down."

"What if they can't trace Demetre's phone?" Camille rambled on. "I can't live looking over my shoulder."

Angelo's cell phone buzzed. It was a text from the ICU intern.

Stanzione just coded. Sorry, he didn't make it.

"Who's that?" she shrieked.

"It's Tammy," he lied. "We're having brunch tomorrow. You should come."

"I don't think so," she said, rising like a sleepwalker. "I can't think about tomorrow right now."

"Come here." Angelo hugged her tightly. She felt so small in his arms, her heart pounding against his chest, and in that moment, he felt an overwhelming impulse to protect her.

But that wasn't possible, because inside, he was falling apart.

◆◆◆

After Camille had gone to sleep, Angelo texted Tammy and invited her to brunch. He didn't mention Stanzione's death or Demetre's threat. Only that he wanted to see her since she had completed rehab. The distraction, he thought, would be good for Camille and him.

The next morning, Angelo met Tammy at a restaurant near Madison Square Park. Camille decided not to join them. She blamed it on cramps, but Angelo suspected she made up an excuse to have the apartment to herself. Two people living in a small studio for months was taking a toll on them. Even though Angelo slept at Jason's two to three nights a week, he tossed and turned, worrying about Camille home alone.

Tammy sat at a table by the window. Just as Angelo approached, she pushed up her sleeve and snapped a red rubber band she wore around her wrist.

"Hello stranger."

Tammy tugged at her sleeve. "There he is," she said cheerfully.

"You look great."

"I'm not as bloated as I used to be when I was drinking. You know I dropped ten pounds my first week in rehab. Ten pounds! Can you believe it?"

"Let me get a good look at you."

She stood up and gave him a stilted twirl. "I'm the new and improved Tammy. Healthy living has transformed me from Chris Farley into Jodie Foster."

The restaurant was in the midst of a brunch furor. They ordered Cobb salads and sipped coffee. Tammy reached under her sleeve and snapped the rubber band again. "What's that you're wearing on your wrist?" he asked.

She offered a strained smile. "Oh, it's nothing. Just a trick they taught us in rehab to deal with stress."

"Is that an anxiety wristband?"

"Hey," she said, "Val and I are thinking about getting a dog."

The abrupt change in conversation caught Angelo off guard. "A dog? Really? Who's going to take care of it?"

"I was thinking of a Yorkie. Call it Bingo. Now, I know what you're thinking. I'm more of the pit bull or Labrador retriever type, but my apartment is too small for a big dog. The only problem is that Val has her heart set on a shelter dog. Figures she would. Good luck trying to find a Yorkie at a shelter."

The sight of Tammy sitting across from him, thin and pointy, wearing a rubber band around her wrist, did not instill him with comfort, not like the old Tammy had. She appeared more fragile now than before rehab. Then again, he thought, isn't that what rehab is, a place to shed those layers of disillusionment, one at a time, until there was nothing left but the deep, dark truth you hide from everyone, including yourself.

Angelo had grown accustomed to recklessly confiding in Tammy. A large sieve, filtering out the unnecessary material, leaving behind the essential elements, something that in the end seemed more manageable to interpret. Hiding under the veneer of a new and improved Tammy, Angelo thought the news of Stanzione's death would be too much for her.

The waitress brought over their salads. Tammy continued to defend her decision to buy a dog even though Angelo hadn't raised a single objection. He tried to focus. His head buzzed with a combination of noise: the clatter of utensils, the shrill laughter of girls at the next table, Tammy snapping her rubber band, and all at once he blurted out, "Dr. Stanzione is dead."

How awkward it felt to hear those words out loud.

Tammy stared at him, mouth gaping. "Jeez, Ange. I can't believe that bastard keeled over." Reaching under her sleeve, Tammy snapped the rubber band twice.

The news hung there. It was then, Angelo realized, that in one short year all the people in his life had met with some form of tragic circumstance: Camille, Tammy, Demetre, and now Stanzione. The wrath of humanity had claimed a life, made another a fugitive, and spared the rest. Perhaps Tammy sensed this coincidence too, struggled with it like some thorny abstraction, just as Angelo had.

Together they had navigated through many obstacles over the years, but it was these past twelve months that proved to be their biggest challenge. Yet, even the most durable of friendships are not impermeable to damage. The tether connecting Angelo to Tammy, to each and every one of them, was as thin and tenuous as that rubber band around her wrist. Still, they clung to it fiercely, petrified that if they didn't, they'd fall backward into the wrath of circumstance itself.

They finished their salads in silence and paid the bill. Leaving the restaurant, Angelo cursed himself for sullying their reunion with the news of Stanzione's death. It should have been a celebration for Tammy. Angelo had been too weak to maintain control. At least he held back from mentioning Demetre.

"Hang in there, old friend," Tammy said. "Give my love to your sister."

"Let me know when you buy the pooch."

Tammy smiled, but he sensed she was holding something back. Then she walked away but stopped after only taking two steps. She turned around and walked back. "Listen, Ange, you probably feel like I've been giving you the ole runaround. The truth is that I've been trying to get my life back on track and sometimes . . . and well, sometimes you're more than a handful. I know you lean on me like a big sister, but I need someone to lean on for a little while. We're still besties. It's just I need to be stronger. I need to change." Tammy threw her arms around him but did it in such a way that made it impossible for him to hug her back. She let go but kept staring at him, taking step after step backward until finally, she hailed a cab and drove away.

Angelo walked back home, feeling the tug of loneliness. Something pooled inside his chest. It was guilt, feeding the obsidian like blood because, of course, it was still there.

It was indestructible.

When he returned to the apartment, Camille was in bed, writing in a small black book. "How's Tammy?"

Seeing her in bed in the middle of the afternoon, reading, made him wonder if Camille hadn't made up an excuse to avoid brunch. "She's good. How are you?"

Camille gave him the thumbs down sign. "I think I have some kind of stomach flu."

He sat on the edge of the bed and felt her forehead. "Do you want me to make you some tea and toast?"

"Tea and toast," she repeated. "Remember Mom and her famous toast triangles? It almost made me want to get sick so that I could stay home from school and watch TV because I knew that Mom would serve me tea and toast in bed."

"That settles it." He walked into the kitchen. "What's that you're reading?"

"I'm writing poetry."

He pivoted around. "I didn't know you wrote poems."

"A few of the women in my group suggested that I write down my emotions. You know, to get them out of my head. It really helps to clear your mind. You should try it."

Angelo set the kettle on the stove and dropped two slices of bread in the toaster. "I've never written poetry before."

"Neither have I."

"Maybe I will. There are more than a few things I'd like to get off my chest." He leaned against the counter. Arms folded. This was one of those microscopic moments where he glimpsed himself at some future place. "I've been thinking," he began. "We should think about looking for a bigger apartment."

Camille didn't respond right away. "Are you sure? I was thinking once I found full-time work, I would get my own apartment, somewhere like Brooklyn."

The toast popped up from the toaster. Angelo walked assuredly to the refrigerator and took out the butter. "Eventually you may want to do that, but for now, we can't continue living here."

"What about Jason?"

"What about him?" Angelo asked. "It's too soon for us to think about living together."

Camille appeared satisfied with his response. "Whatever you think is best. I feel awful enough that you've been sleeping on that lumpy pullout bed for months."

He carried the toast over to her and set the plate on the nightstand, feeling slightly renewed as if he'd shed some of his lingering fear and guilt. "I'll start checking websites tomorrow," he said. "It's time for a change.

CHAPTER SEVENTEEN

Monday morning, Angelo sat on the subway, debating where Camille and he should live. Over the weekend, he gathered information about the different neighborhoods in Manhattan, Brooklyn, and Queens, trying to figure out which was the most convenient and affordable. The thrum of the subway coaxed him into sleep, gently jostling him with a dizzying pleasure as the subway car careened through the dark. A sharp jab in his side woke him. Sitting very close was Yossi, grinning. Angelo didn't say anything, his stomach in knots, he felt as if he'd jumped off a cliff. "Are you following me?"

"Why didn't you call me back?" Yossi asked.

"I have nothing to say to you."

Angelo grabbed his backpack and ran to the other side of the subway car. Yossi followed him. "You need to speak to me," Yossi said.

Angelo stood by the door, waiting to exit at the next stop. "You need to leave my sister and me alone. I already informed the police."

"No, you didn't." Saliva pooled in the corners of Yossi's mouth. "I know things you wouldn't want the police to know, like what you said to Demetre the day that girl died."

Only in the bitter cold silence of the morning does the screech of a halting train sound like a scream. Angelo stood in front of Yossi, his heart pounding. The subway doors opened. Angelo bolted, but Yossi was right behind him. "I have Demetre's phone!"

Yossi gripped the back of Angelo's arm, swinging him around.

"Your message said, 'Text me the address,'" Yossi said, grinning. "'I'll come right away.' You were going to help him."

Staring into the dark subway tunnel, Angelo felt like he was looking down a throat gurgling up the past that he so badly wanted to forget. He paused to eye Yossi with the unabashed curiosity of a physician. Eyes dilated to the size of pennies, jaw jittering, distorting his smile or what was left from the tooth decay.

"And then you called again after midnight," Yossi taunted. "What were you two up to?" He made kissy noises. Yossi's breath smelled putrid, like curdled milk.

"What do you want from me?" Angelo pleaded. He hated himself for asking, for giving in to the intimidation of a drug dealer, but hearing Yossi string those two separate, although true statements, out of context got him worried that the police might investigate if presented with this evidence. And that fear was crippling. "I don't have any money if that's what you're looking for."

"No," he said. "I don't want money. I want you to write me prescriptions for oxycodone."

"And what if I don't?"

"I'll send Demetre's phone to that detective," he explained. "I'm sure they'll be very interested hearing your voice message."

"I have to get to work," Angelo said, hoping another train would come so he could escape.

"I'll be in touch," Yossi warned. "Call me in two days, otherwise, I'll escort your sister to work. See how she likes to ride the train with Yossi."

Angelo got back on the next train, trembling, not sure if it was Yossi who had rattled him or the speeding rush hour subway. When he got to the office, he stepped inside his exam room and collapsed into tears.

He texted Jason and said only that he needed to speak with him about an urgent matter. Nothing else. When Jason arrived in full uniform, Angelo perked up. He forgot how sexy Jason looked in his uniform, those muscular arms stretching the cut of his shirt. "What's wrong," Jason asked, sitting across from Angelo at a cafeteria table. "Your text freaked me out." Angelo could only nod as though he was still memorizing the lines he planned to say. Turning his coffee cup in the saucer, he could hardly bring himself to look at Jason, and when he did, his heart melted seeing those crystal-blue eyes pressed under eyebrows heavy with concern.

"First," Angelo began before Jason even had a chance to sit down. "Any word on tracing Demetre's burner phone? It's been weeks."

Jason sighed with evident frustration. "These things take a while, and I'm not as confident as Farrell." He gave Angelo a peck on the cheek and sat. "One thing struck me as odd. You asked him if he had been reading the newspapers or watching the news. Didn't he say, 'When I get them in English?'"

"Do you think that means he's not in the country?" Angelo ventured.

"I do, which may explain why they're having trouble tracing the burner phone." Jason swiped a hand down his face. "Listen Angelo, you didn't drag me down here to talk to me about Demetre's phone. What's up?"

Angelo reached out to hold his hand. "Remember we said no secrets?"

"Yeah."

"Something happened today, and I need to tell you."

Jason sat upright, leaned forward, his hands kneading. "The suspense is killing me."

"I'm being blackmailed."

"What?'

The cafeteria was tiny, with yellow fluorescent lights highlighting the deep crevices of worry etched in Jason's face. "One of Demetre's fuckbuddies," Angelo whispered. "A drug dealing trainer named Yossi Cohen."

Jason sat against the booth and sighed. "I really thought you were breaking up with me."

"Why?" Angelo felt as shocked as Jason looked.

He waved his hand dismissively. "That's not important. How did this Yossi guy find you?"

Angelo explained how he first contacted Camille at work, and mysteriously appeared on the subway to frighten him earlier that morning.

"Obviously, he's casing your apartment," Jason ventured. "How else would he know your comings and goings? What sort of collateral does he have, and how damaging is it?"

This is the part Angelo dreaded. He was absorbed in thought, recalling the reason they had broken up was due to Angelo withholding information about visiting Demetre's house the night of the murder. *They had gotten into an argument, and Jason decided it was best for him not to see Angelo anymore.* But he forced his panic into calm because he had no reason to feel this ridiculous anxiety. He hadn't told Jason everything then because their argument had escalated before Angelo had the chance to fully explain.

"Demetre called me while that woman was seizing," Angelo explained. "He begged me to come over . . . to help, but I pleaded with him to call 911. The minute I refused he panicked, said she was better, and hung up. I called him back and left a voice message, asking him to text me his address. I said I would come over, but I planned to call 911 myself. I had no intentions of going there. Yossi said he has Demetre's phone and will show it to the police if I don't supply him with prescriptions for opioids."

"So, he has a text message contradicting the story you told the police?" Jason tapped a finger to his chin. "I really don't think you have anything to worry about. Your explanation will make total sense to everyone."

Angelo paused, because he was preparing to tell Jason the worst part of the story. "The phone records will show that I called Demetre after midnight that night."

Jason gazed at Angelo for a long moment, silenced by the shock of this new disclosure. "You called Demetre that night?" Jason shot him a confused look. "Why?"

"I couldn't sleep," Angelo explained, now on the verge of tears again. "I kept thinking about that woman, and so, I called to hear his voice again . . . ."

Jason drew a long breath through his nose. "Hmm."

"No, nothing like that," Angelo insisted, squeezing Jason's hand.

Jason pulled it away, crossing his arms over his chest. "And now this clown wants you to supply him with opioid prescriptions?"

"He threatened Camille," Angelo added. "Who knows what he's capable of? You should have seen him. He's cracked out."

Jason laughed mockingly. "Fuck him. There's no way you're giving him prescriptions."

"What should I do?"

"You need to call Farrell and report Yossi," Jason said. His voice sounded mechanical like an operator reciting prompts.

"Okay," Angelo replied.

Jason appeared absorbed in his thoughts. His expression unreadable to Angelo.

"We need to distance ourselves from Demetre and everyone in his orbit," Jason said in a savage tone. "We need to put this behind us once and for all. Okay?"

"Agreed." Looking into Jason's eyes, he had this eerie feeling the human part that loved him had detached, and the suspicious part now stared back at him.

CHAPTER EIGHTEEN

After that catastrophic week, Camille and Angelo decided to visit their mother's grave on Sunday. Angelo invited Jason. He found himself crossing his fingers with hope as he waited for Jason to reply. When Jason agreed to drive them to Staten Island, Angelo took that as a good sign. Jason's final evaluation was less than a month away. After their last conversation, Angelo swore to himself that he'd never bring up Demetre's name again until after Jason was cleared by his counselor.

That day, Angelo stared out the window at the never-ending strip malls, diners, dry cleaners, Italian grocery stores, bakeries, and tattoo parlors. Even the air smelled different to him. Once he moved away, he saw his trips back to Staten Island as a regression, a forfeit of everything he had learned since leaving, and with every subsequent return, there was a recurring dreariness, like when he was a boy on Sunday night faced with returning to school on Monday.

His childhood was a drab existence full of muted colors, coupons, Salvation Army shopping and meals that came out of a can. Camille and Angelo shared a small bedroom, their twin beds forming a right angle while their mother slept on the couch. Such a gentle soul, their mother was attractive with pale skin, gray eyes, and honey-colored hair. She spoke in a breathy way and laughed in a lilting tone that sounded as though she was about to start singing.

As Jason drove over Todt Hill, the cemetery appeared on the right. "There it is," Angelo said. He lowered the window. Outside the air was breezy with the sun shining overhead. At the base of the hill, Moravian Cemetery sprawled out with its lush knolls and valleys, dotted with tombstones like stars on a green flag. Angelo hadn't been to visit their mother's gravesite in years. Not because he didn't have respect for her. He simply didn't believe in burying the dead. That brown lacquered casket resting deep in a plot of land did not contain his mother, but a collection of her remains that, by now, had decomposed into bits of dust and bone chips, scattered among layers of decaying cloth that once made up the blue dress they buried her in.

Standing over her grave that morning, Jason's arm slung across his shoulder, Camille holding his hand, that's all he thought about.

"I know this is going to sound crazy," Jason said, "but this is one cool cemetery."

Angelo smiled at Camille. "You and my mother would have gotten along so well," he said, smiling.

Angelo understood his mother's fascination with Moravian. Long stretches of winding roads, manicured lawns, and the lake surrounded by cherry blossoms. The white circular leaves floated in the spring breeze like confetti.

One of their mother's shopping rituals dictated they drive over Todt Hill so that she could see the pretty houses, but more, so she could gander at the grounds of Moravian Cemetery. "Doesn't it look like Ireland?" Camille said, imitating their mother's voice.

"How would you know?" Angelo replied, imitating a bratty, young Camille. "It's not like you've ever been there before."

"I know what the Eiffel Tower looks like, and I haven't been to Paris either," Camille continued. "When I die, I want to be buried in Moravian Cemetery. You guys can come visit and have a picnic on my grave."

"Can you believe mom wanted us to have a picnic in a cemetery," Angelo said, thinking how ridiculous that sounded hearing Camille say it again out loud.

"You think she was serious?" Jason asked.

"Without a doubt," Camille said, brushing the dead leaves off the headstone.

Something caught Angelo's eye. "Camille, look," he said, kneeling. Angelo pointed at a four-leaf clover growing out of a corner of the headstone.

"It's a sign," Camille said, bending forward to get a closer look. "It's just like Mom said. Ireland."

Angelo suppressed the urge to poke fun at his sister. Instead, he said, "Maybe it is."

Glancing at their reflections in the headstone, the two of them with their dark hair and epicene faces, Angelo thought they still looked like twins. More so now with the scar on Camille's face. She rested her head on his shoulder, and he knew she was thinking the same thing.

Hours later, they returned to Manhattan. Camille asked Jason to drop her off at the apartment, having refused their invitation to dinner. "You two go. I had enough excitement for one day."

Jason and Angelo bought wine and ordered cheeseburgers, then headed back to Jason's apartment. After they ate, Jason spooned Angelo on the couch as they listened to music. "You and your sister are so cute when you're together," Jason said in Angelo's ear. "It's like you're two sides of the same coin."

Angelo pulled Jason's arm across his belly. "I feel guilty when I'm not with her, especially after Yossi showed up at her office."

"I doubt he'll bother either of you again," Jason said as he rubbed his groin against Angelo's buttocks. "Farrell said they went by his apartment, but he wasn't there, and the gym where he worked said he hadn't shown up in days."

"You should have seen him," Angelo said, subtly shifting his backside against Jason's growing erection. "He was in no shape to train a monkey."

"What I don't understand," Jason said, letting out a soft moan. "Is how did he get Demetre's phone?"

"Demetre must have left it at his apartment the day Mia died," Angelo offered.

"But you called him after midnight," Jason said, grabbing ahold of Angelo's hips for traction.

The last thing Angelo wanted was to discuss this case. He felt more inclined to getting naked in bed with Jason, feeling aroused now himself.

"Think about it?" Jason continued. "Demetre called you from Yossi's apartment, right? Then, after he killed Mia Garcia, or so he thought, he packed her in a suitcase and drove back to New Jersey." Jason hopped up and began pacing. "We know he didn't leave his cell phone at Yossi's because you called him after midnight." Jason stopped pacing. He stared out the window, arms folded, deep in thought. "The only possible explanation is that Yossi was with him while Mia seized and when you called later that night."

Suddenly, Angelo's interest was piqued. "So, he doesn't have Demetre's phone. He only knows what he heard?"

"I bet you a million bucks he doesn't have Demetre's phone," Jason said, his eyes searing with clarity. "Yossi helped Demetre dispose of Mia's body. I don't care how small she was, digging a hole in a garage and pouring concrete is not a one-man job."

Angelo marveled at the way Jason pieced together the crime. Though it was fascinating, Jason's theory had one major flaw. "The homicide detectives ruled out Yossi," Angelo said. "He was training a client. Remember?"

Jason plopped back on the sofa. "I wonder how airtight his alibi is?"

"Airtight?" Angelo repeated, kissing Jason's neck. "Do cops really talk like they do on television?"

Jason chuckled, his erection returning. "Yeah, we say lots of things like, 'keep your hands up, spread your legs, don't make a move.'"

"Is that an order?" Angelo asked. He reached down to massage Jason's bulging groin.

"You bet your ass it is."

"I just hope Yossi doesn't bother Camille or me again," Angelo said, turning serious again.

"Tell you what," Jason moaned, grinding up against Angelo. "I'll call Farrell tomorrow to confirm Yossi's alibi is airtight, and if that asshole bothers you again, tell him your boyfriend is a cop."

"Boyfriend?" Angelo began unbuttoning Jason's jeans to slip his hand inside. "I like the sound of that."

"Oh, so now you like that word?"

He firmly wrapped his hand around Jason's cock. "I like it only because you're referring to me," Angelo replied.

"Come here, boyfriend." Jason stood up and clumsily led Angelo to the bed, his jeans puddled around his ankles. Collapsing on the mattress, they kicked off their shoes and shed their pants. They slid under the duvet. Angelo wriggled over to press against Jason and held him. Angelo reveled in the feelings of this newfound love and the protection his boyfriend provided.

The next morning, Angelo awoke feeling light, thinking at last he was seeing a way through this long dark corridor that had been his first year of practice. How grateful he would be once he closed the door and moved beyond these tragic twelve months.

Climbing up the subway stairs, the door Angelo hoped to close suddenly flung wide open. That optimistic streak faded once he saw Yossi across the avenue, waiting outside the clinic. He was leaning against the wall, wearing a black leather motorcycle jacket, mirrored aviators, and a tight, white T-shirt. He dropped his head and glared at Angelo over his sunglasses. "You're making a big mistake ignoring me."

Angelo summoned all the strength he had and confronted Yossi. "The police are looking for you." The clinic security guard caught Angelo's eye. "Can you help me?" he shouted to him.

The guard stepped outside. "Is everything okay, Dr. Perrotta?"

Yossi took off his sunglasses and hung them on the neck of his T-shirt. "So, you want to play?"

"This man is bothering me," Angelo told the security guard. "Can you call the police."

The security guard pulled out his cell phone.

"You fucked with the wrong person," said Yossi, inching closer to Angelo. "They're going to take your license away. Say bye-bye to your career."

That last part roused a prickly sensation in Angelo's chest, not the obsidian, but something more like fear. Still, Angelo felt he needed to remain steadfast. He walked into the clinic and never turned back.

That night, Angelo returned home to find Camille sitting on the couch, biting her thumbnail. "What's wrong?" he asked. She jutted her chin at the kitchen table. A certified letter sat in the center. Angelo picked it up. It was from the Office of Professional Medical Conduct (OPMC). Angelo felt a twitch of pain in his chest. He tore it open and read it out loud.

"What the hell does any of that mean?" Camille asked after he finished reading.

"It means the OPMC is investigating my professional relationship with SkinDem."

"What are you going to do?" she asked, still biting her nail.

"There's a number," he said. "I'll call them now."

"It's after five," Camille said with obvious distress. "They're probably closed."

"Then I'll call them in the morning," Angelo said, trying to maintain an even tone of voice. "Camille don't get worked up over this. I'll call them in the morning and explain everything. Please, don't get upset." Even as he said those words,

Angelo could hear the quavering in his voice. He was sure Camille heard it too. "I have to tell Jason."

"You think Yossi's behind this?" she asked.

"I don't know, Camille," Angelo said, reaching for his phone but stopped short, remembering Jason's final evaluation was coming up, and his promise not to burden him unnecessarily. "On second thought, I'll call Jason after I speak with the OPMC."

"Why is Yossi doing this?" she continued. "What does he want?"

"He's desperate," Angelo replied. "Jason told me that Yossi is here on an expired visa. Not only does Farrell want to speak with him but now, so does immigration."

"Yea, but the damage is done," Camille said, gesturing toward the certified letter.

"Camille, relax," Angelo insisted. "I'll call the office tomorrow. They'll understand after I explain my side."

The next morning, Angelo called the office of the OPMC. An operator connected him to his case director. "Kraemer here."

"Hello. My name is Angelo Perrotta."

Kraemer cut in. "Doctor, you should contact your malpractice carrier and speak to a lawyer."

"There must be some misunderstanding," Angelo said. "I haven't done anything wrong. Why do I need a lawyer?"

Angelo heard the frustrated sigh of someone who'd heard that response a thousand times. "Doctor, we really shouldn't be having this conversation. I'm telling you what to do. Call your malpractice carrier and inform them you're being investigated by the OPMC. Trust me. They'll know how to advise you."

"You can't even give me an idea what this is all about?" Angelo pleaded.

"I think you know exactly what this is about." He chuckled, disconcerting Angelo by seeming to mock him for playing dumb.

Angelo knew many physicians who went their entire careers without being investigated or sued. He had managed to achieve both in twelve months. Of course, he needed legal representation, but the thought of calling his malpractice carrier seemed like a bad idea. He couldn't afford another increase, not after the Violet Trautman lawsuit. Worse, they could drop him completely, and that he couldn't afford. He needed to work now more than ever.

He confided in a colleague at the clinic who suggested he retain a lawyer on his own and recommended one named Joe Rudnick. Angelo called Rudnick's office immediately and made an appointment. The receptionist informed Angelo he had to pay a five-thousand-dollar retainer that day. Angelo didn't have the money. Knowing Camille, she would have happily borrowed against her 401K, but he wanted to involve her only peripherally. Angelo still hadn't told her about the malpractice case, so he decided to charge the retainer on his credit card.

Rudnick's office was on East Fifty-Seventh Street. The receptionist escorted Angelo to a room with frosted glass walls. Seated at a long conference table, he sipped water as he admired the audiovisual equipment, the stack of yellow legal pads, an assortment of refreshments, and a plate of soft-baked, chocolate chip cookies.

Rudnick entered the room abruptly. He was tall, tan and wore thick framed glasses. Behind him was a petite, younger woman, wearing a crisp navy suit and shiny, brown flats. Rudnick shook Angelo's hand and introduced the woman as Ilene Van Gortz. "Ilene will be assisting me on your case." The thought that Angelo had a case, which needed a team of lawyers, unnerved him.

Rudnick listened to Angelo while Ilene took notes. His intense eye contact made Angelo feel like he was sitting in the principal's office. "Why don't you tell us about your relationship with Mr. Kostas."

Angelo started to speak, hearing the familiar quaver in his voice, but the more he spoke, he began to regain his confidence. All the while, his eyes wandered over Rudnick, stealing glimpses of his gold cufflinks, the faded scar that cut through his left eyebrow, and the peculiar way his pinstripe suit bunched up behind his neck. Once Angelo finished his story—the one he had carefully prepared and rehearsed staring in the bathroom mirror—Rudnick frowned, glancing briefly at Ilene. "I spoke with Mr. Kraemer this morning," he said.

"Yes, and?"

He flashed an accusatorial smile. "Are you sure there's nothing more you want to add to your story?"

"Like what?"

"Did you have a sexual relationship with Mr. Kostas?" Rudnick asked.

"No!"

"Did you perform medical consultations for SkinDem clients?"

"Demetre once asked me to look at someone's mole," Angelo replied.

"From now on please refer to him as Mr. Kostas." Rudnick's self-confidence was daunting. Then he leaned forward, discharging more questions in a cannonade. "How many times did Mr. Kostas ask you to assess suspicious lesions? Were you paid by SkinDem to perform these duties? Did you supply Mr. Kostas with prescriptions for his clients?"

The jolt of his questions caused Angelo to push his chair away from the table. "No! No! No!"

Rudnick sat back, smiling self-assuredly. "That's exactly how Mr. Kraemer is going to question you. What you need to do now is tell us everything. You're safe here, but we can't protect you if hold back anything. This is not a malpractice case, and the pending outcome of Violet Trautman's case may have some bearing on the OPMC's decision. But their primary focus is whether or not you did anything unethical."

Ilene rhythmically tapped her pen as she listened. "By the way, what is the status of that malpractice suit?"

"My lawyer said Trautman had surgery and requires no further treatment," Angelo replied very quickly. "We're waiting for them to agree on a settlement."

Rudnick's eyes rolled. "As I see it, the OPMC's investigation can go one of three ways: one, you can be found innocent of any wrong-doing, two, you can receive a letter of censure, which would go on record, or three, they can suspend or revoke your license."

"Revoke my license, but I haven't done anything."

Rudnick's concerned expression faded into harsh frustration. "Dr. Perrotta, the OPMC has in their possession a copy of all of Mr. Kostas's emails. You realize, oftentimes, we write things in an email we might not want anyone else to read. Since you no longer work for Dr. Stanzione, you don't have access to those email exchanges. So, I'm asking you, do you recall writing anything, *anything*, that might be incriminating?"

"What sort of thing?"

Rudnick and Ilene exchanged smirks. "Come on Angelo. You can drop this babe-in-the-woods routine."

His directness was chilling. "Listen, I'm sure you've seen and heard it all before, but I'm not playing dumb," Angelo said, sitting forward. "I haven't done anything unethical. Demetre and I were friends. We had drinks after work. One time. Nothing more."

"Nothing more?" Rudnick repeated like a mother questioning her teenager with liquor breath. "It's not illegal to screw your colleague, but I need to know."

"I didn't screw around with Demetre," Angelo insisted. His heart palpitated. For a moment, he thought he might pass out. The stress of it all weighed heavily on him. More than he knew. He pressed a hand to his chest and poured a glass of water.

"I'm not being cruel," Rudnick said softly. "I'm on your side."

Angelo half-listened, gulping down water until the light-headedness passed. "Has anyone spoken to Laura Ellis?"

Ilene jumped in and explained that after Demetre's arrest, no one had been able to locate her. She had changed her phone number, and the certified letters mailed to her address were returned.

"Laura ran Demetre's practice," Angelo explained. "She would be a key witness to support my argument that I was not the medical director and that Stanzione was the acting director."

"Rudnick held up a finger. "The OPMC is only interested in knowing whether or not you were a paid employee of SkinDem or received gifts in-kind for services."

"I never received a dime from SkinDem."

"Good," Rudnick said. "Because frankly, Dr. Perrotta, I couldn't care less what the nature of your relationship with Mr. Kostas was as long as you did it on your own personal time and with your own money. However, if there is any shred of evidence that you were SkinDem's medical director or wrote prescriptions for Mr. Kostas, then you can forget all about practicing medicine ever again."

Riding the train home that evening, Angelo felt like he was being shipped off to a prison camp. He was bereft of emotion, not feeling angry or sad, but numb. A complete sense of detachment had overtaken him. Defeat seemed inevitable, and there was little more he could do than allow the process to play out. The only sliver of hope he clung to was the idea that regardless of the outcome, he could pick up the pieces of what was left of his life and move forward.

Kraemer had informed Rudnick that a witness accused Angelo of having a sexual relationship with Demetre Kostas.

Yossi Cohen had testified during the initial police investigation that Demetre and Angelo had discussed opening a medical spa, but other than that, he had no idea who was SkinDem's medical director. When Rudnick pressed Kraemer further, he said that despite the Mr. Cohen's testimony, it was the consultation with Mrs. Trautman, the discussion about opening a medical spa, and the prescription pads found in Mr. Kostas's possession that forced the OPMC to launch an investigation.

Rudnick had tried to assure Angelo that Yossi's testimony held little weight, but he felt he was only being optimistic for his benefit. Angelo had a gnawing sensation how this would end. "Regardless of how this unfolds," Rudnick had said. "The good news is that you will never do anything wrong again."

Angelo found no comfort in that thought. None at all.

CHAPTER NINETEEN

Angelo called Jason after his meeting with Rudnick and informed him about the OPMC investigation. "Why didn't you tell me once you got the letter?" Jason asked.

"You have your final evaluation coming up," Angelo explained. "I don't want to put any extra pressure on you."

"Don't worry about that," Jason said. "As long as I have you, I'll pass that evaluation with flying colors."

That night, with Jason by his side, Angelo told Camille everything, including the part about the malpractice case. "The basis for the OPMC investigation," Angelo explained, "has only to do with my professional relationship with Skin-Dem. Nothing more." She accepted the news. Still, Angelo could see the lines of worry on her face. Angelo never told Tammy he was being investigated by the OPMC. No point. They hadn't seen each other since that awkward brunch. From that day on, they only communicated through texts. Angelo was lost in reveries when Jason called his name. "I'm sorry," he said. "What did you say?"

"Didn't you say you advised Demetre to consult with a dermatologist about Violet Trautman?" Jason asked. "Something about erring on the side of caution, right?"

"It doesn't matter what I said at this point."

"You sure you didn't say that inside the exam room?" Jason pressed.

Angelo felt so exhausted, he hardly had the strength to answer. "I'm sure because I remember Laura shushed us."

Camille's eyes widened. "Who's Laura?"

Angelo hung his head. "She was the office manager of SkinDem."

Jason leaned forward. "Do you think she heard you?"

"You know . . . I hadn't thought about it," Angelo replied, lifting his head. "Laura has the hearing of a dog."

Camille bounced in her seat, patting Jason on the back. "Good thinking, Officer Jason.

"Chill, Camille," Angelo cut in. "No one's been able to locate Laura. Besides, the inquiry is next week. Even if we found her tomorrow, there's a good chance she won't cooperate."

Jason winked at Camille. "It's worth a try."

Camille hugged Jason's arm. "I love you."

The next day at work, Angelo found it impossible to concentrate. He kept glancing at his phone, hoping Jason would call to say he'd located Laura Ellis. By lunchtime, any lingering hope had withered away, leaving behind the dashed remains that even if he found her, she would never agree to help him.

Why would she?

Later that afternoon, he received a call from an unknown number. The phone trembled in his hands. Two versions of Angelo debated whether to answer it or not. In the end, curious Angelo won. "Yes."

"You fucked with the wrong person." Immediately, Angelo recognized Yossi's accent.

He didn't respond. What more did he have to say? He quietly hung up and sat in silence. A few minutes later, Angelo called Jason to check in. "Any luck finding Laura?"

"No, babe," he replied. "My partner and I drove to Ellis's apartment. The super said she moved out weeks ago once reporters started showing up outside the building. But don't worry, I'll find her."

"Okay, will I see you later?" Angelo asked. "I'm meeting Camille to look at an apartment. We'll be home around seven if you want to join us for dinner."

"I'll text you," Jason said. "There are a few leads I'd like to follow up on before calling it quits for the day."

"One more thing," Angelo said. "Yossi just called me."

"What did that asshole want?"

"I don't know," Angelo said. "I hung up."

"You did the right thing," Jason said. "Text me later."

Once Angelo had seen the last patient, he threw on his jacket and grabbed his backpack. Outside, the night was chilly and rainy. Pulling up his collar, Angelo hurried across the street toward the subway station.

"Oh, doctor . . . ."

Angelo caught a glimpse of the metal as he turned his head, just as someone struck a pipe into his temple, baring his teeth like a rabid dog.

Sometime later, flashes of glowing streetlights blinked on and off. Angelo's head throbbed. Face down on the sidewalk, blood puddled around his head, sticky like candy apples and stinky like pennies. Strange voices spoke to him. He wanted to answer them, but he remained quiet, breathing heavily. A siren approached, and he sighed with relief.

He woke up fully in the emergency room. Camille stood over him, needling her eyebrows. He wanted to make a joke, but when he opened his mouth, the pain shot to the back of his neck. "Thank God you're awake," Camille said. Tears streamed out of the corners of his eyes. "You're in the hospital. Someone attacked you."

Angelo attempted to speak, but it came out garbled. He reached up to touch the spot where he had been struck, but he only felt the gauze wrapped around his head. Jason appeared, panting. He leaned in and kissed Angelo on the lips. "I came as soon as I heard." Angelo attempted to speak again, but they couldn't understand him. His mouth felt like it was packed with cotton. "Don't talk," Jason urged and turning to Camille asked, "What happened?"

"We had an appointment to look at an apartment," she began. "Angelo was late, so I called his cell. A nurse answered and explained he had been attacked. Someone had struck him in the head. A policeman said they didn't think it was a robbery because Angelo still had his wallet."

"I'm going to see if anyone knows more," Jason said, but Angelo refused to let go of his hand. "Babe, I'll be right back."

Angelo squeezed his eyes shut, shaking his head. He raised his hand and scribbled in the air. "He wants to write something," Camille said, fishing in her handbag. She handed Angelo a pen and a paper towel. His hands were shaky, but he only needed to write one word.

Camille raised her hand to her mouth. "Yossi?"

A strained silenced followed, broken only by the voice of a nurse, "Dr. Perrotta, we're going to send you upstairs for a CAT scan. Your family can wait for you in the lounge."

Angelo watched his boyfriend stretch his arm across his sister's shoulder as her eyes welled with emotion. He could only imagine what they saw looking at his face as the nurse wheeled his stretcher away.

The hospital discharged Angelo after a night of observation. He had sustained a minor concussion and a laceration above his left eye. They took a cab home, and Angelo lay in bed for hours silently brooding. When he woke up sometime later, Camille was staring at him. He moved to get up to use the bathroom. Camille hopped up to help him. He splashed cold water on his face. Staring at his reflection, he thought his appearance looked monstrous: gauze wrapped head, left eye swollen, and the surrounding skin mottled with red and blue bruising.

Angelo willed himself to remember those final moments before he passed out. Lying on the sidewalk bleeding, Angelo recalled Yossi's expression being ferocious in its intensity. Angelo popped two painkillers in his mouth. He wanted nothing more than to get back in bed, pull the covers over his head, and sink blissfully into a state of numbness.

Angelo heard his cell phone ringing. Camille knocked on the bathroom door. "It's Detective Farrell. Do you want to speak to him?"

"Yes," he uttered, thinking his voice sounded unlike himself. Angelo took the phone from Camille and got back in bed. "Hello?"

"I heard what happened to you," Farrell said. "Just so you know, two detectives went to Mr. Cohen's apartment. It was a mess, like someone had burgled it."

Angelo's jaw trembled as he responded, "Should I be worried?"

"We're doing our best to find him," Farrell continued. "I do have good news."

Angelo couldn't see beyond his own pain to believe there was anything that would qualify as good news other than informing him that Yossi was behind bars.

"We've located Kostas."

A shocked silence enveloped the room as Angelo stared at Camille. She mouthed, 'what', but Angelo, lost in reveries, was to too overwhelmed to speak.

"Where did you find Demetre?" he asked.

Camille's knees buckled, and she sat down on the bed next to him. "Oh, my God!" she shouted.

"He's in Venezuela," Farrell said.

"He's in Venez-fucking-uela?" Angelo said, his voice rising.

The news didn't make Angelo as excited as Camille. A part of him always believed they'd find Demetre, but he no longer wanted to hear his name again. It only brought on the grinding nervousness in Angelo's chest. For weeks, Angelo had fought so hard to make Demetre a weak memory of a disastrous mistake. A guilt he had endured and wallowed in, which finally had receded, but now rushed back like being struck by a tidal wave.

"How were you able to trace his phone to Venezuela?" Angelo asked

"We didn't," Farrell said. "You're not going to believe this story, but Demetre was stripping at a gay bar. The club owner recognized him from the news and reported him to the local police."

"Stripping?" Angelo repeated. "This is beyond all comprehension."

"Well, it's true," Farrell said. "We sent two detectives to Caracas today. I'll follow up with you when I know more. I just couldn't wait to give you the good news. I figured you deserved it after what had happened."

"Thank you, Detective Farrell. Thank you so much."

STRIPPER QUACK FOUND DANCING GO-GO
IN SOUTH AMERICAN GAY BAR

Venezuela – Fraud Doctor suspected of killing twenty-eight-year-old Mia Garcia during a botched plastic surgery procedure was found living the gay high life. New York City detectives believe Demetre Kostas fled the United States after Garcia's death. Kostas became the prime suspect after Garcia's body was found buried in a suitcase under a concrete slab in the garage of his New Jersey home.

Kostas entered Caracas three days after Garcia was scheduled to see him at an apartment on West Twenty-Second Street in Manhattan where he was performing illegal procedures. Kostas had been out on bail while awaiting sentencing for practicing without a license.

One week after Garcia's death, Kostas was seen stripping at a popular gay hot spot in Caracas. The owner of Fuerza identified Kostas from his pictures. A bartender said that Kostas could be seen lounging by the pool and sipping cocktails by day, then go-go dancing in the club at night.

Immigration officials state that Kostas entered under a visa and hasn't left the country using the passport he showed to enter. Since Garcia's cause of death is still pending, an arrest warrant can't be issued. The District Attorney's office intends on nabbing Kostas for bail jumping. New York prosecutors said the charge is not an extraditable offense, but it would keep the quack surgeon in jail until they can charge him with an offense that is. Two NYPD detectives are planning to hunt for the fugitive in Caracas today.

Camille and Angelo sat on the couch reading the newspaper with amused bewilderment. The idea of Demetre dancing go-go at his age at night and sipping cocktails by the pool during the day, while on the run for murder, was absurd. Angelo kept telling himself he had nothing to do with Mia's death, but he couldn't deny he felt some strange connection to the woman bullied as "rabbit girl." In the aftermath of her murder, he knew that when they finally arrested Demetre, the story wouldn't be over. He had to see it through to the end.

♦♦♦

Demetre's lawyers fought his extradition but lost. Two weeks after the news broke the story, Demetre arrived in New York. The newspaper ran an article with a photo showing him being led into custody wearing a Hawaiian shirt, beige shorts, and handcuffs. He was much thinner than Angelo remembered. The article suggested that Demetre had been mistreated in prison. His lawyer stated that the Venezuelan police prevented him from taking his HIV medication, and he had lost nearly fifteen pounds.

Once the court set the hearing date, Angelo called Farrell, insisting he wanted to attend. Initially, Camille didn't understand why, but then she came around. Angelo knew it had to do with her therapy. She had been seeing a psychologist and attending a support group for battered women at Val's recommendation.

Here was a woman abused for years who finally found the strength to confront her harrowing past. Had it not been for Val's influence, he didn't think Camille would have felt confident enough to file for divorce. She might have even gone back to Trace, but that clearly was not the case once she started speaking to the other women in her group.

A few days after Detective Farrell confirmed Angelo could attend the hearing, Camille made it a point to tell him that she had a change of heart. "I was wrong," she said one night at dinner. "You should go. It'll bring you closure."

Even more surprising, Jason agreed. "I think seeing him now, you'll see the real Demetre and not the man you created in your head."

That night in bed, Angelo thought about closure. What a peculiar concept. Angelo wondered how many people thought their happiness was derived from their proximity to closure. And now, he too was hoping, like a cripple visiting Lourdes, to be rescued from this burden of guilt, this nightmare, if only he could witness Demetre's hearing.

Angelo sat in the back of the courtroom, away from the eager eyes of news reporters all drawn for a glimpse of the murderer. Apart from the fact there was no jury, the only thing that struck Angelo as peculiar was the smell—a mixture of mildew and paper, like a library after a flood. Sitting in the courtroom, Angelo wondered what Demetre would look like in person.

A tall man in his midfifties brushed past him and sat down at the prosecution's table. He turned around and spoke to an old woman seated in the front row. It was Mia's mother. Angelo hadn't noticed her until now. Scanning the courtroom for other familiar faces, he wondered if Tim was present. Perhaps he, too, needed closure to free him from an onerous existence, just as Angelo was hoping for, but there was no sign of him.

A flurry of activity drew everyone's attention to the front of the courtroom. A door opened and a guard escorted a man into the courtroom. It was Demetre, dressed in a suit. He was clean-shaven, hair styled, but his face was gaunt and his complexion leaden. Angelo sat up, hoping to get a better look as Demetre shuffled into the courtroom, eyes fixed on the floor as he sat down quickly. Within minutes everyone rose as Justice Emilio Valentino entered the courtroom. A short, dark-skinned man wearing round, wire-rimmed glasses, Valentino took his seat on the bench.

Just as Angelo sat back, his eyes veered over to Demetre who stared back at him. The room fell quiet, and amidst that brief moment of silence, Angelo marshaled every bit of courage he had to hold his stare. He seemed to look through Angelo, enduring this hearing with the incomprehension of someone who had decided long ago that he was impervious to the law. Demetre dropped him one of his trademarked slow winks and turned away as soon as the judge began to speak.

Demetre was charged with murder and pled guilty to first-degree assault as part of a deal with prosecutors in exchange for a twenty-year prison sentence. "Mr. Kostas," Valentino said. "Were you under the influence of cocaine while attempting to perform a procedure on Miss Garcia?"

"Yes, Your Honor," Demetre said woefully.

Valentino dropped his chin to leer at him over his glasses. "In order for me to accept your plea I would like to hear, in your own words, exactly what happened that day."

Demetre cleared his throat, then coughed into his fist. "Miss Garcia came to the apartment that morning." His tone was coarse but still as low and soothing as Angelo remembered. "I injected her lip with 3cc of lidocaine. She began to shake. That's when I called a friend."

A sense of dread rose in Angelo's throat.

"This friend," Valentino said, "was a doctor?"

Demetre tugged his shirt collar. "Yes."

"And what did this real doctor tell you to do?"

Demetre looked at his lawyer and back at the judge. "He told me to call 911."

Mia's mother began to sob. It seemed as if the entire courtroom turned in unison to gaze at her.

The sound of the gavel caused Angelo to flinch. "Why didn't you call 911?" Valentino asked.

Now full attention was back on Demetre. "Because . . . ." He was silent for a moment. "Because I had already been arrested for practicing medicine without a license."

A grumbling arose from the crowd. Valentino's gavel came down again, twice. Angelo could feel the entire weight of it, shooting throughout his body. "So, you ignored the advice of a true medical professional to spare yourself the indignity of a longer prison sentence." Valentino shook his head in slow emphasis of his disgust. There was a long pause. Mia's mother's muffled sobs were all Angelo could hear. "You realize, had you listened to that doctor, Miss Garcia could very well still be alive?"

Demetre didn't say a word. No flippant remark from the man who always spoke his mind. But there, in that moment, he braced himself against the table as his knees buckled, collapsing helplessly forward. A guard stepped forward to catch him before he fell to the ground. "I think we need a medic!" the guard shouted.

More grumbling. Another strike of the gavel. "Order! Order!"

Angelo turned away. He had had enough. Closure was not to be gained from observing this hearing. Did he really think Demetre was going to offer an analysis of his inscrutable behavior? Or had Angelo simply wanted to see him again, and now that they had looked each other in the eye, realized that there was nothing between them any longer? That vibration he felt the first night they had drinks in his office had stilled.

Walking to the subway, the sun shining brightly in the warm April sky, Angelo realized everything had changed for him. For years he had worked hard and studied long hours to become a doctor so that he could enjoy the sweet riches of a lifestyle he felt had alluded him. He thought he had chosen wisely throughout his career. The truth was that he had made mistake after mistake, and the damage those poor decisions wrought would haunt him forever.

Angelo was not liberated from guilt listening to Demetre tell everyone in the courtroom that he acted on his own, because he did not see it that way. The way Angelo understood it, a woman died because of an addict's false confidence, and there was no denying Angelo's peripheral involvement in her murder. Deep down inside, Angelo still believed this tragedy was partly his fault.

That night, Angelo and Camille ate dinner at Jason's apartment. They were celebrating. As Jason had predicted, he passed his final psychiatric evaluation. "Raise a glass, please," Angelo said. "To my wonderful boyfriend, Jason. Congratulations."

They clinked glasses. Just as they were about to start eating, Angelo received a call from his lawyer, Rudnick. He informed Angelo that the OPMC had granted Angelo a two-week extension, but as Angelo suspected, they were still moving forward with the inquiry.

"Maybe when they see my face," Angelo said, "Kraemer will take pity on me."

"You can hardly see the bruising," Jason insisted, "but if you're going to play the sympathy card, why not go full tilt boogie. Rewrap your head in gauze and hobble in using crutches."

"Or maybe," Angelo said, "Kraemer will judge me harshly for associating with a nefarious group of lying, stealing, cheating, drug using blackmailers."

"Don't forget murderers," Camille chimed in.

Angelo hung his head, suddenly he failed to see the humor in this conversation.

"I'm sorry," Camille said. "That wasn't funny."

Angelo stood up and put on his jacket. "I'm gonna head home."

"No," Jason begged. "We're celebrating."

He couldn't explain why he'd reacted so dramatically. But Demetre's hearing earlier that day and his own with the OPMC felt like he was on an endless journey through a quagmire of human misery.

"I'm not mad," Angelo said, "I'm just in a bad mood. Whatever Yossi said to OPMC doesn't matter anyway. I signed a letter stating I was the medical director for SkinDem. I consulted with Demetre's client and failed to document my recommendation. That woman could have died because of me. The OPMC has everything they need. I have to face the fact that I might lose my license."

Jason stood up and held Angelo, but his body was stiff.

"I know this is hard for you," Jason said, "but you've got to find the strength to get past this, and you *will* get past this."

"I'm beaten down, Jason," Angelo said. "I don't have any strength left. Literally, what else could go wrong? With my luck, I'll probably get hit by a truck crossing the street."

"Look on the bright side," Jason encouraged. "Now that we have an extension, I have more time to find Laura Ellis."

Angelo broke free from Jason's embrace. "Stop trying to make me feel better. You're not going to find her. I have to face the fact that this will likely end badly for me."

Jason took Angelo's hand and led him to the couch. "Sit down."

Angelo obliged, but he refused to take off his jacket. "I've hit my breaking point."

"You know what you need?" Jason asked. "You need a break from all of this. Why don't we get out of town? Let's go away for the weekend."

"Sure," Angelo said sarcastically. "Why don't I call Steven and see if he's renting rooms in P-town?"

"Come on," Jason urged. "It would be good to go away. Maybe New Hope or Asbury Park. We can stay at an inn or a bed-and-breakfast."

"That sounds like the perfect idea," Camille interjected.

Angelo's eyes glazed over with the kind of vacant expression seen on zombies. "Inn?"

"Or a hotel," Jason offered. "Whichever you like."

Angelo stood up. "I just remembered something. Laura Ellis said she grew up on the Cape. Her parents owned an inn."

The three exchanged surprised glances. Jason hopped up and ran to his computer. His fingers ran across the keys like a pianist. "I wonder if that's where Laura is now?" Jason ventured. A search online identified hundreds of inns on the Cape.

"Talk about finding a needle in a haystack," Angelo said, peering over Jason's shoulder.

"Let's try narrowing it down." Jason added *Ellis* to the search, and there it was: The Ellis Island Inn, owned by Lydia and George Ellis. The three stood there gaping at the website like a portal to another dimension had opened. They were free-falling toward excitement but soon crashed as if they hit a wall when they saw that the Ellis Island Inn had closed.

"Maybe Laura's parents got too old to manage it?" Camille speculated.

Further searching by Jason revealed that George Ellis had died right before the inn officially closed.

"Well, there's your answer," Angelo said.

"Check if Lydia has an obituary," Camille urged. Jason typed her name, but nothing came up. "That's a good sign."

"How is that a good sign?" Angelo asked.

"I bet you the old lady still lives there," Camille explained. "Too many memories. You know how old people get about leaving their homes."

"Camille makes a good point," Jason said. "It's still worth a shot. We can stay at a bed-and-breakfast nearby. What do you say?"

"A road trip?" Angelo asked. "Looking like Frankenstein's monster?"

"It would be good for you to get out of the city," Camille pointed out. "Good for all of us."

Angelo was running on the remaining fumes of endurance fueled by too much caffeine. He could hardly deny the ridiculousness of taking a trip at this time, looking the way he did, but he could not resist the tug of excitement a weekend away would provide.

Angelo conceded. "Okay, but only because Jason deserves this trip for putting up with all the Perrotta drama."

"Pack your bags, Camille," Jason broke in. "We're heading to New England."

At six o'clock Friday morning, they packed Jason's car and headed to the Cape for the weekend. Camille stretched out across the backseat. Within minutes she conked out. Angelo scanned the radio for music. It began to rain, soaking the road signs and windshield in a dull, bathwater light as the tires thrummed along the highway.

No one felt like speaking. As much as everyone wanted to believe this was a weekend getaway, the fact remained that they were on a mission to save Angelo. Six hours later they arrived in Harwich, where Jason had reserved joining rooms at the Breezy Point Inn. A two-story building, each room had its own entrance, like a motel, but the Breezy Point Inn had a traditional lobby entrance, a café, and a restaurant overlooking the ocean.

Steps away stood the Ellis Island Inn. A Victorian house with a strip of motel rooms around back, it had darkened windows and a stillness that chilled them as they stared from across the street. The sign had a banner that read: CLOSED.

Checking in, Jason chatted up the Breezy Point innkeeper as Camille and Angelo stood by in silence.

"Is this your first time visiting the Cape?" he asked.

"Not mine," Jason said. "My family and I came here every summer when I was younger. We used to stay at the Ellis Island Inn. I see it closed down."

"It was too much for Mrs. Ellis after George died," the innkeeper explained.

"George," Jason repeated. "I remember him. Whatever happened to Mrs. Ellis?"

The innkeeper's eyes narrowed. "She still lives in the house."

Jason glanced over at Camille and Angelo; their eyes were wide with excitement.

"Poor Mrs. Ellis," Jason continued, hoping the innkeeper would take the bait. "All alone in that big house."

"Oh, she's not alone," the innkeeper corrected. "Her daughter returned from New York."

"Her daughter . . . Laura?"

"That would be her," the innkeeper confirmed. "She quit her job as a nurse and moved back to help her parents."

"Thank you," Jason said to the innkeeper as he accepted the keys.

"Enjoy your stay."

After settling into their rooms, they ate dinner at the Crown and Anchor. The sound of the waves crashing, the salty air filling their nostrils, had finally cracked through the cocoon of tension that had formed around them.

"I can't tell you the last time I had lobster," Camille said, wiping her buttery fingers on the plastic bib.

"Tomorrow, after breakfast, you and I will pay a visit to the Ellis house," Jason said to Angelo.

Angelo nodded, feeling somewhat solemn and content to be out of the city with Yossi still on the loose.

"Did you know Laura was a nurse?" Jason asked.

"I had no idea."

"Why would she work as a receptionist slash manager if she's a nurse?" Camille asked.

"Good question," Jason said. "I don't know the answer. At least we know there's a good chance she's here."

Angelo half-listened, hypnotized by the outgoing tide leaving foam on the sand as it receded back into the ocean. He ate the rest of his dinner in silence—still intoxicated by the surroundings—acknowledging that even if Laura refused to speak with them, this trip would not have been in vain.

CHAPTER TWENTY

An attractive, elderly woman with silver hair answered the door. She had Laura's steely blue eyes. Though her skin was creased like parchment, Angelo thought the resemblance was uncanny.

"Mrs. Ellis?" Jason inquired.

"Who wants to know?" she asked with a thick New England accent.

"I'm Jason Murphy, NYPD," he replied, flashing his badge.

Her expression soured like she smelled an onion. "How may I help you?"

"We'd like to talk with your daughter, Laura," Jason said.

"I'm afraid I can't help you there."

Her maternal instincts kicked in, thought Angelo. Expected, considering they hadn't provided Mrs. Ellis with any context for their surprise visit. Two strangers appearing at the front door of an old woman's house in a small New England town. What other reaction had they expected from her?

"Mrs. Ellis, my name is Dr. Angelo Perrotta. I used to work with your daughter. We mean no harm. I simply want to speak with Laura. Please, can you tell us how to find her?"

The old woman didn't answer—she seemed too busy fumbling to close the door. Somewhere inside the house, a voice called out.

"Let them in, Mother. It's all right."

The old woman stepped aside, and there stood Laura Ellis. She wore khaki shorts and a faded blue T-shirt. Her hair was brushed back into a high ponytail. This version of Laura stunned Angelo. He had never seen her look so casual.

"Well, look what the cat dragged in," Laura commented with sarcasm.

Angelo didn't take the bait. "Can we talk?"

She surveyed Angelo's face curiously and craned her neck to see if there was anyone else, reporters perhaps, waiting in the bushes. "What do you want?"

"Just to talk," he assured her. "We'll only be a few minutes."

Glancing furtively over her shoulder—where her mother stood in the shadows—she turned back to them. With a quivering lip, she stepped aside to allow them in. Laura led Jason and Angelo through the bleach-scented foyer and into a large living area with the sun streaming through a bay window. Their footsteps creaked against the floorboards. The peeling wallpaper gave the house the appearance of scaly skin, but this home thrummed with life. Poised beyond, the chilly ocean awaited them.

"How'd you find me" Laura asked. She motioned toward the sofa as her mother politely offered tea. Without waiting for them to reply, she retreated to the kitchen to fetch some.

"You said you grew up on the Cape," Angelo explained, "and that your parents owned an inn."

"Good memory," she said, offering a taut smile. Looking at Jason, she asked, "Are you really a cop?"

"He's here unofficially," Angelo said, placing his hand on Jason's knee. "He's my boyfriend."

Laura smirked, sitting back. "How sweet."

Mrs. Ellis returned, carrying a tray. The cups rattled as she set it down on the coffee table. Wringing her hands, she stared expectantly at her daughter.

"Mom, can you give us some privacy?" Laura reached up and gave her mother's hand a squeeze.

Mrs. Ellis had a pained expression on her face. "Whatever you say dear. I'll just be in the kitchen."

Once Mrs. Ellis exited the room, Laura's demeanor shifted sharply. "You got a lot of nerve coming here looking like you were knocked out in a prize fight. Nice touch bringing along a police officer to intimidate my mother and me."

"We're here to ask if you recall the day Violet Trautman came in to have a mole removed?" Jason asked.

Laura offered him a narrow-eyed look. Angelo liked the way Jason commandeered the conversation, maintaining an offensive approach to keep Laura on the defense.

"Violet Trautman, how could anyone forget her," Laura said. "What about it?"

"Mrs. Trautman is suing me because Demetre documented that I had said her mole was benign," Angelo said, "but outside the exam room, I said he should send her to a dermatologist. After Demetre was arrested, her lawyers want a bigger settlement, and on top of that, I'm being investigated for medical misconduct."

"Do you know Yossi Cohen?" Jason asked.

The whistle of the tea kettle caught Laura's attention. On cue, Mrs. Ellis entered to pour. "Thank you, Mother." Once Mrs. Ellis retreated back to the kitchen, Laura said in a curt whisper, "Of course I know Yossi."

"He contacted the OPMC alleging . . . ." Angelo saw Mrs. Ellis hovering in the kitchen doorway and decided to edit the part about sex and drug dealing. " . . . many sordid and untrue claims. The OPMC launched an investigation into my association with SkinDem. Yossi even tried to blackmail me."

"Yossi Cohen," Laura said with contempt. "Did he do that to your face?"

"Yes."

"Laura," called Mrs. Ellis.

"Mother, please," Laura insisted. She stood up and walked to the front door. "I'm afraid I can't help you."

"Can't, or won't," Jason said.

"You watch your tone in this house," spat Mrs. Ellis.

"I'm sorry," Jason said contritely.

"If you want my advice, Angelo, stay away from Yossi," Laura cautioned. "He's more dangerous than you think. He's one of the reasons I left New York. Him and all those damn reporters."

"Did Demetre falsify his notes about Violet to justify not getting a dermatology consult?" Angelo pushed on. "You must remember what I had said to him that day?"

"I'll say this, and then you'd better leave. I blame Yossi for Demetre's downfall. Had he not gotten him hooked on drugs again, Demetre would have never made so many stupid decisions and taken such foolish risks. That poor girl . . . she would still be alive if it weren't for Yossi allowing Demetre to use his apartment as an office."

"My career is in jeopardy." Angelo turned to pleading.

"I'm serious now." The steeliness of her voice startled Angelo. "I want no part of this." Before he could react, Laura opened the front door. "My life was upended once; I won't allow that to happen again."

It was going wrong. Angelo had thought out a long conversation between himself and Laura that even made room for her indignation, but which allowed him to plead his case. Now she was throwing them out of her house. Angelo wanted a private moment with Laura—maybe then she'd listen.

"Laura," Angelo began in a hushed voice. "Can we talk alone . . . somewhere in public?"

"Laura," Mrs. Ellis interrupted again.

"Mother, please," Laura snapped.

Angelo heard the falter in her voice and was moved to declare with feeling, "It's all right, Mrs. Ellis," meaning it, despite the morass of discomfort that had inserted itself amongst them. Even now, Angelo felt the persistence of whatever worry he'd seen in Mrs. Ellis's face.

"They're leaving. Isn't that right, Dr. Perrotta."

With a last glance back at Mrs. Ellis, Laura had made herself clear. Her mother was already carrying the tray back into the kitchen.

Angelo and Jason walked back to the Breezy Point Inn, defeated. Angelo tried to even out his breathing. His thoughts spilled over, running randomly in all directions. "What were we thinking?" Angelo said. "She must have thought we were out of our minds."

"Did you see the way her entire demeanor changed when Yossi's name came up?" Jason asked.

Angelo stood on the curb as Jason continued walking across the road. Once he noticed Angelo wasn't behind him, Jason turned around. Angelo gazed at him, thinking how handsome he looked. *The blond hair. The light eyes. A body like a suit of armor.* All Angelo wanted to do was rest his head against Jason's chest. Melt like a pat of butter.

"I want to go home," Angelo said.

"We are."

"I mean back to New York."

Jason sighed with frustration. "I know you're upset. So am I, but let's give it another day or two? Maybe Laura will come around."

"Were you in the same room with me two minutes ago? That woman is petrified. In all likelihood, Yossi threatened Laura too. She's never going to come around."

"You don't know that."

"Jason, you need to stop doing this. You raise my hopes only for them to get dashed, and the disappointment is crushing."

"Okay," Jason said. "Let's stay the night. In the meantime, let's find Camille and have a few drinks and some oysters."

They sat on the terrace of the Blue Coral Grill, the three of them, drinking beer and slurping oysters. The sun was high, and a crisp breeze made sitting outside feel very comfortable that early afternoon. Gulls hovered overhead, waiting to swoop down to snag scraps. Angelo hated their squawking. It grated on him like walking with a blistered heel. Everything annoyed him, even the children at a nearby table. Their shrill laughter synched with the gulls squawking so that he felt immersed in one endless screeching terror. After several minutes of gloomy contemplation, he realized Camille had asked him a question.

"What did you say?" Angelo asked.

"What do you think Laura meant by dangerous?" Camille asked. "Do you think Yossi threatened her?"

"I'm not a detective," Angelo said, "but the minute I mentioned Yossi, she shut down."

"Angelo's right," Jason said. "We were literally being served tea, and the next thing we knew, Laura was pushing us out the front door."

"Yossi is an intimidating guy," Angelo added. "Demetre said he was in the military."

"I'm so sorry, Angelo," Camille offered.

He gave her hand a squeeze, sipped his beer. "I'll just have to accept whatever the OPMC decides. Now who wants another round?"

Later that evening, Camille and Angelo stayed up talking in her room while Jason turned in for the night. Once again, the conversation focused on the timeline of events that led them to the Cape. It felt like they were fumbling through a cornfield maze with voices luring them down dead ends. Paths littered with husks that twisted so that they ended right back where they started. Angelo was reminded of when they lived on Staten Island. He and Camille stayed up for hours, talking through their never-ending series of misfortunes, wrestling to find a path moving forward, and choosing the best one from among their limited options.

That night, every time Angelo was about to suggest they head to bed and resume their endless, winding conversation again in the morning with rested eyes, there was another speculation, *but what about* or *why would she*, that kept them up.

The next morning, Angelo woke up in bed next to Camille. They had both fallen asleep fully dressed. He slipped quietly out of her room. Jason was in the shower when he unlocked the door. Angelo stripped down and got in with him. "Mind if I join you?" Angelo began kissing Jason, reaching down to stroke his growing tumescence.

"Be my guest," Jason said, soaping up his hands. Angelo's cell phone dinged on the nightstand. His head twitched. "Don't even think about it." Jason reached for Angelo's erection, drawing him closer. They kissed deeply and passionately, the hot water spraying over them. The shower steam filled up the entire bathroom until they could hardly see each other, enjoying the touch of the other's hands on their cocks.

Their release came quickly, and as satisfying as it felt, it was just as fleeting. They held each other for several long seconds. They were back in reality again, where everything was exactly the same. A jarring abruptness that felt like the shower water had turned ice cold.

Toweling off, Angelo checked his cell phone. "Holy shit!"

"What is it?" Jason asked.

"It's a text from Laura."

Angelo held out his phone for Jason to read.

Meet me in your motel's restaurant, alone.

For most people, Angelo assumed, this was the break they were hoping for. And yet, would it be? Of course he would meet Laura; on some level he expected it would come down to this. He had proceeded through these past several months along an obstacle course, navigating each challenge with mounting apprehension, his stride growing more tentative. "What do I say?"

Jason wrapped a towel around his waist. "Tell her you'll be there in five minutes." Angelo chewed his lower lip, all too aware of the odd sense of foreboding. When he looked over at Jason, he found him staring back expectantly. "Angelo, what's wrong?"

"What do you think she wants?"

"You'll find out soon enough."

Several minutes later, Angelo entered the crowded restaurant and scanned the room. Each table displayed a different portrait of an America family: Mothers coddling their young children, fathers studying tour guide brochures, teenagers texting on their cell phones, and elderly couples observing it all with a warm sense of nostalgia in their eyes. Laura was sitting at the coffee bar when Angelo tapped her on the shoulder. "Good morning."

Laura wore a white, button-down shirt and linen pants. Angelo thought she looked skinny. In the bright light, he saw lines in her cheeks. Her eyes seemed weary, as though she hadn't had a good night sleep in weeks.

"Morning," she said. "Please, have a seat."

"Thank you for meeting me," he said. "I'm so sorry about yesterday. I hope we didn't upset your mother too much. I should have known better than to arrive at your house unannounced, looking like this and with a policeman no less."

Laura shook her head. "Don't worry. Lydia's a tough lady."

"Like her daughter."

The server came by. "Good morning. What can I get you?"

"Due cappuccini," she replied, turning to Angelo, "if that's all right with Dr. Perrotta."

Angelo nodded. "Yes, that would be lovely, *Nurse* Ellis." The server turned around to fix their drinks.

Laura chuckled. "I see you've visited the townie gossip mill on your whistle stop tour of Harwich."

"Why did I not know this?"

Laura squinted, as if Angelo had thrown her off balance for a moment until she had surveyed the situation from all angles. "Why would you?"

"You would have thought it might have come up."

"That's how Demetre and I met," she said. "I was his nurse many years ago when he was admitted to the hospital for PCP."

"Pneumocystis pneumonia?"

"Demetre was very sick for a long time," she continued. "We got to know each other very well. After weeks of listening to me complain about my job, he said, 'Why don't you come work for me?'"

"And you quit your job just like that?"

Laura stared at Angelo challengingly. "HIV was killing off men faster than we could keep count. I was burnt out. Demetre offered me an escape, and I took it."

Her explanation stymied Angelo. He realized that it didn't match with any of the explanations he had made on his own. "Do you miss it?"

"Not one minute." The server returned with their cappuccinos. "Thank you."

"Do you miss Demetre?"

Laura's eyes welled up immediately. "I lost everything after he murdered that girl, including my best friend."

"Yesterday, you said that you blame Yossi for getting Demetre hooked on drugs again."

Laura squeezed her eyes shut as if the very mention of Yossi's name filled her with disgust.

"I do blame him," she managed, still holding back the tears.

"How far back do they go?"

"Who can remember?" Laura went on, "When Yossi came along, I thought at first it was another harmless fling. Demetre was such a whore back then, and Tim allowed him certain liberties. That changed with Yossi. I think Demetre pushed the boundaries of their relationship when he invited Yossi in."

"You mean—"

"They became a threesome," Laura cut in. "Of course, I didn't offer my opinion. No one asked. Just like no one asked me if they could bring Yossi to the inn on vacation. You see, Demetre and Tim summered here. My parents closed the inn for two weeks after Labor Day and went on a cruise every year. Demetre and Tim vacationed with me every summer, and then, one year, Yossi showed up. I hated him immediately. He was the one who introduced Demetre to crystal meth."

"What did Tim think of Yossi?"

She licked the foam from her lips. "Tim didn't say anything. He loved Demetre too much. We both did. But Demetre's addiction spiraled perilously out of control. It got so bad, Dr. Eichhorn fired him."

"Demetre said he quit."

Laura offered a shrewd look. "That's what he tells everyone, but I was there. I saw it unfold, and there was nothing I could do."

"You worked for Dr. Eichhorn after you quit your job at the hospital?"

Laura broke in, "As Demetre's assistant."

"What happened?"

"He left, and I quit," Laura said. "Demetre had hit rock bottom. That's when Tim and I agreed to back his long-standing dream of opening his own practice so long as he gave up Yossi and got clean, which he did. Thank God."

"Whatever bad decisions Demetre made, that has nothing to do with you or Tim or me. Demetre is where he is now because of only one person. Demetre. But the rest of us shouldn't have to suffer. That's why I'm begging you to testify at my OPMC hearing. You know the truth. Won't you please help me?"

Angelo's cell phone dinged. It was a text from Jason.

How's it going?

Angelo texted him back.

Going well. Have breakfast with Camille. I'll join you.

Jason texted back a heart emoji.

Laura had paid the check and was swallowing back the last of her cappuccino when she said, "I have to get back home. Why don't we talk there . . . where it's private?"

"That would be great."

They walked back to the Ellis house. Laura unhitched the gate latch and walked up the path. Angelo followed closely behind. The windows were dark. He squinted, trying to see inside. Unlocking the door, Laura glanced back with a hint of hesitation that confused Angelo. *Something doesn't feel right.* When the front door shut behind him, the room was dim. He squinted until his eyes adjusted. Angelo immediately experienced an unnerving pulse of vertigo.

"I'm sorry," Laura choked out.

A flashlight clicked on, blinding him. This nightmare had hit an old snag. Through the white light, Angelo made out the pastrami skin, the shaved head, and crazed eyes going wide. Yossi held a knife in his gloved hand, raised as if ready to charge.

"Sit down," he hissed.

Angelo glanced nervously between Laura and Yossi.

"Listen to me," Angelo pleaded. "You're not thinking straight. It's the drugs. You don't want to get yourself in deeper trouble."

Yossi shot him a contemptuous look.

"How do you know what I want?" Yossi shouted back. He lurched forward, startling Angelo, who crossed his arms over his face in defense. The blade nicked his forearm, but no pain registered. All Angelo felt was heart-stopping panic as he stumbled back and slammed to the ground. Yossi reared up, the knife raised above his head. Angelo tried to scramble away, but Yossi dropped his body down on Angelo's chest, pinning his arms with his knees. "What are you going to do now?" Yossi asked with a great deal of indignation.

Angelo's hands were going numb. Pins and needles shot to his fingertips. They were face-to-face when Angelo experienced an uncanny sensation of déjà vu. Angelo recalled arguing with his ex-boyfriend, Miles, many months earlier. High and drunk, Miles had thrown Angelo to the floor, pinning him down just as Yossi was doing now. Back then, Angelo was consumed by a familiar state of humiliation and shame, but he didn't feel that way staring up at Yossi. An unnatural calm came over him as Yossi raged. Angelo wondered what Yossi saw when he looked into his eyes? Did he see the sorrow? The compassion? Not likely. Not in his condition.

But then, as if a switch had been pulled, light streaked into the darkened room. Laura gasped. A figure emerged from the darkness.

"Drop the knife," Jason demanded. He pressed the barrel of his gun against Yossi's temple.

"Who the fuck are you?" Yossi shouted.

"Put the knife down," Jason warned. He sounded too nervous. Angelo heard it. The gun trembled in Jason's hands. A gouge of memory made Angelo recall the story Jason had told him. The one that put him on probation for a year due to his impulsiveness, which led him to discharge his firearm, killing a man.

"You bitch," Yossi spat at Laura. "You set me up!"

Jason cocked his gun. "I said, drop it. Now!"

"Go ahead." Yossi's voice was low, dangerous, and to prove it, he thrust the tip of the knife to Angelo's neck. "Shoot me."

Angelo's eyes flitted from Yossi to Laura to Jason. He was compelled to gain control of this situation, knowing one or all of them could get hurt.

"Jason," Angelo spoke in a monotone. "Why don't you take a breath and put down the gun?"

"Yeah, listen to your boyfriend," Yossi mocked. "You little bitch."

"Shut up!" Jason snapped.

The tip of the knife pierced Angelo's skin superficially but just enough for a trickle of blood to spiral down his neck.

"Jason," Angelo called again. This time his voice was more commanding. "Look at me. Put the gun down. Yossi's not dumb. He knows how this will end." Then Angelo turned to Yossi. "If you don't put down the knife, Jason is going to shoot you. Trust me. I know him, and if you kill me, you're looking at a life sentence." Angelo felt the diminishing pressure from the knife as Yossi relaxed. Jason withdrew his gun and pointed the barrel down. "See," Angelo breathed. "Now it's your turn." Yossi was taking jagged breaths through his mouth, looking to Laura as though he was waiting for her to give him a sign.

"Yossi, listen to Angelo," she said, pausing after each word. "It's over."

The knife hit the floor.

Laura ran into the kitchen and called the police.

"Put your hands behind your head," Jason ordered, pointing his gun again at Yossi. "Sit down on the sofa and keep your fucking hands on your head."

Yossi glared at Angelo. "What the fuck is he doing?"

Angelo struggled to his feet. He stood behind Jason. "It's all good, babe. You don't need to point the gun at him. He's following your orders."

Jason slowly dropped his arm, staring at Yossi. Sweat dripped off his forehead. His eyes never veered away from Yossi's face until the police finally arrived.

◆◆◆

They drove behind the police cars in a pageantry of flashing lights. It began to rain. Everything was coated in a hazy fog. Angelo stared at Jason's profile. He was so fixated on the road. "Babe, are you okay?"

One side of Jason's mouth slid into a grin. "You never call me, babe."

"I am now," Angelo said. "Are you okay, babe?"

"How were you able to be so calm?"

"Years of practice I guess," Angelo said.

If residency had taught him anything it was to remain focused in the maelstrom of chaos. Over the years, he learned not to get swept up in the hysteria. He didn't fear it. He embraced it. Only the violence was new to him. A force so dangerous he couldn't comprehend how Jason dealt with it daily.

Jason's mouth opened in shock—seemingly surprised by Angelo's response. "I . . . I think I'm in love with you."

"What?"

"I think . . . no, I mean, I know. I'm in love with you."

Angelo was beaming but considering the circumstances, he was also concerned for Jason. "We can talk about this later."

"No, I want to talk about it now," Jason said with clear emphasis. "When Camille and I didn't see you in the restaurant, I had this awful feeling something went wrong. Very wrong. That's when I grabbed my gun and headed straight for the Ellis house. When I saw Yossi holding a knife to your neck, all I thought was, if he killed you . . . if I lost you . . . I don't know what I would do." Jason quickly wiped at his eyes, but Angelo saw the tears. He heard the swell of emotion in Jason's voice.

It was an unusual experience to hear another man declare his love, but it was more than that. Angelo felt the love. He was swathed in a warmth he had never experienced in his life. A heat so intense he could feel the obsidian melting. The crystalized cocoon that had encased itself around his heart dissolved, and his heart surged, sending rolling waves of euphoria throughout his body.

Angelo slid over and rested his head on Jason's shoulder. "I love you too. I love you. I love you. I love you."

Jason reached his arm across Angelo's shoulders and gave him a squeeze. "From now on, whenever you call me 'babe', I'll know something's wrong."

They drove the rest of the way in silence.

Even in accepting this was finally over, still, something gnawed at Angelo. He had come to believe that he had been beguiled by a man who, according to Laura, had been seduced by a drug dealer. Two vibrant men drawn together for the same reason—an unrelenting sense of envy and greed—only to be imprisoned for it.

A strange emotion gurgled immediately in Angelo's throat. It might have been a sob or just as easily a belch. Because, he realized, staring Yossi in the eyes at the Ellis home and at Demetre in the courthouse, he was staring at two different versions of himself, at what he might have become had he not slipped through a crack on his way down the winding ruthless road of degradation.

Angelo imagined how his life might have turned out had he accepted the invitation to join Demetre and Yossi that night he discovered them in the office having sex and snorting cocaine. What grisly consequences awaited that foolish version of himself? He shuddered thinking about it, and he recalled something Rudnick had said to him at their first meeting.

The good news is that you will never do anything wrong again.

Angelo realized now; no truer words had been spoken.

◆◆◆

Laura spilled it all.

Yossi wasn't only having sex with Demetre and supplying him with drugs. In return, Yossi funneled stolen prescription pads obtained by Demetre to support their expensive habit and for Yossi to sell to his clients. Their addiction had escalated to the point where they were using the office after hours to host men they met online, luring them with the promise of raw sex and illegal drugs. Laura had been on the verge of quitting when the news broke the story of their undercover investigation.

"It's finally over," Laura told a reporter outside the police station. "Now I can finally focus on taking care of my sick mother."

Angelo and Jason offered no comment. A reporter with a cameraman followed them to their car. Angelo got behind the wheel, squinting through the lights as they filmed them driving away.

"We should eat something," Angelo suggested.

"Do you want to pick up Camille first?"

"She already ate," Angelo said. "We passed a burger place on the way here."

Jason moaned. "I could totally go for a burger right now."

"That settles it."

They decided to eat in the car. Angelo experienced a silent implosion of emotion. It was strangely hard for him to remember his life before Demetre. He tried to recall the months before he started working for Stanzione. A carefree existence he didn't appreciate at the time. He had been too focused on his career and less on the people in his life. If anything, this experience had taught him not to take his life for granted.

How are you feeling, Angelo?"

The question seemed to linger before Angelo spoke up. "Laura said Demetre had worked a deal with the district attorney and named several doctors he claimed provided him with prescriptions in exchange for money. Just like the claim he made against Stanzione, but he also claimed these physicians were committing insurance fraud."

"Why does any of that matter now?" Jason asked.

"An investigation into insurance fraud can take months." Angelo imagined Steven copying hundreds of pages from patient's charts, cursing, and thinking how much this would all cost them in the end.

"You think Demetre made it up to lessen his sentence?" Jason asked.

"Probably."

"What I want to know is why did Demetre protect Yossi from the homicide detectives?" Jason probed.

"Maybe Demetre felt some paternal sense of protectiveness," Angelo offered. "Laura said that after Demetre was arrested, Yossi grew more paranoid, fueled by drugs and guilt, thinking everyone was conspiring against him. He began showing up at Laura's apartment, threatening her with violence if she mentioned anything about the prescriptions or their late-night parties to the police. That's when she fled to the Cape."

Still running through the sequence of events that led them to this take-out burger parking lot, something nagged at Angelo, like a tuning fork thrumming in his ears. "Are you going to eat that?" Jason asked. Angelo realized he had hardly touched his food. He handed over his burger and started the car.

"Let's get back to the inn," Angelo said. "I could a use a drink."

What little Angelo had eaten formed into a solid ball in his gut. He felt alarmed by the extent of his dissatisfaction with the outcome of this nightmare when he should be feeling relief. Turning the corner, flashing red lights bathed the street. "What's going on?" Jason asked. An ambulance was parked outside the Ellis Island Inn. "Jesus, what next?"

Laura stood outside the ambulance doors, rubbing her arms. Camille watched from across the street. Angelo parked the car and headed toward Laura. "It's my mother," she cried. "She was unresponsive when I got home. I think with all the stress, she had a heart attack." Just then, the medics carried a stretcher out of the house with a white sheet covering Mrs. Ellis's face. Laura turned and cried into Angelo's shoulder. "Fucking Yossi. I blame him for this."

A medic walked over and asked Laura if she was going to ride with them to the hospital. "Would you like me to go with you?" Angelo asked.

"I can't believe she's gone," Laura said. She followed the medic into the back of the ambulance. Sitting next to her dead mother, her eyes wide and glassy, Angelo thought she might collapse. The driver secured the door shut. Angelo approached him.

"Excuse me," he said. "My name is Dr. Perrotta. I'm Mrs. Ellis's physician. Was she dead when you arrived?"

"Nice to meet you, doctor," he replied. "No, Mrs. Ellis was unresponsive. When we got the EKG leads on her, she was in V-tach. Then she coded. We worked on her for a while, but . . . we couldn't bring her back. Sorry."

"Thank you."

The driver got in the ambulance, and Angelo, Jason and Camille watched as it drove away, leaving them in the dark except for the streetlamp light reflecting in the water just beyond the inn.

Jason put his hand on Angelo's shoulder. "What did he say?"

"Mrs. Ellis had a heart attack." Angelo shook his head.

"And?"

"You saw Mrs. Ellis yesterday," Angelo said. "She looked pretty healthy to me."

Jason raised a finger. "What is going on in that head of yours?"

"Take Camille back to the room," Angelo said. "I'll meet you there in five minutes."

"Five minutes?" Jason repeated. "Are you out of your mind?"

Angelo grabbed Jason's arms. "Please, do this for me."

Jason fixed his eyes on Angelo's. "What aren't you telling me? I thought we had a deal?"

Angelo begged, "Please."

Camille interrupted them. "What are you two talking about?"

"Jason is going to walk you back to the room."

"Where are you going?" Camille asked.

"I want to be alone for a minute," Angelo replied. "Clear my head."

Camille raised an eyebrow. "Angelo, you are the worst liar I have ever met. Now tell me what's going on?"

"Your brother needs to be alone," Jason said. "I'll walk you back to the room. Let's give him a few minutes. It's been a rough day."

"Okay," Camille said, sounding still somewhat unconvinced. "Don't be long."

Angelo watched them walk away. Once they were out of sight, he headed toward the Ellis house. He unhitched the gate and walked to the front door. With all the excitement, he imagined Laura had forgotten to lock it, and he was right. He turned the knob and stepped inside the darkened house. It was a hauntingly chilly moment, standing in the same room where just hours earlier he had been nearly murdered. He moved toward the kitchen, floorboards creaking under his feet.

What was he looking for?

Angelo wasn't sure.

The kitchen was clean. No dirty dishes in the sink. The table was spotless. He was about to search the bathroom when he heard footsteps on the front porch. His heart was galloping in his chest. Angelo ducked behind the dining room table, staring at the door, trapped in the feeling that somebody was about to storm in. The door creaked open. The streetlight outlined the silhouette of broad-shouldered man.

Yossi?

Stunned, Angelo shrank into the corner of the room.

"Angelo!"

He quickly realized it was Jason.

Thank God!

"I'm behind the table," Angelo said, standing up. "You scared me to death."

"I knew you were coming here. What is it you're looking for?"

Angelo pressed a hand against his chest, catching his breath. "Didn't you think it was a coincidence that Laura's father died just after she had moved back home?"

"No," Jason said. "I didn't know the guy."

"Okay, point taken," he conceded. "But what if we hadn't thought this through thoroughly?"

Jason crossed his arms over his chest. "Go on."

"Laura was a nurse who assisted Demetre when they worked for Dr. Eichhorn."

Jason shrugged. "So?"

"So, what if it wasn't Yossi who was assisting Demetre that day Mia died?" he continued. "We just assumed it was Yossi because it was his apartment. But Yossi had an alibi. He was training a client."

"You think Laura helped Demetre carry a dead body, dug a grave in his garage and poured cement? She's not strong enough. It had to be Yossi." And then, Angelo's eyes alighted with an unerring focus. He took the stairs, two at a time. Jason followed closely behind him. "Where are you going?"

Maybe it was a consequence of having reached the end, finding out when Angelo did, a mad glistening tale of greed, murder and betrayal that concluded in way that was too neat—with two abnormal men doing abnormal things until they were both arrested. But Angelo ran heedlessly through a dark house where a woman who had nearly fooled him lived.

Angelo entered the first of three bedrooms. One that was unmistakably Mrs. Ellis's. Quilted comforter. Lace throw. A worn antique red and blue area rug. The bed had been disturbed. There was a wet spot on the side where Mrs. Ellis had slept. On the floor were the discarded remnants of a resuscitation. Latex gloves. Gauze. Needle caps.

The other room had to be Laura's old bedroom. A time capsule of her teenage years minus the posters of Billy Idol and The Damned. What remained was a single bed. Walls papered with a pink rosebud pattern and white lacquered furniture.

Laura was a fastidiously neat person, Angelo knew. The bed was made. He found her suitcase in the closet. He checked the drawers as Jason stood in the door staring at his every move. "What are you looking for?" he asked.

"Drugs," Angelo explained. "Check the bathroom medicine cabinet."

"For what?"

"Anything suspicious."

Angelo pulled open the nightstand drawer. Everything tidy and in its place. Paper. Pens. Pencils. Even a diary. He moved swiftly to the dresser. Again, everything—blouses, undergarments and socks—folded with such precision and stacked upon one another, arranged with such care. Angelo thought it must have taken hours for Laura to do her laundry.

He was overcome with a sudden burst of anger.

How could he have been so stupid?

Laura hadn't delivered Angelo to Yossi. Laura had delivered Yossi to him, knowing either Jason would follow and come to save the day or Yossi would kill Angelo and get arrested. Either way, Yossi would be removed from her life.

Slamming the sock drawer shut, he heard the distinct clank of bottles. Angelo opened the drawer again, spilling the contents on the floor. Throwing the darned socks back into the drawer one by one, he picked up an unusually heavy pair of gym socks. Tucked inside, he found exactly what he had been looking for. "Jason!"

Jason appeared in the doorway, breathless. "I found a bunch of prescription bottles, but it's all Chinese to me."

"Look what I found." Angelo held up one of the bottles for Jason to read the label.

"Lidocaine." Jason shrugged. "Could it be a coincidence?"

"It's not a coincidence," Angelo snapped as though the word was an insult. "She told me that she and Tim put all of their savings into SkinDem. Once Demetre was sent to prison, they lost everything. An overdose of lidocaine can cause ventricular tachycardia, which is exactly what caused Mrs. Ellis's heart to stop. The woman we met yesterday did not look sickly. Laura had thought of everything, down to the cleverly planted comment about her sick mother to the news reporter outside the police station."

And then as if a slow dawning were occurring within Jason, he concluded, "So she killed her father and then her mother, so she wouldn't have to worry about money."

"Tonight's fiasco with Yossi wasn't a coincidence," Angelo said. "Our unexpected visit provided Laura with the perfect opportunity do away with her mother to avoid drawing any suspicion."

"While simultaneously removing her Yossi problem,"

Jason finished. "Let's get out of here."

Angelo placed the bottles in his pockets. They hurried down the stairs and into the streets. No one saw them, even as they entered their motel room. Sitting on the bed, silent, panting, they discussed what they should do next. "We have to go to the police," Jason began. "In fact, I'll call them now."

"I'll go check on Camille," Angelo said as he opened the door."

"Wait," Jason said, standing up. He walked over to kiss him. Angelo felt Jason's hot, wet, mouth, but he pulled away. "You're right. Go."

"I love you," Angelo said as he closed the door behind him. He rapped lightly on Camille's door. "It's me. Are you awake?" There was no answer. He knocked louder. "Camille?"

Angelo didn't wait for her to invite him in. He reached for the doorknob and burst into the dark room. Angelo flicked on the light switch.

"Close the door behind you," Laura said. She sat on the bed. Camille's head trapped in the vise-like grip of Laura's arm. In her other hand, she held a scalpel to Camille's throat. "If you say a word, I'll kill her."

Angelo raised his hands. Camille's mouth was gagged with a sock, her arms tied behind her back. Angelo wondered how long Laura had been terrorizing his poor sister.

"What do you want me to do?" he asked.

Laura's eyes darted over to the chair by the television. "Sit down." Just as Angelo was about to move, she added, "Lock the door first."

Angelo obeyed. "It'll be okay," he said to his sister.

"I hate to break up this tender family moment, but this situation is not okay." Laura tightened her grip around Camille's neck, twisting her body so she couldn't see her brother's face. Camille let out a squeal of fear. "You are so smug. You know that? I mean, who else would be so cavalier as to lie about being my mother's physician."

Smug or stupid, Angelo thought now in hindsight.

"Laura," Angelo whispered. "My boyfriend . . . the cop . . . is in the other room right now calling the police. You won't get away with this."

Laura's mask of control slid off. She began weeping, muffling her cries by pressing her face into Camille's hair. "Why?" she gritted. "Why couldn't you just go home? You had your revenge. Yossi was arrested. It was over. Why couldn't you just let it go?"

There was a knock at the door. "Angelo," Jason called. "The police are on their way. I'm meeting them in the lobby."

"Okay," he replied calmly. "Camille's in the bathroom getting changed. We'll meet you there, *babe*."

They heard Jason's footsteps walking away.

Laura's face relaxed.

"Now what?" Angelo asked.

"Take out your car keys?" Laura demanded.

"I don't have them."

Laura yanked Camille's hair, so her head fell back, exposing her neck. Camille let out a muffled shriek as Laura pressed the scalpel against her throat. "You were driving the car. I saw you."

"All right. All right." Angelo stood up. "I'm going to reach into my pocket." He produced the car keys. They jangled in his shaking hand as he held them out. "Take them. Just leave me and my sister alone."

Laura threw her head back and laughed. "Don't be a fool. You're both coming with me."

"No," Angelo shouted. "No, we're not." At once, Laura raised the scalpel and stabbed Camille in the thigh. Her muffled scream echoed in the room. "What are you doing?" Angelo cried out, sobbing now himself. Blood seeped into the fabric of Camille's nightgown, plastering it against her skin.

"If you don't take me seriously, I'm going to kill her," Laura warned. "What's another dead body?"

"Okay!" Angelo said, gripping his hair. "Just don't hurt her!"

"Your car is parked out front," she began. "I want you to pull it around back so we can get in. Understand?"

"Yes, yes." Angelo didn't have time to think it over, he just reacted. Walking to the door, he peered over his shoulder. Laura pulled Camille to her feet. Angelo felt a lump rising in his throat. He swallowed down hard as he reached for the doorknob. Behind him, Camille whimpered.

He only hoped that Jason would see him get in the car. He turned the doorknob and opened the door. A gust of wind shook Angelo hard so that he fell to the floor. A whip-crack sound blew in the night. The bullet had gone right past him, striking Laura. She was frozen, mouth ajar. Most of her right cheek was missing, exposing her white teeth imbedded in pink gums. Gunsmoke wafted from the hole in her face. Once it faded away, Angelo saw the bullet had gone clear through her head.

Laura's legs buckled, and she sat down, hard.

Camille skittered over to Angelo. They huddled together on the floor as Jason entered the room holding his gun.

"Is everyone all right?" he shouted. Eyes still focused on Laura.

A police siren blared in. Jason let out a gusty sigh. As if it had awakened her—maybe it had—Laura lifted her head and looked at Angelo. Her eyes were leveled, but now pointing in opposite directions. Blood poured out of her mouth, and she slumped forward.

The room filled up quickly with two local police officers. The static noise of their two-way radios filled the air. A command for an ambulance. Report of a death. Angelo untied Camille's hands and removed the gag from her mouth. Jason reached out to Camille. "Take my hand," he said. She looked at Angelo still somewhat in shock.

"It's okay," he said to her. "It's okay.

Jason escorted Camille to their room so she could rest on the bed until the ambulance arrived. Angelo moved to stand, but he felt faint. He pressed his head in between his knees and began gulping air. Once it passed, he stood up, careful not to move too fast. He entered his room and found Jason applying pressure to Camille's wound using a bathroom towel.

"You saved our lives," Angelo said still heaving.

Jason looked up and smiled wanly. "Who knows, you might have still talked your way out of it, *babe*."

"No, you did, Jason. You really did. My life anyway," Camille said. "Angelo, make sure nothing happens to this guy. He's a keeper."

"I won't," he replied to Camille. "Promise."

CHAPTER TWENTY-ONE

They entered the apartment Sunday night, dropped their suitcases, and slept for twenty hours, a sleep as deep as a coma. Angelo woke up around twilight the next day; purple, pink, and blue hues streaking across the city's horizon, making the world outside appear more like a dream than a reality.

Angelo's old life was waiting for him: stuffed mailbox, spoiled milk, and a message from his lawyer, Rudnick, reminding Angelo of his upcoming Office of Professional Medical Conduct hearing later that week.

When Jason and Camille awoke, they had dinner. None of them spoke about what had happened. Beyond the black stitches on Camille's thigh and the fresh bruises on Angelo's face, there was something altered deep inside each one of them. Something they weren't quite ready to deal with. Maybe certain basement floorboards in the brain had snapped—free falling, crashing into an unknown crawlspace that was never supposed to be invaded.

One thing was certain: they were grateful for each other's company, for the light conversation, the delicate chiding that pushed boundaries ever so slightly, and the welcomed euphoric wave of inebriation as they sipped wine.

Only when they returned to sleep later that evening did Angelo stumble back to the Cape, retracing his steps through the cornfield maze of events. Though he felt rested and relieved that Demetre and Yossi were in jail, there was the vague, residual regret that he would do everything differently if given the chance. Only so that Mia would still be alive.

Tuesday morning Angelo returned to work, though he felt more like a ghost than a physician, seeing patient after patient, and subsisting in a daze that clouded his conscious so that he had to ask the clinic manager to reschedule his afternoon appointments.

Camille had taken the rest of the week to recover, so when Angelo returned to the apartment, he found her on the couch writing in her journal. "You're home early," she said.

Angelo shook his head. "I'm not in the right headspace to take care of myself, let alone sick people who need my undivided attention."

Camille patted the cushion next to her.

"Sit down." Angelo reclined on the couch with his head in Camille's lap. "Good or bad, everything will be decided on Friday. For now, there is nothing you can do other than remain focused on the OPMC hearing."

"You're right."

Camille combed Angelo's hair to the side. He recalled his mother used to do the same thing when he was little. His sister's resilience was something that never failed to surprise him. He wondered how he would have gotten through this without her.

"I want to read you something I wrote," she said, clearing her throat. "When we finally returned to our real lives after experiencing such a traumatic experience, it was as if everything—our apartment, the neighbors, the streets—all the colors seemed muted. We felt things less profoundly, as though we had left a part of ourselves at the Cape. Maybe we needed to leave that part behind so that we can begin to grow another part to replace the old one?"

"That's very good." Angelo managed to find some scintilla of comfort in Camille's observation. At least he had a sister and a boyfriend who loved him. At least, he told himself assuredly, he had that.

Later that night, Angelo and Jason strolled through the streets of his neighborhood. They passed restaurant windows, alive with lights and noises. Glasses clinking, people chatting as the restaurant doors opened, spilling patrons into the streets radiating with ebullience—these sounds seemed to follow them as they passed.

"When did you first become suspicious of Laura?" Jason asked.

"It was while we were at the police station," Angelo said. "I kept wondering, how did Yossi know we were there? And then it occurred to me, Laura told him. When Yossi said, 'You set me up.' I thought he meant she had tricked him, knowing you would come to save the day, but that's not what he meant. Laura knew that even if Yossi came clean and admitted he was working with Laura, if she didn't confess, no one would believe Yossi over her."

In the end, Yossi had confessed to helping Demetre dispose of Mia's body, but Angelo had been correct in his assumption that Laura was the one who had been assisting Demetre when Mia became unresponsive. Angelo wondered why Laura's nursing training hadn't kicked in. Succumbing to panic is a trained healthcare provider's worst nightmare. Agreeing to dispose of the body, instead of calling for an ambulance, was the worst path Laura could have gone down.

The night before the OPMC inquiry, Camille, Angelo, and Jason dined at a French brasserie in Chelsea. They piled into the red leather booth. Camille stared at them like she was the proud mother of two heroic sons.

"I have a good feeling about this inquiry." Camille took Angelo's silence as disappointment for her bringing up the subject and added, "Me and my big mouth."

"Why they even need to proceed with this inquiry is beyond me," Jason said.

"This inquiry has nothing to do with Mia's death," Angelo recited as if he were reading lines. "They're investigating my relationship with Demetre and whether there is any evidence I acted with misconduct."

The server welcomed them, but Camille asked if he could give them a few more minutes.

Angelo took a long sip of water. "I figure if I lose my license, I'm going to rent a farmhouse and rescue dogs from kill shelters."

"Dogs?" Camille laughed.

"Farmhouse?" Jason asked.

"Why not?" Angelo said somewhat hysterically. "Dogs can't be harder than people to care for." After a few deep breaths with Jason rubbing his back, Angelo experienced a peculiar fear.

It was Mia.

Across the room she appeared alone, sitting at a table. There was no escaping her sweet presence, those soft brown eyes, the cascade of chocolate hair. She didn't frighten him. There were no milky eyes, no ghoulish sneer like one might expect from a ghost. She materialized as a young woman in his presence, asking for nothing, just raising a quick hand, *hello*, and when he returned the gesture, she disappeared back into her secret world.

Neither Jason nor Camille saw her, and, in the end, Angelo decided that he hadn't either; a subconscious hallucination he feared would haunt him like a ghost forever.

◆◆◆

Friday morning, Angelo arrived at the offices of the OPMC in New Rochelle. Rudnick was waiting for him outside. Angelo had forgotten how tall he was. Rudnick greeted Angelo warmly, and they went inside. The lobby appeared trapped in 80s décor. Salmon-colored fiberglass chairs. Plexiglass wall-mounted magazine rack. Linoleum floor tile. Rudnick stood out with his tanned skin and gold cufflinks.

Kraemer met them in the lobby. He was an obese man in his mid-fifties with a meaty head, no neck, and a thick 70s porn star mustache. He escorted them to a small room with white walls and no window. They sat at a foldout table. The room reminded Angelo of a hospital psychiatric intake room; except this time, he was the one being analyzed. That shift in power was disarming, and the gravity of the situation was not something he took lightly. If his actions were deemed unethical, Angelo would lose everything. Or maybe not everything, but his career, and that was a lot.

Kraemer offered them coffee, but Rudnick and Angelo refused. "Well, then let's begin," Kraemer said. "As it's been explained to you through your lawyer, Dr. Perrotta, we are investigating your involvement with Mr. Demetre Kostas, and your role with his practice, SkinDem. Do you understand?"

Angelo nodded.

"Dr. Perrotta," Kraemer said. "I need you to reply verbally so the stenographer can record your response."

Angelo complied, "Yes, I understand."

"Let's begin."

For the next two hours, Kraemer read email exchanges between Demetre and Angelo. All the while, the walls of that small room felt like they were closing in. Angelo heard his emails imbued with whatever it was that had snared Kraemer's suspicions. Although there was nothing incriminating, it was still a horrible invasion of privacy. Each time Angelo looked over at Rudnick, his lawyer offered him a subtle, yet, encouraging smile.

By noon, the interview was drawing to a close. Kraemer pulled a letter from within a stack of papers.

"Have you seen this document before?" he said, sliding it over to Angelo. Immediately, he saw the Jeune Toi letterhead. Angelo willed his eyes to remain fixed to avoid drawing any suspicion. "Did you inform the Jeune Toi representative that you were the medical director of SkinDem?" Kraemer asked.

"No."

"Then can you explain why she thought you were?" Kraemer pressed. "It says so at the bottom."

Rudnick picked up the letter and handed it back to Kraemer. Then he looked at Angelo expectantly.

"Mr. Kostas lied and told her I was the medical director," Angelo admitted.

"Why would Mr. Kostas lie about that?" Kraemer asked.

"Lunch," Angelo said flatly. "Demetre. I mean, Mr. Kostas, wanted her to take him to a fancy Japanese restaurant for lunch."

"And you agreed to go along with this charade and signed the letter?" Kraemer clarified.

"I didn't think much of it at the time," Angelo said. "It was just another drug rep lunch."

Kraemer placed the letter back within the stack. Angelo sensed his disapproval.

"Dr. Perrotta, you were asked to consult with a Mrs. Violet Trautman. Do you recall why?"

"Yes," he replied. "Mr. Kostas wanted me to look at a mole on Mrs. Trautman's back before he removed it."

"Currently, you are being sued by Mrs. Trautman for delay in diagnosing her melanoma?" Kraemer asked.

"Yes."

"Dr. Perrotta was an employee of Dr. Stanzione's practice," Rudnick explained. "He was instructed to spend time with Mr. Kostas because there had been several meetings to discuss merging the two practices. My client had no way of knowing Mr. Kostas was performing illegal procedures, particularly since the burden was on Dr. Stanzione to check Mr. Kostas's credentials."

"I understand, but Dr. Perrotta had every right not to offer his medical expertise. Plus, he failed to document his consultation in which he should have recommended that Mrs. Trautman seek the advice of a dermatologist. All we have is Mrs. Trautman's testimony in which she states that Dr. Perrotta said the mole looked benign. Her testimony is corroborated with Mr. Kostas's notes obtained from SkinDem." Kraemer then focused his attention on Angelo. "Were you paid for this consultation?"

"No." Angelo's mouth was parched. He filled a Styrofoam cup from the pitcher of water on the table. He took a sip but struggled to swallow without coughing.

Kraemer pulled another page from his stack. "That Saturday, after you consulted with Mrs. Trautman, Mr. Kostas took you to a department store for a makeover." Kraemer placed a photocopy of Demetre's calendar in front of Angelo. The date was circled with the words, *Makeover with Angelo at Barneys*, written in the center.

"Do you recall this?"

"Yes, I do," Angelo said, "but I bought everything myself. Mr. Kostas didn't pay for a thing."

"His credit card statement shows that he bought you dinner at Mr Chow's that afternoon."

"So, he paid for dinner," Rudnick said. "That doesn't mean anything."

Kraemer eyed them both for several long seconds. "Why don't we pause here for a ten-minute break?"

Angelo excused himself to use the restroom and slipped into one of the stalls. He sat with his head between his knees, taking deep breaths. Someone entered the bathroom. A shiny pair of mahogany Oxfords stopped in front of the stall door.

"Angelo," Rudnick said. "You're doing fine."

Angelo pressed his forehead against the wall, feeling the cool aluminum on his skin. "I'll be done in a minute."

Rudnick was waiting by the sink when Angelo stepped out. "Kraemer showed me your prescription records. I have to say, I was very impressed. You should be proud of yourself. You can't imagine what I've seen. Some doctors make a living selling prescription drugs. Your records are impeccable."

Angelo washed his hands and smiled at him in the mirror.

"So far they've got nothing on you."

"Then why are we still here?" Angelo asked. His tone was unabashedly snarky.

"It'll be over soon," Rudnick said. "Just stay calm."

Rudnick walked out and left Angelo alone. He began the tortuous process of regaining his composure, hoping to instill confidence when all he felt was dread. Once he returned to the conference room, Kraemer and the stenographer were whispering to each other. There were teeth marks in Kraemer's Styrofoam cup, and Angelo hoped that meant he was hungry. Maybe this nightmare would be over soon.

"Are we all here?" Kraemer asked, looking around. "The sooner we get started, the sooner we can finish up."

Angelo wondered what else Kraemer had up his sleeve, what document he was waiting to pull out that would unravel this entire proceeding and prove without a doubt that he was an unethical doctor who should have his license revoked.

"Dr. Perrotta," Kraemer began. "Did you have a sexual relationship with Mr. Kostas?"

"No."

"Did you go to gay discos with Mr. Kostas and use illegal drugs?"

Angelo wanted to laugh when Kraemer used the word disco, but he was gripped by a panic so sharp and unexpected that it felt like a slap. He looked beseechingly at Rudnick.

"What does any of that have to do with whether or not Dr. Perrotta acted unethically?" Rudnick asked.

"We have a witness who stated Dr. Perrotta and Mr. Kostas were lovers, that they danced at discos and took drugs. They hatched a plot to open their own medical spa, cutting out Dr. Stanzione." Rudnick focused his attention on Angelo. "Although you weren't paid directly by SkinDem, Dr. Perrotta, you were the medical director. Documents, including several invoices, list you as the medical director." Kraemer supplied copies of those invoices, which Angelo reviewed closely.

The muscles in Rudnick's face tightened. "I don't see Dr. Perrotta's signature anywhere."

Angelo felt a gurgle of acid rising in his throat. The sight of Kraemer, looking smug and self-assured, had awakened pieces of himself; horrified, angry pieces coming together to formulate the picture of how Kraemer saw him.

"Excuse me," Angelo said, clearing his throat, "but who the hell is this witness? Is it Yossi Cohen? Because he was just arrested for assisting Demetre . . . . Fuck! Mr. Kostas, in disposing of a dead woman's body." Angelo lost his grip, gimping along instead of maintaining a controlled stride.

"Angelo," Rudnick said in a hushed, strained voice. He picked up the invoices and handed them back to Kraemer. "This doesn't prove that Dr. Perrotta was the medical director, and knowing that Mr. Kostas is an admitted liar, thief and murderer, it would stand to reason Mr. Kostas was capable of resorting to extraordinary measures by using my client's name without his permission. We already know Mr. Kostas stole his prescription pads."

"Dr. Perrotta," Kraemer said, ignoring Rudnick and maintaining a laser focus on Angelo. "Did you and Mr. Kostas discuss opening your own medical spa?"

"We may have had a discussion," Angelo said, "but it was just talk. Demetre didn't want to merge with Dr. Stanzione if it meant giving up his autonomy. He didn't want to be—"

Kraemer cut in, "Like a shelter dog." Kraemer eyed Angelo with a tinge of appraisal. Only then did Angelo realize Kraemer was toying with him.

"This is ridiculous," Angelo said with disgust.

He watched the corner of Kraemer's mouth curl up because he'd won. He had succeeded in rousing the obsidian, and now it was slowly churning. Angelo's heart beat against his chest. He could hear Kraemer's voice, but as if from far away, and then, suddenly, very close as though he were speaking directly in his ear.

"I couldn't disagree with you more," Kraemer said. "Dr. Stanzione offered you your very first job out of training, and you repaid him by plotting with Mr. Kostas to go out on your own, even ridiculed him in emails. The invoices, the letter from Jeune Toi, and the consultation with Mrs. Trautman indicate you were acting as SkinDem's medical director. Not to mention the makeover and expensive meals. Seems to me you had a taste of the good life and wanted more than what the late Dr. Stanzione had to offer. There is nothing ridiculous about that."

"You're right," Angelo replied with an unexpected spate of anger. "This isn't ridiculous. This is fucking bullshit!"

Angelo was unaware he had stood up but quickly realized it once he felt Rudnick's hand pressing down on his shoulder. "Can I have a moment with my client?"

"Who are you to judge me anyway?" Angelo continued. "I looked you up online Mr. Kraemer. You're not a doctor. What happened? Couldn't get into medical school?"

"Angelo!" Rudnick gripped his arm and pulled him out of the room.

He fought to stay, enraged by the lengths to which he had been insulted. "Do you like your job, Mr. Kraemer? Does it make you feel powerful, judging doctors?"

In the hallway, Rudnick pushed Angelo against the wall. Such feelings of anger and frustration had been building up inside, Angelo hardly recognized his own actions. Angelo had committed the cardinal sin of medicine. *First, do no harm.* Kraemer's derogatory summary, characterizing Angelo as someone who befriended a murderer and betrayed his boss, was meant only to humiliate. His integrity had been scrutinized and built upon the testimony of a drug dealer and now, an accomplice to murder. Never had he felt so small as sitting at that table listening to a man with a gnarly mustache disparaging his choices for wanting a better life.

Suddenly, Angelo was depleted of any emotion. He stared blankly into Rudnick's eyes. He couldn't hear a word he was saying, lost in the frenzy and fury of his alternate self, the one that took over; the same one who may have just ruined his life.

Rudnick asked to meet with Kraemer in his office alone. Sitting in the waiting room, Angelo felt a beat of anger rise up his neck, realizing insulting Kraemer so horribly, so publicly, was the final nail in his coffin.

Rudnick stood over him. "We have a problem." There was a stretch of dubious silence. Angelo was about to vomit when he saw them walking through the door. He slowly rose as they neared, grinning and sobbing—deliberately walking to greet them. Jason escorted Tim Meadows, Demetre's ex. Angelo threw his arms around Jason's neck. "What's going on?"

"We'll talk later," Jason said. "Is that your lawyer?"

Angelo beckoned Rudnick. "This is Demetre Kostas's former partner," Angelo explained, "both personally and professionally. He owned half of SkinDem along with Laura Ellis."

Rudnick shook his head in disbelief. "I hope you're here to save the day."

Tim smiled—a bright, big white smile. "I'm only here to tell the truth."

"Please, come with me." Rudnick escorted Tim into the conference room.

Angelo gave Jason the tightest hug and kissed him repeatedly on the cheek, which made Jason blush. Standing in the busy hallway, they were drawing a lot of attention.

"I love you more than anything. How did you get Tim to agree to come all the way here?"

Jason wiggled his fingers in front of Angelo's eyes. "Mind control."

"Well, it worked on me," Angelo said. "Hopefully, it will work on Kraemer."

"Actually," Jason said. "You inspired me to reach out to Tim. After you said Tim and Laura lost everything after Demetre was arrested, I wondered how Tim felt, particularly after he heard Laura and Demetre were involved in Mia's death. To my surprise, Tim had a lot to say. I didn't want to tell you until I was sure he was coming. I couldn't let you down."

Angelo stood teary-eyed before Jason. "I can't thank you enough."

"Don't thank me yet," Jason said.

"Just take the compliment," Angelo said, kissing him. "Once again, you saved the day."

An hour later, Rudnick escorted Tim to the waiting area. "Mr. Meadows is leaving."

"Tim," Angelo said. "Thank you so much for taking the time to testify on my behalf. I know you've lost so much already. It couldn't have been easy to relive it again."

"My pleasure," Tim said. "I hope all goes well with your inquiry. It would be such a loss. No one deserves to have their dreams stolen from them. I should know."

Once Tim had exited the building, Rudnick took Angelo and Jason to a nearby coffee shop to talk. Rudnick used the word "magical" to describe Tim's testimony. They sat at a booth by the window. A waitress brought over three coffees. Rudnick ordered a slice of apple pie. Angelo and Jason were hungry, but Angelo could hardly catch his breath, let alone eat.

Rudnick explained, "Tim recounted years of Demetre's drug addiction, which inhibited his ability to differentiate right from wrong. Demetre had stolen money from the practice to buy drugs, and when Tim put a limit on how much Demetre could withdraw, he resorted to stealing prescription pads to obtain opioids, which Yossi sold to his clients."

"Well, he certainly stole prescription pads from me," Angelo said.

"For years, Demetre had stolen and swindled from the very people who trusted him," Rudnick continued. "But it was an incident involving a patient with a mole that Demetre removed without recommending a dermatology consult that snagged Kraemer's attention. Tim said that the patient went to a dermatologist to assess another mole, which was cancerous. Once Demetre heard, he amended his notes, to state that he recommended a dermatology consult when in fact, he had never given that advice to the patient."

"Unbelievable," Jason said.

"You're a lucky man, Angelo," Rudnick sang through a mouthful of pie.

Glancing at Jason, Angelo knew exactly how lucky he was.

That night, they had dinner with Camille at the apartment. Angelo told her the entire story. "You're a hero," Camille said to Jason. "Twice. How do you do it?"

"Mind control," Angelo said, wiggling his fingers at Jason, who wiggled his back.

"Oh, to think you can finally put this awful mess behind you." Camille grabbed her arms and shivered. Angelo wondered if she was thinking about her impending divorce. Wouldn't it be great when that was over too?

CHAPTER TWENTY-TWO

It was a clear day; blue skies, blinding sun, fresh grass, and blossoms swaying in the breeze. They arrived in Staten Island with the intent of pulling out all the stops. They ordered Italian heroes from Vertucci's, stacked with a ridiculous amount of deli meats and cheese—salami, ham, and provolone—on fresh Italian bread as long as a child's arm. They bought two bottles of Chianti and set out for Moravian Cemetery.

"Let's lay the blanket under the tree," Camille suggested.

The mane of lush green lawn looked blue as it stretched out under the clear sky. They ate and drank for long periods without talking. Angelo stared at them, assailed by a brief inebriated sense that what they were doing was attempting to work through their damaged past, not by revisiting it, but through actions moving forward. He felt he had taken a page from Camille's reflections she wrote in her journal: *They had left a part of themselves at the Cape in order to grow another part to replace the old one.*

A picnic at Moravian Cemetery would go down as the most macabre thing any of them had ever done, and yet it felt completely normal in the moment. Angelo pitched his head toward the sun, closing his eyes. Envisioning his mother, he thought about her smile, her honey-colored hair, and those wide eyes. Seeing himself reflected in her eyes, he imagined a world of endless possibilities.

For as long as he could remember, Angelo dreamed of living the good life, and all the years it took to build that dream had been dismantled in only twelve months. Though he hoped to distance himself from that clapboard bungalow on South Beach, imagining himself living happily somewhere else. In reality, he had never been more contented sleeping alongside Camille, talking after lights out, cuddling on the sofa with his mother watching TV, and walking along the beach with Don after dinner.

Standing over his mother's grave while Camille and Jason loaded up the car, he whispered a solemn promise to live a life that would make his mother proud, not just for her, but for himself.

Behind him he could hear Jason calling. It was time to go. At last, Angelo could say he was ready.

ABOUT THE AUTHOR

Frank Spinelli, MD is a licensed physician, and the author of The Advocate Guide to Gay Men's Health and Wellness, as well as Pee-Shy: A Memoir, which has been optioned to be developed into a limited series. He appeared in the Emmy-nominated 30 Years from Here, Positive Youth, and I'm a Porn Star. He also hosted a season of Dueling Doctors.

Frank lives in New York with his husband and their two four-legged adopted sons.

Acknowledgements

Finishing a book takes a team of generous, talented, and honest people.

I want to express a massive thank you to my early readers: Josephine and Paul. Without their encouragement, I would have given up years ago.

I'd also like to thank Chad for kindly tolerating my ramblings about new plot twists at dinner when all you really wanted was to eat in peace.

Nicole Kimberling is a boss. She pushed me well beyond the confines of my comfort zone, forced me to be patient, and did it all with a sense of humor. I love your collaborative spirit. At least I can say something good came from being holed up at home during a pandemic. I'll miss waiting for your Friday night emails.

Finally, my profound gratitude is to Dianne Thies and her eagle eyes. And to everyone at Blind Eye Books. This wouldn't have been possible without you.